SO-BVP-047

Love is
a time of enchantment:
in it all days are fair and all fields
green. Youth is blest by it,
old age made benign: the eyes of love see
roses blooming in December,
and sunshine through rain. Verily
is the time of true-love
a time of enchantment—and
Oh! how eager is woman
to be bewitched!

SUMMER SECRETS

The story of three generations of women, the men they are drawn to and why. In particular it is about the youngest, twenty-three-year-old Tessa Selway, who is building up a Chelsea flower shop into a thriving business. But her love-life is disappointing. Sensing this, her grandmother—a captivating personality—decides to step in. She introduces Tessa to a forty-year-old journalist, worldly, cynical and quite unsuitable, and Tessa falls headlong . . .

SUSAN GOODMAN

SUMMER SECRETS

Complete and Unabridged

ULVERSCROFT
Leicester

First published in Great Britain in 1989 by
The Penguin Group,
London

First Large Print Edition
published May 1990
by arrangement with
Michael Joseph Ltd.,
London

British Library CIP Data

Goodman, Susan, *1935–*
Summer secrets.—Large print ed.—
Ulverscroft large print series: romance
I. Title
823'.914[F]

ISBN 0-7089-2208-2

Published by
F. A. Thorpe (Publishing) Ltd.
Anstey, Leicestershire
Set by Rowland Phototypesetting Ltd.
Bury St. Edmunds, Suffolk
Printed and bound in Great Britain by
T. J. Press (Padstow) Ltd., Padstow, Cornwall

For Charles

Part One

Dorset, July 1945

1

THE train, which was on time, thundered in—hissing, disturbing the peace of the countryside on a warm summer's afternoon. Standing alone, very straight in her sky blue slip of a dress, hands clasped behind her back, Tessa waited. Doors opened, a few heads stuck out, sacks and luggage landed on the platform. The stationmaster, who had been dozing, ambled out shouting good-naturedly at the guard.

A very tall man appeared in front of Tessa. He seemed to blot out the sun and cast a dark shadow. He was appallingly thin. His khaki uniform, decked out in scarlet braid, hung on him.

"Is it Tessa?" this person enquired. "Just Tessa?" His voice was very deep.

Tessa, whose knees had suddenly turned to jelly, looked up at him. Jutting chin met jutting chin. She stood her ground. She started to put out her right hand.

"How do you . . ." she began, when

3

this extraordinary stranger—*Papa?*—gave a harsh bark of laughter and lifted her right off her feet and hugged her and whirled her around.

Then she saw his face and the wiry, reddish hair—her own—and everything suddenly seemed perfectly all right and she shouted down at him.

"They sent me to meet you by myself. *Me*. Not Tom. Wasn't I lucky?"

When she was older, Tessa was sure, quite sure, that sweet peas had been placed all over the house that morning. A huge bowl on the round table in the middle of the hall; in the drawing-room; between silver candlesticks on the dining-room table. And after, whenever she smelled their rainbow perfume, she was immediately transported back to her childhood, to Chalcot House in Dorset . . . and to the day her father came back from three years in the army, in Burma.

It was the day, she also sometimes thought, which changed all their lives dramatically—and forever.

For, to the astonishment of the rest of the household, Jennie Selway, Tessa's mother, decided—*no, insisted*—that Tessa should be taken to Chalcot station to meet her father when he arrived on the 3.15 train from Southampton that afternoon. *Alone.* Jennie Selway, in her soft, girlish voice, broke this to the family over lunch.

"But Jennie," her aunt, Flora Flood protested, "surely after all these years George will expect . . ."

"And she's only nine, my dear girl; she hardly remembers George." Hubert, Flora's husband, interrupted. "You must go with her, at least."

"Tessa will go by herself. I've quite decided, Hubie."

Sunlight streamed in through the long open windows and a pair of Victorian Floods, painted in their Sunday best, looked down—unsmiling—from above the sideboard.

"Very well, my dear."

Jennie Selway, whose face reminded everyone who saw her for the first time of Botticelli, smiled radiantly in his direction. Flora and Hubert Flood exchanged glances down the long table. Since they had received George Selway's telephone call that morning, which they had expected all week, saying that his boat had docked and he was on his way to Chalcot, Jennie had scarcely mentioned her husband's name.

Jennie Selway and her two children—Tessa, and Tom who was five years older—had been living with the Floods in the village of Chalcot in a remote part of Dorset for the past three years. The Selways' house in London had been damaged early in the war and Jennie and the children had moved to a rented flat in the suburbs. George Selway sailed for Burma soon after.

But Jennie loathed the flat which she found cramped and inconvenient. Without the authoritarian George and several servants—particularly a nanny—she was managing badly. Vague and inefficient, she had one minor illness after another—colds, 'flu, sore throats. Both of the children got out of hand. Her mother, Vi Delmore, who was living in Eaton Square and working at the War Office, having the time of her life despite the intermittent bombing, was no help at all.

So when Vi's sister, Flora Flood, and her husband Hubert suggested that Jennie

6

and the children spend a summer with them at Chalcot House, Jennie jumped at it. The Floods had a large house and no children; they also had a dour but faithful French cook-housekeeper, Marie. It seemed a sensible arrangement under the difficult wartime conditions. By August, the flat had been given up, Marie had more or less taken charge of Tom and Tessa, and the weeks at Chalcot stretched into years.

It was Marie, now, who was serving the cottage pie at lunch. It was a dish of which she strongly disapproved—but made magically with her special blend of fresh herbs. One of her legs was shorter than the other and she lunged about, dodging the chairs, with what Hubert Flood described as her "drunken sailor gait."

"Mange toi," she hissed at Tessa, giving her a dig with her elbow. Her face was set and sour as ever, although it was Tessa, her favourite, who managed to produce an occasional glacial smile.

"Why can't we *all* go and meet Papa?" Tessa had gone red in the face, matching her gingery hair. Her strong chin stuck out dangerously. Beneath the table, her long

7

and skinny legs, which ended in sandals, scissored away. *"Why only me?"* she wailed.

Jennie Selway smiled gently, and said nothing.

"It's absolutely stupid," Tom jeered. "Tessa's just a baby . . . I jolly well think you should go Mum. He's your husband, anyhow," he said rudely, miffed at being left out of the homecoming drama. He had rather looked forward to bragging at school about his father turning up in a cap with red braid and all the trappings.

"That will do, Tom," Hubert Flood said pleasantly. Tom was still growing, much too fast. He had his mother's fine features and very light blue eyes beneath well arched brows. Although he was doing brilliantly at his boarding school—and was also a handy athlete—he was going through an awkward, nervy stage.

"Well that's that then," Flora Flood said, eyeing her niece disapprovingly. She privately thought her shallow and irritating; sometimes wondered if she was all there in the head. Certainly she was hopeless with her children; that was plain to see. As an artist—and Flora Flood was a

8

considerable one—even her perfection of features bored her. Her face was a beautiful expressionless mask. Of late, she hadn't even considered her interesting enough to paint.

"I suppose so, my love," said Hubert. A linguist, he had been thought one of the cleverest men of his year at Oxford; but he had never quite lived up to academic expectations. He had inherited a sizable chunk of the Flood brewing fortune, including Chalcot House, at a young age. Full of charm and zest, with countless friends all over the globe, he enjoyed the good things his money could buy.

But wherever they were, however frantic their social life, Flora Flood painted every day. Hubert was passionately convinced of her talent and she was now being mentioned as a leading British artist. They were an exceptionally devoted couple—both very tall with long, aquiline noses. Over the years they had even developed the habit of finishing each other's sentences.

Their home in Dorset, Chalcot House, was a solid, rather plain, Georgian building fronting on to the main street of the village. It had a large walled garden stretching behind towards fields and distant hills; a pleasant stable block had been converted into a studio for Flora.

During the war, Hubert, with his fluent French and deep knowledge of the French countryside, was conscripted by the SOE. While the Selways were at Chalcot, he came and went mysteriously—saying nothing, Flora drawn with worry—often undertaking dangerous missions into occupied France. But now that the war in Europe was over, and George Selway had been invalided out of Burma, the two families would separate and pick up the threads of their former lives.

Flora Flood sighed. She saw Tessa, looking rebellious, was staring hard at the bowl of sweet peas. She fancied that she was not far off tears.

"Don't worry, lamb," she said to her comfortingly, through a cloud of cigarette smoke. "Your Papa will be utterly thrilled to see you."

Bobbing around the table, Marie gave Tom and Tessa second helpings. Her dark eyes, black as the dress she wore winter and summer, missed nothing. She had come to England with the Floods when they fled from the South of France in the ominous late summer of 1939. And because of the war—or so she said repeatedly—she had stayed. Although her command of English was limited, she never failed to get her meaning across. It was half believed by the locals that she was some kind of witch . . . She had already noticed that Jennie Selway had done no more than toy with her lunch, and that she looked pale, passing a crumpled handkerchief repeatedly over her smooth, high forehead.

"That's all right then," Jennie said, smiling distractedly round the room. "If you could deal with the taxi please Hubie . . . tell Fred . . . And ask him to come on the early side."

Soon, Flora Flood rose from the table, cigarette in mouth, ash drooping precariously. She was a stately figure with a large bosom and white hair piled on her head like a mad bird's nest. As always, she wore a long gown in a rich fabric—and stout boots. Her eccentric clothing was accepted by the locals "on account of her being an artist."

11

"We'll have coffee outside, Marie," she said. "Pull the table and chairs into the shade, would you Tom, please? It's turning out quite warm."

"I suppose so," Tom said gracelessly, scraping back his chair.

"A bit later on we'll go down to the cellar, old chap," Hubert Flood told him, putting an arm round his shoulders as they left the dining-room. "Just you and I. Marie is planning a special meal for tonight and we want something decent to welcome your father safely back."

"Oh jolly good, Hubie," Tom said, brightening, pushing back the hair that had fallen over his forehead. "That's a super idea."

Tom sprinted ahead on to the terrace, and Hubert and Flora Flood were crossing the stone-flagged hall when Jennie clutched Flora's arm—and started to crumple. Hubert Flood caught her, only just preventing her from falling to the ground.

"Heavens, Jennie," Flora Flood said, appalled. "Are you all right? Perhaps you should go upstairs and lie down. I'll get Marie . . ." Jennie's face was chalky; with a huge effort, she held herself upright, shaking off both their arms.

"No please," she said quickly. "Don't bother Marie. I'm quite all right. This warm weather . . . and I'd love a cup of coffee."

They sat on the heavy white iron chairs that Tom had dragged into the shade. Jennie Selway, who never bothered with her appearance, had on a shapeless creamy dress and old sandals. She had pinned her long hair into a bun; tendrils, darkened by sweat, sprung around her face.

She could make *some* effort to look presentable, Flora Flood thought crossly, particularly today of all days. Really, Jennie was impossible. The war in Europe over, three years in Burma . . . She hoped, but was by no means sure, that she was going to pull herself together and behave. Even Hubert, bless him—and she knew the signs—was nervous. He wasn't talking much for one thing. A name, which none of the three would dream of mentioning, hung between them. She looked away.

Down on the lawn Tom had started mucking about with the croquet set and

Tessa was on the swing which hung unevenly from the great green beech tree. Both children, in their different ways, were beginning to feel apprehensive about this barely known father who was returning to their lives.

"Jennie dear," Flora asked, feeling that some show of concern was called for. "Would you like Marie to get you a glass of water? Mrs. Selway hasn't been feeling very well, Marie. All the excitement . . ."

"No thanks, Aunt Flor," Jennie began. "I'm sure . . ."

"I know that she has not," said Marie, in English, for once.

By a quarter to two, Tessa was dressed, her hair brushed tidily, waiting for Fred in the hall. With one hand on the bannister, Jennie Selway said only, "Do pull your socks right up, Tessa . . . not folded round your ankles. That's better." And she started to drift up the stairs.

"See a change in you, your Dad will. Just a nipper you was when 'e went off." Fred looked at Tessa through the rear mirror as his ancient Ford, which he used as the local taxi, ground towards the station.

Nice little kiddie this one, he was thinking. Fred also ran the village bicycle shop and he'd mended her bike—punctures mostly—often enough. Fancy sending 'er off alone to meet 'er Dad. Not to be wondered at from what 'e'd 'eard put about. Three years in bloody Burma, no respect. Shocking, if you asked 'im. That hoity-toity Mrs. Selway. And she no better'n she ought to be, neither.

2

WHEN Fred's taxi spluttered to a stop outside Chalcot House, the family welcoming party was lined up to greet them. The house was separated from the street by a shallow, semi-circular drive; a very old magnolia, which was never cut back, clung tenaciously to the front. The door was open and through it—beyond the wide, dark hall—the sunny splash of the garden could be glimpsed.

Flora and Hubert stood on the top step. Tom, almost as tall as Hubert now, stood fidgeting and blinking beside him. Marie, tight-lipped, glowered to one side with young Connie who did the cleaning and had come to help her with the preparations for tonight's dinner. Connie, a sentimental girl, was tearful with excitement. Sensing that something was up, Orlando, the Flood's marmalade cat, patrolled the group.

Jennie Selway was not there.

16

Hubert was the first to reach George Selway as he emerged from the back seat, closely followed by Tessa. He pumped away at his hand, "My dear fellow, welcome home." Tom followed, looking awkward. George Selway grabbed him by the arm.

"Tom! Good God, how you've grown . . . what a big chap you are!" He gave a piercing glance at Tom's lank fair hair which had fallen over his eyes, and went towards Flora.

"George dear, this is simply marvellous." They kissed briefly on both cheeks. "And such a lovely surprise for you to find Tessa waiting . . ."

"Indeed it was. I hardly recognised her. And Jennie?" George Selway's eyebrows were raised. Tessa, feeling rather pleased with herself, kept close to her father's side.

"Upstairs George, in your room. You remember—on the left at the top of the stairs. I said we'd send you straight up."

While George Selway and the Floods chatted briefly, Fred carted out the battered luggage under Marie's direction as she pushed and pointed. Connie watched the reunion, sniffing hard. Such a

17

sight he looked, Mr. Selway—a brigadier he was now they said, not far off a general —with all that red and gold on his uniform. Thin as a rail, needed building up, anyone could see that . . . And little Tessa, not that she wasn't a handful mind, clinging away . . .

After a few minutes, George Selway went inside, his children at his heels. *The heat and the stink; the alien colours and voices. In the jungle—sheer heart-stopping terror; threatening silence broken by sudden wild shrieking. A bird? An animal? A human being? The undergrowth crackling—was it this way? Over there? Silence again. Humidity pricking the skin, melting the pores. Illness: the agues of malaria; dysentery sapping the body and weakening the mind . . . how he had longed for coolness, for greenness, for Englishness. For this. His wife.* He tossed his cap on to the hall table. His face was gaunt and his wiry red hair, like Tessa's, was shot through with grey. Although he looked strained and tired, he nevertheless gave the impression of considerable authority. He took the stairs two at a time and when he reached the landing, looked down at the raised faces of his children. Tessa was happy and smiling, Tom blank. He gave them a quick wave.

"Tea on the lawn, Aunt Flor says. Your mother and I will join you. And I want to hear all about school, Tom." He knocked lightly on the bedroom door. "Jennie?"

"Yes."

When she had seen that Tessa was ready to go off to the station in Fred's taxi, Jennie Selway had gone straight up to her room. She was sitting on the chaise by the window overlooking the garden, still wearing the same loose, light dress she had put on that morning. Wisps of hair had fallen on to her shoulders. As the door pushed open, she faced her husband across the pretty, sun-dappled bedroom. Her cheeks, which earlier had been so pale, were now slightly flushed.

"Jennie."

George Selway strode across the room and fell on his knees beside her. He was not a demonstrative man. He had always considered Jennie more child than wife; malleable; ineffectual; infinitely decorative. But seeing her beside the window— so calm, so beautiful—after an absence of more than three years, he was deeply moved. His throat became choked as he buried his face in the stillness of her lap. Although he fought for control, his body was racked by rasping sobs.

"Jennie," he gasped.

"George . . . please don't."

"Don't? Jennie . . ." He looked up at her, his arms on her shoulders, pulling her face down to his. She resisted. "My dearest Jennie . . ." He reached up and touched her hair. She recoiled instantly, turning her face away from him. A small moment of infinite coldness.

"Do not touch me." Each word cool and precise; her arms kept close to her sides; still looking away.

"Not *touch* you, Jennie?" George Selway leant back dazed. He seemed not to understand. "Not touch you?"

"Do get up, George. You look ridiculous on your knees like that. There is something I have to tell you." Despite her high, girlish voice she spoke briskly and with such composure that George was left speechless. He felt as though he had been winded. His mind was a blank; no words —or thoughts—formed. He got heavily to his feet and groped for a chair and sat facing her. He was the colour of parchment.

"Of course, I'm sorry that it had to happen like this but I felt that I would prefer to tell you myself, not simply write it. So I have waited."

She paused. The room was very still. A mere two feet away from her, George Selway stared. He moistened his lips. She went on.

"I do not consider myself to be your wife any longer. I am leaving you, you see . . . today, immediately, and in time I shall want a divorce." She spoke calmly and lightly as though what she was saying was the most natural thing in the world.

"Jennie—why?" He thought he might choke—or vomit—on that single word. The room heaved around him and he could feel sweat on his forehead; all day, despite the warmth, he had felt chilled.

"Because I am going to live with someone else—with Felix Morgenstern." Still the sweet, tranquil voice; her nearness —the loved and passionately wanted familiarity.

"With. . . ? Jennie, I cannot believe this

21

is happening." He took a handkerchief out of his pocket and wiped his face. Certain facts from their letters registered mechanically. Morgenstern. Old friend of Hubert's. Colleague. Some kind of professor. Jewish refugee. Helped him get out of Austria. Or was it France? Lent him a cottage on his land.

"It has all happened George. As I said, I'm sorry. Really I am."

Such finality. And such uncharacteristic decisiveness. She looked at him with indifference, a gentle smile curving her lips; pale eyes distant. His arms began to shake and he made a tremendous effort. Swallowing hard he said, "We have been living, all of us, under exceptional circumstances. I appreciate that—fully." The words sounded thick. "In all of our interests, I am prepared to overlook this relationship you may have had . . ."

Jennie put her head back and started to laugh.

"To overlook? But I want nothing overlooked, nothing." She sounded genuinely amused, happy even. "How can you be so stupid, George? I am going to live with Felix Morgenstern. When I am free, we

22

will marry. I simply wished to tell you so myself. The years *we* lived together—our marriage, our life in London—are as though they had never been. Don't you hear, don't you understand what I am saying?"

She leant towards him—radiant. He watched the outline of her full breasts, nipples taut, straining against the whitish dress. Each syllable twisted slowly in his gut. He changed his position painfully in the uncomfortable cane chair.

Night after night he had tossed in his bunk on that confounded, crowded troopship. Often feverish. His body unpleasantly excited at the thought of Jennie's cool presence; soft, naked coming closer every hellish, stifling day . . .

He crossed and uncrossed his legs.

"I see." He inclined his head, playing for time; marshalling his forces to control, once and for all, this chaos, this madness. He spoke carefully, as he would to a recalcitrant child. "But nevertheless, Jennie, we—you—have responsibilities. The house in London to be opened and repaired. Our belongings brought out of storage. The children . . . and what of the children?" He was a strong man; he had already recovered some of his judgment.

"Tom is in boarding school. He's a clever boy. And Tessa . . ." She shrugged. "She is a confident, independent child. And as for the house in Parloe Square; I always did hate it so . . ." Her voice trailed off and she looked out of the window on to the lawn and the spreading beech tree. "Those gloomy grey curtains in the drawing-room." Again, the soft, secret smile.

George Selway wrenched himself out of his chair, started to walk towards the door, then wheeled round and faced her.

"Now stop this nonsense. Stop it, I say. Your duty is as my wife and the mother of our children. You will break off your relationship with this Felix. We'll go away. Without the children. Forget all this ever happened. Then go back to London—I've work to do there in case you may have forgotten. A business to rebuild, a family to support—in some style. We will get the house going, settle the children, find a school for Tessa—and resume our lives. This sordid alliance is absurd. Damaging to everyone concerned, the children in particular. And to me. You are my wife and I love you," he finished stiffly. "I may be inadequate at expressing it—but indeed I do." His grey eyes bore into her, blazing.

Jennie shook her head. "I have told you, George, I have no intention of returning to the life we had. Ever. In any case, it is not possible." The light had gone out of her voice and she sounded tired.

"But of course it is," George Selway thundered. "Of course it is. Do you imagine for one moment that you are the only woman to have formed an attachment under these wartime circumstances?"

"It is not possible," Jennie repeated. She was rubbing her hands together in her lap, for the first time showing some consternation.

"And why is that, may I ask?"

She paused, then said quietly, "Because I am having Felix's child."

One by one the words, so gently spoken, dropped between them. The room was bright and peaceful. Pretty pastel chintz covered the beds and framed the window. On the dressing-table lay the silver mirror and brushes—one of George's wedding presents to her. Next to them, Marie had put a vase of yellow roses. They could both hear faint sounds of the household below. Some way off in the garden the children were shouting.

"In that case, I shall divorce you. Citing Morgenstern." George Selway's voice was clipped and icy, his mouth clenched into a hard line. He turned away from her.

"Of course." All Jennie's hair had fallen on to her shoulders now. Her face—lips parted—was glowing. Her hands were motionless in her lap.

"I shall want custody of the children. You realise that." He looked back. He saw that she was smiling. Her beauty astonished him. *How could she do this to him? How could she?* Her face was a perfect oval, her high forehead; smooth ivory skin; silvery hair hanging loose. He shut his eyes against it all.

"Yes, oh yes, I expected that. It would be better, I'm sure."

Her face was brilliant with—what? Happiness? he wondered bitterly. He thought: she's mad, quite mad. Felix Morgenstern. For God's sake—why? She was always vague and odd. He had known from the beginning that she had needed help, needed organising. He had, or so he thought, provided all this. But she had become unstable, deranged. Lost whatever grip on reality she had ever had. *Felix Morgenstern*. Did Flora know? Did Hubert? Peacetime and this lovely day, his first in England for years, had become a grotesque, half-waking dream.

In sudden revulsion, he wanted her out of his sight—with her beauty, her remoteness, her maddening defences which he had never quite penetrated. (He knew, he had always known, that his sexual ardour had never moved her.) The child, not his, growing inside her.

"Get out," he shouted. "Go."

She rose. For the first time since he had entered the room she showed uncertainty.

"George, I—the children . . ." One hand touched her throat.

"No. *I* will tell the children. Take what you wish. Telephone for a taxi. Go to— that man. And never, never come back."

3

THE Floods and George Selway were in the drawing-room—tea, barely touched, cooling in their cups. Marie's lightest of light sponge cakes, dredged in snowy icing sugar—hoarded through the war and brought out only for special occasions—was uncut. Since George had come down and, standing to attention in front of the fireplace, delivered his bombshell, none of them had spoken much. The Floods knew that the last thing he wanted at that moment was their sympathy. They sat in the deep, rather uncomfortable chairs—tense, listening.

Flora silently thanked Heaven that the children, bored with hanging around, had decided to pay a visit to the neighbouring farm where they would undoubtedly be given tea. George Selway took a handkerchief from his pocket and mopped his forehead several times. His teeth were chattering; he would need to start taking those damned pills again. Hubert Flood thought, irrelevantly, how satisfying was Flora's large and colourful still-life (zinnias stuck in a ceramic jug) on the far wall.

After what seemed an eternity they heard, with relief, the sound they had all been waiting for—Fred's taxi, so unexpectedly summoned to Chalcot House for the second time that day. The bell clanged. Above them a door creaked. Jennie Selway, carrying one small suitcase, a shawl draped round her shoulders, ran lightly down the stairs and through the hall to the front door. She was smiling, her face shining with happiness. As they drove noisily off, she did not give Chalcot House —or its occupants—a single backward glance.

Only Marie saw her go. Clacking back and forth between the dining-room and the kitchen, shouting incomprehensible orders at the flustered Connie, Marie stopped when she heard the doorbell and pressed back in the shadowy passage. Seconds later, *she* came floating down the stairs, almost running through the hall, slamming the door behind her . . .

Marie had made it her business to listen to Madame Selway calling for Fred on the upstairs telephone. She was not surprised. For weeks, her keen black eyes had noticed the fainting spells and the morning nausea, skilfully hidden from the rest of the family. And she had guessed the reason. Madame's reluctance to have anything to do with her, even to look at her directly, had also not escaped her notice. Marie's insight was accepted—and feared.

She was familiar, too, with village gossip. She knew very well where *Mademoiselle Jennie*, as she described her contemptuously, had been spending her afternoons . . . for months. At Mr. Morgenstern's cottage or, according to one source, openly, flagrantly, in the flowery fields once the weather turned warmer. *"'er naked on 'er back down in Long Meadow and 'im on top of 'er"* was the way it was put.

"Dégoutant," she muttered angrily, banging about in the larder.

As the noise of the taxi dwindled, George Selway and the Floods started to breathe more easily. Flora Flood rose, refilled their cups, and cut firmly into the cake. No reason everything should be spoiled on Jennie's account, she thought crossly.

"Well," said George Selway, "that seems to be that. An unexpected home-coming—if you can call it that." His voice was sour with bitterness. "I take it you both knew what was going on?"

Hubert Flood cleared his throat. "We weren't blind, of course. We suspected . . ."

"Yes," said Flora Flood. "We knew."

But how to tell him—George?

Felix Morgenstern: a friend of Hubert's since their student days. A Jew from Vienna, his family destroyed by the Nazi régime. While he was abroad at a conference, given special permission to do so by the Nazis, his wife and child disappeared from their apartment in Vienna—into the camps. Contacted somehow by a friend; he never returned. For two years he was hidden in a cellar in France by the Maquis. They got word to Hubert. And through Hubert's underground contacts he eventually arrived in England. He had nothing; he knew nobody. The Floods offered him the use of that shabby cottage, miles from anywhere, and gave him

31

introductions to one or two publishers to get work doing translations . . .

And one bitter night he cycled over to Chalcot for supper. He was friendless, stuck out there, and Flora thought: *we really must ask him* . . . Hubert was away; she at her wits' end with worry. The war was dragging on, going badly. The nine o'clock news more sombre every day.

Then—Jennie. Coming into the warm, ill-lit kitchen, hugging her cardigan, looking half frozen after putting Tessa to bed. Felix crossed the room when they were introduced, his brief salute dropped towards her hand, barely touching. He was nothing to look at—there could have been no hint then of the special charm of the man. But the change on Jennie's face was plain to see, even in the gloom. Her eyes suddenly focused on him—and she so rarely actually looked at anyone or anything. A bit of colour in her cheeks; something about her indefinably altered. The French had an expression for it. *Coup de foudre*. It had happened, just like that. She, Flora, had seen it. There was nothing more to be said.

"We knew she had been—foolish,"

Flora elaborated carefully. "We knew that and naturally we were extremely concerned. For all of you. You, coming home . . . the children . . . But we never seriously thought she would act upon it. Never."

Which was not strictly true either, as she and Hubert had been increasingly worried by Jennie's unrestrained behaviour—and its possible consequences. But there was no point in wounding George more than he had been already. Flora's anger towards Jennie mounted. At that very moment, as they were talking, there she was—tiresome creature, cruel too—being transported on the taxi's bouncing springs, through hedgerows sweet with wild summer flowers, to her lover. Leaving the rest of them, particularly George, her husband, to deal with reality—*with her own children*. Fuming, she fumbled in the long folds of her gown for a pack of cigarettes.

"Frankly, I'm feeling somewhat responsible," Hubert began awkwardly. "After all, Felix is, or was, my friend. It was my idea to offer him the cottage when we eventually managed to get him out of

33

France. He had nothing, absolutely nothing. Family, country, career, all lost. The cottage, such as it is, was vacant. It seemed, at the time, the least one could do for a former colleague—a victim of all we were fighting against."

"Indeed. My dear Hubert, you could hardly be expected to foresee these events," George Selway said drily. He got to his feet and began pacing up and down the carpet, an incongruous figure in that richly furnished country drawing-room, still in his khaki uniform and red trappings. "The next order of business is the children. They must be told the facts quite simply: that their mother has left them— us—and gone to live with another man. Morgenstern."

At the mention of the children, Flora burst out, "I blame Jennie. Almost completely. She threw herself at him. I saw it with my own eyes. And what could he be expected to do? A man on his own, desperately lonely and unhappy, besieged by this beautiful young woman . . ."

"Who had very considerable loyalties and responsibilities which she chose to ignore." George Selway's voice was like a whiplash. There was an uncomfortable silence. He looks shocking, Flora thought. Not an ounce of flesh on him and a dreadful colour.

"Divorce." He went on pacing. "And custody. She'll have nothing more to do with the children if I can help it. I warned her of this. It was my distinct impression that she didn't much care . . . however, apart from this misfortune, there is much else to be got on with. The house in London to be opened. The business—God only knows what has been happening there."

Every few paces, he turned smartly on his heel. The Floods, watching, said nothing. He was a hard man, George Selway, they both knew that. Able, resourceful, ambitious. He wasn't, well, a favourite with either of them. But for him to be faced with this shocking affair; that appalled them both. He was a proud man —would this pride recover? And the children . . . Who could estimate how this ghastly situation would affect either of them in the long run? Tom was such a highly strung, nervy boy . . . and protective of his mother, they both thought.

"When do you think they'll be back—Tom and Tessa?" George Selway asked, looking at his watch.

"Any moment now, I should think. I'll just ring for Marie to take these things . . . and then, Hubert my love, shall we leave George for a while? One thing, you must do as you wish, George, but perhaps it would be wise not to mention the child just at the moment, do you think?"

He nodded curtly. "Quite."

George Selway continued to stride restlessly about as the Floods went off. A little later, he saw them cross the lawn, both wearing large and battered straw hats. He stood and watched them. A good sort, Flora, he thought. And Hubert. They had opened their home to Jennie and the children; in no way could they be held responsible for this madness of Jennie's . . . (the thought of her—and what had happened —cut through him like a knife). They were an eccentric pair, but something about them—their obvious harmony perhaps—evoked in him a feeling close to envy. If he had allowed it, he would have described himself at that moment as a very lonely and embittered man.

Shortly afterwards, the children came sauntering towards the house from the direction of the farm. Calling sharply from the window, he told them to go straight into Hubert's study. He strode in after them, closed the door, and explained briefly and tersely that their mother had left them. From now on, and when they moved back to London, he would be looking after them. He did not expect that they would be seeing her again for some time. He added, by way of an afterthought, that she had gone to live with Felix Morgenstern. And that he would divorce her.

There was a dreadful silence. Neither of them could think of anything to say at all. They were too stunned even to ask questions. Tom reddened and blinked and stared at his feet. Tessa, bewildered, said, "Has she gone already? From her room I mean?"

"Yes."

After another silence she piped up clearly, "Oh, I knew she was always with Felix. I shadowed them to the cottage on my bike a couple of times. They went upstairs to the bedroom. I watched from the hedge across the road and then I biked back to Chalcot."

"Nonsense Tessa, you're imagining things. Be quiet," Selway barked. Tom looked nervous. Tessa stood with her feet planted firmly apart.

"No I'm not. Anyhow, it's all in my diary." She looked her father full in the face. They looked absurdly alike with their red hair and determined jaws.

"Diary? What diary is this, then?"

"My diary. It's got a key. Aunt Flor gave it to me for Christmas. She sent away to Harrods for it. I shadow people sometimes—grown-ups mostly—and then I do notes on what I've seen. Things like that. It's a sort of game," she added, twisting about awkwardly.

After a moment George Selway rapped out, "Bring it here. This diary. And the key. I want to see it, Tessa."

"But you can't," she said indignantly. "A diary is private. Especially when it's got a key."

"Bring it here. Immediately. Do as I say Tessa."

"I won't."

Tom, unnerved, fighting back tears, muttered, "Go on, Tess, do . . . it doesn't matter now."

"All right." Tessa flounced off. "But it's wrong, wrong, and I'll never forgive you," she shouted back at her father. The door slammed.

"Get off with you then," he told Tom testily. With a look of fury, Tessa came back, threw the diary on Hubert's desk and flew out of the room before her father could say anything.

Making sure the door was quite shut, George Selway then placed two long distance telephone calls, one to his lawyer in London, one to the manager of the family electrical business. When he had finished—and both calls took some time— he went upstairs to the bedroom which his wife had so recently and so unexpectedly vacated.

He threw off his uniform, put on a dressing-gown, and gulped some pills— thirstily drinking the tumbler of water beside the bed. On the lawn outside, Tom was yelling, showing off, tossing a cricket ball much too close to the windows.

39

George Selway went to the window and shouted, quite harshly, for him to stop that noise immediately.

Silence.

He drew the curtains and lay down, pulling the covers right up to his chin, and slept like the dead for two hours.

4

NEWS of Mrs. Selway's flight from Chalcot House within an hour of her husband's return from Burma was round the village in a flash. Her philandering with "the foreign chap" was old news. But nobody seriously thought she would up and leave Mr. Selway (yellow as mustard, poor chap, invalided out. Ended up a brigadier something—or was it a colonel?). *And* those two nice children.

"They" were wrong.

"Well you just listen to this now," Fred gasped when he returned from depositing Jennie Selway and her one suitcase at the ugly, primitive little house—not much more than a shack, thrown up before the war and abandoned—with a lean-to kitchen and a lavatory at the bottom of the garden. And after being waited on hand and foot at Chalcot House.

He staggered into the Goose and Duck, badly in need of a pint, and quickly became the centre of the bar's attention.

"Mr. Morgenstern runnin' out of the door and down the path to meet Madam— runnin' 'e was—with 'is arms out wide . . . like this look."

Because despite his incomprehensible foreignness, Felix Morgenstern had become popular in the district in the eighteen months or so he had lived there. Some evenings, wobbling along on his bike, he would drop in for a pint with the locals. He liked to talk, too. Lonely out there for a man on his own, it was. With his guttural accent and roundabout way of putting things, he asked all kinds of questions about farming and politics. Anyone could see that he was an educated gentleman. And he was friendly to anyone, didn't matter who. Lovely manners he had, kissing the ladies' hands as though it wasn't anything out of the ordinary. And kind. Turn his hand to anything he was asked—the village school play, even harvesting last summer, though his build and his age didn't really allow for it.

Now Mrs. Jennie Selway was altogether a different kettle of fish. Everyone liked Mr. and Mrs. Flood. Mr. Flood particularly. And they were used to Mrs. Flood's funny, arty ways. But that niece of hers down from London and the bombing, just drifted about like a half-wit when she did anything at all; hardly a word to say for herself, only that daft smile. Connie, who should know, said she was that simple she couldn't even boil a kettle straight. Everyone knew Marie looked after those children; anyhow, the little girl.

And even Jennie Selway's remarkable beauty was not much thought of in Chalcot where the opinion was that she should go off and get herself a good perm and a proper red lipstick.

So as "Time" was called that night, to a man (and woman) the sympathy in the matter lay not with George Selway or the children. But with Felix Morgenstern. He was now saddled with *her* . . .

At Chalcot House, the homecoming dinner which Hubert and Marie had planned so meticulously took place all the same. Sweet peas—which Tessa would later remember so vividly—trembled between the silver candlesticks. When they first sat down, Jennie Selway's extraordinary absence gave the proceedings an eerie feeling. Flora and Hubert, facing each other at either end of the table, both talked a shade too brightly. Once Tom said, "Don't you think Mum would . . ." and stopped and bit his lip. There was a short hush until Flora started chatting about the holiday in Cornwall which George Selway was planning for himself and the children; and the conversation became general again.

George Selway, feeling rested and surprisingly well, enjoyed Marie's cooking —and said so.

"Marvellous," he exclaimed, helping himself to more cheese soufflé. "Superb. If you only knew, all of you, how I had longed to be here again." He gave Tessa a pat on the shoulder.

Tessa, her tantrum over the purloined diary forgotten, was enjoying herself. She sat next to her father feeling very grown-up. She said to Flora Flood that she wished the dining-room could always look pretty like this with candles and flowers and the good china which they never used . . .

"It will now, lamb, with the war over

and everything getting back to normal. You'll see."

Tom was flushed and bright-eyed and slightly excitable. He held out his glass frequently for more wine. Given the circumstances, Hubert decided to be on the generous side. It was after all, he thought with a sigh, an occasion of sorts.

It was a good deal later, close to midnight, when George Selway and Hubert Flood sat in the study enjoying Hubert's best brandy. Moths fluttered round the single, dim lamp. Books, chairs, Hubert's desk, were silvered with moonlight which slanted in from the warm darkness outside.

From the depths of an armchair, George Selway said, "Thank God, at least, that we've almost got through today. I can't say it was the homecoming I had pictured." He sounded bitter. "Tom and Tessa seemed all right at dinner, didn't you think?"

"It's early days yet, old boy. Tom's a clever lad—and sensitive. We both think that. He needs careful handling. A bit like a racehorse. He'll miss Jennie—rather more than Tessa will, I fancy, even though she's younger."

"Yes, well, there we are." He leant forward to pour another brandy. "He does well at school so he obviously responds to discipline. The first thing he needs is a haircut . . . Flora told you about Tessa's diary, did she?"

"Er—yes." (She had also said, alarmed: "I do hope George isn't going to start treating them like the Fourteenth Army.")

"It made unpleasant reading," Selway said grimly, "despite the inkblots and the misspellings. I shan't need to use it, but at least I'm convinced that I'm taking the right line concerning custody."

"You'll see, in time, how it all settles down," Hubert Flood ventured cautiously. "Some limited access . . ."

"For the present—*none*. All the same," he leant back and closed his eyes. He was dog-tired; drained. The brief gaiety of dinner had turned to ashes in his mouth. He felt cold and shaky; the pills he had taken were wearing off. "I am tremendously grateful for the way you and Flora have looked after—the family—while I was away . . ."

"My dear chap. We've enjoyed it. It's a big place, much too much room for us. It's good to have young life about. And it was company—and interest—for Flora when I wasn't here. If there was only some way we could have forestalled this calamity of Jennie and Felix."

"Don't." Selway dismissed any further mention with a sharp gesture. Then, "What do you suppose the locals are making of all this?" He sounded drily amused.

"Not very interested, I should say," replied Hubert Flood who knew better and would frankly rather not think about it. Rumours of various rendezvous had reached his ears too. And the thought of the Morgenstern household more or less on their doorstep—and the expected child —horrified him.

Soon after, Flora drifted in and sat on the arm of Hubert's chair in a haze of smoke.

"I suppose I shall have to tell Vi—warn her—before she gets here on Sunday." She sighed. "She's coming down for lunch, George. Did I tell you?"

"I'm glad. I'm fond of Vi; there's lots

of go about her. Yes, she'll have to be told before, and she'll have to lend a hand in London with the children too. Especially Tessa. I was desperately sorry to hear about David. To think that he survived so much—seemed to be recovering from the frightful burns—and then to die in a crash that should never have happened, a stupid accident. Terrible for poor Vi. Terrible."

"Yes—yes it was. Although she has been very brave about it and has carried on. What else could she do? She seems to have quite a gay life in London. But she always doted on David. And he seemed such a golden young man with everything before him—looks and charm and brains."

"It's a tragic waste. Does she ever see Sam these days?"

Vi Delmore had been amicably separated from her husband Sam (Viscount Delmore)—David and Jennie's father— since long before the war; but they had never divorced.

"I rather think she does from time to time. She says he comes for lunch now and again. I think David's death brought them together perhaps, but there's never truly been anyone in her life except Ben Levson,

48

as you know. As it happens, he's over from New York for the summer, staying with her in Eaton Square, and they're both coming down on Sunday. Ben has a car and driver. And petrol. He always manages *everything*, does Ben."

And money, thought Selway. Big money. Ben Levson had inherited an American cosmetics fortune which he had doubled many times over. He and Vi Delmore met in the South of France in the mid 1920s. They had never married, largely, as Vi used to say so amusingly, because Ben was almost always married to someone else (which was true); but they had remained the best of friends—and lovers. And it was Ben who had provided her with the elegant flat and the lifestyle that went with it when she parted from Sam Delmore.

"I'm sorry to keep harping on the subject but I always told Vi there was something odd about Jennie. I don't mean to hurt your feelings, George dear, but I used to say to Vi: there's something not natural about that girl of yours. Lovely to look at I daresay . . . but impossibly shy. As though she was always somewhere else, a curtain between her and the rest of the world. Vi found her quite tiresome herself." Flora stopped. "I'm sorry, George. I'll say no more."

George Selway shook his head. He was beyond tiredness, almost beyond caring. Numbed. With an effort, he pulled himself out of the chair.

"I'm all in. Bless you both. I'm off to bed."

He paused on the landing. Through the tall window he could see the full white moon cutting a luminous swathe through the trees. England. A deep, aching regret, promptly stifled, stirred within him. How he had longed for this night during those gruelling days and years; and how bitterly unlike his imaginings it was ending. He thought wearily of the problems ahead—a sickening divorce, the house, settling the children. Reconstructing the business— and commercial times were going to be far from easy for years to come.

It was essential that he got back his health. He must find the best man in Harley Street and see him as soon as possible. And he must take those goddamned pills. Now.

Abruptly, he turned into his room, took something from a table and continued up to the third floor where Tom and Tessa slept. Very quietly, he opened Tessa's door. Here, too, the silvery moonlight spilled on to the bed. He touched Tessa's hair, briefly and tenderly, and placed the diary on the chair beside her.

Tessa, who was over-excited and still awake, waited until the door had shut again and then her hand shot out, seized the diary, and stuffed it under her pillow.

Mum's gone, poor Tom, was her last waking thought.

The full summer moon shone, too, through the bedroom window of Felix Morgenstern's cottage. It blanched the bed and splashed the bare floor. Her arms around Felix, who was sleeping against her, Jennie lay awake. She was in a state close to bliss; transfigured by happiness. Safe at last; the past sloughed off like an empty skin.

Rapturously, she watched as the moon grew paler and the pink flush of morning appeared. Felix stirred and sighed at her breast, restless, muttering German words. She heard the dawn chorus—very faint at first but growing louder and louder—in the trees and hedgerows around the isolated dwelling. It was only when the light was already strong that she drifted into sleep . . . But at Felix's first urgent touch—*"Mein Liebchen, mein Liebchen"* —his hand sliding across her stomach, parting her thighs, she was awake at an instant. He moved and entered her.

5

"HERE we are, my darlings," trilled Violet Delmore as she got out of the car at the front door of Chalcot House. It was late on the following Sunday morning. She held on to her hat, a minuscule and frothy creation, worn tipped fashionably forward. "I thought we would *never* get here, neither did Ben. We've been on the road since the crack of dawn. It was absolutely endless." Small and chic, she was wearing a navy linen dress and navy and white shoes. Tom and Tessa, who had been waiting around irritably all morning, flung themselves on her. "Gran, Gran, we thought you would never get here . . . Did the car break down?"

"Were you lost, Gran?"

"I don't think so, darling. It just felt like it. What an adorable blue frock, Tessa. Ben," she called over her shoulder as Tessa clung round her neck. "Come and meet my divine grandchildren. Now this is darling Tessa . . ."

Helped by his driver, the elderly Ben Levson emerged stiffly from the back seat. Although he was a short man, he had very broad shoulders. He was wearing a light tropical suit, a brown felt hat and dark glasses. There was a lighted cigar in his hand. He looked at Tessa closely, nodded— and put the cigar back in his mouth.

"And Tom . . . I told you how handsome he was." Tom went bright red as they shook hands. Ben Levson looked morose. His heavy, rather fleshy face was deeply grooved. His skin was tanned and leathery.

"All I can say is," he remarked, shuffling into the house, very bent, "that that was one hell of a journey. Jesus, don't they know how to build highways in this country? Where's Hubert?"

"Coming, coming . . . welcome, my dears, Vi . . ." Hubert Flood came out of his study, kissed his sister-in-law and warmly greeted Ben Levson. "Ben, such a long time—a war ago at least. Come in, come in. Flora's in the studio—she'll be out directly. George is on the phone I believe."

Vi addressed the children who were stuck on either side of her. "Now you two —we've got lots to talk about . . . and you've grown again, Tom, I do believe. I can't wait to see your Papa. *Isn't* it all exciting. But I *must* see Flora first."

Hubert tactfully chivvied the children out of the way, saying that he was sure Gran and Mr. Levson wanted a bit of peace and a drink before lunch.

"You can say that again," Ben agreed, blowing rings of cigar smoke.

"So later, my darlings," Vi called after them as they went off out into the garden. "We'll have a lovely talk later. But I must chat to your father and Flora first." And when they were out of earshot, "*Jennie* . . . Hubert my dear, I'm in a state of total and utter shock. When Flora rang to tell me, I nearly fainted dead away. Didn't I Ben?"

She caught sight of herself in a mirror and adjusted her hat slightly. She had never been good-looking; she had sharp features and a long nose like her sister Flora's. But she was always superbly groomed; her hair swept up off her face and the most expensive accessories money could buy.

"I mean, it's too dreadful for words. I do feel for poor George, coming back to face all this; and as for the children . . ."

"She's a bolter." Ben Levson's teeth, surprisingly white against the dark skin, flashed in a sudden—and enormously persuasive—smile. "Like her mother."

"Really, Ben. My leaving Sam wasn't like this at all. It was all extremely dignified," she told him reprovingly. "And I certainly didn't leave him with two children on his hands, after three ghastly years in Burma. What are we to do?"

Hubert, who had sensed that Vi had no intention of being put out by her daughter's flight said, "Do? Well of course we must all do whatever we can to support George and help Tom and Tessa. Jennie is quite out of the picture for the time being. But my first suggestion, Vi dear, is a drink outside. It's warm enough for you, is it Ben? Ah—here come Flora and George . . ."

"Goodness me, Ben, how the years do go

on," observed Hubert. "When was it we first met? When Vi came out to stay with us with the children, Jennie and David, in Antibes. 1926 was it?" They were sitting on the terrace with drinks while George Selway, his mother-in-law and her sister held a council of war in the garden.

"'25."

Ben Levson lifted his glass and sunlight caught the heavy, and very beautiful, gold ring which he wore on his little finger. Watching him, Hubert saw little resemblance to the flamboyant entrepreneur they had met that first summer which seemed a lifetime ago; he looked as though he had recently lost weight—his suit hung on him. Only the full head of hair and the accoutrements of cigar and dark glasses remained the same. Hubert thought he must be well into his seventies.

They had met when they were invited, through friends, to a luncheon on his yacht—*The Andromedes*—which was the talk of the Riviera that year. The parties, the music, the starlets that came and went —Noel Coward's "cocktails and laughter" generation all right. Ben Levson's squat, ugly, powerful figure presiding over it all.

Loving it; exuding confidence. And money. A Midas touch in all his enterprises—the early talking films at that time. Or so everyone said. The cosmetics empire which he inherited and expanded vastly became simply a front for his other many, and varied, activities. There were lots of stories about him, hinting at all kind of shenanigans and perversions. It was said that he had connections with the Mafia; that he had a penchant for the girls in a club in Harlem . . . Largely envy, Hubert supposed.

Because there had been something truly mesmeric about Ben in his heyday—his wonderful dark eyes; the dazzling smile (with a flash of gold) which seemed to break his face in two. Hubert could see him now in the Casino, raking in the chips, laughing hugely, waving that cigar about. He was that rare breed—a lucky gambler. And he had—what was the expression?—animal magnetism. Vi thought so at least. She was hooked from the first by Ben Levson, who was notorious with women and proud of it; after that luncheon, which was all it took, nice dull Sam Delmore in his hideous gothic house in Hertfordshire never had a chance.

"That was it. July and August 1925. David had broken his arm badly and the doctors thought the warmth and the swimming would do it good. So Vi came alone with the children," Hubert said tactfully, omitting mention of Sam. "I remember we got hold of a very staid mademoiselle so Vi could enjoy herself." He went on hurriedly, "How do you think Vi is looking—after David? Flora and I were dreadfully worried about her. They were so very close those two. We were all utterly heartbroken."

"She keeps going. She's a great gal, Vi."

Ben Levson had once told Hubert that Vi Delmore was the only woman he had ever known who never bored him.

"She certainly knows how to enjoy life, but we did wonder how David's death would affect her. She was very brave. She doesn't seem to talk about him much, which I suppose is natural enough. Anyhow, we now have this extraordinary —and very nasty—situation of Jennie going off. And Felix, as you know, an old friend we tried to help which makes it even more embarrassing . . ."

"His family—destroyed?" Ben turned the black glasses towards Hubert. He was never a man to use more words than were necessary.

"Yes." He nodded. "Yes, he knows that definitely now. His wife and daughter both died in Thérèsienstadt. His wife apparently died of malnutrition. I don't know about the rest of the family or friends and colleagues."

"*Bastards,*" Ben Levson said briefly. He stubbed out his cigar and took another from a silver case in his pocket. After he had carefully cut and lit it, he said, "Not like her mother as a kid. The girl. I looked."

"Tessa? No—no, she's the image of George, we think. It's Tom who has taken after Jennie and the Delmores."

"Pretty little thing she was, Jennie." Ben Levson drew on the cigar and swirled his glass, the ice cubes clinking. "Blonde. Cute." He drained the scotch. "I used to take quite an interest in her—take her about a bit. The galleries. Vi never bothered much, not about the girl . . ."

Vi, Flora and George decided on the rose garden. They walked slowly, heads down, deep in discussion. Tessa skulked nearby, cross at being kept away from the grandmother she adored. Tom glanced at the grown-ups (of whom he felt himself almost, but not quite, a part) from the other end of the parched lawn. He alternately bit his nails and tossed a cricket ball. *Jabber, jabber, jabber*, he thought irritably . . .

They were discussing Jennie, of course.

"The most extraordinary behaviour; I simply couldn't believe my ears," Vi was saying, one eye on the roses which had been particularly good that year. "I intend to have nothing to do with her for the present. Nothing."

"Good," said George Selway.

"And a *child* . . . What on earth do they intend to live on?"

"Not much," George Selway muttered grimly, his hands behind his back, staring fiercely at the ground. "One thing I do want to make clear." He stopped and looked from one sister to the other. "*I* am getting custody—and Tom and Tessa will be seeing as little of their mother in future as possible."

"Quite," said Vi Delmore after a very short pause. "She may be my own daughter, but given the circumstances, I'm very relieved to hear it."

Flora frowned and said nothing.

"I've already made arrangements to get the house in London opened," George Selway continued. "One of my managers went over it yesterday and he doesn't think there's too much wrong with it, fortunately. Shabby, of course, but then what isn't? I'll have to find a school for Tessa. Tom is well settled at Marlborough which is a relief. I'm just hoping I'll stay fit. This damned malaria is hard to shake off."

"I've got the most marvellous doctor—he's a friend, really," said Vi. "As a matter of fact, I've got Ben to see him recently—he's been most awfully under the weather lately, not himself at all. I've been quite worried. Shall I ask him who he thinks you should see, George?"

"I wish you would, Vi. I've fixed three weeks in Cornwall for myself and the children. The sea air should do us good at least . . . And then I've got to get back to work." He straightened—grey eyes glaring under bushy red brows, his jaw obstinate. "From what I can deduce, Selway Electric has run down rather badly. It's going to take a lot of hard work to put it right again. So much is out of one's hands . . . It depends how quickly the country can pick up the pieces and get going again, what sort of national willpower we've still got left."

He went off to join Hubert and Ben Levson, and Flora and Vi loitered on their own.

"Flor, do tell me, I've been dying to ask, what on *earth* is this Felix person like?" asked Vi.

"Delightful. We've always liked him enormously—so this business has come as a great shock. He's very charming, warm, clever. I think I feel rather sorry for him. He lost everything, absolutely everything, in the war. His wife, his only child . . . He's such an honourable man, truly, that after everything Hubert has done for him, I'm afraid he must be feeling so frightfully guilty and uneasy."

"For goodness sake, I can perfectly well understand Jennie having an affair with him," Vi said impatiently, stepping carefully round a pile of weeds, keeping to the path, mindful of her smart shoes. "After all, for the last five years almost everyone has been sleeping with everyone else in a manner of speaking. One took a bit of comfort where one could . . ." She glanced at her sister who remained silent. "But as Felix is an intellectual, what on earth can he see in Jennie? She can't be any sort of companion for a man like that. I mean, she hasn't got two words to say for herself, she's scarcely read a book . . ."

"Loneliness, Vi. And Jennie is young and beautiful. Odd but beautiful. I tell myself I blame *her*—Jennie. And then I wonder . . ." She sighed, "It's all a mystery. Anyhow, the 'cottage' really is quite ghastly. Badly built red brick put up to house workers on one of the estates, I believe. A lavatory at the bottom of the garden. No telephone. Felix gets a bit of work doing translations, but it's poorly paid. And a child coming . . ."

"Tom and Tessa don't know about that?"

"No, no. Much better not for the moment, we all agreed."

"I can't see Jennie coping in that set-up. She's hopelessly impractical. I always assumed George practically ran the London house."

"We all did. Hubert and I feel that with Jennie gone, the sooner Tom and Tessa are back in London with George, getting on with things, the better. Away from the local gossip here, too. And he's going to need a good housekeeper. You'll have to help there, Vi."

"I will—although it won't be easy. Hmm . . . you know, I did hear of someone like that available recently. Now who was it? I'll have to think—and I'll ask around. Don't worry. I'll find someone. George will simply have to pay up—which he won't like—and behave himself. He can't go ordering people about any more in the way he likes to."

Shading her eyes against the sun, Flora saw the dark figure of Marie on the terrace. Tom and Tessa had joined their father, uncle and Ben Levson.

"Lunch," Flora said to Vi. "We must go in. Marie has been cooking and scheming like mad and we must put a good face on things. It's important for the children. No mention of Jennie, of course."

"Naturally not. I'm going to talk to them about it a bit later—saying Heaven knows what, but there it is. Tell me something, Flor."

Half way across the lawn, Vi Delmore stopped and looked at her sister.

"What?"

Flora was looking very handsome in her dotty, exotic way, Vi decided. Hair piled high, long wild silk gown in fuchsia and white stripes. The inevitable cigarette in a long holder. She's aging well, Vi thought. She said, "Why, *really*, has Jennie gone off with Felix?"

Flora considered. It was the very question that had woken her at four o'clock that morning.

"I think—because she adores him," she said simply. "I think she felt she couldn't live without him. What I don't understand is *why*."

"Exactly. After all, George may have his shortcomings, but he's so competent—just what she needed, we thought."

Flora sighed. "She was determined on Felix, nothing else mattered. Husband, children, how she lived, what people would say. And that's all there is to it."

"I know you're still painting away. Anything nice in the studio, Flor?" Vi asked. Everyone had wandered off into the warm, cloudy afternoon and they were sitting together in deckchairs on the lawn. "Ben and I were only thinking last night that the flat looks a bit bare. It badly needs redecorating—like everything else in London. One of your big, bright pictures would cheer it up."

"I've got quite a few available just now. I keep getting asked by dealers, even these days. And Hubert has been talking to one of the London galleries about an exhibition. I'm pleased with them." Flora blew out a cloud of smoke. "I'll go and find Ben and take him over, see if there's anything there he fancies, if you like. Perhaps you ought to find the children and have a chat. Tom's friend Oliver Bingham is coming over for tea, so you should have a word with him first."

"Right you are. And don't let Ben beat you down. You know what a haggler he is. Oh there's Tom. Cooee!" she called out. "Wait for me, Tom, and we'll go off for a walk—but nothing too taxing . . . and then I want to see Tessa."

Linking arms with Tom, her head bent confidentially, Vi stuck to the jolliest subjects she could think of—the proposed holiday in Cornwall, getting back to the London house, a new day-school for Tessa which she would help her father choose. She mentioned Jennie briefly and tactfully. *Of course* the children would be seeing plenty of her once everything settled down . . .

"I doubt it," Tom said seriously, sounding like an adult.

"Nonsense, darling. I know it's very upsetting for you—it is for all of us. Frankly, I'm simply horrified—but we've got to count the blessings and get on with our lives. Awful for Papa, the divorce, but you may be sure that he will manage it as well as he can. And once school starts again and you're occupied it won't seem so—well, dramatic."

Vi Delmore had a particularly buoyant

personality and invariably managed to instil optimism; even David's death had not quenched it completely. She suspected that Tom, not Tessa, would be the one who would brood over Jennie's desertion.

"It won't be the same, ever," Tom said, blinking and tossing back his fair hair. "I can't understand what could have made her do it. And she didn't tell us—not even me."

"It's very difficult, I know, but try not to be too hard on her. I'm glad we've had a little chat about it. Look, Tom, isn't that your friend who's come over for tea?"

A boy of Tom's age, wearing a cricket sweater, was jogging across the lawn towards them. He was shorter than Tom, but well-built with a determined, manly air.

"Sorry. Hope I'm not interrupting. My aunt dropped me off a bit early because the cousins had to go to a birthday party."

"Oh hullo Oliver . . . Gran, this is Oliver Bingham. He's at Marlborough with me. We're in the same house."

Oliver and Vi shook hands. He had a firm grip and he looked her straight in the eye with a nice, open smile. Although the two boys must have been much of an age, Oliver seemed noticeably more mature to Vi.

"You live round here, then, Oliver? Isn't that lucky for both of you."

"Actually I don't. My mother died last year and my father and I live in London. But my cousins—there are five of them, all girls—live outside Porchester and I spend some of the holidays with them. So when I'm staying, I come over quite a bit. Five is an awful lot of girls to be stuck with for too long."

Vi smiled, liking him instinctively. "I expect they're thrilled to have a young man about, and spoil you like mad. I'll leave you with Tom because I want to find Tessa. See you at tea, then."

Tessa and Vi walked round the garden, Vi looking at the flowers with keen interest and Tessa skipping, talking nonstop, and clutching her grandmother's hand. She hadn't really been able to see what all the fuss was about Mummy. She had known for months that she was spending a part of every day with Felix. She didn't miss her company because she hardly ever

70

spoke to her. For as long as she could remember, ever since they had come to Chalcot, if there was anything she needed, anything important at all, she had gone either to Marie or Aunt Flor. So *that* hadn't changed . . . She was slightly apprehensive about returning to London; she sensed the days of her running about, doing more or less what she wanted, sitting reading in the back row of the village school, were over. And she wasn't sure she liked the sound of a strict London day-school. But the good thing was that in London they would be nearer Gran.

"And that's really the nicest thing about going back to London. We'll be able to see you whenever we want, won't we Gran?"

"Of course, my darling, of course. We'll have lots of gay outings," Vi replied a bit vaguely.

Marie and Connie had brought the tea out on to the terrace. Ben Levson, who dearly loved a bargain despite his enormous wealth, was jousting with Hubert over two of Flora's pictures which he had seen in the studio and wanted to buy for Vi's flat. For all his charm, Hubert was a canny adversary and they reached an amicable agreement not far off the asking price.

"That's a deal then. I'll get a cheque down to you tomorrow." Tom and Oliver Bingham and Vi and Tessa, in pairs, converged simultaneously on the terrace from opposite directions. Flora appeared from the studio (smelling faintly of turpentine) and George Selway emerged from Hubert's study where he had spent the afternoon, studying papers and telephoning.

It was then that Hubert, squinting up at the sky which was rather overcast, rubbed his hands and announced, "Just time for one good snapshot now everybody's here." He was holding a camera, his newest toy. Tom and Tessa groaned. *Must we?* It's so *boring* . . . can't we have tea? Oliver and I want to go fishing."

"In a moment. Patience, patience." Hubert busied himself with the camera. "Now come along all of you, you'll be amused by it one day."

"Very well." Flora sounded resigned. "Up you get everyone, before the tea gets cold. Where do you want us Hubert?"

"Over there, I think. On the balustrade.

Adults sitting." Vi heaved Ben Levson to his feet.

"That's right . . . Tom and Oliver on one side, Tessa on the other. You, Flor—and George. And Vi and Ben."

"I say, sir, what about Orlando?" Oliver called out enthusiastically. "We don't want to leave him out. Look—there he is."

He was rubbing his thick ginger fur against the table where the tea tray was, sniffing. They all looked at him and laughed. Even George Selway.

"We *must* have Orlando, Hubie . . ." Tessa pleaded.

Orlando paused, looking back at them; composed; very dignified.

"Quite right Oliver. Get him, will you, before he scarpers." Hubert readjusted the camera as Oliver dived, scooped up Orlando, and gave him to Tessa.

"You hold him Tessa. Hang on tight so he can't jump." And he went back and stood next to Tom who was glowering and fidgeting.

Tessa, who had had a crush on Oliver all that summer, went very pink.

"Oh come on, Hubie," Tom moaned. "Get it over with."

"That's enough, Tom," barked his father. He was sitting on the grey stone balustrade, his arms crossed, looking grim again.

"Still everyone . . . Good, good. Quite still. Say cheese. Right—all over."

"We must be off, Flor," Vi said. The sisters were in Flora's bedroom, tidying themselves up. Vi smoothed her dark hair, which now had white wings swept up from her temples. Outside on the lawn, Tom, Oliver and Tessa were playing croquet. "It's after five and the journey takes ages. And Ben seems to get so exhausted these days."

"I don't think he is looking well, although it's been so long since I last saw him. Why don't you stay, Vi? We could lend you everything you need for one night. The weather is quite pleasant—it would do you both good. And we've masses of room as you know, even with the Selways here."

Vi shook her head. "We must go, really. I did talk to the children—rallied the troops, as it were." She sighed. "It's sad for them but they're so young and, whatever else, George *is* reliable. Tom seems the most perturbed . . ." She looked down at them. The croquet was going well and they were shouting and cheering alternately. Tom was teasing Tessa while Oliver was clearly lending her an encouraging hand.

"Which is what we expected," Flora said. Vi turned away from the window.

"We're giving dinner tomorrow night to one of David's old RAF buddies. Marcus Reardon. He was his greatest friend, you know. They learnt to fly together straight from university. Throughout, they were inseparable. He used to bring him up to Eaton Square whenever they both had leave. I like to keep in touch with David's friends, particularly Marcus."

Flora thought: that's the first time she has mentioned David's name all day . . . that rouge and red lipstick make her look quite haggard. She said, "Yes—yes I'm sure you do. Marcus . . . I think I remember . . ."

"He was at the funeral. He's rather good-looking. Interesting. Anyhow, he's at a bit of a loose end at the moment; can't seem to settle, like so many of them. He's thinking of journalism and Fleet Street. He's got a Celtic way with words all right. I thought—I don't know—that Ben might have a few ideas. It's a contact for Marcus, anyhow. So you see . . ." she began gathering up her bag, her gloves. "We must be off, Flor. The driver will want to get back, too."

On the way downstairs, Vi remarked what a delightful boy she thought Oliver Bingham was. Flora agreed.

"Hubert and I think he's a good influence on Tom, too. He's very steady—quite old for his years. And such a pleasant personality."

"Yes, I do *so* like him . . ." She started to draw on her gloves. "And I've remembered where I heard of that housekeeper. It suddenly came to me. She was with the mother of a friend of mine at the War Office. The mother died and I know she was looking for another position. If only she's still available . . . I'll get right on to it tomorrow."

Which was how Ella came into all their lives.

When they got down to the hall, Ben was

already in the back of the car with a rug tucked round his knees.

"We've wrapped the pictures in a blanket and put them in the boot," Hubert told Vi as he kissed her goodbye.

The driver, who had spent the day under Marie's suspicious stares and couldn't wait to get on the road, held the door while Vi hugged everyone. They stood at the door as the sleek car purred slowly away from the house and up the road. Vi turned and looked back through the window, her dotty hat bobbing, waving a pale gloved hand. They all waved cheerfully back—Flora and Hubert, George Selway, Marie, Tom. All except Tessa and Oliver who were standing a little to one side—and seemed to be enjoying a private joke.

Part Two

London, 1960

1

TESSA. On a cloudy, sultry afternoon late in May. Face flushed and angry, flung across her bed in Parloe Square. In her father's house. Sulky, smarting from her latest words with him.

"I can see no reason for you going to the funeral, Tessa, none," he had just told her, glaring from behind the large partners' desk in his study below. "You hardly knew him . . . you won't know anyone there."

"But Sam Delmore was my grandfather," Tessa found herself yelling back at him, defensive, angry, both hands on the desk, leaning across. "I saw him sometimes. You know I did. And what about Gran? She's his widow—even if they hadn't lived together for years and years. She's going—so is Tom. He's making the effort. And I want to go—to be with *her*. Didn't you think of that?"

Silence.

Unspoken between them the unmentionable name—Jennie. Both of them knowing that Jennie Morgenstern, Sam's daughter, would naturally be at the funeral. At least, in so far as you could count on her ever doing anything normal. Since the divorce, all that time ago, George Selway still bitterly resented even the intermittent contact between her and their children. Even now, now that they were adults. Old wounds, his wound particularly, reopened.

"Tom's coming," Tessa repeated. "He's got a case on in Winchester but he's going to do everything he possibly can to get away."

Selway's grey eyes, so like her own, lighted on her clenched hands. Tessa looked down. She knew what he was going to say before he said it.

"If you must work in a flower shop, isn't there any way you can prevent your hands looking like pieces of meat?" Tessa immediately snatched them off the desk and put them behind her back. Her chin jerked up. Then he said gruffly—hating these rows that seemed to blow up between them as much as she did.

"All right, all right . . . I suppose

someone should go down with Vi; a bit of an ordeal for her. You must do as you wish. Now—off you go. I've got papers to go through."

George Selway, chairman of the board of Selway Electric, one of the miracles of British industry since the War—now poised, so the business world had it, for a major acquisition in the United States. Dismissing her; both of them miserable. As she reached the door, he said testily, "Get a wreath sent down if you think it's the thing to do—ask your grandmother." Rustling papers about, putting on his glasses . . .

So there was Tessa, having rushed straight up to her room at the back of the tall London house, lying contemplating the striped pink wallpaper. *And feeling, very seriously, that it was about time she took stock of what was happening in her life.*

It was a bit faded now, the wallpaper, like the matching curtains—chosen by whom? Aunt Flor? Hubie? Soon after that dreadful summer when, as children, she and Tom had been frogmarched from the country freedom of Chalcot to the fashionable, though war-weary, London square. Minus Mother of course.

Not that she had minded, really; although Tom had. She realised that more and more. He had been bitterly, openly rebellious. (They both felt friendless and restricted—missed the Floods and Marie; and those long hours when they had disappeared, doing whatever they wanted, no questions asked.) There were daily arguments with Papa over everything—Tom's haircuts, friends, his allowance. It had been a relief to Tessa when he had gone back to boarding-school. She remembered him waiting in the hall, neat in his grey suit, trunk locked and roped—fiddling around, never still for an instant. A ring at the doorbell, the taxi driver—and Papa appearing from his study, shouting instructions in all directions.

"That's the trunk, off you go. Not that way, Tom. Look sharp . . . got your ticket, have you? And I want a better report this term, young man." Tom flinching visibly as he grasped the handle.

Ella, dear Ella, bustling out from the kitchen, soothing, comforting, pouring oil in every direction. Somehow mollifying everyone—an encouraging hug for Tom, Tessa sent off on some errand. George Selway calmed into feeling that the household was running efficiently, under his control—setting out for his office after taking the medicine discreetly handed to him by Ella. (For years after Burma he was wracked with bouts of malaria.) Tessa summoned by Ella for a special lunch, a treat, at the old scrubbed pine table in the kitchen; for an hour of Ella's sympathetic, wholehearted attention. And it was to Ella, of course, that she had taken her troubles ever since . . .

For, as though in answer to the family's prayers, Ella had arrived on the doorstep towards the end of that first chaotic summer, pounced on by Gran Delmore who had, as she had promised, tracked her down through an acquaintance.

Their first morning back in London, after a forlorn and rainy holiday in Cornwall, Vi Delmore telephoned.

"A treasure, George. I've found her at last. Now look after her and give her everything she wants." She sounded triumphant—and rightly so.

It was Ella, and she was quite definite

about her requirements: a small flat in the basement into which she could move her own furniture and her cat. An efficient cleaning lady engaged by herself. A reasonably free hand with the children. About her wages, which were generous for the time, she was less bothered. Selway agreed readily and she arrived at Number 34 Parloe Square, small and neat in her navy blue suit, with two suitcases and a cat-box. She took one look at the children standing about self-consciously and beamed.

"So this is Tessa . . . and Tom." A firm handshake, brown eyes friendly and direct. White curly hair and red apple cheeks. "Your Granny told me what a tall chap you were. Take Morgan for me, then, would you?" She handed Tom the cat-box. "Watch out, he's a heavy old thing."

She moved in, established her authority with intelligence and humour, and got to work on them all. Within weeks none of them, including George Selway, could imagine life without her. Morgan—large, black and majestic—took one look round the establishment and decided it would do.

The furniture, which turned out to be good dark oak left to her by an aunt in Wales, arrived soon after. The basement was painted white, curtains found in the attic and re-lined. "Ella's place", as it became known, turned into a comfortable home and was often envied by the young Selways. Particularly, Tessa reflected, after the awful Poppy Renfrew—her father's "friend" of many years, the constant escort he had never married—persuaded him to give over the furnishing of the rest of the house to a fashionable interior decorator.

Ella had accomplished so much, so unobtrusively, in that first difficult post-war year. Most of all, she had reassured Tom and Tessa after their mother's sudden disappearance and their painful uprooting from Chalcot House. She refused to let the general shabbiness of everything, the lack of heating, the acute food shortage, get her down. (Tessa remembered it all dimly, just as she remembered shivering in a gymslip in her fashionable Knightsbridge day-school). Ella made the London house a real home.

And it was Ella who had told her and

Tom about Max's birth. The telephone rang one murky November evening. It was Aunt Flor and Hubie from Dorset. Tessa had been hustled up to her room; then Ella and Papa were closeted in the study for what seemed like hours. Tucking her up in bed later Ella had said, "Your mother has a fine little boy, born this morning. Now isn't that nice news? Quite a bit earlier than expected, but never mind, and Mother right as rain. I'll be writing to Tom at school in the morning to tell him . . ." Drawing the curtains briskly against the foggy night, no questions allowed, Tessa was left alone to puzzle out the strange antics of grown-ups' lives.

In all the years, Tessa had never once heard Papa refer to Mother or Felix or Max by name.

And thinking of Ella, she wondered if it was too early to pop down and see her; have yet another comforting chat about Papa's impossibility—even though she loved him dearly. Ella—calm, practical, intelligent—understood. But it was an unspoken rule of the household that Ella's afternoons were kept free. Tessa looked at her watch. It was five o'clock now, a bit after. She badly needed her sympathetic ear. She could see in the dressing-table mirror that her face was still red and cross-looking beneath the mop of gingery hair. She really ought to wait for another half hour or so.

"We must have some house rules, my dears," Ella always said about the after-noon freedom.

Tessa sighed. Would she ever fully come to terms with Papa? Today their clash of wills was reasonably resolved; but it had left, as always, a sour taste in the mouth. The root cause, she knew, was knotty enough. Since he re-entered their lives, almost as a stranger, Tessa had felt deeply ambivalent towards him. As she became an adult, the love and pride which she felt for him were mixed with the need to assert herself; for independence. Tessa thought she knew what her mother's desertion had done to his soul. She had always known— although she had never put it into words —that only *she* provided some solace.

Tom, who had never got on with his father, had escaped. After a brilliant record at Oxford, he had become a barrister and now shared a large and untidy flat with old university friends. He rarely came to Parloe Square any more—except, surreptitiously, to see Ella.

George Selway adored Tessa, would give her anything, show her his steely charm, his intelligence, his wide-ranging mind. But he had to dominate everyone, *particularly* her. Tessa longed to break away. But short of marriage, which showed no signs of happening, how?

A continuing bone of contention between them was her job. She had run away from a finishing school in Switzerland and refused to finish a secretarial training. As Selway correctly pointed out in both cases, she was better at knowing what she didn't want to do than what she did. Then, quite by chance, she was asked to help out in a small, up-and-coming flowershop in Chelsea which was beginning to get a reputation for imaginative flowers and unusual arrangements. It was owned and run by an unmarried middle-aged woman called Joan Bell who chain-smoked, swore like a navvy—and had a talent for friendship.

Joan and Tessa met at a Christmas party given by mutual friends three years before.

"I don't know why I bother," Joan told Tessa cheerfully, referring to the shop which was deluged with holiday orders, and the assistant who had left unexpectedly that morning. "It's bloody masochism, that's what it is."

Tessa soon discovered that she bothered because she loved it—and did it exceptionally well.

"If you need a hand, let me know," Tessa had told her. "I'm not doing anything at the moment." (The secretarial course had recently collapsed and she was longing to get out of Parloe Square.)

Joan grinned. "Okay. You've got a deal." She stuck out her hand. "When can you start?"

"Well," said Tessa, slightly taken aback. "Tomorrow, if you like." She had started—and stayed and stayed . . . She and Joan developed a warm, but unlikely, friendship. Tessa was the only daughter of a rich man; Joan, a lot older, brought up on a farm in Sussex, had driven an ambulance during the worst of the Blitz. She had inherited part of her parents' farm which included a cottage. And it was the large and beautiful garden, which she cultivated expertly, that had given her the idea of opening a shop in the first place.

Joan's Garden, as it was so logically called, was a success. Surprisingly successful, in fact. Everything about it was countrified and natural. Joan preferred simple, weedy flowers—mostly white—and soft, unstructured arrangements. "My country bunches," as she called them, were her favourites; freesias, gypsophila, cornflowers, lupins, dianthus; all mixed with grasses and lots of fresh greenery. A world away from the stiff, much wired flower arranging which was considered fashionable.

The shop itself, in a charming little Chelsea street, looked more like a cottage living-room. Bouquets of dried flowers, tied with long ribbons, hung from the ceiling; prettily planted baskets were dotted among the vases; all kinds of pots and containers, many of them antiques, were piled on every available surface. Joan always took special care with the small bow-fronted window, with a seemingly artless spray or basket, carefully lit, plonked on a tapestry stool or by a gilt mirror. Even the small note-cards sent with deliveries had designs in the corners, hand-painted by an artist friend of Joan's.

Joan's Garden had a style of its own and, largely through word of mouth, was becoming popular.

George Selway never really approved. "No time for yourself, keeping those hours. *A shop* . . . and you'll ruin your hands." However, for the first time in her life, Tessa felt useful. Her enthusiasm grew. She took herself off on a flower-arranging course and quickly found that she had a natural flair for colour and line and what looked appropriate where, and good ideas of her own. After assimilating the basics, she left and went back to the shop. With her horticultural knowledge and her collector's eye, Joan was a good and patient teacher. She and Tessa worked well together. Soon Tessa, who had previously thought she could hardly do simple arithmetic, was tackling the books as well, leaving Joan to get on with her garden and special customers.

Tessa also started doing some of the supplementary buying in Covent Garden. She enjoyed this too. She didn't mind getting up at five, driving through the empty streets in the half light or even the dark during winter. She revelled in the edge-of-day feeling, the camaraderie of the market—the crates and boxes tossed hither and thither by the porters; the cut-and-thrust of buying, the lively Cockney humour; her hands clasped thankfully round a steaming mug of coffee, always at the same stall, before getting back to open up the shop.

Then, last winter, the crunch came. The lease on the shop was running out and they were offered a new one. They had just bought a second-hand delivery van, so further bank-borrowing was out of the question, no matter how well the business was going. Tessa went straight to her father. Taking Joan.

"I'll have to think about it Miss, er . . ."

"Joan," said Joan, smiling at George Selway across the first floor drawing-room in Parloe Square, stubbing out one cigarette and lighting another. "That's better."

Appalling woman, Selway was thinking sourly. Trousers like a land-girl and that cropped hair . . . looked like one of those odd creatures that went for other women. Heaven forbid. What a friend for Tessa, I ask you, yet his daughter seemed devoted to her.

All the same, he could never resist a bargain when he saw one. The property, not the shop—even though it made a reasonable profit—was the nub of the thing. There wouldn't be many more years when a long lease on a central London property could be picked up for a couple of thousand like this. And if it kept Tessa occupied, he supposed he could do worse for the moment. Not what he had expected of his only daughter at twenty-three, frankly, but she seemed to have a couple of decent young men in tow and she was still very young, after all.

So the solicitors were called in, an agreement drawn up and George Selway guaranteed the bank loan. Tessa and Joan became equal partners.

Which was one very pleasant aspect of her life, Tessa thought, getting up and staring in the mirror.

"You're a big, tall girl, darling," Gran always said. "Now stand up straight and be proud of it."

"So why do you feel such a lump, then?" Tessa asked of her reflection, grinning, and deciding that her hair needed a good cut. "Answer me that . . ." No knight in shining armour had appeared, that was certain. But she had her share of dinner dates and invitations and weekends at large and mostly uncomfortable country houses. One young Guards officer had taken her out for months and asked her to marry him; but he, certainly, although fun, was not the particular knight she had in mind—whoever that was. Having Tom, who was six years older, had helped her social life too. While he was at Oxford, she had often been asked up to parties and was always the youngest there, enjoying the interest in her being Tom's sister. He was bound to get a First and was already a cricketing Blue.

And she had admired his friend, Oliver Bingham, ever since she could remember. She saw him, off and on, at parties or when he was staying with his cousins near Chalcot. He was very gregarious and popular and had made an impressive start at the Bar, Tom said. Whereas he, Tom, seemed quite bored and disillusioned by it,

Tessa thought. Once or twice Oliver had asked her out in a friendly sort of way.

So she was very surprised at how complimentary he had been at the hunt ball last winter. She was wearing a shocking pink swirling taffeta dress. ("Divine with your hair, so clever of you," a sophisticated fellow guest had murmured to her in the Ladies.) She knew she looked good. Oliver asked her to dance again and again and said how he couldn't believe she had grown up, really grown up, and was so beautiful and he hoped she didn't think he was a fool for saying so.

The night flew by, one of the happiest Tessa could ever remember, and she was sure she would see him again, or that he would phone, very soon. But nothing happened. And Tom mentioned casually that he had fallen madly in love with a flighty débutante called Julia and was making a complete ass of himself. All his friends thought so. So that, Tessa supposed, was that.

She had Joan and the shop; Ella; Gran; a lovely home, even if it was presided over by an overbearing father. Tomorrow— who knew?

Turning away from the sight in the mirror which depressed her, she tucked her blouse into her skirt, powdered her nose—and cautiously opened the door. No sign of Papa. While the coast was clear, she ran down the stairs to the hall. She could hear her father bawling into the phone in his study as she slipped down to Ella's flat and knocked on the door. She was already feeling much more cheerful.

Ella was sitting in her comfy chair reading the paper, a decent brown teapot by her side. Morgan, who wasn't very active these days, was curled up asleep on the flowery sofa.

"Gracious me, Tess, what's been the matter? You look as though you need a good strong cuppa. Fetch the hot water from the kitchen, dear, would you? Has his highness been creating—or what?"

"A bit . . ." Tessa came in with the kettle. "If only I could get a place of my own, Ella."

"That wouldn't be right, Tess," Ella said quickly. This was one of the few points on which she and Tessa disagreed. "Not a young woman on her own . . . now where would you go to? He'd never agree to it, never. And not with this great big house here." She poured a strong cup.

"Tom has," Tessa said resentfully.

"That's quite different, love. He's a man and so much older. Now what was all the shouting about earlier then?"

"Grandpa Delmore's funeral. He doesn't want me to go, but I am. It's just that he's afraid I'll see Mother and he hates anything Delmore—you know—but of course I'm going."

"Well, I should just think so," Ella said indignantly. "It's Friday, isn't it? I remember reading in the paper. You'll have to find out the trains and arrange it with Lady D."

"He came round in the end—he always does—and said perhaps we should send a wreath. Which I've done, in any case, from all of us. Not that I bothered telling him. Can I use your phone and have a word with Gran, Ella?"

"Help yourself. And Tessa, love . . ."

"What?"

"Don't forget to use that cream on your hands, will you? The new one I got at Boots last week."

"Oh Ella."

2

"THAT was my granddaughter, Tessa," Vi Delmore said to Marcus Reardon, putting down the phone. "We're going down to Winterton to Sam's funeral together on Friday and we'll have to study a timetable to get the trains right. I shall leave it to Tessa. She's such a practical girl. More tea?"

Marcus shook his head. They were sitting in Vi's drawing-room in Eaton Square talking, as it happened, about the late Sam Delmore—and he had something stronger than tea in mind, sooner rather than later.

He had been a dear, a sweet man if none too bright. Wonderfully handsome with those dazzling fair Delmore looks, but of course they had both been far too young and disastrously ill-assorted, Vi had been saying in her bright, brittle way when she was interrupted by the phone. Marcus, who had never met Tessa but knew her

100

background, assumed her to be the spoilt only daughter of a wealthy man. So he was mildly surprised to hear her described as "practical".

He had seen the announcement in *The Times* that morning and decided to drop in and see Vi—as he often did, these days, when he was at a loose end. Or in some kind of fix, which was not uncommon. (As today.) They had developed a good, very open friendship—odd, Vi sometimes thought, because in the beginning they had sought each other's company for one reason only: David. Each represented to the other a tangible and precious hold on his memory, but over the years the relationship had taken on a texture of its own. Both lived alone through choice. And quite simply they got on extremely well together.

Vi had been particularly pleased to see Marcus at the door that afternoon. She had been thinking of phoning him and asking him round for a chat, for company, although she had long been parted from Sam when David first brought Marcus to Eaton Square. Marcus and Sam had never met; but with Marcus, somehow, she

101

could be herself. And Sam's death had affected her in painful and unexpected ways. Old memories of their early married days, when the children were young and when she was trying to cope in a large and ugly country house she detested—funny, sad, trivial things she hadn't thought about for years and years had recently come back to haunt her in the early hours. A fickle beast, the human mind, she had decided. Despite a strong pill, she slept very little of late. And she had had some nasty breathless bouts during the long nights which she put down to grief and anxiety.

"The new Delmores have been very correct. They insist that Tessa and I come back to the house after the service. I said we would, but not for long. I really must see that Tessa organises the trains so we don't get stuck in that ghastly house, The Towers. I really couldn't bear that . . ."

"The new Delmores?"

"Of course. Cousins of Sam who lived in Canada for years. Otherwise," she said coolly, her hands moving expertly over the tea tray in front of her, forking a wafer of lemon, "otherwise it would have been David."

Oh Christ, Marcus thought. How could he have been so dense? Of course, if David had been alive he would be the new Lord Delmore. Not this unknown male hauled back from Canada.

Poor Vi, it was rotten luck that David's death had come searing back in such a subtle, insidious way. Sickening. Painful. And after struggling with it, and nearly winning, over the years. As indeed they both had in their different ways. He felt the familiar, guilty, downward drag of depression himself.

"Poor Vi. I hadn't thought, how terribly stupid of me . . ."

Because the fact was, he was feeling very bloody-minded and out-of-sorts. After years of precarious freelancing on the fringes of Fleet Street, he had recently landed a steady job as part of a team on the gossip column of one of the tabloids. It was hack work, unchallenging, the kind of thing he could do standing on his head; but it meant a routine and a steady income. That morning, he had had a nasty personality clash with his immediate editor, told him to go to hell and take his crappy column with him—and been fired.

Again. He had meant to break it to Vi who had long been his confidante in these matters. But now he wasn't so sure.

Marcus sighed. He was looking his age, nearly forty, these days. He had prominent cheekbones and very straight brown hair which he always kept more than a shade too long. His eyes were a wintry grey; wary, giving nothing away. He dressed casually and stylishly. In public places people, mostly women, tended to stare. They could swear they had seen him somewhere before, on television, in some film or other . . . Not knowing that he was a journalist, most people would have placed him as an actor; his unusual looks—and he was very thin—did have something theatrical about them. Although he was extremely attractive to women, and always had a steady mistress or two on the go, he had never married. The mere thought of taking responsibility for anyone else appalled him.

"Well, I *am* the widow—even though it seems a curious rôle to have thrust upon one. In a manner of speaking. We had a legal separation—very discreet, years ago. Ben got his lawyers to deal with it, I remember." She replaced the delicate cup and saucer on the tray and gazed down adoringly at the plump King Charles spaniel who was dozing at her feet. "So I must be seen to attend the funeral. For Sam. And for David." She reached down, fondling the dog called Charlie—who was snoring gently—with her clawlike scarlet-tipped hands.

David Delmore.

Marcus glanced over at the photograph in the silver frame on the sidetable—handsome, glossy, empty. The young flying officer, not long down from Oxford. Ready to take on the world—which he did in a way. As I did myself, with him, Marcus thought bleakly. They had both been much decorated, pilots in the Battle of Britain, instant heroes. If he had lived, by now who knew what he would have done? All the doors were open to him—the foreign office, the law, even journalism he had thought in the end. He had been trying his hand at writing, quite seriously, right up to the accident.

Whatever he had chosen, he would have done it spectacularly well. There couldn't have been much doubt about that. A brace of angelic children, the right wife—Pamela perhaps, the pretty Pamela he fell in love with that summer before the hun got him. Somehow, he hoped not . . .

Marcus thought moodily: surely it was not possible that David Delmore really had been more charming, more life-enhancing —and, yes, braver—than the rest of them? And yet many people, including Marcus himself, had thought that he was.

He flung one leg impatiently across his knee and looked at Vi. She was sitting on the brocaded sofa opposite him, petite, very upright, hair swept up, her tightly corseted figure encased in bright blue silk. She's a gutsy old thing, he thought with a rare burst of warmth. Gallant. Bags of style.

"I'll think of you, and wish you luck," he told her, smiling as he always did slightly out of one corner of his mouth.

"There you see, you can be nice if you want to be, Marcus dear. I tottered out and bought the most wonderful black hat today specially for the funeral. Wildly expensive. A picture hat they call it. I just felt like it. Here you are Mama's precious diddums . . ." The fat, spoiled little dog had crept up on to her lap and she started to feed him crumbs of biscuit from the tea-tray.

Marcus's sympathy vanished. He said crossly, "For God's sake, Vi, treat him like an animal. For Heaven's *sake!* It's so unlike you, all this drivel. What he needs is exercise and discipline, not this slobbering. He'd be a healthier hound for it too."

He pulled himself out of the deep armchair and stood over her, tall and cadaverous, glaring down.

"It's been ages since tea, hasn't it?" Vi said quickly. "Surely the bar is open somewhere . . . Australia, perhaps? Why don't you get us something fortifying?"

Completely at home, Marcus walked through to the small bottle-green dining-room which was scarcely used any more. Since Ben Levson's death from cancer, more than ten years ago now, Vi Delmore rarely entertained. Most of her meals were taken on a tray in front of the television—and shared by Charlie.

Marcus had first come to the flat, with David, on one of their early, frantic leaves sometime in 1940. He had been brought up by his widowed clergyman father in Ireland. His father had since died and he had no living relatives that he knew of. He had been to university in Dublin; literature had been appreciated during his upbringing—but there had been no money. So Vi Delmore's Eaton Square pad, bestowed upon her in the late 1920s by her lover, Ben Levson, had seemed to Marcus the height of luxurious chic. Which it was for its time. More like a set in a Noel Coward play than a home, he had thought, staggered.

"I'm glad you'll have your granddaughter with you, anyhow, on Friday. Nice to have a bit of support. What about your daughter?" He walked over and handed her the glass of whisky. "She'll be coming, I suppose?"

"Oh, *Jennie.*" On the rare occasions she mentioned her daughter it was with a mixture of exasperation and displeasure. Marcus knew a little of the background and gathered that Vi considered her highly unsatisfactory in every respect. "I suppose so . . . she's insisting on coming by car and it's sure to break down, hers always do. I like her husband, though," she said surprisingly. "And their boy, Max. Tom, my elder grandson, is hoping he can get there. I must get Tessa to find out about the trains . . ." She paused and frowned and pulled the cigarette box towards her. "You know—I'm worried about Tessa, really quite worried."

Marcus leant forward to light her cigarette.

"What on earth for?"

"I wish . . ." She exhaled a long stream of smoke. "I wish somehow that she was happier."

Marcus laughed sardonically, amused. It wasn't like Vi to bother much about anyone else, not deeply, these days. Whatever could she mean?

"That's up to her, isn't it Vi?"

"I suppose so . . ."

"How old is she, then?" he asked, curious.

"Twenty-something, two, three . . . I get vague about ages. Yes, twenty-three. That's right."

"Does she do anything?" Unlikely with Selway Electric money behind her, Marcus thought. A débutante-type most probably.

"*Indeed* she does," Vi said indignantly,

sitting up even straighter. "She and a partner run a charming and very successful flower shop in Chelsea. Tessa works *extremely hard*. I believe she's doing all the buying in Covent Garden now, so she's up and off at the crack of dawn. And she's clever with the arrangements too. They do all kinds of things—dances, weddings, lovely pots and baskets for houses. I'm very proud of her for her work."

"So you should be." That was why she was thought of as "practical", no doubt. "Pretty?" Marcus raised his eyebrows. The good scotch was definitely mellowing. Even the furious scene with his editor that morning was blunted. Good old Vi.

"Nice looking. Or could be if she bothered about herself. Tall, splendid shoulders. Pleasant features. A bit hefty. There's something unusual and distinguished about her. It's that awful father—George—he's dreadfully possessive. And he squashes her. Or tries to."

"Poor little rich girl . . ."

"Don't tease," Vi said sharply. "You're far too cynical for your own good. I've told you that before. Anyway, about my Tessa.

She's not as happy as she could be, and I mind about it. Get us the other half, would you?" She handed him her glass. When he came back she said, "I've had a thought. You know my sister, the artist?"

"Flora Flood. Of course, I like her work very much." He looked over to the mantelpiece where one of her striking flower paintings drew the eye and beamed out over the huge, high room. "That's a real beauty."

"Yes, Ben bought it on a visit to Chalcot right after the war. It's my favourite, I think. She's having a new exhibition, starting next week."

"I think I read about it somewhere."

"Very likely. We're all terribly pleased because her husband, Hubert, hasn't been well at all and we think it will cheer him up. He utterly adores her, you see." She stopped—then plunged on, "Why don't you come to the opening? Quite a few of the family will be there. And I'd like you to meet them. You never have . . . The Floods, George Selway, Tom . . ."

"And Tessa?"

"And Tessa. Actually, Poppy Renfrew, George's chum, is giving a bit of a fork

111

supper in a room at the side. It's at the O'Lana Gallery. The card's up there somewhere. Have a look."

He walked over in that elegant, fluid way he had. Quite as though he was crossing a stage. Beige twill trousers, navy turtleneck sweater. He's an attractive man all right, Vi thought, watching him. I wonder . . . She groped for another cigarette.

Marcus shuffled through the jumble of stiff white cards on the mantelpiece—most never replied to, he guessed, much less accepted—and found Flora Flood's. It was in front of a small, rather faded framed snapshot.

"That's the one. Bring it here. Oh you've found Ben. Bring him over too would you?"

Vi had been missing Ben Levson badly these past days—his companionship, his dry humour. She had thought that one of the few good things about aging was that one minded less about everything. Not true, she had discovered. Pain could still twist the knife cruelly enough. Stubbing out her cigarette, barely lit, she held the invitation in one hand and the photograph in the other.

"There you are: 31 May 6.30. The O'Lana Gallery. I'll get them to send you a card and I'll tell Poppy to expect you."

"Won't anyone mind?" He took the card and perused it.

"Certainly not. You'll be my escort. And Poppy Renfrew may be a cow but she knows how to do things. It should be an amusing evening. The Floods, in their day, knew everyone."

"Thank you, I'd like that very much," Marcus said politely thinking what the hell, he could always get out of it at the last moment if he wanted. "I can't say I'd have recognised Ben Levson from that." Vi was studying the snapshot, inches from her nose.

"If only I could find those damned glasses. But that's my Ben all right." She smiled affectionately at the old sepia-coloured picture. Tanned, arms akimbo, Ben grinned confidently out at the world of the 1920's, in his ridiculous yachting get-up and rakish cap.

The first time Marcus met him, soon after the war, was when Ben and Vi had

113

taken him out somewhere very grand for dinner. One of the big hotels. He had been at a terribly low ebb then; it wasn't long after David's death, when he was plunged into a real depression. In blacker moments, he wondered if he had really ever got over it.

Anyhow, Vi had known he was miserable and tried to help. She had always been a good sort in that way. Ben, whom Marcus found ponderous and pernickety —it was the beginning of his fatal illness, it turned out—thought he might have been able to fix him up with a subsidiary of one of his English companies. He chewed away at a disgusting cigar non-stop, Marcus remembered. He had thanked him and said he would think about it and had decided then and there to put his trust in words, for better or for worse—both of which it had certainly been.

It had to be said that, although he had had his successes, Marcus had never stuck at any job for long. He was good, very good, and both he and his procession of editors knew it. But just when he was getting settled, like today, he would lose his temper or decide he didn't like the feel of the place and chuck it up. Or arrange, somehow, to get the push. (He followed a similar pattern with his women.)

After a long article for an American magazine which paid very well, Vi had bullied him into buying a small flat in a dingy block in Soho. This had become his lair and his sanctuary; he had never regretted it. And it was Vi who, without being asked, when he had been jobless for some months, would pull her cheque book out, start writing and say, "This is about all I can manage . . ." No ceremony; he always paid her back. He wasn't always fussy how he made money on the side—he knew his way round the underbelly of the London Press all right. Remarkably, through it all, he knew Vi truly believed in his particular journalistic talent. He did himself.

Into the second scotch, relaxed, he said, "By the way, I got the sack this morning."

Traffic thundered past through the square. The window boxes were bright splashes against the white stucco of the buildings. After a cloudy day, a last burst of sunshine was filtering through the new leaves of the trees.

"I thought there was something," Vi said. "I didn't imagine you had come just because of Sam."

"Well . . ." He tapped his glass against his suede shoe. He wore these always, unrepentantly, making a lot of men think that he was a bounder. Which in a way he was. "Put it like this." That maddening half-smile again that the women seemed to like. "I would have come anyhow—it's just that not having a job gives me more time."

"You can't go on like this you know," she said severely. "You're getting too old. You're throwing away your chances." She was right.

"Lots of irons in the fire." He put down his drink and looked at his watch. "I must be off. I won't let the grass grow under my feet, I promise you."

Vi looked sceptical.

"All right. I'll see you out." And as he followed her into the hall. "Don't forget about Flora's opening. I'll deal with an invitation for you tomorrow."

"I shall look forward to it. I don't know what to say about the funeral except that it will soon be over—and I hope it isn't an ordeal for you." As he bent down to peck her cheek, Marcus thought she looked frail and somehow shrunken despite the brave make-up and the colourful dress. Contritely for him, he gave the disliked dog which Vi was holding a quick pat.

"Good old Charlie. Honestly Vi, calling a King Charles spaniel Charlie must be one of the few unoriginal acts of your life."

Marcus drove his green sports car—an unexpected bonus he had bought with royalties from a series of interviews for a magazine later adapted for radio—through the rush-hour streets back to Soho. He parked with difficulty and arrived at the door of his third floor walk-up feeling decidedly jaded. The effect of Vi's excellent whisky was beginning to wear off. The reality of being once again without a job and forty this year hit hard.

Keys in hand he stood stock still in the gloomy corridor. The unmistakable beat of rock and roll was coming from inside. "I'm gonna rock around the clock tonight, gonna rock, rock . . ." Dammit. That girl —Angie Gordon. He had only met her a couple of times, once at Guy Loden's place

117

and once in a nightclub. That was last week. He must have been very drunk because when she started to complain that Guy Loden, with whom she had been living for some years, had taken to beating her up—he handed her his spare key. He knew that Loden was a very nasty piece of work indeed and he felt, briefly, sorry for her. "Just in case you're desperate," he had said, getting up and leaving. He then forgot all about it.

Madness. He felt like groaning. It was the kind of thing he was always so careful never to do; never to let down his guard; always keep his essential privacy. Well, he would deal with it. He didn't bother to knock.

"Hello there," she drawled, her long, lean body still twisting sinuously to the music; smiling at him with her slanted green eyes; her exquisite pouting mouth lifted towards him. "Talk about taking a girl unawares. Anything the matter?"

"Not a thing," he said shortly. He turned off the radio in mid wail and looked round for her coat. She didn't look "desperate" at all; what she did look was slightly drunk. And even so, remarkably beautiful.

"I've had a hellish day, and I've got some phoning to do," Marcus told her. "So off you go, there's a good girl."

"Marcus." She sashayed towards him and put her hands on his shoulders. Marcus was impervious. "Just one little drink . . ."

"Not even one. Sorry. Now where's your coat?"

Angie Gordon was the top photographic model of the day in London. In a thousand different poses, her heart-shaped face and raven hair blanketed the better magazines and newspapers. The camera adored her. She had also recently been voted by some spurious group, The Spirit of Mayfair. Although she took her work very professionally, she also loved the high life. Taken up by the shadier elements of café society, she drifted elegantly through the social round of balls and nightclubs and fashionable race-meetings.

No-one knew where she came from. She had assumed a plummy accent, which only occasionally slipped into suburban cockney. Good luck to her, Marcus had thought when he met her at Guy Loden's house in Aberdeen Road. She seems to have done all right for herself. The dressy clothes and the jewels provided by Loden, he assumed, looked marvellous on her. She was very tall for a woman; she had style. And a pampered, cushy life. That was, if you didn't count Guy Loden, her "protector". He was a well known and somewhat sinister figure around town with his Edwardian suits, dark glasses and blue Rolls Royce. Always a red carnation in his buttonhole. Boxes at the best race-courses; the most desirable table in one or two nightclubs he favoured.

His large house in Kensington was the scene of endless parties which involved gambling—illegal at the time—limitless champagne, low lights and pretty women. (Marcus had no doubt at all that the police were waiting to pounce.) And it was over these "happenings" that Angie presided; a beautifully dressed bogus hostess drifting from table to table, chatting a bit, flattering, keeping the champagne on the move. While Loden—always in dark glasses, always cold sober—watched every move at the tables. He was reputed to make thousands at each sitting, mostly in cash. A posse of thuggish men, Loden's minders, mingled with the guests.

Marcus had been there once and seen Angie doing what was expected of her. So he knew. It was at their second meeting, in a club, that she had told him about Loden's violent temper—and he had ridiculously given her the key.

"Spoilsport," Angie made a face. "I thought we could have dinner."

"Another night. We'll paint the town. But tonight I've got to think things through. And Loden will expect you to be on show, all dressed up, doing your stuff. You don't want to ask for trouble. Oh— one other thing," he held out his hand, "my key, darling," he said pleasantly. Angie ignored his hand and dropped it on a table. "Thanks. I'll come down and get a taxi with you."

He put her coat round her shoulders and steered her out into the hall and down the stairs. He fancied that she was none too steady on her feet. He hoped Loden would find her up to scratch once she got back to Kensington. He hailed a taxi and bundled her inside where she collapsed in a heap of black clothing and long, skinny legs. He felt just the slightest qualm sending her back like that—to Loden. But really, it was none of his business. He hardly knew her; she was a big girl who had knocked about a good deal . . . surely she knew how to look after herself by now.

When he got back to the flat he opened all the windows as wide as possible to get rid of Angie's sultry scent and tried not to think of some of the more unpleasant rumours he had heard about Guy Loden. Then he put a Mozart record on the gramophone and went into the kitchen to make scrambled eggs. Just as he was finishing, the phone rang. An old editor friend, now running a decent middlebrow daily, had heard about this morning's firing. He wanted him, no beating about the bush. But he would have to behave himself. They arranged to meet for lunch the following week—on Wednesday, 31 May.

3

"WE have done well, darling. Timed it just right," Vi Delmore said late the following Friday afternoon, climbing into a first-class compartment of the London train at Winterton Station. They had attended Sam Delmore's funeral and gone back, briefly, to pay their respects to the family. "Thank Heavens we asked that nice taxi driver to pick us up at The Towers, otherwise we would have been there for hours . . . and all those people came up to me whom I hadn't seen since the year dot."

Tessa collapsed into the seat opposite her, the whistle blew, and they were off.

"You were marvellous, Gran. I was so proud of you. You looked so elegant and you chatted to everyone. Honestly—they were all staring, even in church. They aren't used to anyone looking like you in Winterton. That was quite obvious." Tessa laughed. "Who was that old lady you were talking to for quite a time?

The one who was very red-eyed and tearful."

"Oh—Florrie. Dear Florrie. She was our cook and after I left she was marvellous to Sam. Took him over completely. I believe they lived together quite happily in the kitchen for years. They made a bedroom in the scullery next door. And Sam had the library. His head was always stuck in a book. But I don't expect you realised that when you and Tom occasionally went there."

"Heavens! No we didn't. I think we used to have lunch in a dining-room. It's nice to think Grandpa Delmore wasn't rattling around there, lonely, all by himself."

"Oh, I *quite* agree. I'm so grateful for dear Florrie—although I can't recall she was much of a cook, very given to rabbit stews. Not that your grandfather would have cared. Or known. Apart from doing bits and pieces in the county, he lived in a world of his own. I felt I ought to put on a bit of a show, you see. Except for David's funeral, I hadn't been back for well over thirty years." She fished in her bag for her compact. "I think the hat was

124

a great success. I wasn't sure when I got it." She tilted it slightly. "Remember, everyone *local* thought I was the most awful scarlet woman going off like that when I did. Very 'fast'. One day I just wasn't there. No more garden fête openings or visiting the cottage hospital or trying to deal with that grotesque house."

Tessa giggled.

"It really is awful, isn't it? A sort of gingerbread Gothic pile. It's hard to believe you ever lived there."

"It's leaky too, and colder than charity. No proper heating. And I very much doubt if it's had a new roof since my time. When it poured, we used to put umbrellas up in the upstairs corridors. I expect they still do. The new Delmores looked very simple and tweedy, I thought. Perhaps they won't mind, being used to Canadian winters. David always said the only thing for it was a bomb."

She snapped the compact firmly shut and replaced it in her black bag—her best. And she did look spectacular, Tessa thought, watching her as they swayed along. Black from head to toe, wonderfully made up, her superb single row of big pearls, perfectly matched, which she always wore. Every inch the widow—which of course she was. And she would be seventy, Papa had told her privately, later that year.

"I saw David's memorial in the church," Tessa said. "So sad, Gran . . ."

"Yes. One thing about getting old is that things don't hurt quite so terribly, not *quite.*" She looked out of the window. She was by no means always sure that this was true. She had managed to avoid seeing the plaque for David that Sam had insisted on; in any case, her eyes were too bad these days. "I was glad Tom managed to get there. It was sweet of him, I thought. I hope he got back to Winchester in time. I don't think he's enjoying law very much, do you?"

"No, I don't. I think he finds it quite boring. *Oh Gran*, I nearly *fainted* when Mother turned up at the same time as the coffin. When I heard the commotion at the back I knew it was her. I didn't dare look round. I was much too embarrassed. And I could hear her apologising in that silly, flutey way . . ."

"Ridiculous of her not to have taken the

train," Vi said crossly. "I knew that car of hers would break down. And the sight she looked—sandals and no hat, a woman of her age."

"I feel quite sorry for Felix and Max having to put up with her," Tessa said. "She's so gushy and she smiles all the time in that starry-eyed way and never says anything sensible."

Vi Delmore sighed and looked tired. She felt suddenly, achingly, glad it was over.

"She was the most enchanting-looking child I have ever seen, Jennie. Absolutely ravishing. Quiet—but composed. Like a naiad, is it? A nymph. One would never never believe that she would have turned out the way she has. Did she tell you that Max is going in for a music scholarship to that boarding school in Dorset? Hubert thinks he's very talented. He's been extremely generous in paying for his music lessons since he was tiny."

"I hope he gets it. I like Max. He's normal and he's got a good sense of humour. He must take after Felix. When we were all going back to The Towers Mother did say that the reason she had to rush off was that she had to pick up a whole lot of plants on her way back. Apparently, she sells produce from the garden at market stalls round the county. It must be jolly hard work."

Vi closed her eyes.

"My daughter is a complete mystery to me," she said finally—and after that seemed to be lost in her own thoughts.

They stopped at a couple of country stations and then the train picked up speed. Soon, the dreary outer suburbs of London stretched on either side of them. Coming back to the present with a start Vi said, "Getting along with George all right, are you?"

Tessa grimaced.

"Not too bad. I try to keep out of his way as much as possible. Ella's a great help there. Otherwise he tries to interfere in everything. You know how he is. Luckily, Tom thinks this American deal with the business should keep him pretty occupied for the time being. I'm so glad I have my work and the shop. I really do enjoy it, Gran. And it's going awfully well. The other day, Joan mentioned something about opening another shop. We've got more work than we can cope with. And I've got quite a lot of experience now."

"I think it's marvellous, darling." Vi looked at her, alert. "You should feel very proud and pleased. I know I am. And you *must* look after yourself, too, take a bit more interest in your looks."

Tessa blushed. She knew very well what was coming. It did.

"Pay attention to your clothes, darling." Vi looked, without enthusiasm, at Tessa's grey coat pulled over a flowered cotton dress. "I don't mean work clothes for everyday so much . . . but you're young and you want to dress yourself up a bit. Enjoy it. Now don't roll your eyes up to the heavens like that. *Listen*. If I don't tell you, nobody will. And stand up straight. You're a lovely big tall girl. Statuesque. Be proud of it."

"Yes, Gran, yes, yes, yes." Tessa—half exasperated, affectionate. "I will."

"Some young men about, are there?"

"One or two. I go out quite a lot Gran, you know I do. But no one special."

Tessa suddenly wondered, a bit regretfully, if Oliver Bingham was still involved with that girl Tom didn't approve of. She must remember to ask Tom when she saw him next.

"You've got plenty of time. You mustn't make the same mistake I did . . . I was so young and then there was that dreadful war, all the boys we danced with going off to the trenches, the casualty lists in *The Times* every morning. All the same, I think I knew it was wrong, marrying Sam. Unless you're terribly unlucky, I think one does, somehow." She seemed to remember something important. "Darling—you are coming to Aunt Flor's opening party next week, aren't you? I do hope so."

"Of course." She gave her grandmother a conspiratorial look. "You know Poppy is putting on some kind of a buffet . . ."

"I know darling. Very appropriate. After all, Flor *is* one of the foremost artists in the country. And Poppy does manage entertaining very well. She has her points."

"Not many," Tessa, who loathed her, said glumly.

"Anyhow, Tessa, promise me one thing. Before the party. *Promise* me you'll get that mop of pretty coloured hair nicely cut. Now promise, darling. It would make all the difference to your appearance."

"OK Gran." She sighed and grinned. "I'll be a whole new me."

Which she wasn't exactly; but standing with her father in the O'Lana Gallery at Flora Flood's preview, she did look very charming indeed. Her hair had been shaped and brushed and burnished to a dark copper. Her nails were manicured. She was wearing a new blue and white silk dress and filigree gold earrings, a recent birthday present from Vi.

The brightly lit gallery was very full and getting noisier by the minute. Flora Flood, wearing a flowing silver caftan, dominated easily. She stood, glass in hand, in front of the colourful flower painting which had been reproduced on the cover of the catalogue—splashy dahlias, pink and yellow and crimson, spilling out of a blue jug. A short queue had formed beside her as old friends pressed to offer congratulations.

"No sign of Tom," George Selway rapped out. "High time he was here."

"Don't *fuss* Papa," Tessa told him. "Who on earth are all these people?"

George Selway looked over the chattering groups with a shrewd eye.

"Oh, arty types. People who want to be seen to be in the swim. One or two looking to pick up investments for the future." He looked very distinguished with his erect, soldierly bearing and immaculate dark suit. There was still some ginger in his head of wiry hair. His expression was forbidding. He nodded so curtly to a couple about to approach them that they faltered and moved away.

Hubert Flood, leaning heavily on a stick, was at the centre of a group of people, his head bent courteously. Several friends had already remarked to each other, discreetly, how gaunt and shaky he looked. But he kept going gamely—introducing, pointing out one picture, explaining another . . .

Tessa went on wondering who all these people were—old friends of Aunt Flor's and Hubie's, she supposed; dealers and critics in the art world. Whoever they were, they seemed to have a lot to say to each other. The noise intensified—so did the heat from the well-lit pictures. Apart from a few obviously artistic types, all

132

the women, most chattering away like magpies, seemed to be wearing smart black suits. She caught sight of Poppy Renfrew, highly visible in a skinny bright red dress, hopping about from group to group, revelling in the excitement. Silently, Tessa prayed that she wouldn't come their way—she didn't.

"They'll want us to eat shortly," Selway shouted into Tessa's ear. "Looks bad that Tom's not here—family, after all."

"He *said* he'd probably be late, Papa," Tessa shouted back. "You know he's got a case on."

Tessa was getting slightly uneasy herself that he hadn't turned up. He could have tried. After all, she was the one who suffered from Papa's short fuses.

Just then, Vi Delmore appeared out of the crowd. Her head was bound up in what seemed to be a turban, fastened with a diamond clip. Her make-up, for once, had gone awry. She snatched Tessa by the arm shrieking, "I want to borrow Tessa, George, and show her off. *Doesn't* she look sweet? Come with me, darling . . . this way."

She pulled her into the crowd and they

struggled to the other side of the room where a man was standing alone. Tessa knew instinctively that he had been waiting for Vi to bring her over. Even at her first glance she was aware that he looked like no one else in the room—or indeed like anyone she had ever seen. His mouth was curved in a sardonic smile, as though he was enjoying a thoroughly good joke that only he could appreciate. His hair reached almost to the collar of his pale blue shirt.

"Tessa," Vi was saying beside her, very faint in all the din, "this is Marcus Reardon, David's friend in the war and now a great chum of mine. Marcus this is my granddaughter."

Self-conscious, not knowing quite how to respond to his strange smile, she put out her hand. Her eyes met his and held them.

"Hello, Tessa," he said easily. "So you're David's niece . . . well, well. I can see all the nice things Vi said about you are right." Dropping her hand, he immediately touched her on the shoulder, manoeuvring her out of the way of a cruising waiter. He took two glasses of champagne off the tray and handed her one. Tessa had decided there was no way to reply to that, but it didn't matter because he went on, "We can't let all this lovely booze go to waste on these ageing Bright Young Things of the Twenties. The bulk of our fellow guests . . . Anyhow—cheers." He tipped back his head and polished off the wine.

"Do you know the Floods very well?" she asked.

"Not at all. I've just met them briefly tonight. Great characters, aren't they? I've admired her pictures for a long time. Your grandmother has a couple of magnificent ones in her flat, don't you think?" He replaced his glass on a passing tray and expertly took another. He had had a very good day—and he was enjoying himself.

"They're lovely. We've got some at home too." Tessa felt unaccountably shy —big, rather clumsy. She remembered what Gran had said and stood straighter.

"Vi tells me you run a flower business. Good for you. I approve of working girls."

"My father says it ruins my hands—you know, cutting and wire—and they're always in water. But I love it, I really do."

She kept both hands wrapped tightly round the stem of her glass.

"Let me see."

"All right." Colouring, smiling, she held one out. It looked a useful, well-shaped hand to him, and he said so.

"Thank you. That's enough about me. Tell me what *you* do," Tessa said boldly.

"I'm a journalist."

"That sounds exciting. Should I know?"

"Only the paper."

Rather to his surprise, Marcus found himself telling her about today's leisurely lunch which had ended in a firm job offer, instantly accepted. What he didn't, couldn't, tell Tessa, or even put into words, was that he had a good gut feeling about this one; that despite all odds, this outfit was going to be the making of him professionally. And he wanted recognition; he wanted it badly. His beat on the paper hadn't been defined yet; if he played his cards well for once he might be able to wangle exactly what he wanted.

"That sounds marvellous," Tessa was saying, a bit breathlessly. "How terribly exciting. Well done. Does Gran know?"

"No, I haven't mentioned it to her yet, actually."

He had intended to tell her when he took her home; perhaps he would stay on for a nightcap. But he was thinking: Vi's quite right. The girl had something. Not least was her total unawareness of the effect of her clear grey eyes shining out of that nice young face. Pretty hair. And a quality of sympathy. As far as he could judge—his eyes lowered a bit—a beautiful body underneath the dress that wasn't somehow quite right. Unusually for him, he went on talking about himself; about the particular journalistic niche he hankered after, had done for years. Such a sweet, attentive kid. *David's niece, good God*. He had drunk the champagne very quickly and was beginning to feel a bit light-headed. He was still talking when Vi interrupted. She looked sharply from one to the other and said, "Marcus, this is Tessa's father, George Selway . . . George, Marcus Reardon."

The two men shook hands, nodded, murmured—disliking each other on sight.

Arrogant, humourless bastard, thought

Marcus—who was, in any case, allergic to successful businessmen.

No gentleman—that hair, those shoes . . . What could Vi be thinking of, bringing the fellow here? thought George Selway.

"Poppy is trying to get us into the next room to eat. Mounds of forks and food," Vi piped in her scatty, social way. "So do come through, you two. Most of the ones who aren't staying on have left."

Tessa looked round. While they had been talking, the gallery had thinned out considerably and the twittering had levelled off.

"We will, Gran." She looked straight at Marcus. "But shall we have a quick look round the pictures first? Aunt Flor was working on these when I was last down at Chalcot and it was too crowded to see much when we arrived."

"What an excellent idea," agreed Marcus. He half smiled at Vi.

George Selway shot him a distrustful look.

"Vi must be pleased that the funeral is over. She was delighted, by the way, that you went with her." Marcus put down his plate, having barely touched the food, and picked up his glass. "Such a *practical* girl, Tessa, she told me . . . she's very fond of you. And proud." Lightly ironic; amused. The fact that they had been standing alone for a good part of the evening, Tessa Selway and this interesting-looking, and apparently unattached man, had attracted glances—from Flora Flood; George Selway; family friends. Of this Tessa was oblivious.

"I know."

"Anyhow, she got through it all right, did she? I thought it might evoke sad memories of David. She might be badly upset. But she's a trouper is Vi, she knows how to put on a good face."

"She did. Everyone else looked so dusty and drab, and there was Gran—all pearls and picture hat looking as though she was on her way to Buckingham Palace."

Marcus laughed with her, appreciating the image. And it was then that Tessa happened to look towards the door and saw Tom. (She had forgotten all about him.) He strolled in just as the guests who had stayed on, divided into small groups, were finishing the supper.

Watching him, Marcus experienced an extraordinary sensation of déjà-vu. This very handsome, very fair young man who walked calmly through the gallery entrance was the image of David Delmore—and it gave Marcus a nasty jolt. He hadn't expected it somehow. Uncle and nephew, about the same ages, were dead ringers. He hadn't been prepared for it. It was an eerie feeling.

"There's Tom. At last—thank God," Tessa was saying nervously. Her hand went involuntarily to Marcus's elbow. "Better late than never, I suppose. I only hope Papa doesn't make a scene."

He did. George Selway broke from the man he was speaking to and marched over to meet his son. It was immediately clear that father and son were having an angry exchange. Selway's pent up rage carried.

"An insult . . . disgraceful . . . where have you been, for God's sake? No message? You will apologise to your aunt at once." The harsh, ringing tones of George Selway silenced the general conversation. There was an embarrassed hush.

"Very well, if that's how you feel, then I'll leave."

Tom Selway turned on his heel and walked out.

Tessa and Marcus reacted instantaneously. Marcus went straight over to Vi Delmore. And Tessa, heels clattering awkwardly, half walked, half ran through the heavy glass doors after Tom. Moments later, Marcus found them standing on the pavement in the warm twilight.

"You could have turned up earlier, Tom." Tessa was saying, not far off tears. "It's so unfair of you. You know you goad him into these awful rages—you do it on purpose. And then he takes it out on me and Ella. He can't even help it—he's just *like* that. And it was all going so well for Aunt Flor . . ."

"It damn well wasn't my fault, Tess," Tom replied quite violently. "I was late back from court, then I had to change in the flat, and the car wouldn't start. I waited for a bus or a taxi and neither came, so I walked from Kensington. How the hell can I help a flat battery? Answer me that."

They were in the middle of Mayfair, and

couples on their way to dinner or the theatre turned round, regarding them curiously.

Tessa became aware of Marcus standing beside them.

"Sorry," she said briefly. "Family temperaments. Tom this is Gran's friend, Marcus Reardon. And this, as you will have gathered, is Tom."

Tom held out his hand, smiling ruefully at Marcus. "How do you do? Sorry about this. Bad show. Awful rumpus in there—or has everyone decided to ignore it?"

Avoiding the question, Marcus said, "I had a quick word with Vi and suggested that I took you home, Tessa. She thought it was a good idea. Your father can drop her back at Eaton Square later." Striding out of the gallery past a nonplussed and furious George Selway had given Marcus, who was inclined to be anti-establishment, a certain amount of pleasure.

"Terribly decent of you," Tom began. Marcus interrupted.

"I think after that we could all do with a drink or a cup of coffee. As you're without transport, Tom, why don't we all go back to my place in Soho—I've got the car

142

round the corner—and then I can take you both back wherever you're going."

"I'd like that," Tessa said. "Thank you very much."

143

4

CROUCHING, Tom squeezed his long legs into the back of the raffish sports-car—and slumped. It had been a hellish day, apart from this scene with Pa. He was less and less sure that he was cut out to be a barrister. Much of the work that came his way was trivial and bored him. He had come down from Oxford, where he had done extremely well, and made an enthusiastic start; but increasingly, he was finding the daily grind unrewarding. He'd been at it five years already. Looking ahead, he couldn't see himself sticking at it, frankly.

Not like Oliver. He could see that now. *He* was totally committed, ready to master the enormous amount of detailed paper-work that a top legal practice involved. Confident on his feet in court; an excellent voice and good delivery. And he was getting the big cases, moving up; spoken of as one of the young men to watch. It wasn't simply a question of ability; *he* had that. It was more a feeling, a deep feeling, for the work. That was what he doubted in himself. His present case—he was defending a man accused of assault on the underground—had gone to the jury late that afternoon. He was pretty sure his chap was innocent; but he had an uneasy feeling that he hadn't really done his best for him; not brought the skill and imagination to bear on it that he might have.

Sticking his head between the front bucket seats, he shouted above the noisy engine, "We've always heard from Gran that you were a close pal of David's. You were in the same squadron, weren't you?"

"That's right. We met the first day we turned up for training. September '39. It seems a long time ago now."

"Brave lads."

"It didn't seem so at the beginning. It was exciting—a job that had to be done. It got pretty hair-raising later."

"I'll bet."

Marcus drove fast and confidently around Hanover Square and across Regent Street. Tessa hoped that they wouldn't get to wherever they were going too soon. She was beginning to enjoy herself again—or perhaps was just relieved to have been spirited away so efficiently from the family tensions. Funny to think that in a few hours from now she would be on her way through the pale morning light to Covent Garden. They were specially busy that week at the shop, and she needed to buy masses of stuff including greenery for a twenty-first birthday party they were decorating.

Changing gear, Marcus's hand accidentally touched her thigh. Confused, excited, Tessa bit her lip and turned her head.

She liked and was flattered by the way he had followed her out after Tom; taken charge as they stood bickering miserably on the pavement.

She liked watching his hands which she thought looked sensitive. He was in every way different from the young men she met at parties and went out with. Older, experienced, hard to place.

She suspected that although he was a great friend of Gran's, Papa would not like him—perhaps not consider him "a gent".

All sorts of unsuspected emotions churning about inside her, she managed to say calmly enough, "Gran never talks much about David. And I don't like to ask her. Wasn't David engaged when he was killed? Someone—it may have been Gran, or perhaps my mother—told me once that he was."

"Well, more or less . . ."

"He was dreadfully badly wounded when he was shot down, wasn't he?"

"Terribly."

The car slowed as Marcus negotiated a maze of streets obviously looking for somewhere to park.

"I'd like to know more about him," Tessa said hesitantly. "After all, he was our uncle. I've seen the photograph in Gran's drawing-room so many times."

"Tom looks astonishingly like him, by the way."

"Yes, that's what everyone says."

Marcus gave her a quick sidelong look. "You'd like to know about David? One day, Tessa," he said, "one day, I'll tell you."

The three of them walked up the dark flight of stairs in silence, their footsteps echoing through the shabby corridor.

Marcus stopped, produced a key and flung open the door. He switched on a light. "Here we are. My old bachelor hideout." It was a surprisingly large room with dazzling white walls. It was simply and pleasingly furnished, reflecting literary tastes and a sense of order. "Let's get some more lights on and then I'll think about something to drink."

Two entire walls were lined with books from floor to ceiling. The furniture was sparse—two sofas covered in what looked like old tapestry, a desk, one or two functional tables, a chair of unusual modern design and a Persian carpet.

"I say, how very nice," Tom said, cheering up. He went straight to the bookcases. "It's got a very good feel to it. I like it." Head cocked, he was already going through the shelves, reading titles.

"It's a super room," Tessa said shyly. "I hadn't expected it to be so big."

"I played about with the walls when I bought the place," Marcus said, moving round the room turning on lights, partially drawing the curtains. "They were only partitions. And I was left with this, a small bedroom, bathroom and kitchen. The building is a bit dreary but the flat, and the position, suit me. Tessa—sit . . . What can I get you? Coffee?"

"I'd love one."

"Good. What about you, Tom?"

"Could I possibly have a whisky and soda. I've had a rotten day in court and Pa on top of it."

"Of course. I'll deal with that first."

Drink in hand, Tom flung himself on the sofa, long legs stretched out. He looked exhausted. On his way to the kitchen, Marcus thought: he's got David's looks but not his verve. Pity. Bad luck for the girl, too, having that sod of a father. He hadn't liked the sound of him from the things Vi said.

Looking round the room, Tessa was surprised at how impersonal it was. There were no photographs and few ornaments of any kind. One or two framed posters on the walls; a good charcoal drawing of a nude girl. A neat pile of papers and magazines. No correspondence visible on the desk—just a portable typewriter, notebooks, pens and pencils.

"You've got to get away from Pa, Tess," Tom said sombrely. "He's far too

149

controlling—particularly of you. If anything, I think he gets worse." Tessa, who had been feeling intrigued and oddly excited and had forgotten the scene in the gallery, was instantly depressed. The thought of her father always did that to her.

"Let's forget about it, Tom. I can't move out for the moment, even Ella thinks that. He's bad enough about the shop, but I've got that at least. And Joan and I couldn't have taken on the new lease without him. My still living in Parloe Square is a sort of compromise. Anyhow, I'd miss Morgan too much," she said jokingly, wanting to get Tom out of his black mood and recapture the exhilaration she had felt in the car with Marcus. "He's my talisman—and Ella."

Soon, Marcus came back carrying a tray with coffee and a plate of bread and cheese.

"What a heavenly smell," Tessa said, sniffing the coffee.

"This is for you, Tom, you must be starving," Marcus handed the plate to Tom. Tessa noticed how competent he seemed to be in ordinary domestic matters.

Again, she thought of her father. She couldn't remember ever seeing him in the kitchen except to shout at Ella for something.

"I say, this is terribly good of you," Tom said, sitting up and preparing to attack the cheese. "I can't actually remember when I ate last. A sausage roll for lunch possibly."

"When Vi and I were talking the other night and she mentioned the private view, I didn't think I'd end up by kidnapping her two grandchildren." Marcus sounded amused.

"Rescuing, more like it," Tom said through a mouthful of bread and cheese.

"Papa must have been apoplectic," Tessa said, feeling weak and giggly, taking the coffee. "He always has had a terrible temper, hasn't he Tom? He does have his good side," she added loyally, reaching for a biscuit. "He just has to order everyone about, particularly me, and goes off the deep end when he thinks he isn't in total control."

"The right kind of personality to succeed in the business world," said

Marcus. "Which he certainly has—and I'm sure he hasn't finished yet."

"I suppose so. We adore Gran, though," Tessa said. "She's a character, isn't she?" From the opposite sofa, Tessa appealed to Marcus with her fresh wide-eyed look; prettier, more relaxed than she had been standing around in that hot, noisy gallery, he thought. Although the dress did nothing to display what were undoubtedly beautiful breasts.

"I'm devoted to her—and she's always been the most marvellous friend. Another drink, Tom?"

"Please. But not as stiff as the last."

Marcus was disappearing into the kitchen when the doorbell rang. Tom made a quick, startled movement. Marcus turned into the narrow hallway.

"Now who on earth?"

Tessa automatically glanced at her watch. Almost ten o'clock. She looked at Tom.

"I wasn't expecting you," they heard Marcus say coldly. "As a matter of fact, I have guests . . ." Then, *Jesus Christ, what has he done to you?*"

So utterly unexpected, the horror in his

voice alarmed both Tom and Tessa. Instinctively, they jumped up, crossed the room and stood behind Marcus by the open door. Just outside, in the ill-lit corridor, they could see the shadowy outline of a young woman. She seemed to be wearing a long black cloak. Marcus took her arm and pulled her roughly inside.

"Angie," his voice was hoarse. *"Good God!"*

Appalled, they stood motionless. Marcus stared, they all did—at the girl's face, stark between the cloak and her long black hair. One side was pale and perfect; the other savagely bruised—hideously swollen, livid blue and crimson. That eye was completely closed.

Shocked, Tessa turned to Tom. His face was ashen. For a fleeting moment, Tessa wondered if he was going to be sick. Marcus shut the door, still holding the girl's arm, and said quietly.

"We'll get you help, a doctor . . ."

But when she swayed and the good eye closed and she started to fall slowly, slowly forward, it was Tom, not Marcus, who stepped forward and caught her and carried her to the sofa. Tessa and Marcus followed. Kneeling beside her, Marcus said quite loudly.

"Angie—you're safe now and away from him. It was Loden, wasn't it?"

She gave a barely perceptible nod.

"OK, look—can you hear me?"

Another slight nod.

"Good. Now I'm going to ring for an ambulance and get you to a hospital. Your face needs looking at."

She began to move her head from side to side despite obvious pain.

"No," she half breathed, half slurred. "No, no, no . . ." She opened her eye and they saw that she was genuinely terrified. She began to shake. Tessa, who had recovered from the initial shock and stayed calm said, "I'll have another look, but I can't see any cuts. Only terrible bruising —which will probably get worse as it comes out." She looked at Marcus. "Ice is what we need. And a flannel or small towels. Can you get them? Then we can decide what's best to be done."

Marcus looked from Tessa to Tom and said very quietly, "I'm desperately sorry

154

about this. I'll explain as soon as I can. You understand?"

Tessa nodded and he went off to the kitchen. The unknown young woman on the sofa was now moaning softly. Tessa leant over her, examining the swelling contusions. Tom sat at the bottom of the sofa watching intently.

"She's cold, Tess, whoever she is, poor thing, look, she's shaking like a leaf."

"Go and ask Marcus for a blanket," Tessa said without looking up. "And ask him to put the ice in a bowl and bring it here."

Tessa spoke clearly to the nastily battered face—which seemed familiar; only she couldn't quite place it.

"I think it's going to be all right. The skin isn't broken, only very badly bruised. And I'm afraid you've got an awful black eye. In fact, it looks as though the other one is going that way too. Can you hear me?" No answer. "We're going to put a cold compress on your face. I think it will help."

Marcus came back.

"Is this what you wanted?" He put the towels and a bucket of ice cubes on the floor beside her. Tessa wrung out a flannel in the cold water.

"Can you take her cloak off?" Tessa asked Marcus. "She'll be more comfortable and the water might dribble down."

Tom appeared with a blanket.

"Hold on," he said. Very carefully, he put his arm under the girl's shoulders and pulled off the cloak. Laying her back against the cushions, he removed her shoes. She was dressed entirely in black. He tucked the blanket round her.

"I'll be as gentle as I can," Tessa told her. "I won't press hard. Yell if it hurts too much."

Goodness knows what she's hearing, if anything, Tessa thought. She seems to have practically passed out. She must see a doctor tomorrow, if not tonight. Barely touching the livid skin, Tessa put the cold flannel to her forehead, cheek and round the damaged side of her mouth. Although she avoided the spots which seemed angriest, almost raw, the girl winced. Every few seconds she dried the skin with a clean towel and wrung out the flannel in the bowl of icy water which Marcus was holding.

After about ten minutes, she had stopped shivering and seemed more comfortable. The puffed, blackened eye opened slightly. She was alert. She tried to smile at Tessa and managed quite a distinct "Thanks."

"That's more like it," Marcus said, grim-faced. "You've been a brick, Tessa." He put his hand on her shoulder. "I think that's the most that can be done for the moment. Here, let's get rid of this stuff." He waited while Tessa finally dried off the girl's face and neck. "Brandy all round wouldn't go amiss."

In the small, neat galley kitchen Marcus chucked out the ice. Tom followed them in.

"For God's sake, who is she?" he demanded. "Who on earth has done this to her? That's no accident, that's assault and battery."

Marcus turned and faced Tom who was standing in the doorway. He had taken off his jacket and rolled up his sleeves. He motioned to Tom to shut the door and folded his arms, leaning back.

"Quite so. Her name is Angie Gordon,"

he said quietly. "She's a top model, mostly photographic."

"But of course," Tessa burst out. *"Of course . . .* There was something about her . . . I knew I'd seen her before somewhere. I mean, she's in all the glossies, she's absolutely gorgeous. Wasn't she named Spirit of Something the other day? Her picture was in all the papers, I remember."

"That's right." Marcus nodded. "That's her. She was picked up in a coffee bar by some freelance photographer a few years ago, I believe. And she's highly photogenic . . . the cover of *Vogue, Harpers,* the lot." He opened a cupboard and took out a bottle of brandy and glasses. "But she keeps bad company, I'm afraid," he added drily.

"Loden," Tom said. "I heard you ask her. Is that Guy Loden?"

"Yes. *The* Guy Loden. He has a house in Aberdeen Road which he runs as a sort of private gambling casino. He attracts the seriously rich in this country—and plenty from abroad. It's an open secret, really. Because of course it's illegal. His reputation is pretty rum. He dresses in a very dandified manner, always seen in the 'best' places, that kind of thing. He's perfectly correct, to meet, but I've heard very unpleasant things about him."

"I know," Tom said. "I've been to the house."

"Not gambling, Tom?" Tessa said.

Tom ignored her.

"Really?" Marcus raised his eyebrows. "It's a good place to avoid, I should have thought. I was after some information recently and I looked in . . . and met Angie. You might have seen her there yourself, Tom. She lives there—with Loden, or so it appears. At least she acts as his hostess, swans around the bored rich with a taste for gambling. That is, when she's not modelling. I rather think she's got into some bad habits—matching the company."

Angie had indicated to him, when they met for the second time at that nightclub, that Loden could get violent—which was why, in a not entirely sober moment, he had lent her his key. And why, presumably, she had turned up on his doorstep tonight, hoping to find him in. And a sympathetic port in a storm. Well, he would have to think about how best to deal with that one.

"The swine," Tom spat out, looking fierce and handsome, a high colour in his face, more than ever like David, Marcus thought. "Bloody animal . . . only worse. The police are on to him, by the way." His jaw was clenched tight. "They've got enough on him to send him down for years."

"Not too loud, old boy. But I daresay you're right. In the meantime we—or rather I—have a problem on our hands. I'm extremely sorry, by the way, that this should have happened while you two were here. Just one of those things. I'll get it sorted out, but first brandy." He had poured three and handed one each to Tom and Tessa.

"What about Angie?" Tessa asked. "She's obviously dreadfully shocked. A drop wouldn't hurt, would it?"

"I'll take it in to her," Tom said. "She might not be able to manage a glass. Have you got a teaspoon?"

The brandy burnt comfortingly in Tessa's throat. Neither she nor Marcus made a move to follow Tom back into the sitting-room. Marcus stared at the floor, frowning. He was wondering whether Loden had any idea that Angie would have turned up here . . . he had been at the table when he had had that long and revealing talk with Angie; it was likely that he would make it his business to know who Angie might be friendly with in her "off" hours, so to speak. And he, Marcus, had not the slightest intention of getting caught up in Angie's sordid little life. God, how he loathed messy, emotional situations.

Tessa stood miserably, gulping down the brandy. Marcus's nearness disturbed and excited her. She wanted, desperately, to make him aware of her. She had kicked off her shoes while ministering to Angie, and the silk dress was now badly creased. Angie's dramatic entrance, their combined attempt at first aid—and now the large brandy drunk much too quickly—seemed to have catapulted her into a strange intimacy with Marcus. Misinterpreting his frown, and the silence, she said, "Poor Marcus . . . how awful for you. Do you love her?"

For a second, Marcus looked at her, his

face completely blank. Then he threw back his head and laughed, really laughed.

"You silly little goose." He spoke, for him, quite tenderly. She looked so young and fresh and vulnerable. And hopelessly untidy. "Angie? I hardly know the girl. And as for loving her—I never *love* anyone, ever . . ."

They were so close that Tessa could see that there was a lot of grey in his hair. He leant over, arms still crossed, and kissed her lightly on the nose. "I'm a selfish bugger," he said. "I let everyone down in the end. Remember that, will you?"

When they came back into the sitting room they found Tom on the arm of the sofa holding a spoon and a brandy glass. Angie was now upright, looking into a small make-up mirror and showing distinct signs of having returned to life.

"She's feeling rather better," Tom informed them. "She asked for her bag, and the brandy helped."

Angie, meanwhile, had dived into the bag and come up with a black and white silk scarf which she folded and wound skilfully round her head, partially obscuring the bruised side of her face.

"In that case," said Marcus, "it's time for some introductions. This is Tessa Selway and her brother, Tom. Angie Gordon." Holding the silk across the worst of the bruises, Angie did her best to smile —first at Tessa, then Tom. Her look in Tom's direction seemed to last a long time. "Tessa and Tom are the grandchildren of a very old friend of mine."

"Hi—sorry about this. Thanks for the help. You've both been marvellous. And you Marcus."

Although somewhat indistinct, the words were comprehensible enough. The green eye, the still beautiful curve of one side of the mouth, entreated. Tom reached across the sofa, removed Angie's empty glass, and took her hand. Tessa watched —astonished.

"You can't possibly go back to him under any circumstances," he said fervently. "Not tonight, not ever." Intense; his fair hair falling over his fore-head. "The police have got their eye on him. I happen to know that. Quite apart from this ghastly business . . ." His eyes flickered over her face, the silk scarf. "You can't get mixed up in that. You've got to cut and run."

"But where to?" Marcus asked coldly, looking Angie straight in her good eye. She sighed but said nothing. "I suppose this happened tonight?"

Angie nodded. "There was a party . . . you know . . . people from abroad, important. He wanted me to dress up, be amusing, you know—all that jazz. But I was too tired. I'd been working all day and after we'd finished in the studio we all went out for a drink." All this muffled through the silk scarf.

Too tired? Tight is more like it, Marcus was thinking, remembering her like a rag doll in the back of the taxi; recalling, less pleasantly, the fact that they were both rather drunk when they met at that night-club. It had occurred to him then that she probably drank too much to dull the loneliness of her life with Guy Loden, despite its superficial glamour.

"Don't go on talking; it must be bad for your face. It's got to heal." Tom moved closer.

She continued, "I didn't remember all those suckers were coming. I was late back and Guy was furious and he told me to go upstairs and dress. I was so tired I just went to sleep. He came up later . . ."

"Spare us the details," Marcus said icily. "How did you get out?"

"I climbed through the bathroom window. The bedroom door was locked. I must have passed out after he left. It was nearly dark when I woke."

"Will he know you've come here? The truth please, Angie."

"I don't think so." She looked at him directly in the face. "I think it's very unlikely, but you know he does have—people, men, who watch all the comings and goings at the house, follow people if necessary."

"Heavies," said Marcus.

"Yes. But I honestly don't think anyone could have seen me leaving. They knew the bedroom was locked," Angie said quickly. She dropped her head in her hands. "But he'll try and make me go back, I know he will. I know too much, and I can't, I just can't . . ."

The panic rising in her voice was unmistakable. Watching her, sitting next to Marcus, Tessa leant forward in helpless sympathy. The whole situation dumb-founded her.

"Family?" Marcus asked.

Angie shook her bowed head. "I . . . can't go there . . ."

Marcus sighed. He had thought as much. So many of these attractive young women round London, making their way as best they could on youth and looks, seemed to spring, fully grown, from nowhere.

"What about a girlfriend?"

"No."

All her social contacts revolved around Aberdeen Road, Marcus supposed. Which was why she had latched on to him.

"Well, you can't stay here, you realise that," he said crisply. "If you like, I could fix you up with a room. There are plenty of small hotels round here—clean, adequate—no questions asked."

"Absolutely not. I won't hear of it." Tom put his arm round Angie and looked across at Marcus. His chin was thrust out. "There's no problem about tonight. Angie can come home with me."

"*Tom,*" Tessa cried, aghast. "You can't possibly . . ."

166

"Shut up, Tess. Why on earth not? There's plenty of room. Three bedrooms —Oliver has moved out. And also," Tom went on, full of confidence, "Will is away up North on a course for two months . . . So what do you say, Angie? If you think you can put up with the pigsty—and me —you would be extremely welcome."

Angie raised her head, looked at Tom briefly—and burst into tears. Tom put his other arm round her as well.

"Now that's not going to help anyone," Marcus said to Angie, irritated, looking at his watch and wanting to get finished with the whole business. "Tom, look, you can't possibly take on that reponsibility. I mean, it's extremely kind and chivalrous, but why the hell should you?" He ignored Angie who was now sniffing into a handkerchief which Tessa had passed her and was leaning against Tom.

Tom said, "I think it seems quite sensible. Loden won't have the slightest idea where she is. If he asks you, you can say you don't know what he's talking about. I'm in court tomorrow finishing off a case so she can have the place to herself, rest up a bit, find a doctor if it seems necessary . . . and take it from there."

Marcus and Tessa looked at each other.

"Well—what do *you* say, Angie?" Marcus asked. "It's most awfully kind of Tom . . ."

Angie murmured brokenly, "Yes, please . . ." and started weeping silently again. Marcus had had enough. He stood up.

"I want to get Tessa home. I promised Vi. Now let's get you on your feet," he said to Angie.

As Tom helped her up he asked her, "You've got enough gear for tonight in that sack thing, have you?"

"Yes, I have. But are you quite sure?" she asked Tom softly, holding the scarf to her face, looking at him with that limpid green eye. "I won't get you into trouble or anything?"

Tom ran his hand through his hair.

"God no. And it's just between the three of us. Right then, we'll pick up a taxi and we're off to South Ken."

Tessa put on her shoes, attempted to smooth her dress, and ran a comb through her hair which was by now quite tousled.

She looked over to Angie and drew in her breath. She was almost as tall as Tom. Her thick, shiny hair, very dark, fell down her back. She flung her cloak over her shoulders, and turned up the collar so that part of her face was hidden. Then she drew on black gloves and picked up the holdall.

She is completely, utterly stunning, Tessa thought. Even now. Immediately, she felt lumpen and awkward.

"Ready," Angie said to Tom, throwing him part of a smile. He took her arm. "Coming Marcus?"

Marcus had gathered up the glasses and put them in the kitchen. He started switching off the lights.

"Thanks, Tessa," Angie held out the borrowed handkerchief. "It's in a bit of a mess, I'm afraid. And thanks—honest—for helping me. I was in a tight spot."

"Not any more," Tom said firmly, walking her towards the door.

Tessa stared.

"Ready everyone? Lead on Tom," Marcus said. And it was then that the telephone rang. Angie turned sharply and looked at Marcus. There was naked fear in her face. After the second ring, Marcus said smoothly, "I'm not expecting anyone to need to get hold of me at this hour, so I think we'll ignore that. Be careful going down—the stairs are badly lit." He shut the door and locked it.

As they filed along the shadowy corridor, Tom and Angie going ahead, they could hear the phone ringing and ringing, fainter now. Tessa paused at the top of the stairs, treading carefully downwards. Beside her, Marcus took her arm.

The streets of Soho were crowded, bright with neon signs. Restaurant doors opened as diners left—briefly spilling noise and smoke and good cooking smells out on to the pavement. A man was hawking the last editions of the evening papers at the corner. Marcus automatically stopped and bought one, tucking it under his arm. An empty taxi came along immediately. Tom grabbed it, helped Angie in, called out a quick goodbye to Tessa and Marcus—and they were off, almost before Tessa realised what was happening.

"Stay in touch," Marcus called, seeing Tom's head stuck out of the window.

"Will do," Tom shouted back. "Cheers."

"Well, that's that. Good old Tom. The car is just round the corner." She had the feeling that Marcus was smiling, obscurely. He sounded infinitely relieved. He steered her into the next street.

Tessa suddenly experienced a strong sense of unreality—and heightened consciousness—*here, now, walking with Marcus through Soho in the warm May night* . . . It had nothing whatsoever to do with her everyday life: her family, Parloe Square, friends, Joan and the shop . . . It was as though, through meeting Marcus Reardon, leaving the gallery with him earlier that evening, she had stepped out beyond her normal, safe routine.

"Here we are. Hop in. I told Vi I'd look after you. *Take care of my Tessa*, she said. I'm not at all sure I have." He walked round the car and slithered into the driver's seat. She watched his hands. A slight tremor went through her.

"Too bad about poor Angie." Marcus reversed expertly. "I think we'll keep the whole bizarre incident to ourselves, don't you?" He smiled at Tessa in that lopsided way he had which made something thump about inside her. "Particularly Tom's gallantry."

"I won't say anything. Except to Tom, of course."

"You were absolutely marvellous—coping with Angie. I see why Vi says you're a practical girl. Pretty too." He touched her hand lightly. "It wasn't the sort of evening I had anticipated when I whisked you and Tom away from the gallery . . . But I'll make it up to you, I promise. How about a good lunch one day soon—without interruptions?"

Tessa experienced something close to bliss. She turned to him, her eyes shining. "Lovely."

"Good. We'll fix it soon. Often like that, your father, is he?"

They had passed Eros, swooped round Piccadilly and were heading towards Hyde Park Corner.

"I'm afraid so. Particularly with Tom. He got quite a lot worse when our mother went off when he came back from Burma —but I expect you know all that . . ."

"A bit."

"I sometimes wonder if he ever got over it."

They were silent as Marcus negotiated the traffic flooding down Knightsbridge.

"It was splendid of Tom to solve the Angie problem tonight. But I hope he knows what he's doing. I get the impression that Angie Gordon is a very tough girl indeed. Steely," Marcus said.

"I can still hardly believe it."

"What?" They were stopped at a red light and he turned and looked at her.

"Tom disappearing with Angie, a complete stranger. And he seemed, well, to know exactly what he was doing . . . no hesitation or anything."

The car purred forward.

"I'll keep an eye on the situation if I can. Actually, I'm thinking of taking the car over to France for a few days. I shan't be starting on the paper for a week or so . . . and I have friends whose house I borrow from time to time. In Normandy."

France . . . And who with? Not alone, surely. Tessa's heart plummeted. He would never remember his promise of lunch. Already he was sounding offhand —as though he had put tonight's episode,

and her—behind him. Vi's grandchildren
. . . he had meant well . . . an odd incident. All a bit unfortunate. No more to it.
There was no hint of the sudden intimacy
that had arisen between them in his
narrow kitchen. For sure, for sure, she
would never see him again.

"Here we are," she said in a small,
desperate voice as they turned into the
square. "Number 34. On the right. Thank
you so much."

"I've delivered you back safely after
all . . ." They shook hands. "And thanks
again, so much, for your help, Tessa," he
said quite formally. He stood by the car as
she walked up the steps to the front door.
Lights were shining under the curtains in
the drawing-room on the first floor. She
rang the bell.

"Goodnight Marcus."

He ducked back into the car. "Tell Tom
to keep in touch," he called through the
window. "I'm in the book. We'll meet
again. Goodnight, Tessa."

The door opened, with Ella's face behind
it, just as the car moved off from the kerb.
She answered the ring so quickly that

Tessa knew she must have been hovering, expecting her at any minute. Ella held her finger up to her mouth. Her voice hardly above a whisper, she said, "Happy as a sandboy he is now with his paper and a nightcap. I hear there was a bit of a to-do with Tom."

"There was a bit," Tessa whispered back. "He was dreadfully late; we'd almost finished Poppy's old fork supper. Papa pacing up and down like a mad thing. Anyhow, when Tom did arrive, Papa started shouting and he walked out again."

Ella tut-tutted, well used to Tom and his father's dust-ups.

"He *is* a naughty boy, our Tom, the way he asks for trouble. And such an important night for Mr. and Mrs. Flood." Although Tom could never do much wrong in Ella's eyes. "They are very pleased by the turnout—Mrs. Flood sold lots of pictures and there were all the grand critics there . . ."

"Yes, I *am* glad. Actually, a friend of Gran's rather saved the day after the scene with Tom. The three of us went out for a coffee and he dropped me back. Tom's car wouldn't start—that was why he was so late."

"I see. I didn't think that was Tom's car outside. If I were you, I'd nip upstairs, Tess. I'll pop in on his lordship before I lock up and tell him you're back. He was saying earlier that he might have to drop everything and go to New York very soon on some important business."

"Really?" Tessa yawned. "Night, Ella. I've got one of my early starts tomorrow."

On the first landing, she tiptoed past the drawing-room doors, avoiding the bit that always creaked. She had had enough of Papa for one night. Ella had drawn her curtains, turned back the bed and put the light on in her room. Comforting . . .

She got ready for bed quickly and lay with her hands behind her head, wide awake again, her mind blazing with a jumble of images.

5

ALL the next day, odd disconnected thoughts kept intruding as Tessa skilfully massed vases for a church wedding—lilies and the palest pinks and roses, apparently artless greenery cascading . . .

"Damn," Tessa said irritably in the part of the shop they used for making up the arrangements. "They won't *bend* like I wanted—or fall properly. They look so stiff." She stood back, considering, frowning, her head on one side.

"They're smashing," Joan assured her stoutly. "And they're going to look wonderful in church. Very dramatic. Honestly." One hand stuck into corduroy breeches, the other dragging on a cigarette. "What's up with you, Tess, anyway?" She looked at her knowingly. "Late night? The old boy acting up again —or what?"

"Nothing like that," Tessa assured her, sighing, pushing strands of hair behind her ear. "Pass me the bucket with the roses in, would you? No, the deeper pink ones . . . thanks." Snipping and cutting, she began sticking them, apparently at random, into the huge, overflowing urns. "Do you think Jilly will be able to help me with the centrepieces later?"

Jilly was the part-time assistant they had taken on some months before. She was pretty and scatterbrained and not very efficient; but both Joan and Tessa liked her and hadn't the heart to let her go.

"Sure. With luck, the shop will be fairly quiet."

But it wasn't. The small space by the pine table that passed for a counter was crowded for most of the day, often with three or more customers. The phone rang constantly. Joan, pleasant and calm, dealt with one order or enquiry or desperate, last minute need for *something*—one after the next. Always a cigarette to hand, always an open smile and some cheerful personal comment. It was no wonder, Tessa often thought, that so many people who wandered into the charming, individual little shop had soon become friendly with its owner.

Eventually, Jilly arrived and the centre-pieces began to take shape, devised partly by Tessa and partly by shouted suggestions from Joan. "Tiny white bows . . . scatter them all over, tucked in. That's the way Jilly." For once, Jilly stopped giggling and pulled her weight. Late in the afternoon, the driver arrived with the small delivery van they had recently bought. Despite the rush, everything was delivered, exactly as ordered, on time.

"I'm off," Tessa announced at five. She had been up since the same time that morning.

"Off you go," Joan agreed. "We'll lock up. Got your list for tomorrow's buying? Good girl. See you."

No two days were ever quite the same. And thank God for that, Tessa was thinking as she parked her car and let herself into the house. The weather was dull and heavy and she had a splitting headache.

"Hello Ella, dreadful day but we got it all done somehow. Any phone calls?" she asked hopefully. There were. An old school friend and a young man called

James who had, Tessa remembered, asked her to go out one night that week.

"That's all. Except Tom. He said not to 'phone. He will ring later."

"Oh, Tom told me last night that Oliver Bingham's grandmother has died. She's left him a house somewhere—Maida Vale I think—and he's left the flat and moved in. Did Tom tell you?"

"I can't say he did. Well—that's nice for Oliver, isn't it? And he's such a dear."

"I really ought to write to him. I will tonight. I do remember meeting his grandmother, and he was very fond of her. I'm *exhausted* Ella . . . We're not eating late, are we? I think I'll go and have a bath. If Tom rings, tell him I'm in all evening."

Tom rang, much later, clearly hoping to avoid speaking to his father. It happened that George Selway was conducting a late, informal business meeting in his study and Tessa, waiting edgily, picked up the upstairs phone at once.

"Tess? Tom here." He sounded very brisk.

"What's happening? I'm upstairs. I can

talk." She held the receiver close to her mouth.

"Is the old man about?"

"He's got a meeting in his study. How's —er—Angie?"

"She's still here. There's masses of room, so she can stay as long as she likes."

Tessa said nothing.

"Tess? Are you there?"

"Yes. How is her face?"

"Worse today actually. I walked her round to the chemist and he gave her some stuff to put on it. But it's a matter of resting up and waiting for it to heal, apparently. She's very grateful for what you did, by the way."

"It wasn't much . . . any sign of Loden?"

"None. We spoke to Reardon and he thinks he'll let it go for a bit—expect Angie to cool off and come crawling back to Aberdeen Road. Fat chance. It's not the first time something of this sort has happened—but never so badly. *Pig*. Reardon is definitely off to France, he said."

"I see." The world suddenly seemed inexpressibly dreary to Tessa. "By the way, Pa's going to New York with Poppy next week—suddenly. It's about the Selway Electric deal. They're taking me out to dinner tomorrow night so I'll hear all about it."

"You don't sound very cheery . . . hang on, Angie's shouting something. She wants you to come and have supper with us on Monday. Is that OK?"

Tessa swallowed hard at the "with us".

"I'd like that. Thanks. Tell Angie I hope she feels better soon," she said politely.

"She will. She's brighter already—less shocked. She's told the agency she can't work for a bit because she's got 'flu. Any word from Pa about the scene last night?"

"Nothing."

"That's all right then," Tom said cheerfully. "By the way, we got a quick verdict this morning and my chap got off. I was very pleased, actually."

"Well done, Tom."

"See you on Monday then, Tess. 'Night."

Expensive and exclusive London restaurants were Poppy Renfrew's

182

favourite stage. She played them, each one slightly differently, with style and assurance. Part of the act was table-changing—which was practically obligatory. The following night, the first table at Lorenzo's shown them by an obsequious head waiter was found, unsurprisingly, not to be to Poppy's liking.

"What, sit in this draught with the door banging away behind me, George *dear*, how could you possibly allow it?" This was in her high, grating voice—which carried. So they were moved, ceremoniously reseated, and began studying the vast menu. Champagne was brought and found to be satisfactory. Tessa picked up her glass and sighed. She wondered how soon she could get away.

"Now Tessa, darling, you're a big healthy girl . . ." Hidden by the menu, Tessa glared. "You must be longing for a lovely meal. What about those divine Russian things they do so well here, a sort of creamy pancake, just to start with . . ."

Poppy, who starved her skinny figure with a will of iron, encouraged everyone else to eat their heads off.

"Something simple," Tessa said through gritted teeth.

After studying the menu through an antique lorgnette, Poppy ordered, as she always did, grapefruit and grilled lamb cutlets. And while these were being prepared for the second time—when they first appeared they were waved away as being too something or other—George Selway explained to Tessa the gist of the takeover Selway Electric was attempting in the States. "If we can bring it off," he said, fixing her from beneath bushy eyebrows, "we'll have acquired a mass manufacturing base and a mass market—without having to relinquish the technical knowhow which we have here. And too much of that pioneering knowledge, in my opinion, has been allowed to drain away from this country—and be fully developed, commercially, elsewhere."

Tessa had heard it all before; his business pontifications always made her and Tom yawn or giggle; but she was impressed that he was now, evidently, about to put these privately held theories into very public practice.

"Your father is right, Tessa. And

184

it's *because* this trip is so important for British industry as a whole, not *just* Selways, that I'm giving up *all* my social arrangements for the early part of the summer. *Poor* little old me—and going *just* to be with your father, to support him. That's right, isn't it, George?" She played about discontentedly with the cutlets.

"I only wish you could come too, Tess," George Selway said gruffly. "You're too committed with that shop of yours. I keep telling you. You must see the world a bit when you've the chance."

"Next time, Papa," Tessa said, smiling at him. "Next time you go over. I'd love to come. Really."

When the coffee was brought—Tessa longing to leave, wondering whether she dared to make the excuse of having to get up so early—Poppy suddenly piped up, "That chum of Vi's. Marcus someone . . ."

"Reardon," said Tessa, looking into her bright, inquisitive eyes. "Marcus Reardon." She didn't miss much, Poppy.

"That's right. The journalist. Such an *arresting*-looking, such an *attractive*, man.

He seemed to take quite a fancy to you, Tessa darling, we all thought so, didn't we George?"

186

6

WALKING into Tom's bachelor flat in Kensington the following Monday evening, Tessa's first thought was: it's all different. For one thing the sitting-room, which was flooded with early evening sunlight, was tidy. The usual jumble of shoes and books and old newspapers, dirty cups and glasses on every surface, had gone. The rickety table in the corner was laid for supper. And the furniture with its faded loose covers and sagging springs had been rearranged. The place really looked quite homely. Tom, shambling about in corduroy trousers and an old sweater, said that he had opened a bottle of red wine and would Tessa like a glass?

"You bet," said Angie coming out from the kitchen. "Hi there, Tessa. Surprise, surprise. So, how do you think this dump is looking?"

Tessa started. She could hardly believe it was the same girl who had landed on

Marcus's doorstep last week. Her face was still discoloured—more yellow than blue-red now—but most of the swelling had gone down. There were very dark circles under her eyes; both must have eventually turned black. Unlike the other night, there was no disguising the loveliness of that face. Her hair, which had evidently just been washed and was still damp, hung loose. She wore black trousers and a scarlet tunic overblouse.

She seemed totally at ease in the surroundings.

"It's a great improvement," Tessa said, looking about. And it was.

"And what about Tom?" Angie linked her arm through his with unmistakable possessiveness, turning her face to him, provocatively tilted.

He looked back at her adoringly.

Embarrassed, Tessa mumbled, "Oh fine . . . glad about the case you won Tom . . ."

"Hell, the sauce . . ." Angie fled back to the kitchen. Tom handed Tessa a drink and she sat on the dilapidated sofa. Delicious smells—spicy, garlicky, tomato—wafted about.

"Angie's an amazing cook. You wait . . ." Tom sprawled comfortably in an armchair, his long legs stretched. He looked unusually calm, not nervy at all. And Tessa knew that he had been moody of late; unsure about his career and even more irritated than usual with their father. Now he seemed happy and relaxed. "Come in and be sociable," he called out to Angie. "Whatever it is you're concocting smells tantalising . . . I've poured you a drink."

Angie reappeared, this time covered in a blue and white striped apron, picked up a glass, and perched on the arm of Tom's chair. Tessa watched this picture of domestic harmony in disbelief.

"So when is Pa off to the States?" Tom asked. "I know a bit about what he's trying to do over there. If he manages to acquire the company he's after and keep control through Selway Electric he'll be in the major business league."

"He seems to think it's a possibility anyhow," Tessa said. "Poppy is going too . . ." She made a face. "To *support* him, she says. God, she was ghastly at dinner last night. Does Angie know about the 'constant companion?'" It seemed awkward somehow not to include her in a casual family chat.

"I've got the picture. Will he marry her, Tessa?" Angie asked keenly.

"I doubt it. The arrangement seems to suit them both, sort of permanent royal escorts with their own establishments. We've been lucky there, haven't we, Tom? Imagine being brought up by that creature . . ."

"All the same, she's a clever woman, Tess, whatever our feelings may be. And she's shrewd. They'll be doing a lot of entertaining in the States, meeting people . . . and I think he relies quite heavily on her personal judgments."

"I suppose so . . ." Tom had never taken the slightest interest in Selway Electric, in fact, quite the reverse, so she was surprised to hear him discuss the forthcoming possible merger so thoughtfully.

"You must get in touch with him before he goes, Tom," Angie said, looking down at him, her arm along the top of his chair. "After that row. The night we all met. Tomorrow. I'll remind you. You'd be a fool not to."

"Your face looks enormously better," Tessa said shyly, changing the subject. "It's hardly swollen at all any more."

"It's more or less OK now. I'm hoping to get back to work next week. Whatever you did with the cold flannel was the right thing. Anyhow, thanks again." She sounded a bit offhand. Tessa thought, as she had the other night, that her manner wasn't very agreeable. Something about her voice didn't sound quite right. She was direct but not at all charming. Not that anyone would notice much about Angie except her looks.

Because she did look very lovely sitting there, swinging a leg, hair tumbling; the curve of her cheek; long neck; slanted green eyes. All the times Tessa had seen that face from different angles, with different hairstyles, staring or smiling out of one magazine or the other . . . And here she was, sitting on the chair opposite, more or less glued to Tom.

"I expect you're a bit surprised to find me still here," Angie said briskly. "But we're getting along fine, aren't we Tom?" She looked down at him again, her hair falling over her face.

191

"Never better," agreed Tom. He put his hand up and touched her bruised cheek. "No rush," he said gently, "but when are we going to be fed? Frankly, I'm damned hungry."

Angie gave a mock salute and went off to the kitchen.

"Can I help at all?" Tessa called after her.

"OK—if you like. Come and take this to the table, would you? And ask Tom to bring the wine and light the candles. Tell him to do *something* useful at least."

Minutes later, Angie appeared with a large oblong dish of steaming spaghetti covered in a rich and fragrant sauce.

"I've run out of crockery so I had to put the parmesan in an egg cup. You can tell nobody ever cooked here before. Pity— because the market round the corner is fabulous, though you have to watch them. They try to get away with murder."

She served the spaghetti with almost professional panache, and fetched in the warmed bread and unsalted butter. When Tessa commented on her effortlessly good cooking she said casually, "Oh I love cooking. I learnt when I was a little kid.

My mum pushed off soon after I was born, you see, and my Auntie, her sister, took me on." Tessa glanced at Tom who was looking only at Angie in between shovelling the excellent spaghetti. "It was she who brought me up."

"Did you ever see your mother?" Tessa asked.

Angie shook her head.

"Wouldn't know where to start looking. She was a one for the lads—nobody knew for sure where I came from. I wouldn't want to know anyhow, not my parents. Some things are best left alone. And Auntie and Paulo gave me a good home, you could say."

"Who's Paulo?" Tom asked through a mouthful, reaching for the cheese. Angie's background seemed to be unknown to him as well as Tessa.

"Paulo's a lovely man—more than I can say for most of them." She held out her glass to Tom for some more wine. "He's Italian, a waiter at Lorenzo's, been there for years."

"At *Lorenzo's?*" Tessa almost choked.

"That's right. Know it, do you? I expect you lot would."

Tess and Tom exchanged amused glances.

"As a matter of fact," Tessa said, "Poppy and Papa took me there for dinner last night. How absolutely extraordinary."

Angie gave the salad an extra toss and helped herself.

"I can't say I'm surprised . . ." She shrugged. "They've got a good clientèle, the same people have been going there for years. And it's not far from your house."

"Go on," Tom said, taking the salad bowl from her and passing his plate for more spaghetti. "About Paulo . . ."

"Well, Paulo and Auntie have been together for years, ever since I can remember. They've got two kids, Marco and Sharon, fourteen and fifteen they are now . . . a nice semi in West Borwood. They can't get married. Auntie knows that, always has. Paulo has got a wife in Italy and a grown-up family there." She shrugged again. "No divorce. When the restaurant closes in August, he goes back to Italy—it's a huge family, cousins and grandparents and God knows what. And he loves them. He sends them money the rest of the year too. Auntie doesn't mind.

194

She's got a good man and nothing's perfect —and she knows it. *Reelly* she does." (Her refined tone of voice was slipping away).

"This food is so good, Angie. Amazing. Did Paulo teach you to cook?" Tessa asked. Angie's background, and the brief, forthright way she discussed it, fascinated her.

"Not so much teach. I just watched how he did it. Naturally. He loves good food and cooking—he always cooks on his days off. Auntie always said she reckons she eats better than the Queen of England."

"She probably does," Tom agreed. "Angie . . ." He reached out for her hand. "You never told me all this, just that your mother had gone off, and that a photographer saw you in a coffee bar . . ." They looked at each other in the soft candlelight —one so dark, the other fair, both strikingly good-looking—like a young couple in one of those grainy, romantic French films, Tessa thought sentimentally.

Nobody spoke and suddenly, for no apparent reason, she remembered Marcus. Something caught in her throat and she gulped down her wine.

"You know it all now, anyway," Angie said. She and Tom smiled and smiled at each other and Tessa was starting to feel that they had completely forgotten about her when Angie turned to her and said, "That's right about the coffee bar. Simple as that. I got fed up with school and I pushed off to the West End—made up to the nines, wearing Auntie's high heels and black stockings . . . and the very first day I bumped into this geezer. Bill Owen the photographer, as it turned out. Not that it meant anything at all to me then. I thought he was shooting a line to start with, and he was in a way . . . but within a month I'd done my first job and I had a portfolio of pictures to drag round. I met Loden a couple of years later."

Tom scraped back his chair and stood up.

"I'll clear the table and make the coffee. That's my one domestic accomplishment. You two girls go and make yourselves comfortable over there."

While Tom messily piled the plates and glasses, Angie and Tessa moved to the other part of the room. Angie lit a cigarette.

"Guy Loden. He's a clever bastard, Guy —and when I met him . . ." She lay back in the chair. "He seemed the most glamorous man in the world . . . to a kid coming from West Borwood. I was starting to know my way about a bit by then and it was champagne all the way, all the clothes I wanted, cars, posh restaurants. I was dazzled. Who wouldn't be? Modelling for the glossies in the day, the top photographers—Pailey, Midgefield, Nevis —and dressing up every night."

"But where did you go?" Tessa asked.

"Nightclubs mostly, in the beginning. Then he started those boring, bloody non-stop gambling sessions and I had to walk around, like you see those models in grand tea places like Fortnums, keeping the boys interested. He knew I hated it, so if I got too stroppy it was off to the Bahamas or in a private plane to France for the races . . . then I'd have drunken lords in Guy's box who couldn't put two words together trying to pinch my bottom." She laughed. "As for Guy . . ." Her face became inscrutable. She said very quietly, "I thought he was God. I really did. I learnt different."

"You were very young," Tessa said, not

quite sure how to take it at all. And incredibly beautiful, she thought. The whole evening, watching Angie, she had felt dull and ungainly.

"I was good raw material—and he worked on me. Like that 'My Fair Lady' chap. Correcting how I spoke, teaching me the social ropes . . . clothes, hair, that sort of thing was never a problem. I always knew how to put myself together."

"What did Auntie and Paulo think?"

"That I was making the big time as a model, had a boyfriend or two. They come from different worlds." She sat up straight, flicked ash—and laughed with a cutting edge. "And I'll tell you something else. Guy got everyone at Aberdeen Road sooner or later—everyone, believe me, from royalty down—and a right load of trash they were."

"You were better off in West Borwood, my love," Tom said, coming in with three mugs of coffee on a tray. "Except that I wouldn't have met you and carried you off."

"*Listen,*" Angie said, taking one and ignoring Tom's last words. "You're talking more sense than you know. At leas they've got values there. Not much money, and that's not fun, but he looks after her, Paulo does. And the kids. He's tender, Paulo is. He's all man . . . but he's not afraid to be gentle."

If it weren't for the constant hardness in her voice, Tessa could swear her eyes were wet. "So you see, I couldn't have gone back to them that night, not in the state I was in. They only know about the photographs, the pretty clothes, the holidays. Not the other side, the ugly one. They're proud of me. I couldn't let them down."

"No. I understand." Tessa thought she did.

Tom took her hand. "I don't see why they should ever know about that part of your life. There's no need. It's over now." He dropped a kiss on her hand and went on holding it.

Tessa said, "Has Tom told you about Mother? That she left us as well?"

Angie nodded. "I can't figure out what for. I mean your father's got everything . . . and there she is stuck down in some lousy cottage in the country. I wouldn't like that," she said crisply. "Get the milk Tom, there's a love."

199

Tom rose obediently.

"What about your shop then? Like the work, do you?"

"Yes I do. Most of the time."

"I know what you mean. It keeps you going, makes you respect yourself. Especially you—not *having* to do it. Tom says it's going well. Just a drop," she said to Tom who had brought in the milk bottle. "What about you, Tess?"

Tom sat next to Angie and put his arm round her. "We were talking about Tessa's shop," Angie said. "I must go and see it one day. There's a studio I do a lot of work in just round the corner. We'll have lunch."

"Let's do that. Tom can give you the address."

"The shopping round here is smashing. I love that market . . . Paulo always shops in markets when he gets the chance. You wouldn't find anyone putting anything over on him—rotten apples or sour tomatoes. Not Paulo." She laughed . . . Then she said seriously, "You know, I had the feeling that I was being followed today, Tom. Trailed from shop to shop. Don't laugh. I'd forgotten all about it until now.

200

But Guy's ruthless enough for that. He won't let me disappear from his life, from the house. Not just like that. He'll find me."

Tom pulled her closer. "I'll look after you. Did you actually see someone— someone you recognised?"

"Not really." Angie frowned. "It was more a feeling, but I don't think I was wrong. I rushed back here and double-locked the door."

"What about your belongings?" Tessa asked. "Surely you'll need some things?"

"I packed a bag before I left and we sent a taxi round to collect it the other day. We had it brought to my agency. Anyhow, Tom," she turned to him, "if Guy really means to find me, that's how he can do it. He knows the agency. And I'm going back to work as soon as my face is cleared up."

"You've got nothing to worry about," Tom said stubbornly. "You're finished with him. Through. There's no law against that, for God's sake."

"Does Marcus think he'll leave you alone?" Tessa had been waiting for an opportunity to use Marcus's name all evening. She could feel herself colouring.

"He doesn't know or care," Tom said. "We tried to get him today and there was no answer. He must have gone to France. We spoke to him the day after Angie came here. He said he thought Loden was a sinister character and we should be prepared for anything. Frankly, he didn't seem much interested."

"He was a lifeline that night, I'll say that for him," Angie said. "Because he was out of the Loden circle. And I've been so drawn into the net over the years, I hardly know anyone else. He's clever, Marcus is. People say he's a talented journalist. But he's a cold fish—he's got a bad reputation, Guy told me. More coffee anyone?"

"No thanks," Tessa said, ignoring her mention of Marcus. "I must be on my way. Joan—my partner—is having her garden in Sussex enlarged so I'm doing all the buying in the market for the moment. And we're terribly busy. So I have to be up at the crack of dawn."

On her way out, Tessa glanced into Tom's bedroom. The twin beds had been pushed together and an obviously new bedspread draped neatly over them both.

Tessa looked discreetly away. She could never remember Tom—not far off thirty now—having the same girlfriend for more than a couple of months running. With his worship of sports, they simply took up too much time. They seemed to come and go from all over the world—Australia; girls met skiing in Switzerland. A pretty South American actress. One or two girls he had been up at Oxford with turned up quite regularly at his parties. But nobody he was even slightly serious about. And now this, with Angie . . . And he had fallen head over heels in love with her from the first; that was very obvious.

She left them standing very close in the doorway, for all the world as though they had been together for years.

"I'll give Pa a ring in the morning," Tom said, yawning. "Mend the fences . . . after all, why not?"

"Why not indeed?" Angie echoed tartly. "Cheerio, Tessa. Be seeing Marcus again will you? I suppose he must have taken you home that night."

"Yes he did." She turned, one hand on the bannister. "I've really no idea." She started down the stairs calling, "Good

203

night and thanks for the delicious supper."
As she let herself out into the street she
heard the door of the flat slam shut. Life
was very odd. If someone had told her
Tom would take up with a girl like Angie,
the model girl of both male and female
fantasies, she would never have believed
it. And what to make of Angie? She
frowned. She wasn't sure. She seemed
honest enough; she had believed the story
about her background. It sounded plaus-
ible. But where did Tom come into it? He
didn't seem at all the kind of man she
would be attracted to—not after the kind
of high living she was used to.

Had she fallen for him too? When he
dashed to catch her before she fell at the
doorway of Marcus's flat? Perhaps it was
a case of truth being stranger than fiction
after all.

As she drove towards Parloe Square, she
thought about Marcus starting on the new
paper—and when he was likely to return
from France. A week or so he had said.
She started counting the days . . .

7

TESSA saw her father and Poppy off on the liner to the States. She drove down with them to Southampton, squashed into the car with their expensive luggage. Ella waved them off from Parloe Square on their way to pick up Poppy at her flat. George Selway, impressive in a dark suit, looked depressed. He had a dread, even then, of leaving Tessa, despite Ella's presence in the background.

"You have the itinerary," he told Ella gruffly for the hundredth time. "And I can be reached at any time through the office." Ella nodded and smiled and murmured reassuringly while the chauffeur stowed several heavy briefcases. The scene at Poppy's was similar. She appeared in a chic navy suit carrying a sable stole and dressing-case and screeching last minute instructions to her housekeeper. Passers-by turned and gaped as the porter appeared with a mountain of matching luggage. After much pulling and pushing and rearranging, all of them making conflicting suggestions, the car doors were shut and they set off.

The dockside at Southampton was a hubbub of excitement. The sun glinted and danced on the water; gulls wheeled and screamed high up in the blue sky. The liner's flanks rose like smooth white cliffs from the dock as passengers and crew scrambled over the decks, up and down staircases and corridors, while waiters flashed in and out of staterooms carrying silver buckets with iced champagne. The quayside swarmed with well-dressed passengers being seen off; lights flashed as a film star and entourage pushed through. Luggage, telegrams and elaborate flower arrangements were brought aboard. But when Tessa gave a last wave to the barely visible figures of Poppy and her father at the rail, her relief was palpable. They were away, she was on her own . . . Sitting in the front seat with the chauffeur on the way back to London, she felt lightheaded. This glorious day, the summer ahead and weeks and weeks without her father's constraining presence.

It was late in the afternoon when they

got back to London. Tessa asked to be dropped off at the shop. The tiny space was a fragrant bower of roses and lilies and sweet peas which cascaded out of every kind and shape of container. She found Joan and Jilly coping with as many customers as the place would hold. The phone rang and Tessa picked it up and took the order. Two dozen perfect yellow roses. Yes, she was sure they had them, absolute beauties, she would send them round at once . . . sliding effortlessly back to work. When she at last had a spare moment, Joan poked her head into the back-room where they worked and said, "By the way, a chap came in asking for you this morning. Just before lunch. Marcus someone-or-other. I told him you were seeing the family off in style." She paused in lighting a cigarette and her eyes twinkled. "Interesting looking—fortyish I should think. And a super car. Now who's he, then?"

Marcus. So he had remembered. Exhilaration burst through her.

"Marcus?" she asked coolly, keeping her head down. "It must have been Marcus Reardon. He's a friend of Gran's.

We met a couple of weeks ago at the party for Flora Flood's opening. You remember. What did he want?"

Although she continued calmly snipping the stems off yellow roses, her heart was thumping about ridiculously.

"He just asked for you. No message. A bit grown up for you, isn't he?"

"Don't be ridiculous," Tessa snapped, uncharacteristically. Joan thought hard.

"Reardon. Wait a minute. Is that the journalist? I forget what he writes for. He looked familiar. I think I've seen him on television—or perhaps heard him on the car radio."

"You might have. I honestly don't know. He's just started on the *Chronicle*."

"I'll look out for him. Oh, we're doing a dance and two more weddings. They rang this morning. We'll have to put our heads together about extra help. Come over to the house for supper one evening and we can make a plan."

The rest of the afternoon danced past for Tessa. She smiled and smiled as the customers came in, the doorbell tinkling endlessly, inspired by the long-awaited summer sunshine. Wrapping plants and flowers, fixing their special narrow white satin bows, she took extra trouble to make them appear particularly pretty.

And all the time thoughts tumbled round and round in her head. For all her smiles, she worked away efficiently. Marcus had come looking for her; he had remembered. Walking home through the rush-hour crowds, she thought briefly of her father and Poppy, steaming down Southampton Water, heading for the open sea, trunks and jewels decanted into their staterooms . . . She felt wonderfully free and happy as she swung into Parloe Square. The soft, warm early evening air promised a spell of fine weather. The new leaves of the plane trees in the square garden had reached their full green growth. She ran up the steps, found her key and flung open the front door.

"Ella, Ella . . . I'm back."

She found Ella in her sitting-room in the basement, reading the evening paper and listening to the news. Morgan snoozed beside her.

"Hello, my love." Ella looked up and smiled, white hair short and tidy, neat in her usual grey skirt and blouse. "There you are. I thought you'd go back to the shop. They got off all right, did they? I couldn't imagine how on earth they were going to get all Mrs. Renfrew's luggage in —I'll bet you had a right carry-on with all that."

Tessa threw herself into one of Ella's cosy chairs and giggled. "You could say that. There she was, waving the sable stole, screaming instructions left and right. Everyone was turning round and staring. You know, she reminds me of a parrot, the shrieking and the beady eye. Papa's so used to her. I don't think he listens."

"He does over business. She's sharp, you know Tess."

"I suppose so. That's what Tom says." Tessa jumped up and began to thumb through the papers. "Did anyone phone, by the way?"

"Oliver Bingham did, I was just going to tell you. We had quite a chat. Anyhow, he wants you to ring him—the number is on the pad. He's having a bit of a party, he said."

"That's nice. I've been quite out of touch with him since last winter. Tom told me he'd moved out of the flat into the house."

She scooped up Morgan, who was only pretending to sleep, and waltzed round the room with him.

"*You* seem full of beans, Miss. It's having the place to ourselves for a bit, isn't it? You never know when his lordship is going to start ranting—but he's a good man for all that. I thought we could have a bit of supper on trays if you're not going out . . . there, that might be Oliver now."

Tessa picked up the phone. It was Oliver Bingham.

"I *was* sorry to hear about your grandmother, Oliver, Tom only just told me. I didn't know your new address so I sent a note to chambers . . . good, I hoped you would . . . Not too bad, very busy at the shop at the moment which is a good sign. What about you? Yes, I saw it in the papers, spectacular case, well done you . . . Gosh, yes, it must be the most ghastly strain . . . Papa's all right. As a matter of fact, he's just gone off to the States. I got back from Southampton this afternoon from seeing them off . . . Yes, Poppy has gone too, they're on a corporate raiding

211

expedition. I don't understand it, but apparently it's mega-business stuff . . . A party? This Saturday? Yes I can, sounds lovely . . . I know what you mean, you want to make the house feel like yours . . . Needs painting? Oh, nobody will even notice . . . eightish? Lovely. I'll just write down your address . . . Thanks, Oliver. See you then."

She followed Ella up into the kitchen.

"That was Oliver. I said I'd go to his party, I suppose . . ." She sat at the big kitchen table and watched Ella neatly break eggs in a bowl.

"You don't sound very pleased," Ella remarked as she added salt and a grinding of pepper. "And he's such a pet. He used to come here for tea with Tom in the holidays from school."

"Now Ella, don't matchmake," Tessa teased. "He's Tom's friend and I've known him all my life and besides, he's got a girlfriend—very pretty and very flighty. Tom told me. He doesn't approve."

"That doesn't sound like Oliver," Ella said. "And speaking of Tom, he's sure to be going to the party too, isn't he?"

Now that was an interesting thought. Would he and Angie be there on Saturday? She tried to imagine what Ella would make of their instant cosiness in the shabby flat. She would love to have known. Better to let Tom tell her—whatever there was to tell—in his own way.

The second time the phone rang it was a friend asking her to join the committee for a charity ball. She accepted, sighing, knowing that she would be leant on to do the flowers. All the same, Joan would say it was the right sort of publicity, well worth the extra work and the cost.

The third time the phone went, much later, Tessa was taking a cup of coffee down to Ella's. She knew at once that it was Marcus. She picked up the phone on the hall table.

"Hello," she said. She turned on the light which threw golden beams right across the black and white marble squares on the floor. "Hello?"

A pause. "Marcus Reardon here."

"Yes, I know. I recognised your voice." A bit breathless, colour already in her cheeks. "Didn't you come to the shop today?"

"So she told you? Whoever it was I spoke to."

"Joan. We run the shop together. I'm sorry I missed you."

"I was around there and I just looked in on the off chance—I thought I might have carried you off to lunch." He sounded distant, slightly ironic; Tessa's heart was bumping around. She looked towards the door down to the basement and was relieved to see it was still closed.

"I would have loved that," she said hurriedly. "Actually, I was seeing my father off to the States." She willed the door to stay closed and for Ella to remain safely in her sitting-room.

"What about Saturday then?"

"Lovely . . ." Her voice leapt. "I shan't be working."

"Then let's say around twelve-thirty. I'll pick you up at the house. Would that suit you?"

"Yes, oh yes . . ."

"Good. Until Saturday, then."

"'Bye Marcus."

He rang off and Tessa went on standing in the quiet hall, her hand still on the receiver. When Ella started calling, she

214

didn't hear her voice. Eventually, she switched off the light, picked up the cooling coffee and went into the kitchen where she sat for a while by herself—not really thinking about anything.

8

SATURDAY was warm and fine. For the first time, Tessa felt dismally conscious of her inadequate wardrobe. She should, as Gran said, start paying more attention to how she looked. She thought despairingly of Angie's style, how she made the simplest combination of garments look appealing. Several times in the past week she had seen a dress or a pair of shoes in a shop window and thought: I'm sure that's the sort of thing Angie would wear. And it wasn't that she didn't have the opportunity to buy nice things; Papa had always given her a generous allowance. Neither was it that she didn't have an eye for colour and design. Her work at the shop proved that. She had just never cared enough to take the time and trouble that a good appearance demanded.

She sat down at her dressing-table and stared into the mirror. At least she had had her hair shaped again that week. It was tamed into a becoming red-gold bob. She had washed it the night before and it was pleasingly shiny. Perking up, she peered more closely into the mirror. Her skin looked all right. Perhaps everyone got bored and discouraged with their own faces from time to time. She had never bothered much with make-up, but she would dig out a bright lipstick; if only, just that day, she could look less . . . *girlish*.

Ella left quite early to spend the day with her sister so Tessa found herself alone in the big house which creaked in familiar, friendly ways. She wandered restlessly from one room to the next as sunlight streamed through the large windows on to highly polished chairs and tables. In the narrow garden which her father's study overlooked, tubs of geraniums glowed pink and scarlet.

Tessa was ready and waiting long before Marcus was expected. She had put on a bright pink cotton frock and sandals. As she was alone, it was perfectly safe to ask Marcus in for a drink without questions being asked. She ran up and down from the kitchen to the drawing-room fetching ice, lemon, more tonics. She went up to

217

her bedroom and brushed her hair yet again, added more lipstick. And when she saw the hand of the grandfather clock in the hall move down towards the half hour, she suddenly panicked. The immediate prospect terrified her. Lunch with a man she had only met once in her life, much older, and from a world she knew nothing of . . . What on earth were they going to talk about? How could she ever have thought that this stranger, because that was what he was, could be so beguiling?

She was standing in the middle of the hall wishing for all her worth that she had never made the arrangement, when the bell rang. He was early. Taking a deep breath, she opened the door. The sunlight behind was so strong that for a moment she couldn't see his face. He was taller than she remembered. He seemed quizzical, a little hesitant.

"Tessa . . ." He took the hand which she held out and went on holding it, head slightly to one side. "Tessa in a pink dress, red hair . . . what a very pretty sight."

Smiling back, all her nerves vanished, Tessa said, "Do come in for a drink. It's quite early."

"I know. I was determined to be punctual. I felt I must be on my best behaviour after the fiasco the night we met."

"With Angie, you mean? You certainly couldn't help that." She led the way upstairs. "I had supper with her *and* Tom the other night. They seem very cosy together, I must say."

"I hope Tom knows what he's doing."

"He looked terribly happy. I've never seen him like that before. This way."

She walked into the drawing-room through double doors. The huge, high room had long french windows opening on to a decorative wrought-iron balcony. It was elaborately furnished with some fine antique pieces—mirrors, eighteenth-century side-tables, porcelain, and luxurious upholstery.

"What a splendid room," Marcus commented, looking round. "The proportions are superb." He walked over to the open windows which overlooked the green and sunlit garden square. "And the outlook—magnificent." He turned back towards her, smiling. "A very impressive home indeed."

"It's a lovely house. I'll show you round

sometime if you like . . . We've lived here all our lives except for part of the war when we were with the Floods in Dorset. Can you help us to something?" She indicated the drinks in the corner. "I think there's just about everything there."

While he poured them both gin and tonics, Tessa watched him. There was something—was it his hair which seemed to have lost its parting?—that made him look different from the other men she knew, friends of her father's and Tom's. She couldn't quite put her finger on it. He was wearing a navy blazer and a cravat instead of a tie. She noticed again, as he dealt deftly with bottles and ice and lemon that he had very elegant hands and wrists. And when he gave her the drink, she saw his eyes were pale, almost grey, no colour at all really. They sat on either side of the fireplace and he raised his glass towards her.

"Good health. And here's to an uninterrupted meeting. No dramas this time." They both laughed. "And I thought the shop—Joan's Garden—was really charming, by the way. It's got something about it, quite distinctive. It's certainly no ordinary florist's shop."

"That's what we *hope* people will feel."

"I'm sure they do. And the flowers actually looked like flowers, not cardboard arrangements."

"My father only half approves of my doing it. It's a running battle between us . . . but I've stuck to my guns over that. Joan and I are partners now, fifty, fifty," she said proudly. "I think Papa feels it ties me down too much. He'd like me to be more of a social butterfly. I expect Gran would too."

Marcus put his drink down carefully. "She would like you to be happier," he said.

Tessa stared at him. "Happier? But I am happy," she said. She felt suddenly tremulous; excited in a strange way, not like herself at all.

The clock on the mantlepiece whirred and pinged. On the other side of the square a car started up. Marcus said, "So that's all right, then. I'm wondering about the curtains," he said, changing the subject completely. "Purple. Very dramatic against the grey walls . . ." He had turned to look at them again.

"A friend of my father's, Poppy Renfrew—you know—persuaded him to get in a fashionable interior decorator a couple of years ago. And she talked him into these curtains. The ones before were old and grey and stripey. Tom and I loathe the purple ones. Actually, they're our pet hate in the whole house."

Marcus laughed. "I think I might have preferred the others too—but you can't ignore all those yards of royal purple, they make an impression all right. And I've been looking at the Flora Flood over the mantelpiece and admiring it. It was the first thing I noticed when I came into the room. It's you, of course . . . delightful—fresh and beautifully painted."

Surprised, Tessa looked up at her nine-year-old self staring out of a carved gold frame. "It's funny, but I hardly ever notice it."

Flora Flood had painted Tessa sitting on a chair, in her blue dress, holding a ginger cat on her lap—and looking straight ahead. The colour of Tessa's hair and the cat's fur harmonised pleasantly.

"Aunt Flor did that just before we left Chalcot and came back here. Just after Papa came back from Burma—and Mother went to live with Felix, our stepfather now. That was Orlando—poor Orlando . . . he was run over the next year so it's a nice memorial to him. We adored him. Isn't it funny, the things one remembers? Those white socks, for instance. I remember my mother—who hardly ever told us to do anything—telling me to pull them up straight . . . Sorry, it all came back. Would you like another drink?"

Marcus looked at his watch.

"I've booked a table at rather a popular place—so I think we ought to be on our way . . ." He got up and stood in front of her, holding out his hand to pull her up. She rose—somehow—right into his arms. And for a few moments they stood together, very close, not moving; like old and affectionate friends. Their closeness seemed perfectly natural and they drew apart without embarrassment.

Tessa shut the windows and fetched her bag from her bedroom. Going down the stairs she said to Marcus over her shoulder, "Angie's a very good cook. Did you know?"

"*Angie?* Goodness me, you do surprise me. I shouldn't have thought she knew one end of a kitchen from the other."

"Neither would I," Tessa agreed, laughing. "But apparently she learnt from the man her aunt lives with. He's Italian. They brought her up. She told Tom and me quite a bit about her background the other night."

"She did, did she?" Marcus sounded quite disinterested. "Well, I hope she's learnt her lesson with Loden, anyway."

"Oh, she's finished with *him* and everything to do with him, I should say."

"Good." Marcus opened the front door onto the brilliant early summer's day and Tessa stepped outside. "I hope he's prepared to let her."

The restaurant was in Chelsea—small, full of atmosphere, Bohemian. And it was, as Marcus said, very crowded. A casually dressed group stood on the pavement outside holding drinks, their talk punctuated by bursts of laughter.

"I'll lead the way," Marcus said,

pushing into the dim interior, pulling Tessa by the hand after him. He was hailed at once by a waiter who managed to get them to a table by the window, the only one which was unoccupied. As they made their way over, a couple shouted to Marcus who waved but hurried to his own table.

"Recognise him, did you?" Marcus asked as they settled themselves. "The chap on the television programme, *What do I do?* Drunk as usual, so I think we'll avoid him." He picked up the menu. "I hope you're hungry?"

"I'm not awfully," Tessa said apologetically. "I know who you mean. Frederick Parding. Is it all right if I look round?"

"Wait a few minutes or we'll be set upon. Ah, Bruno . . ." A swarthy, perspiring man in an immaculate white apron was standing over Marcus. "This is a good fellow, Tessa." He leant back in his chair. "And he's going to cook us a fine meal, aren't you, Bruno? Miss Selway hasn't been here before so we want your best form." The chef kissed Tessa's hand with elaborate courtesy and "begged" them both to trust him. He whisked away their menus, tapped the back of the nearest waiter and disappeared into the kitchen. Immediately, two glasses were set before them with a flourish.

"Cheers again." Marcus raised his glass to Tessa.

"You seem very well known here. Or do you always get this kind of treatment in restaurants?"

"God, no. But I'm something of a regular here. And being a member of the press never hurts. Bruno and his brother own this. They're making a go of it as you can see"—he indicated the hubbub around them—"but publicity in the right places never hurts."

"Gosh." Tessa put down her glass, her hand over her mouth. Looking years younger than she was, almost childish, in the simple, crisp pink dress and bright lipstick, the only make-up she was wearing. *Your new job.* And I haven't asked you about it. Have you started yet?"

"Yes, and I feel well entrenched already. I'm working for an old editor friend whom I respect. And *so far* I like the feel of the paper. I've made lots of good resolutions since the night we met.

For one thing, I've decided to be a success. I'll be forty next year, so it's now or never. I'm angling for something I've wanted for a very long time . . . If it comes off, I'll tell you about it. Your Gran will be pleased. She's seen me through enough ups and downs. It's nice this drink, isn't it? White wine with a drop of cassis."

So *that's* what it is, Tessa thought.

"Super. And gone right to my head after the gin. She's splendid, Gran, isn't she? I must go round and see her. I 'phoned the other day and she said she had been feeling exhausted. I expect the funeral took a lot out of her. I saw the memorial plaque for David in the church . . ."

"Don't let's talk about David," Marcus said quickly. He winced as though a nerve had been touched. "Not now. It's too sad for this lovely day. And besides, you'll make me feel more than ever, being with you, that I'm cradle-snatching."

"Silly." Tessa shot him a flirtatious look from under sweeping lashes. Her hand lay on the red checked tablecloth beside a tiny vase of pinks. "I'm having a lovely time," she said.

"I'm glad." He put his hand over hers and their eyes met. "Tessa . . ." The crooked smile; her grey eyes very large, very clear. It was only for a second or two then, "Ah, here comes the food. I wonder what old Bruno has cooked up for us today?"

They ate a delicious Hungarian chicken dish personally concocted by Bruno, and drank from a carafe of red wine. Sunshine poured through the window, splashing the colourful tablecloth and the tiled floor. They talked easily of this and that—the shop, her pals in the market at Covent Garden, current gossip. It seemed to Tessa that quite a few people in the crowded restaurant noticed Marcus . . . perhaps he was better known as a journalist than she supposed; she knew he had been on radio and television programmes. And he did look arresting, there was no getting away from that. The high, well-defined cheek bones, even the slightly too long hair; the air of raffish elegance . . .

Tessa looked at him over the rim of her glass. She was suddenly and quite over-whelmingly glad that she was with him.

"Darling Marcus . . ." A woman with

an actressy voice and a mop of streaked blonde hair swooped down on him. "It's been an age, we *must* meet soon." Marcus barely nodded at her before she was dragged off by her companion.

"Someone I used to know. She became a bore," was his brief, cold comment. "More wine?"

"It's funny to think that Papa and Poppy are supposed to arrive in New York today. I'd have to work out the time change to think exactly when—they're behind us over there, aren't they?" Tessa said, thinking with pleasure of the blissfully empty house on Parloe Square, and particularly her father's empty study.

"Does he trust you when his back is turned?" Marcus enquired, eyebrows raised. "He looked extremely dictatorial—with Tom, at least."

"Oh he is. Gran and Aunt Flor always says he treats us like the 14th Army."

"I can see he and Tom have difficulties. He's got the reputation in the city for being very able, but tough." (Although "ruthless" was the word generally used about George Selway, Marcus reflected.)

"But you get on with him all right, do you?"

"I do and I don't. I'm always coming up against him over something or other, even more now that Tom has gone off. The shop is a bit of a hot potato . . . He doesn't really like my working there. And he didn't want me to go to Grandpa Delmore's funeral. But I think I understand him. I love him a lot, but I don't always like him. And he is *terribly* possessive," she sighed. "Have you got lots of family, Marcus?"

He shook his head. "As far as I know, absolutely none. My mother died when I was a child; my father soon after the war. There are some distant cousins somewhere but I'm not in touch with them." He smiled cynically. "I can never decide if I'm lucky or unlucky."

Something caught his eye at a nearby table.

"Don't look now," he said, concentrating on his food, "but a member of the cabinet has just walked in. I happen to know that his girlfriend lives round the corner. He's with another man . . . I'm sure I've seen him before somewhere too . . ." He frowned. "Anyhow, it's such a marvellous day. Why don't we get out of London and try and find a boat on the river? Or are you busy?"

"No. I'm not. What a wonderful idea."

"That's settled, then." He looked at his watch. "Let's get the bill and be off."

On their way out, the waiter bowing and Bruno calling gaily from the kitchen door, Marcus looked hard at the two men lunching together. When they got to the car he suddenly seemed to remember something. He handed her the keys.

"Get in, I won't be a moment. All right? I want to go back and make a quick phone call . . ."

They drove fast out of London, the top of the car down, the golden sunshine and the warm summer air on their faces, blowing through their hair. Past Windsor, they began turning and streaking over quiet country roads; Marcus seemed certain of the way. He drove with an assured touch and absolute confidence—using the nerve and co-ordination he must have needed in a plane, during the war, Tessa thought. Soon, they arrived at a small boathouse and Marcus negotiated—cannily, it seemed to Tessa—the hiring of a rowing boat.

Marcus and the boatman held it steady for her as she stepped from the wooden jetty. Then Marcus leapt in and started grappling with the oars in a businesslike fashion. He had taken off his jacket and rolled up the sleeves of his shirt. He had long arms which were surprisingly muscular. Manoeuvring the boat into midstream, he settled the oars and began to row with rhythm and concentration. He hit his stride easily and they pushed through the quiet water, leaving silvery white troughs in their wake.

Marcus had appeared to Tessa so urban —and urbane—that she was surprised to see how competently he rowed and handled the boat. It was like being with Tom who excelled in anything athletic. Enjoying the calm rush of the water, Tessa lay back on the mothy cushions and watched the trees spinning along against the sky. She listened to the river sounds . . . the creaking oars, shouts and splashes from boats nearby, couples strolling on the towpath. They passed one or two fishermen sitting quietly, patiently. It was all very peaceful, very serene, drenched in the afternoon sunshine.

Soon, she felt the movement of the boat changing. She sat up. Marcus, using only one oar and turning his head, was guiding them towards the bank. As they hit the earth with a soft thud, he grabbed an overhanging branch and pushed both oars on to the bottom on the boat.

"I enjoyed that, even at my advanced age." He was breathing heavily. "I don't get enough exercise in London. If I remember rightly, this is rather a lovely spot." He stood. "Here, hang on would you Tessa while I tie her up?" Moving stealthily up the boat, Tessa jumped ashore as the boat rocked crazily.

"Throw me the rope. I'll do it." Her clear, crisp voice rang across the river. "Chuck it over."

"Fair enough . . . here." He threw the rope in her direction and she caught it handily. "I didn't know what a tomboy you were."

Tessa laughed, lashing the rope round the solid trunk of a tree.

Marcus stepped from the boat and they

climbed through the shimmering spring undergrowth and emerged on a grassy clearing, a few feet above the water. Tessa saw that they were in a secluded dell on a bend in the river, some way from the towpath. Bright wild flowers grew among the reeds and tall grasses. Marcus yawned and lay full length on the hard, dry ground, folding his hands behind his head, still puffed from the effort of rowing. He closed his eyes. Tessa sat beside him, arms clasped round her knees, the full skirt of her pink cotton dress spreading around her.

"I think I'm going to have a short kip. Would you mind?" He opened one eye and squinted up at her. She shook her head. "You're sure?" Both eyes closed.

"Not a bit. It's so lovely and peaceful here. I'll keep a watch on the boat."

"You do that."

Below, the water flowed and eddied in soothing ripples, green weeds waving in weird patterns beneath the surface. The boat rocked gently. It was a hushed and idyllic spot. Shafts of sunshine slanted through the new leaves of surrounding trees and bushes; there were birdcalls,

234

children playing some way off; on the other side of the river, in the water meadows, a line of poplars rose towards the palest of blue skies.

Tessa pulled at a clump of grasses and looked down at Marcus. He was lying beside her, very close, his face raised to the sunlight. She could tell from his even breathing that he was asleep. His blue shirt, wet with perspiration, clung to his arms and chest. She saw that there were deep creases round his eyes; his hair in the front was quite grey. Sitting there, watching him sleep, she was conscious of a suffocating tightness in her chest; a throbbing excitement; new and disturbing sensations. She wanted badly to touch him. The quietness; both of them so close; alone. She reached out and put her hand on his chest—and she did it so lightly that he couldn't have felt it. But instantly he reached up, eyes still closed, and pulled her down beside him.

"Sleep, sweet Tessa," he murmured, "sleep."

His arms went around her, her face pressed against his shoulder. He sighed deeply, sinking back into sleep. Tessa felt

235

the spikey, uneven ground beneath her, the warmth and sweat of his body next to hers. All around them, the sounds and smells of the awakening countryside—and the persistent, rippling flow of the river at their feet. She felt so light with happiness it was as though the least current of air would blow her higher and higher, somewhere far away, up, up, up in the blueness . . . But the sun and the wine had made her drowsy too. Soon she slept.

She slept so soundly that she only stirred, and did not wake, when Marcus got up. Opening her eyes she saw that he was already back in the boat, fiddling with the oars.

"Come on, you idler," he called out good-naturedly. "It's time we were heading back. I can't leave you here like the sleeping princess forever you know . . ."

Brushing the grasses off her skirt, feeling a bit foolish, Tessa scrambled down the bank, through the bushes and back to the boat. Marcus took her hand as she climbed in.

"Not a bad way to spend a glorious

Saturday afternoon," he said, giving her a quick kiss on the cheek. He looked alert and refreshed; a better colour, almost handsome. She blushed deeply and felt her way, wobbling, to the cushions. Tessa looked at her watch. It was half past five and the sun was much lower in the sky. They must have slept for a good half hour . . . Deliberately, she turned away from Marcus and flapped her hands at the clouds of gnats which buzzed around her head.

"That was lovely," Tessa said too brightly as they got back to the car. "I don't think I've ever done that before."

She meant: rowed on the river near Henley on an early summer's afternoon.

"What? Slept with a man?" Marcus said.

He seemed suddenly much younger; relaxed; almost jovial. He had had some needed exercise and a good sleep; worked off the recent tensions of his life. And he found Tessa's company refreshing. He was teasing her now, enjoying it. He looked boyishly happy. And when Tessa promptly tripped in a rabbit hole he put his arm round her, and she him, to save herself from falling.

"*No,*" Tessa almost shouted, her cheeks as pink as her dress, "what I meant was . . ." They were laughing, stumbling against each other, until he stopped her.

"I'm sorry," he said, with that quirky smile. "I do know what you mean. Forgive me."

They were standing beneath a fullblown chestnut tree, loaded with candle blossoms, towering above a creamy froth of hawthorn hedge. She looked straight at him, chin raised, wide-apart grey eyes very steady.

"But I haven't . . . what you said."

"I know," he answered gravely.

Seconds passed; then one of them—it was Tessa—made a small movement. They came together. He moved his knee between her legs and slid his hands up and over her breast . . .

"Ahhh . . ." she breathed as his mouth came down on hers and he pushed her, not gently, back into the fragrant hawthorn. Instinctively, she moved to his tongue and his touch and clung to him as though otherwise she would surely drown. And

238

she thought: *"Yes, oh yes, yes . . ."* Her body pounded and her head spun and she was lost to everything in the world except for Marcus and the musky sweet smell of the hawthorn.

Then, "Look, I've got to get you back to London." His voice, which sounded thick, seemed to come from some way away.

Still clinging to him, Tessa opened her eyes. Breathing was difficult so she nodded.

"All right," she whispered.

They drove to London with the western sky dramatically streaked in reds and purples behind them. Marcus concentrated on the driving—early evening traffic was flooding back into London. Once in the car and off the back roads, Marcus became remote and uncommunicative. All his warmth and pleasure at being in the country, on the river, seemed to have vanished. It was as though their passionate closeness, just half an hour or so before, had never been. They didn't speak much; he replied to Tessa's strained chatter in monosyllables until she, too, lapsed into silence. He fiddled irritably with the car radio trying to get the news, pressing buttons and turning knobs, wincing when loud rock and roll blared. Eventually, he gave up.

Tessa, her senses in turmoil, sat miserably beside him. She was baffled by his swift change of mood. She shot sideways looks at his set profile and watched his hands move capably between the steering-wheel and the gears.

When they reached the outskirts of London and stopped at traffic lights, he turned to her as though suddenly aware of her presence again.

"Sorry. Am I being anti-social? I often am, I'm afraid. I was thinking out a strategy of how to get exactly what I want at the paper—a column of my own. The ambition I've always had really. Sorry—again." He quickly raised her hand to his lips before the lights changed and they shot ahead. Reassured, her spirits leaping, Tessa said boldly, "Speaking of being social, I'd almost forgotten, but I'm going to a party tonight. Sometime after eight, nothing very formal. Why don't you come along?" She felt, but ignored, warning lights that flickered somewhere in her consciousness. "It's at a house in Little Venice, overlooking the canal . . ."

Marcus said warily. "Whose party is it?"

"Oliver Bingham's. He's a friend of Tom's—his oldest. I've known him forever. And I'm sure Tom will be there too."

"What kind of a party?" Marcus enquired, accustomed to not committing himself.

"A sort of housewarming. His grandmother died recently and left him the house. He's invited masses of people. And there's going to be food . . . he's not married and I expect it will be chaotic . . . but Oliver's good at parties."

"Surely the host—this Oliver—won't want you turning up with someone he's never met?"

"He won't mind."

"I wonder," Marcus flashed past a dithering driver ahead and began to show some interest. "I wonder whether Tom will bring the lovely Angie." Amused, ironic. "Now that would be intriguing . . ."

"I'm sure he will. As far as I know she's

still at the flat—it was Oliver who moved out of there last month."

"I'd love to come," he said. His hand left the steering wheel briefly and felt for hers. "Had we better bring a bottle or two? I lugged some wine back from France recently . . ."

"I think we should. I expect he'll have hoards of people . . . Did you enjoy it in France? Tom and Angie told me you had gone."

In her excitement at his reappearance, she had forgotten her morbid fears about whom he had taken and whether or not he would contact her when he got back.

"Quiet but pleasant. I go off there quite a lot. Friends have this farmhouse in Normandy which they don't use much, and they let me have it whenever I want. It's basic, but the food and drink are superb. It's a good place for thinking things through when one needs a bit of hibernation. And I remembered to send Vi a card. She always complains vociferously if I go away and neglect her." He laughed, apparently in high good humour again. "She's a funny old thing, isn't she?"

They were cruising up the Bayswater

Road, round Marble Arch and into the Park.

"You'll want to change—and God knows I need a wash and a shave. So when would you like me to pick you up?"

"There's no need, Marcus, honestly," Tessa told him quickly. She had thought that one out. Ella and her sister, Maggie, would surely be back soon if they weren't already; instinct told her it was safer, at the moment, to keep Marcus from Ella. Even Ella, dear Ella, wouldn't understand. "It's out of our way and it's so easy for me to get a taxi over to you. What time shall we say?"

"Eight-thirty, do you think?"

He pulled up in front of the house. They both got out and stood on the pavement. The familiar bustle of London seemed strange after the tranquillity of the countryside; Tessa was oddly conscious of the traffic grinding along Knightsbridge at the top of the square.

"Thank you," she said, not quite meeting his eyes. "And for the wonderful lunch . . ."

"Tessa, come here." He touched her cheek and turned her face towards him.

Then he kissed her mouth lightly and swiftly and he was off. Tessa waited until the car, like a long green insect, had turned the corner. She found her key and let herself in, shutting the door quietly. The hall was cool and dim. She stood for a moment with her back against the door. Waiting until she felt more composed, she listened at the top of the steps which led down to Ella's flat. She heard soft voices. Ella and Maggie were back.

"Hey there," she called. "Can I come down for a moment?" Surprised that her new, altered self still sounded so normal, she found them sitting over cups of tea on the little side terrace outside Ella's living-room. "Hello Maggie, hello Ella . . . ," Tessa perched on the wall beside Ella's cherished double begonias. "Did you two have a wonderful day out?"

Maggie, a nursing sister, was a slightly older version of Ella; they were like two peas in a pod, Gran said. They spent every free moment, including holidays, together. "What did you two get up to? Isn't this weather marvellous?" She looked radiant.

"Well," said Maggie, "now let me see . . . we did a bit of shopping in the morning, didn't we Ell? And then we took ourselves off to Regent's Park."

"And you should see the roses . . . Oh gracious me, Tessa, love, I knew there was something." Ella clapped her hands together. "We'd hardly got back when your father and Mrs. Renfew telephoned from New York to see we were all right. They had a good voyage, very calm, lots of interesting people on board . . . and they're settling into the hotel, the Waldorf. They were sorry to miss you but I said you'd gone off for the day with friends."

Long distance telephone calls, particularly ones from America, always threw sensible, down-to-earth Ella into a tizzy of excitement. That's lucky, Tessa thought. She's not going to cross-examine me like Papa would have. If I act naturally, she's not going to notice anything. She crossed her arms and hugged herself in a sudden spurt of excitement.

Ella eyed her keenly.

"You look well, Tess. That new short haircut suits you. You caught a bit of sun, I believe—in the park like us, were you?" She had clearly forgotten what Tessa had told her earlier about "lunching with Gran's friend".

"Mmm, that's right," Tessa answered vaguely, brushing away crumbs. "I've got to go up and get changed now. It's Oliver's party, remember."

"So it is. Isn't he lucky to have an evening like this for it? I expect you'll all be out in the garden. It's a big place, Tom said."

"We might as well make the best of it while it lasts . . . Heavens, Tessa, that dress looks as though it's been through a hedge backwards"—this from Maggie.

"It's cotton and it gets terribly creased," Tessa said hastily. "The blue silk one's ironed, isn't it Ella? I thought it would be nice to wear it tonight as it's so warm."

"Lovely dear. I expect you'll meet lots of nice young people there, don't you?" she asked hopefully.

"Oh Ella, there you go again," Tessa teased affectionately. "She's simply longing to get me off her hands," she said to Maggie. "You can't wait, can you Ella?"

"I only mean, dear, that friends of Oliver's are bound to be the sort of people you *should* be meeting. I agree with Papa about that, you know I do. And I'm sure it will be a good party. Tom will be there, won't he? I expect he'll drop you back. Dear Oliver, he always does *everything* well . . ."

Tessa raced up to her bedroom only just managing to get there in time before she burst out laughing. What was it Maggie had said about her dress: *through a hedge backwards?* She grinned at her reflection in the dressing-table mirror. If only she and Ella had known how perilously close she had come to the truth . . .

Her senses were so heightened that she did not even think of Marcus. Not then, not directly. The evening lay ahead, the party . . . She ran a bath and laid out her clothes on the bed—strappy silver sandals, silver bag, a cashmere shawl with bright threads that her father had brought back from somewhere. The shimmering peacock blue dress, bought for summer parties, intended for a rare night such as this, hung from the wardrobe. Outside her window, in a cloudless blue arc, the golden evening light. She opened and shut drawers and boxes, selecting make-up, scent, a particular brush. Then she went to the bathroom and poured an extravagant amount of perfumed oil into the water. She could hear the muted, city sounds of London—the hum of traffic, a plane, children in the garden next door. (All the while she smiled, expectant, exhilarated.) Feeling the water, she slipped into the smooth and scented bath. Relaxed, she touched her breast, bringing her fingers down across her erect nipple. A physical intensity she had never before experienced pervaded her. She looked down at her body—white and beautiful, the silvery contours distorted by the water. Her hand lightly touched her waist, her stomach . . . her thighs moved apart. Only then did she let herself think: *Marcus* . . .

9

THE taxi seemed to fly across London—up Park Lane, over Oxford Street. The lights were with them all the way and the traffic sparse. Tessa had escaped from Ella and Maggie with a shout and a wave. They had no place, dear though they were, in the magic of this evening. In a flash it seemed to Tessa—heart thudding, anticipating wildly—they were twisting their way through the streets of Soho.

Marcus was standing on the steps of his building.

"Hello there . . ." He smiled as the taxi drew up, opened the door and handed her out.

He looked as she had imagined he would; an unusually attractive man by any standards. Very assured; worldly. He had put on a dark grey suit and a sober tie. And yet there was still something about him—what was it?—almost, but not quite, flamboyant. Perhaps it was the way he

SS17

walked. He didn't stride; he moved fluidly, as though all of a piece. That was one of the first things Tessa had noticed about him.

In the car he turned to her. The afternoon in the sun had given his skin, which was quite sallow, a light tan.

"Don't *you* look lovely," he said appreciatively. "Another pretty dress." He started the engine. "What on earth are Tom and your friends going to think when you turn up with an old roué like me?"

"We'll just have to wait and see, won't we?" Tessa told him mischievously and they exchanged sideways smiles.

He began driving towards north London using back streets which Tessa couldn't remember ever seeing before.

"Was—Ella—in when you got back?" Marcus asked. Tessa was surprised he had remembered her and told him so.

"Journalists are trained to remember things."

"I suppose they must be. Oh, Papa phoned, before I got in, to say that they had had a good crossing and so forth. I was glad I missed him. He gets even more nervous and overbearing when he's away."

"Well, he wouldn't approve of your escort this evening, that I can tell you . . ." He was leaning forward, edging the car carefully into a main road, craning to see past a stationary taxi. Tessa reached over, slid an arm around his neck and kissed him. He turned towards her quickly, looking surprised.

"What was that for, then?"

Tessa laughed and didn't answer. She felt very happy, very at ease, being with him. *Excited.*

"What a funny girl you are . . ."

When they reached the street where Oliver's house was, lights had started to come on here and there and the sunny evening was dissolving into a soft blue mist. Marcus slowed the car. To one side was the canal, lined with gaily painted barges and bordered by trees; to the other, a dignified row of large white stucco houses standing in walled gardens.

"This is the road," Marcus said. "Pleasant, isn't it? I wonder which one . . ."

"It's number twenty-two." She pointed a little further along. "Where all the cars are." They parked on a side street and walked round to the house. It was blazing with lights and they could see through the open windows that it was already crowded. They walked through the gate and up the path. White fairy lights had been strung haphazardly all round the tangled garden; tables and chairs were set out on the terrace and on a few of the paths that were cleared. Rampant climbing roses and starry jasmine gave off delicious scents.

In the hall they pressed into a crush of mostly young people, everyone seeming to talk noisily at once. Several people called out to Tessa, but she was looking up to the top of the staircase, waving at a burly, powerfully built young man who stood there, a bottle in each hand, beaming. She leant close to Marcus to make herself heard.

"There's Oliver, up there . . . he's coming down. Let's go and pay our respects before he gets mobbed."

Oliver had seen Tessa at once, as she had him. They met at the bottom of the stairs.

"Tessa . . . *so* glad you could make it on this short notice. Tom's here some-where—and masses of my cousins whom

252

you know. How *are* you? It's really *lovely* you could come, and you're looking gorgeous."

He had an endearing grin which it was impossible not to respond to. Tessa did. "What a beautiful house, Oliver. I hadn't expected anything so grand."

"It needs lots doing to it. It's very neglected and the roof's in a terrible state. But it's marvellous, isn't it? I'm so glad you've come to see it. I have tried to get you several times." He was in his shirt-sleeves and wearing a jaunty red and white spotted bow tie. He had a pleasant face with nice brown eyes; his ears had stuck out since he was a child. He seemed very happy and excited that night—by the house; the din of the party; his friends around him. He was warm and gregarious by nature. Everyone said that with his personality and his ability he was bound to do well at the Bar.

"I've brought a friend, Oliver, I do hope you don't mind." Behind her, Marcus stepped forward. "This is Marcus Reardon, Oliver Bingham."

Both men shifted the bottles they were carrying to one arm and shook hands.

"Sorry to be gatecrashing like this—Tessa kindly brought me along."

Something quite discernible happened to Oliver's expression; for a moment the wide smile faltered. Just as quickly, he recovered. It all happened in a split second.

"I'm so pleased she did. Any friend of Tessa's . . . As you can see, it's a big bash. The cousins have been asking for you, Tess. Oh Tom's in the drawing-room, I think . . . I say, how terribly kind," he said as he saw Marcus's bottles. "Looks a lot grander than the stuff you'll find here."

Behind them, another wave of guests had arrived, chattering away, laughing, exclaiming over the house, calling out to Oliver.

"Do excuse me," he said, "but I'd better go and see to this lot. By the way, there's masses of food and drink in the dining-room, grab a plate and help yourselves . . . Julia, how are you?"

As they began edging their way through the crush towards what appeared to be the dining-room, Tessa saw Oliver put his arm round an extremely pretty blonde girl. She wondered, briefly, if that was the girl Tom had said he was so madly in love with.

The dining-room walls were very dark, almost black, and in places the wallpaper was peeling badly. Marcus peered in. "This seems to be right." In the centre, a large oval table was piled high with mounds of food. Bowls of rice and meat casseroles, salads and trifles and cheeses—all squashed together round elaborate candelabra lit by white candles, the only lighting in the room.

There were bottles and glasses everywhere—on tables and chairs, the mantelpiece. One or two groups stood around the corners, balancing drinks and paper plates. Marcus picked up a bottle opener and began drawing the cork of one of the bottles he had brought. "Find a couple of glasses, Tessa, will you? I think we could do with a drink."

Tessa came back with two glasses and paper plates. "We'll have to forage about for forks. There seems to be a shortage." She took a glass of wine from Marcus, laughing, catching the spirit of the party. "He's so nice, Oliver, isn't he? Everyone likes him. And what an incredible house."

"Inherited it, did he? Lucky chap."

"Everyone says that about Oliver, that he's lucky. He's so popular and he does everything well. He's much happier doing law than Tom . . . this house belonged to his mother's mother. She died and she was an only child, like Oliver, so it's come to him. His father lives in Menton in the South of France."

"He likes *you* . . ." Oliver's dismay at his unexpected appearance with Tessa had not gone unnoticed by Marcus. "Has he always?"

"Silly. It's just that we've known each other all our lives." A chubby, dark-haired young woman came up to Tessa.

"Tessa," she said breathlessly, "it's been ages . . ." She gave Marcus a fluttery look.

"Oh Fiona, Oliver said you were all here." And turning quickly, "This is Marcus Reardon. Fiona is Oliver's cousin."

"Hello Fiona." As they shook hands, he said smoothly, "I've explained to Oliver that I'm the uninvited guest—brought by Tessa."

"Oh Oliver won't mind. He loves

parties and people, the more the merrier as you can see. Tom's in the drawing-room with an absolutely divine-looking girl. I must go, Oliver has pressed us all into service tonight . . . 'byee." And she was off, moving from group to group, making sure everyone had enough to eat and drink, picking up empty glasses, removing plates. Tessa and Marcus watched her go.

"I told you Oliver was a whizz at getting things done. He's got five—no six—girl cousins on either side. I bet he's got them all working hard tonight while he swans about playing the host."

Marcus laughed. "Sensible fellow. Why don't we investigate the food and then we'll go and find Tom? He's got our friend Angie with him by the sound of it."

Later, they squeezed out into the hall. Marcus, looking over heads, said, "There they are." His arm round her shoulders, he steered Tessa into the drawing-room—high-ceilinged, with an elaborate cornice; sash windows opened on to the summer garden. By then, most of the guests were in the hall or the dining-room and it was noticeably cooler and emptier there. Tom and Angie stood by the fireplace, talking quietly, their profiles reflected in the elaborate gold-framed mirror above. Tom was leaning against the mantelpiece. They were much the same height; both very slim. Two things struck Tessa simultaneously: that Angie looked ravishing—and that they were very much lost in each other's company. The same thought must have occurred to Marcus because he murmured, "We shouldn't butt in, perhaps . . ."

But Tom turned and saw them and called out, "Hello, Tess . . . good heavens, Marcus." He looked astonished. "Come over and join us."

Angie was wearing a black halter-neck dress, the back cut daringly low, which showed off her sinuous white arms and shoulders. Her hair was pulled up in a chignon and she wore enormous fake pearl earrings.

"We thought you'd be here, Tessa . . . but I must say, you're a surprise, Marcus." She sounded cool. "What's that bottle you're hoarding?" She held out her glass.

"I had no idea you knew Oliver," Tom said, rather dazed, as Marcus filled his glass too.

"But I didn't," Marcus smiled. "We'd been off in the country for the day, and Tessa kindly suggested I come along—it seemed a nice idea. What about you two?"

Tom looked at Angie who said, "Well —what about us, Marcus?"

"I mean: have you started working again—and has Loden been giving you any trouble?"

"Yes to the first question, no to the second. Satisfied?"

Tom said into the uncomfortable silence that followed, "Where did you go today? What part?"

"On the river near Henley," Tessa said. "It was lovely, wasn't it?" She looked straight at Marcus. She felt confident and lightheaded, excited by Marcus's presence, well aware of the glances he was attracting —from Fiona for one, as she dashed from room to room. "Oh—and Tom, Papa phoned from New York. I was out but Ella told me."

Tom threw his head back and laughed. Watching him, Tessa thought: he seems really happy, not edgy at all like he usually is. "Do you know," he said, "I haven't

259

even given the old man a thought for days. I'd forgotten all about him . . ."

"You mustn't say that Tom," Angie scolded.

"Why ever not?"

"Because he's your father and because he's—*Somebody*. I mean—Selway Electric . . . you're crazy turning your back on all that. I mean it, Tom." The slanted green eyes flashed at him. Tom leant over and whispered something in her ear. Angie's mouth quivered deliciously on the edge of a smile.

"I hope nobody heard that," she murmured.

"Who cares? Angie darling, if you knew him you'd know how impossible my old man is."

Tessa and Marcus drifted away from them; they seemed—both of them—totally absorbed in each other. Hardly in the same world—even Angie, whose dark, hard-edged elegance contrasted starkly with the soft, pretty girls, girls like Tessa, who floated through Oliver's house that night.

"All right, all right, look lively . . ."

There was a commotion by the double doors as Oliver's shoulders—he was

260

considered a useful chap in a rugger scrum —loomed. He was waving his hands above his head, all zest and enthusiasm.

"Come along, you lot, break it up, there's work to be done," he called out. Angie and Tom looked away from each other, startled.

Tom asked, "What's going on, Oliver?"

"We can't get the gramophone to work in the study so we're going to try a replacement in here for some dancing. Lend a hand with the rug, will you chaps? Shake a leg, Tom. I'm going to pry you briefly from this gorgeous girl . . ."

In the following ten minutes or so, the drawing-room was transformed into a miniature dance floor. Tessa was spotted by Fiona and asked to help put away some valuable china ornaments on a side-table. Most of the furniture was carried into the hall. Tom and one or two others rolled up and removed the huge Persian rug, while Oliver and a friend fiddled about with the gramophone and sorted records. In the corner, Tessa saw Marcus and Angie talking.

"Who *is* he?" Fiona whispered to Tessa. "I think he's frightfully attractive, all the girls do, between you and me. He looks so—*unusual*. What does he do?"

"He's a journalist. I haven't known him long. He was a fighter pilot in the war. If we're going to dance, don't you think that lamp should go?"

"Let's put it behind the sofa. He looks as though he's been a glamour boy. I recognised Angie Gordon at once. We all did. Isn't her dress divine? And wildly sophisticated. All the boys are terribly envious of Tom. He looks besotted."

"I think he is. Actually, she's rather nice, not at all what you'd expect . . . Oh —well done Oliver!" she called out. After much trouble with a wobbly needle, the music was going—an easy, recognisable, swinging foxtrot, a bit scratchy but still liltingly tuneful.

"The lights," Oliver shouted. "God I know just the thing . . ." He tore out and came back with the candelabra from the dining-room. He put them on the mantle-piece, and lit the candles. "Kill the rest, let's try it."

Someone switched the lights off and the effect was immediate—and theatrical. The huge, high room became in an instant dimmed and mysterious. Wavering in the slight summer breeze, the candles were reflected again and again in the mirrors and glass picture frames. They threw flickering shadows on the darkened walls and softened the bare floorboards. Through the open windows, the fairy lights in the garden, strung on trees and bushes, looked like fallen stars. Attracted by the music, couples wandered in from other parts of the house.

All of a sudden, something happened to the foxtrot: it ran down, screeched and stopped. A chorus of groans went up from the darkened room which was now pleasantly full, intimate, like a good night-club. Oliver was working frantically by the gramophone, using a torch. Tessa felt Marcus beside her. He took her hand.

"For a moment I thought I'd lost you," said Tessa. They stood very close.

"I saw you with Angie. She looked terribly serious."

"Oh, she was, she told me in no uncertain terms that I shouldn't be seeing you." He sounded amused.

"But she hardly knows you," Tessa said indignantly.

"True. But she's heard things, she says
. . . and the trouble is, she's right."

"*Marcus . . .*"

From over in the corner Oliver called
out, "Here we go, this is one of the
greats . . ."

After one false start, the persuasive,
sophisticated words dropped like magic
into the darkness.

> *There's a saying old, says that love
> is blind . . .*

The needle skipped, faltered—calls of
"not *again* Oliver"—then righted itself.

> *. . . Haven't found him yet . . .*

The mesmeric entertainer—half singing,
half talking . . .

> *He's the big affair I cannot forget.*
> *Only man I ever think of with regret.*

Tessa turned and Marcus's arms came
round her. "I'm not very good at this.
Want to risk it?"

"Mmm . . ."

There's a somebody I'm longing to
  see
I hope that he turns out to be . . .

Moving very close, her hand round his neck . . .

  Someone to watch over me . . .

They were swaying together in the candle-light, drenched in sweet seductive sound.
  "She is, you know, Tessa."
  "Is what?" Abandoned to the music, the bittersweet lyrics. To the mood of the party. To Marcus. "Is what?" Turning her head, brushing his mouth with her hair.
  "Right . . . Angie, I mean."

  I'm a little lamb who's lost in a
    wood . . .
  I know I could always be
    good . . .

Cheek against his, Tessa whispered, "Marcus, I want . . ."

  To one who'll watch over me . . .

Hardly moving, seconds passing. "I know, my love, I know—me likewise." He held her tighter and sighed into her hair. "But it won't do, will it? You're a big responsibility."

"I wouldn't be," she said softly. She looked up at him in the dimness, her fingers linked behind his neck.

Although he may not be the man some
Girls think of as handsome . . .

"You would, you know. And there's something else."

"What?"

To my heart he carries the key . . .

"I might start to like it, break all my rules. And then where would we be?"

Tessa didn't—couldn't—answer. Overpowered by Marcus's nearness and the corny, infinitely potent music.

Won't you tell him please to put on some speed . . .

Couples sliding over the creaky floor. Tessa thought she glimpsed—over Marcus's shoulder—Tom and Angie dancing on the terrace outside. Despite the open window, the room was getting warm.

Follow my lead . . .

Her mouth by his ear, Tessa whispered, "What did you tell Angie anyway?"

Oh, how I need . . .

Marcus's hands moved down her back. She couldn't see his face. "I told her to mind her own damned business," he said.

Someone to watch over me . . .

When the record finished, there were laughing cries and shouts. "More, more! Keep it going, Oliver." Under cover of the voices and the laughter, still in near darkness, Marcus said quietly, "Look, I think I've had enough. I'm too old for all this. Do you mind? Let's go, shall we?"

They slipped through the drawing-room doors and across the hall, blinking in the

267

light. Tessa snatched her silver bag from the hall table and Marcus took her hand and they walked quickly out under the portico, down the steps and along the wide path.

Marcus put his arm round Tessa and led her across the road. There was a nearly full moon. They stopped in the deep shadows of a plane tree, next to the canal, and looked back across at the house. Except for the drawing-room, it was brilliantly lit; the music and the laughter floated gaily up into a clear, starry sky of midnight blue.

"You were right," Marcus said. "It's a very good party indeed." He sounded surprised. She knew that he had enjoyed it more than he had expected to. She was pleased.

"I told you it would be. Oliver's marvellous at parties. And we never said goodbye," she added guiltily.

"He won't notice—there are too many people."

"All the same . . . Tom and Angie too."

"*They* won't notice . . ."

He pulled her to him, scrutinising her face, touching her hair, her cheek, her throat, in a way he had that was both cold and intense at the same time.

"What is to become of us, you and me?" Half amused; half serious. Then, answering his own question, "I'm going to take you home, my sweet Tessa—soon."

She closed her eyes and waited. His nearness bewitched her. She could hear the faint music from the house, the inky movement of the canal. And then Marcus's hand on her chin, his mouth—she pulled against him, moving with him. His tongue, hers . . . straining together—both of them —lost.

In the car, driving back, they didn't speak. Tessa, in any case, couldn't. It was only when they got back to the West End, stuck in traffic, that she swallowed and asked him, "What do you think is going on between Tom and Angie?"

"I should have thought that was perfectly clear."

Tessa flushed. "But Tom—I mean he's not the sort of man she's used to, surely. He's got to make his own way . . . he's mad about sport . . . he doesn't know anything about the fashionable sort of life she must have had. If he can either play, or watch, some game or other—wild horses wouldn't drag him to a party."

Marcus laughed. "He's very handsome, you know. And as for Tom not being like the men she's used to—frankly, that can only be in his favour as far as Angie's concerned. And as she indicated tonight, there's Selway Electric in the background. That's not lost on her, you can be sure. I think she's probably straight—hard, but straight. And definitely lacking in social graces. She seems to say what she thinks, which is never acceptable. But I shouldn't worry about Tom, my love. He's old enough to look after himself, for God's sake."

"He does look very happy with her. Perhaps it will turn out all right."

Marcus slowed for a red light and turned to her. "I don't think Vi did you two much good when she brought me to the Flood opening." Almost, but not quite, humorous.

Tessa looked away. "Don't say that, Marcus," as the car slid forward again, "please don't."

In the Park, grown mysterious with moonlight and great dark shadows, Tessa began to shiver. In minutes—seconds—Marcus would be gone. She wondered, despairingly, how she would bear the loss of his presence, his touch.

"Cold?"

"I am a bit. I forgot . . . I've left my shawl at Oliver's. I only just remembered. I expect they'll know it's mine and hold on to it."

Without a word, Marcus stopped the car, got out, took off his jacket and put it round her shoulders.

"Marcus . . . we're nearly there. Why on earth did you do that?"

"I think you know." He let off the handbrake and accelerated sharply. Tessa felt tears welling in her eyes.

Neither of them said anything when he stopped again, this time outside the house. Tessa watched his hands splayed on the steering wheel. She thought how long his fingers were.

"You still haven't told me about David. You said you would. Remember?" Her voice was only just steady.

"I will one day. Truly, I haven't

forgotten what I said—or when I said it. I've got a busy week, a lot riding on a couple of important meetings. A particular decision."

He could hear her sigh. She was nearly crying now; emotional; aroused. Longing for his warmth. He knew this.

"Marcus . . ." she turned to him. Almost, but not quite, pleading.

"Don't." He was looking straight ahead. "It's my grey hairs, that's all. And a bit of novelty. I'm extremely unsuitable for you in every way. Tonight—your friends, your background. It was obvious to me . . . And I'm a pal of your grand-mother's as I was of David's. Also, most people who know me wouldn't think so—including Angie—but I do have a conscience. Look," he faced her, "I'll give you a ring and we'll have dinner."

"Thanks for the coat," she said miserably.

"Oh Christ . . ."

He took it from her, slung it on the back seat and again looked ahead—into nothing. His hands gripped the wheel. A shaft of moonlight crossed his face. He looked tired, older than his years.

"Now be a good girl and hop out, would you? Thanks for the party. I enjoyed it. We'll meet soon. All right?"

10

JUST before lunch one day the following week, Angie Gordon walked into the shop and asked Joan, who was massing flowers for a wedding reception, "Is Tessa Selway about?"

"Tess . . . someone to see you," Joan called out—cigarette, as usual, drooping from a corner of her mouth.

Half hoping, half dreading that it was Marcus, Tessa came into the front of the shop. Since that Saturday, she had jumped every time the phone rang; but she had heard nothing from him. Angie was wearing dark glasses and her hair was pulled severely back. She wore no make-up. She was wrapped from neck to ankle in a black duster coat, pulled tightly in at the waist with a wide sash. She looked so different that for a split second, Tessa didn't recognise her.

"Angie . . . Good heavens . . . This is Joan, Joan—Angie Gordon."

Tessa had told Joan, in a vague way,

that Tom had recently acquired a new and very beautiful girlfriend called Angie, who was a top model. Now, she was intrigued enough to stop what she was doing, remove her cigarette and dry her wet hands on her corduroy trousers.

"Hello there . . ." She looked at Angie with frank curiosity. "If Tessa hadn't told me, I don't think I would have recognised you from the photographs. I expect they put all that muck on your face for them, do they?" Joan asked cheerfully.

Angie, who had taken one look at the cropped hair and the grubby trousers, ignored this and looked round the shop. She picked up, and quickly set down, a couple of small planted terracotta pots.

"Don't you do *proper* arrangements— you know, oblong things for tables with carnations and big vases of lilies and glads —like they have in hotels?" She sounded disappointed.

"That's not really our style," Tessa said. "We go for a more natural look, don't we Joan?"

They exchanged glances and Joan exhaled a spume of smoke.

"It all looks natural all right," Angie

said, staring hard at a splash of blue corn-flowers. "We had those in our garden when I was a kid . . . I thought they were weeds."

"Really? I adore them," Tessa told her briskly. "Was there anything you wanted specially—or shall we grab a sandwich somewhere round the corner if you've got time?"

"That's why I came—and I thought we could have a chat. I'm working in a studio near here at two, so I can't be long. Could you come out now?" The black glasses above the perfectly shaped mouth and chin fixed on Tessa. Everything about Angie was gracefully elongated—legs, arms, neck—all accentuated by the simple line of her coat-dress and the plain dark shoes and stockings.

"Go on," Joan said good-naturedly. "I'll mind the shop. And no need to rush back, Tess."

Angie had already headed out of the shop without a backward look so Joan gave Tessa a robust wink—and her heartiest grin. *Have fun.*

"Look, there's a sandwich bar round the

276

corner I go to sometimes," Tessa said. "I expect it will be pretty crowded, but let's try it anyway . . ."

Inside, they pushed past the queue waiting for takeaways and found a table at the back. Angie swiftly commandeered this, although a group of students were eyeing it, obviously waiting to be seated. The place was hot and stuffy and uncomfortable. Angie said loudly, "What a dreadful place . . ."

As soon as she lifted her arm, a sullen waitress materialised and they ordered coffee and sandwiches. "And make it snappy," Angie told her, fishing in her huge black bag for cigarettes. "We're in a hurry."

"How's Tom?" Tessa asked, struggling out of her jacket, uncomfortably conscious of the looks which Angie's imperiousness, as well as her looks, attracted. "Is he getting any interesting cases?"

Angie offered a cigarette which Tessa refused. "If you ask me," she flicked her lighter, "he's crazy wasting his time on these footling cases after all that education. Breaking and entering; someone accused of nicking a bike. He says it takes years to build up a practice at the Bar and earn good money. If you're unlucky, you might never get anywhere . . . And it's not as if he likes the work. He doesn't. Half the time he's bored stiff."

The waitress plonked a plate of sandwiches on the table—and two cups of coffee, most of which was slopped on the saucers. Angie pulled a face at the stale sandwiches and refused the coffee. They wouldn't, she said firmly and none too graciously, do. The waitress flounced off, muttering audibly—*"Some people . . ."*

"It was his choice after Oxford," Tessa pointed out. "I don't think Pa wanted him to go into Law particularly."

"And that's what's so ridiculous." Angie inspected the second cups of coffee which were put down with sarcastic care—and nodded. Tessa tried to smile at the waitress and took a sandwich. "It's one thing not to go into a family business if there's something else you desperately want to do . . . but for Tom to turn his back on Selway Electric for no reason other than he doesn't get on terribly well with his Dad . . ." She shrugged. "I call that cutting off your nose to spite your face.

Amazing, this coffee isn't too bad at all. The sandwiches look dead." She took one, dissected the middle, nibbled a small piece of ham—and left the bread which was smeared with margarine. "Don't you think I'm right?"

Tessa didn't know about "right". But she detected in Angie, even if she didn't much like it, hard, down-to-earth commonsense. No social graces, as Marcus said. But straight? Perhaps.

"It's Tom's life," Tessa said, munching. She had been up since five and she was hungry. "And he's never been keen on business. He either had his head in a book or a ball in his hand when he was growing up. He's looking awfully well, though," she added, not sure how Angie would take this. "Very contented—and he's rather a highly-strung person really."

"We get on," Angie said, "we really get on. I can tell you that." Her face was a beautiful, black-and-white mask. "Auntie came for supper. She thinks he's a dream, so handsome, such a gent . . ." Tessa thought the mask softened slightly—but she couldn't be sure.

"I know. I saw you at Oliver's . . ."

279

"Ah . . ." Angie pushed away the sandwich she had barely touched and fractionally adjusted her dark glasses. "While we're here, I want to tell you one or two things about Marcus Reardon. OK?"

Tessa had been braced for this from the moment Angie appeared in the shop. It was the mention of Oliver; but it would have come anyhow. She could feel herself hardening mentally. "If you like." She looked steadily at the pools of darkness which were Angie's eyes. "But you hardly know him, surely."

"Maybe. But I've been around—a hell of a lot more than you and Tom." Tessa purposely did not dispute this. "And I've heard about him one way and another. And it's mostly bad."

Tessa put her cup down carefully. Inwardly, she was seething. "He helped you willingly enough," she said, her voice steely. "The night you turned up at his flat with nowhere else to go, your face battered to a pulp. We *all* helped you, Angie."

"Fair enough." There was no sign of so much as a flicker behind the black shades. "I'm grateful—and I've said so. I liked

Marcus, in his way, the first time I met him. I admit that. But I also know he's a bad hat. And mostly a bum."

Tessa's mouth tightened. She looked at her watch. She really didn't have to listen to this, she told herself. She wanted nothing more than to get out of this clammy, dreadful café and away from Angie. Her heart pounded, her head buzzed. She almost put her hands over her ears. "He's a journalist on the *Chronicle*," she said icily. "And he is . . ."

Angie interrupted. "You wait. He won't be for long, even though I've heard he's a good writer. He doesn't get on with - people, he won't kow-tow, he ends up getting sacked. He's always hard up—and he isn't fussy about how he makes a bit on the side. He sells gossip to newspapers for one thing—any kind of dirt, true or not. And he can be paid to keep quiet—Guy told me that. That was why he hung round Loden's place last winter . . ."

"I see," Tessa said politely, picking up her cup. "Is that all?"

"Not quite." The cigarette unsmoked, was burning down towards her slender fingers. "He's a bastard with women.

They go for him in a big way, too. He picks them up and drops them dead. And he likes them rich. Although he probably doesn't like them at all very much, come to think of it. I don't mean he's queer or anything. I just don't think he respects women. Most men don't, for God's sake."

I might be sick, Tessa thought. I *might*.

"Look," Angie stubbed the cigarette in her saucer and put her elbows on the table. "I've probably overdone this—tact isn't my strong point . . . I've been told that before. But Reardon is not someone your Dad would want you running around with. And I thought I ought to tell you. That's all." The black shoulders shrugged.

"What on earth for?" Tessa asked coolly. She was angry now, really angry. "Did you know that he's a friend of our grandmother's—and that he was in the same squadron as David, our uncle, in the war?"

Angie nodded. "He had one of the best war records of the lot. Loden told me that. And even *he* was impressed—not that he would have dreamt of getting *his* hands dirty fighting, not him. He got out of it somehow. Pure spiv . . . Sure, I know

Marcus was a hero, but the war ended a long time ago." She looked at her watch. "For God's sake, Tessa, with everything you've got going for you don't waste your time on a second-rate hack like Reardon. Because *that's* what he is."

She signalled for the bill. When it came, Tessa grabbed it and paid, leaving an unnecessarily large tip, while Angie made her way coolly to the door.

While they were in the café, a sudden summer rain storm had broken. Outside it was pouring, there was a blustery wind and already streams ran in the gutters.

"Bloody hell," Angie muttered. "There goes summer. Unless I can get a taxi, I'm going to be late."

"You won't get one in this," Tessa said coldly. She turned up the collar of her coat. Already, she could feel rain on her neck.

"I can try. I'm lucky with taxis."

She stepped into the street, arm raised, and seconds later an empty taxi screeched to a splashing halt beside her. "Come on Tessa." She wrenched open the door. "Get in and I'll drop you. You'll get *soaked . . ."* Tessa stood in the rain, watching, too angry for words.

"Look," Angie shouted. "Don't be an idiot, Tessa. I'm sorry if I spoke out of turn. I meant it for the best . . . *now get in."*

Tessa shook her head and turned, walking quickly back the way they had come—to the shop. She heard the taxi grind off. She was furiously angry—and beneath the anger, pain seared.

What business was it of Angie's what she did with her life? *Angie*—of all people . . . ? How dare she interfere like this—and when she hardly knew Marcus. Everything she said was hearsay—hateful innuendo. Nastiness. *She was tough*, knowing . . . despite that freakish beauty that the camera worshipped. She had always known, deep down, that Tom, for all his gifts, was a weakling. *Angie proved it.*

The driving rain stung her face and a car flung a shower of muddy water across her legs. Her hair was plastered to her head, dripping. Miserable, hardly knowing what she was doing, she dived into a news-agents and bought a *Chronicle*. She stuffed it into her coat and plunged on through the downpour. Without realising it, she was sobbing quietly. She dashed across the street and paused outside a red telephone kiosk. It was empty. Again without conscious thought, she went inside. It was steamy and smelly but at least it was dry.

Without a moment's hesitation, she started fumbling in her purse for change and turned to the *Chronicle*'s masthead. She dialled the number. On the third try, she reached someone who seemed to know what she was talking about. Almost faint with relief, she leant against the glass windows which were getting fogged.

"Trying to get hold of Marcus, are you?" came a cheerful voice. "Hang on, he was here a minute ago . . . Sorry, I gather he's gone to the composing room. He shouldn't be long. Would you like to leave a message?"

Her shoulder hunched against the door, Tessa held the receiver away from her. She tried to think coherently . . . two people were now waiting impatiently outside.

"Hello, hello . . . are you still there?"

"Yes," Tessa said quietly.

"Speak up, I can only just hear you. If

285

you leave your name and number I'll ask him to phone you back." The friendly, matter-of-fact voice carrying halfway across London.

"No, it's all right." She stood upright and spoke into the receiver. She was fully controlled. "Don't bother. Thanks, but I've changed my mind." She fell out again into the chilly summer rain. She was soaked through but the shop wasn't far now.

Phoning Marcus instinctively, without even thinking of the consequences, had been a mistake; lucky she couldn't reach him. Because what did she have to say to him—this moment—or ever?

He's a bastard with women . . .

Angie's ugly insinuation; she had been, she admitted it, digging around for what she could find on him. People she had met through Loden most likely; but what business was it of Angie's who she saw? She had felt on her guard the moment she saw her standing in the shop with Joan.

He sells gossip . . .

She remembered Marcus watching that politician across the crowded restaurant; his preoccupation; the sudden phone call.

It was certainly nothing to do with Angie.

Or her.

It's my grey hairs . . .

Marcus . . . the pain struck again. Oh Marcus—where are you? Help me over this.

Panting—she had run most of the way —she got to the shop; the bell tinkled as she pushed open the door. Her clothes dripped, making pools of water where she stood.

"I'm back," she called to Joan. "I look like a drowned rat . . ."

As she placed the damp newspaper on the desk, something caught her eye. She looked closely. Along the top of the front page, in bold type, she read: *Starting next Monday—a new twice-weekly column, London Life, by Chronicle reporter Marcus Reardon—the lowdown on London high life . . . don't forget— starting Monday.*

She was standing surrounded by vases of summer flowers; rain was beating on the windows; but all she could smell was the heady scent of sun-drenched hawthorn.

"What's that?" Joan enquired, poking

her head round the door. "Blimey child, you look as though you've been swimming . . . now stop reading whatever it is and get in and dry yourself."

"Coming." Tessa went into the small bathroom in the rear where they kept overalls and extra sweaters and a few basic changes of clothing. She stripped off and dried her hair on a towel. Rummaging through a drawer she found a bright blue cotton skirt and an oversize blue and white striped shirt which Joan had acquired in France one summer and never worn. It was miles too big but she pulled it in with a wide belt and, discarding her damp and muddied stockings, put on flat heeled white shoes which she kept for emergencies such as this. She brushed her hair very sleekly and looked into the mirror above the washbasin. She would do.

"Right then, I'm off," Joan announced as she emerged. "I want to beat the traffic getting out of London. Have a nice lunch, did you?"

"Not bad."

Joan raised her eyebrows. "I see. She's a glamour-girl all right. What does she want with Tom then, a girl like her—

modelling and all that stuff? I mean, you'd think she'd go for someone with a big name, pots of money, that sort of thing."

"You would rather, wouldn't you . . . Were you busy over the lunch hour?"

"Not very. Jilly should be in any moment. I've left her a list of orders to be getting on with. And I know what we want in the market tomorrow. My turn this week. You're looking a bit down in the dumps, Tess. Nothing wrong, is there?"

"Nothing at all. Honestly." She smiled brightly. "I must start thinking about arrangements and a colour scheme for that twenty-first party. I'd get going if I were you . . . I think the worst of the rain has eased."

"Okydoke. I say, that shirt looks super on you. Keep it. You see, it wasn't such a bad buy after all . . ."

Once Joan had gone, Tessa took the *Chronicle*, folded it, and put it away in her bag. She wondered, briefly, if Gran had seen it . . . perhaps she would telephone tonight and pop over and see her. She had hardly seen her since Grandpa Delmore's funeral.

It was an unusually quiet afternoon with

few customers so she was able to think out a scheme for one party at least, decide on what flowers and greenery and "props" she would need, cost out the labour. At about four o'clock the phone rang for the first time since Joan left. Tessa went to the desk, pulling over the order book, pencil poised.

"This is Joan's Garden. Hello."

A pause. "Tessa? Marcus here."

Tessa felt nothing at all—not surprise, not pleasure, not excitement. She pushed the order book and pencil neatly to one side.

"Oh, hello Marcus."

"You phoned the paper . . ."

"How did you know it was me?" She was mildly astonished.

"I guessed. Was there anything you wanted?"

"Nothing special. I changed my mind."

"That's what he said you said—Dan, the chap you spoke to. That's how I knew it was you."

"Oh . . ."

He sounded uncharacteristically buoyant—almost euphoric. "Look—this has been a tremendous week for me."

"I know that," she cut in swiftly. "You've got your own column. Congratulations, I know it was the sort of break you were hoping for, wasn't it? You must be thrilled."

"You could say that. *At last* . . . Anyhow, I was wondering if you were doing anything tonight?"

"No, I'm not. I was thinking—I don't know—of perhaps going round to see Gran."

"Tessa? You sound whacked. Feeling all right, are you?"

"Fine."

"In that case, would you risk doing a bit of celebrating with me? I don't mean the out-on-the-town variety. I've been given a couple of bottles of decent champagne to drink to what we hope will be a success. And I thought I'd do the rounds of my favourite local delicatessen. Why don't you join me at the flat and we'll have a sort of pre-midnight feast?"

"Thanks Marcus, I'd like that."

"Splendid. Now what time shall I pick you up?"

"There's no need, really."

"Nonsense. It's sure to be a filthy night

and you may not get a cab." Disjointed thoughts filtered through Tessa's mind—Ella, the traffic, her flat white pumps.

"If I can come just as I am," she said, "I'll wait for you here. It would be easier. Any time after five-thirty, really."

"Good. That's settled then. I'll be there. See you a bit later on . . ."

The moment she put down the phone a regular customer who had a house round the corner dashed in, breathless, her arms full of parcels. She was the attractive, rather scatty wife of a merchant banker and as Tessa knew, was required to do a good deal of entertaining. That evening she had been "landed" with a dinner party for eight unexpectedly—for an American business contact of her husband's who was over with his wife.

Tessa laughed. "I'll do my best; now let's see . . ." She did some quick thinking, considering the house, which she knew, the client's taste and the flowers available. "Let me look in the back just to check what's left. Do sit for a moment . . ."

After a few minutes spent conferring with Jilly, who was working on the greenery for tomorrow's dance, Tessa came back. "It's all right, I think we'll manage. Now what about this . . ."

First she suggested a large basket of planted lilies to be put by the window half way up the stairs. "They'll see them when they come in and going *up* to the drawing-room and *down* for dinner . . . and the whole house will smell divine." She would do a soft, trailing centrepiece for the table, nothing stiff, in different shades of pink. And remembering that this customer preferred white, "I'll put together a big mix of all the white flowers we've got— some lilac, roses, lilies again—and you can plonk them into that pair of magnificent vases you've got in the drawing-room. Oh —and a few pink roses for your dressing-table. They're a bit overblown and they won't last but they'll look pretty. Will that be all right, do you think?"

"It all sounds marvellous—what a relief! Now could you possibly have the flowers delivered—or is it too late?"

"The van has already gone for the day." Tessa sounded doubtful; then in a burst of pleasure and excitement, she remembered Marcus. "Don't worry," she smiled radiantly, "I'm getting a lift so I can drop them myself. About six. Will that be all right?"

Humming to herself, excitement growing, Tessa finished the flowers for the table and began the basket of lilies. To hell with Angie. I won't think about her, I won't . . . Whatever I do is my business. I'll be wary of her from now on whatever happens; I've seen the claws underneath the beauty. Poor old Tom . . . and yet they did, she had to admit, seem so happy together.

Usually, towards closing time, they started to get busy. Keeping enough, but not too many, flowers for the end of the day was always a problem. Husbands guiltily remembered anniversaries and rushed in flapping briefcases and bowler hats; guests who were invited to dinner parties suddenly thought: *I must bring something*. On good days, particularly in the spring and summer, even passers-by looked in the window, hesitated, and came in to buy something, however small, to put in a vase and light up a dull city living-room. This was often the time when the small shop was most crowded.

But that night with the heavy summer storm still gusting, the door opened only a few times after five. Jilly had been working hard and well so Tessa decided to let her go a bit early.

Tessa finished the order, did the till and the books; she tidied up, swept and watered. She rearranged the window for the night, putting a huge basket of pink dried flowers in the middle, lit by a single spotlight. Then she started foraging around among Joan's jumble of containers. It had occurred to her while she was planting the lilies that she would take one to Marcus. Simply planted with a bit of moss in a plain white ceramic pot. She knew exactly the one she was looking for and found it at last—under a new pile of Joan's hoard of junk. He would like that. She could tell from having seen the flat that night that he had strict, simple taste.

Tessa looked at her watch. It was a quarter to six. She locked the door and pulled down the blind on the window. The order to be delivered was waiting on the desk. At the sight of the telephone, she immediately started dialling the number in Parloe Square.

Ella answered. She had met a friend unexpectedly in the lunch hour, Tessa told her. They had arranged to meet and have a meal and perhaps go to the pictures. The French film at the Curzon, the one Tom had told her was *so* good . . .

It was so easy, so simple to mislead Ella that Tessa found herself embellishing. Yes, she had always rather liked her at school but they had lost touch. Yes, she did get drenched earlier, impossible not to. And Oh dear, Ella said, Oliver had rung to say she had left her shawl at the party last Saturday; one of his cousins thought it was hers but he wasn't sure and could he drop it by this evening on his way somewhere and perhaps stop for a drink . . . He'll be ever so disappointed if you're not here.

"Yes—well, I'll see him another time. It *was* my shawl, by the way, that I'd left at Oliver's. And no, *please* don't wait up. See you tomorrow, 'night."

Smiling, feeling as light as air, she went into the pokey lavatory which passed as a cloakroom. In the mirror she saw that her rain-soaked hair had dried and fluffed into a curly halo. It looked rather nice, she

296

thought. And Joan's unusual striped shirt, pulled in at the waist, was a success. Her coat was still damp so there was nothing for it but to borrow Joan's grey suede jacket. She put it round her shoulders and switched off the light.

The bell rang.

He looked infinitely younger and happier. She saw that at once as though some weight or worry had been lifted from his shoulders. He had on an open-necked shirt and a trenchcoat with the collar turned up which accentuated his high cheekbones. In her most matter-of-fact voice, she told him about the delivery which she had promised to drop off and handed him the large bunch of flowers, carefully wrapped, and the centrepiece.

"If you take these to the car I'll bring the rest."

She switched the lights off, double locked the door and followed him over the wet street, her arms full of fragrant lilies.

They delivered the flowers to the house in the next street and began driving across London. By the time they reached Soho, lights were already glistening on rain-soaked pavements. Marcus parked and they emerged into the dank evening. Several bags of groceries were stacked on the back seat, a loaf of french bread sticking out of one of them.

"You forgot a plant," Marcus said, diving into the back of the car and out again.

"No. That one is for you. For the new column—for luck."

Marcus straightened. "Darling Tessa . . . how kind. Here, you take it while I get the rest of the stuff."

He went into the building ahead of her, pushing the doors open with his elbow. At the first landing he said, "Wait, let me put on the light." As the dingy staircase brightened, he turned. She stood several steps below him, colourful in her azure blue and white top; her feathery, gingery hair. She looked up at him, her face glowing above the lilies . . .

"Marcus . . ."

"What?"

"How *did* you know it was me, when I phoned the paper? I didn't leave my name."

He laughed, pushing on up the stairs. "Come on . . . second sight, wishful thinking. Who knows? But I was right, wasn't I? And I do like that shirt, by the way. French, isn't it?"

11

THE flat was as immaculately clean and tidy as Tessa remembered. She put the lily on a table by the sofa next to a neat pile of books.

"It should get enough light there. But you must remember to water it," she called out to Marcus who was putting away the groceries in the kitchen. He came in, saw the plant—"It's lovely, bless you"— and went straight to a pile of records. He took their coats and put on a couple of lamps. Then, against a background of Chopin, he opened the champagne and poured two glasses. He handed one to Tessa.

"Here's to you—and the column," she responded.

"To Tessa," he said quietly.

They drank . . .

"Mmm . . . the most delicious thing in the world. Why to me?"

He planted a kiss beside her mouth. "You ask too many questions. Come

300

along now; we've got to work while we drink."

He opened kitchen cupboards and took out plates. Cold meats—Italian salami, mortadella, Parma ham—were unwrapped. Cheeses were put on a marble slab. Last came salad greens and fruits. Marcus topped up their glasses.

"I'll wash the salad." He rolled up his sleeves and took a salad bowl and servers from a shelf. "You make the dressing. Can you do that properly?"

Tessa giggled. "Any well brought up English girl who has been to finishing school, even for a few weeks like I did, can make a decent vinaigrette."

"Show me, I dare you. I always use that jar." He put the olive oil and vinegar on the kitchen table and began to wash the lettuce. "Salt and pepper grinder are on the shelf. Anything else you need?"

"Mustard."

He turned round, smiling, surprised.

"Good girl. In that cupboard . . . further over. That's right. Any kind you like—you're in charge."

Tessa poured some vinegar. "I had lunch with Angie today," she said. Marcus was splashing water at the sink, shaking the wet lettuce into a colander.

"I see. Enjoyable was it?"

"No. Actually, it was very nasty." She began grinding the pepper. "I didn't enjoy it at all."

"Nasty? In what way?" The splashing halted.

"Unpleasant. Bitchy—*very.*"

"Well, well . . . She has great looks, but she's no lady. I should think she came up the hard way. Assassinating my character, was she?"

Tessa added the salt and stared at the row of different mustards.

"So much choice . . . you do make things difficult." She took one down.

"Well, was she?"

"Yes."

Tessa, with her back to him, heard the lettuce leaves being shaken dry one by one.

"Women, no money, no damn good—that sort of thing?" he asked drily, amused. "Since she knows me so little personally, she must have been doing her homework."

Tessa didn't answer. She had shaken up

the vinegar mixture and was adding the olive oil.

"Poor sweet, I can imagine. I hope she kept her language cleaned up. She doesn't always. I suspect she's as hard as nails under the sleek actressy exterior. Did she upset you?"

"A bit. I thought about poor old Tom." She added a pinch of sugar.

"You and Tom are babes in the wood as far as the Angies of this world are concerned."

"Yes, I suppose we are." She shook the jar for several seconds. "Can I get to the tap? I always add a dollop of water last thing and shake again."

He turned and stood behind her, his hands on her shoulders. Tessa swallowed hard and stayed very still, holding on to the table. She shut her eyes.

"I want you to make love to me," she whispered.

His grip on her shoulders tightened.

"Oh my God," he said. "Oh my God . . ." He pulled her round to him. Her eyes were still closed. He held her tightly. "Poor love, I'm sorry . . . the trouble is, she's not entirely wrong about me—Angie. You know that . . ."

"I know." Very faintly.

From some way above her head he said, "Did you really mean what you just said?"

"Yes."

"Come . . ."

In the early hours of the following morning, when she lay awake watching beams of light fall across the faded pink-striped curtains in her room in Parloe Square, Tessa remembered . . . At some point—and it seemed to take hours and hours, nothing rushed, every touch drawn out—Marcus had said: "I promise I won't hurt you." He didn't. Then: "Is this still what you want?" It was, oh it was. And at the end, beyond control, *My love, you are so lovely.*"

When it was over and he lay beside her, he whispered into her ear, "It's a messy business. It won't be next time." He picked up her hand and kissed it. "Thank you, my darling. Mmm . . ." He licked her fingers one by one. "You taste deliciously of olive oil. Pure virgin, of course," he added wickedly, bending to kiss her breasts which he had already told her many times during that past hour were irresistible.

"*Marcus!*"

"I'm sorry, sorry . . ."

But her laughter, released by the sudden and astonishing physical pleasure, was uncontrollable. It welled and grew and echoed around Marcus's spartan bedroom —peal after peal after peal. It was infectious. Soon, Marcus, too, was helpless, delighted as much by her abandon as the silly wordplay.

They clung together, tousled, naked, still laughing, on the narrow bed.

It was their most loving moment.

"The most *awful* joke ever," Tessa gasped. "And you're supposed to be so good with words. I'll *never* forgive you . . ." Her face was hidden somewhere between his head and shoulder.

"You shouldn't. I don't deserve it." Lying back and starting to laugh again, manoeuvring her gently across him. And as soon as he could speak coherently, "Listen, I'm going to get up. *My love*. Don't move, wait, I'll get you a dressing-gown." With his peculiar, quite unself-conscious grace, getting into his trousers and pulling on his shirt; looking down at her, still vastly amused—tenderly . . . "What am I going to do with you in these fits of giggles?"

Tessa hiccupping, pink in the face, eyes watering.

She sat up. "Throw me something to put on—to make myself respectable—and I'll get up too."

After she had washed and dressed—rather fetchingly, she thought—in Marcus's towelling robe sashed tight at the waist, Tessa came back into the bedroom. She picked up her clothes which were flung about, and folded them neatly on the chair. She could hear Marcus moving in the kitchen. The bedroom was painted white with dark stained wood floors and heavy white cotton curtains. There were bookshelves from floor to ceiling all down one wall. Apart from the bed, there was only a chest, a reading light, a chair and a small rug. She looked at herself in the mirror—Tessa, just the same. No visible difference. She was astonished at how

ordinary, how natural, she felt; how extra-
ordinarily happy.

Picking up one of Marcus's brushes, she
tidied her hair and went into the kitchen.
Marcus had laid the table and put out the
food. He sniffed the remains of the champagne—and poured it away.

"Flat and nasty. A beer for me. What
about you? Let me open another bottle
. . . I'm flush today, remember."

"Could I have a cup of tea? It's what I
feel like."

"Of course. You're all right, darling
Tessa, are you?" He looked at her search-
ingly. She looked back at him—a bit shy,
a bit uncertain, totally trusting; her face
still suffused from the love and the
laughter. He smiled and held out his hand
which she took with both of hers. "Yes.
You are, aren't you? Good." And with his
head slightly to one side, "I do think you
ought to wear my dressing-gown more
often."

"Can you tell me a bit about the column?"
she asked, eating away. "You'll make your
name on it, won't you?"

(She remembered later on that she had never had any doubt about that.)

"I assure you I intend to. I've been given more or less a free hand." He said seriously, "The bottom line is that it's read and talked about. That's the brief really. We won't know that immediately, of course." He paused. "I want this to succeed more than anything I have ever tried—there have been enough failures. No more." He spoke in his normal voice, but Tessa could sense his determination. His expression in the dim light—his pale eyes, his sharply defined cheek bones— was cold and impersonal. She thought of his kisses, those hands, and shivered.

"It's an eclectic sort of diary—politics, publishing, personalities. I've got to get out and about and keep my ear to the ground. I've always done that, of course. And this particular editor, for once, has decided to use the know-how I've got, or developed over the years. He's an inspirational sort of chap and he's got confidence in me, which is nice. He hasn't given me the sort of beat that a lot of other younger men can cover as well, or better. Anyhow, we'll see how the first one or two go . . . And of course, there'll be the old nugget of shock/horror." He was staring into the darkness. He said slowly, as though savouring the thought, "I rather look forward to setting a few cats among the pigeons . . ."

He sells gossip to newspapers.

"But Marcus," she said, "not destructive—gossip?"

That seemed to bring him back to the present—and her presence. "There's got to be some bite, you know." He shrugged. "It's what sells newspapers, after all. Coffee?"

She shook her head. Her elbows were resting on the table, her chin in her hands.

"Cold?"

Under the table, their legs touched. He reached down and lifted up her bare foot. "You are, you know." He rested it on his knee and covered it with his hand. "I'm a selfish sod . . . now don't forget that, will you?"

Tessa started to move her foot. Their eyes met and held across the candle flame. After a while he murmured, "The things you learnt in that finishing school."

"Along with the vinaigrette." Lips

parted; intense. Nothing—no-one in the world for her but Marcus.

"That too." He grimaced, more or less pleasurably. "I'm going to deliver you safely home, of course, but not quite yet . . ."

Exhausted, elated, wordless, they had dressed, and Marcus had driven her home through the late, nearly empty London streets.

Don't, he had said at the end when she had pulled up the sheet and looked away from him . . . The candle, burnt low, flickered on the chair next to the bed . . . please don't—he pushed down the sheet and turned her face back towards him— because I shall want to remember you, you see . . . Like this. Always . . .

In the car, he became impersonal, almost offhand. These sudden mood changes of his caught her badly off balance; alarmed her. He didn't know what the week would bring, he said, he'd just have to play it by ear. The shop would be busy, too, he imagined . . . Ascot coming up, parties

. . . and speaking of parties, he'd have to go to God knows how many from now on—work, not pleasure. Perhaps she wouldn't mind coming with him sometime? Anyhow, he would see what turned up and let her know. He would give her a ring tomorrow.

"And I must go round and see Vi. I don't want her to think I'm not paying her enough attention."

"Me too. I think she gets lonely stuck in that flat with the awful Charlie day after day. She says going about much is an effort. She's happiest just pottering and 'living in the past' as she calls it."

"Yes. I'm sure of that. She's been talking a lot about Ben recently. I suppose your grandfather's death brought everything back."

"It must have. That ghastly house . . . and David would have inherited."

"I'll drop in on her sometime soon. And say that we had dinner together . . . that's all right, isn't it?" She could hear the amusement in his voice.

Her key in the lock (did it always make such a noise?), across the darkened hall

and up the stairs, such loud creaking . . .
a note from Ella on her dressing-table left
unread.

In bed at last, so childishly familiar,
hands behind her head, eyes staring.

*Because I shall want to remember you,
you see. Like this. Always . . .*

When she finally got to sleep the milk
float had already turned, rattling, into the
square. And she was smiling.

12

TESSA overslept, turning off the alarm and going back to sleep until she was awakened by Ella banging on the door.

"It's after eight, Tess," she called out. "You're going to be late . . ."

Tessa leapt out of bed and threw back the curtains on to a shining June morning —and remembered. Marcus . . . Even the weather echoed her bursting high spirits. Yesterday's storm and greyness had been swept away and replaced by this superb jewel of a morning—the sky washed blue, the sun gleaming.

She bathed and dressed in record time and was doing her hair when she noticed Ella's note on the dressing-table for the second time.

"Oliver dropped by with your shawl," she read. "I've put it back in the drawer. He was ever so sorry to miss you. Can you phone him late this afternoon in his chambers?"

She would, of course she would. She had been feeling a bit guilty about Oliver. They hadn't said goodbye last Saturday—and she hadn't phoned or written to thank him for the party. And she did like Oliver, she liked him enormously. She wouldn't ever want to lose his friendship. She slipped the note into her pocket and leant over to look at herself closely in the mirror. Exactly the same Tessa; she didn't look the slightest bit different despite—Marcus, olive oil, God only knew what else . . .

Stifling laughter, looking remarkably fit and rested after no more than three hours' sleep, Tessa ran downstairs to the kitchen.

"I've got to dash," she told Ella who was sorting laundry. "Thanks for the wake-up call. I needed it. Any interesting post?" She helped herself to coffee and sat on the table, swinging her legs, riffling through a selection of bills and letters.

"A card from Poppy. She's doing lots of shopping in New York, she says. The shops are *divine*." Tessa swallowed a mouthful of coffee. "How on earth is she going to lug anything else home, for heaven's sake."

"Well, I expect she has lots of time to kill during the day while your father is in meetings," Ella said patiently. "Did you enjoy the film, Tess? I must say, I didn't hear you come in."

"I was rather late, actually. Yes—the film is very good. I think you and Maggie would like it, you ought to see it," Tessa replied blandly. "And thanks for the note about Oliver. I'll ring him from the shop. Goodness, look at the time . . . I must be off."

She put on her jacket and slung a bag over her shoulder. "Just let me see I've got all my keys . . . right." She turned by the door. "I'm not sure what I'm doing tonight, Ella. I might even go round and see Gran. So don't bother about supper. If I'm in I'll have a boiled egg."

"You look full of beans," Joan said as Tessa practically waltzed into the shop. "Just as well when you see our order book. I got some marvellous buys in the market this morning; the boxes are all in the back, go and look, and Tess . . ." She was coughing, spluttering, lighting yet another cigarette. "I've had the bank manager on the phone already. We're badly overdrawn and only because we haven't sent out a mountain of bills. Be a good girl and get it sorted out, would you?"

"Heavens, yes. We're dreadfully behind on bills. I'll get out a few local ones and spend an hour on them today if I can."

"Good idea." Joan inhaled deeply. "And I'll tell you something else, Tess. While I had that bank chappie on the phone, he made a couple of interesting suggestions. We're doing well—if you don't count inefficiency—and we've got a lot more business than we can comfortably handle. We were chattering on about this, and he said why don't you open another shop? Keep the style which appeals and is getting known—spread out a bit—get some more (and more experienced) help. Put the whole thing on a bigger and more 'cost effective'—his expression, blimey— basis. The sort of thing we've been thinking about ourselves."

Tessa grinned. *"Joan's Second Garden . . ."*

Joan grinned back. "Exactly, or *Tessa's* or *Joan and Tessa's Garden*. I like the sound of that."

"I'm game, why ever not? No point in just talking about it. Will he back us? The bank manager?"

"You bet. Why else would he have suggested it? After all, he needs people like us to make some money out of," Joan declared confidently.

"Then let's get going on it. Really, Joan." As they had begun to realise, their idea, the way they did the work, was unique. It made sense to expand, to capitalise on their style. "Let's investigate it seriously. And now that I've proved that I can stick at it, I don't at all mind asking Papa—at least for some advice. I might as well make the most of having one of the best businessmen in the country for a father. The problem will be finding the right place. OK partner—you're on."

They shook hands, laughing.

"Just get those bills out, young lady, or we won't be looking for a new shop, we'll be out of business altogether . . ."

In the early afternoon, when Joan had left for Sussex and Jilly was holding the fort in the shop, Tessa dashed out to deliver some of the bills she had drafted hastily that morning. Much of their clientèle was local. She enjoyed being out in the sun, walking through the streets with their pretty terraced houses.

"Oh Tessa," Jilly said, all bubbly and excited when she got back. "I shouted after you but you didn't hear. The moment you left someone called Marcus phoned for you. Can you give him a ring at his home, he said. I've got the number here. Lucky you. I must say he sounded heaven. Older. Very sexy. Is he?"

"Jilly, you're impossible. You're supposed to be wildly in love with some young Guards' officer. But as a matter of fact he is—very. Sexy, that is. Now give me the number before you lose it."

"That's a very dizzy young lady you've got there in your shop," Marcus told her, amused. "A sort of breathy ingénue type . . ."

"Oh she is. She gets the orders hopelessly mixed up but we like her so much we can't sack her. As a matter of fact, I've just been out to deliver a heap of bills. I'm supposed to be the bookkeeper among us —but we're horribly overdrawn so I'm

trying to get some money in quickly. I
don't seem to have inherited my father's
business brain. Not yet at least."

She was chattering to cover her nerves
and excitement.

"You seem very practical to me." He
paused. "Among other, infinitely more
attractive, attributes. Are you all right,
sweet Tessa?"

A sudden drop in his voice affected her
powerfully. After a moment or so, "Yes."

"Once more with feeling, please."

"*Yes.*"

"That's more like it. I have been
thinking about you—longingly. That is
true, Tessa." He sounded so near, so intimate; her heart thumped about. "Look,
I've got a round of duty parties tonight
—a couple of book launches and a new
restaurant—and I wondered whether you
wanted to risk coming with me? I warn
you, I'll be on the prowl—working, really,
though it mightn't look like it. I may not
be very good company. But the restaurant
should be amusing."

Tessa thought quickly. She could phone
Oliver—and Gran—and go home for a
quick change.

"I'd like that."

"Good—that's very satisfactory. Because I'm on to a nice, murky little nugget and I expect I'll be working flat out on it for a week or so. I'm waiting for a couple of calls on it from France now. As a matter of fact, the whole thing started in the restaurant last Saturday. I'll tell you about it if it ever comes to anything . . . so could you come round, say, six-thirtyish?"

What on earth am I doing here anyway? Tessa thought gloomily at the second of the publishing parties Marcus took her to that night. At least, she supposed, Marcus had warned her. Both parties were, to Tessa, indistinguishable—noisy, hot, full of almost drunk men and young women with white faces, heavily made up eyes and dangling earrings. Most of whom looked decidedly grubby. She knew nobody—and introductions appeared not to happen. Apart from telling her "For God's sake don't touch the wine whatever you do, pure gut-rot. We'll eat later. I'm going to cruise around for a bit," Marcus ignored her. He seemed to know, or be known, by everyone. Tessa watched, feeling inadequate and unhappy, as at least three women greeted him with very public intimacy. Then she lost sight of him completely. The party was in a house, going strong on all three floors, so he might be anywhere.

In desperation, she headed for a trestle table in the corner which was piled with books—the publication of which they were presumably celebrating. Elbowing her way through the crowd, at one point stepping over a group who had retired to the floor, Tessa reached the table and picked up a book. It was a novel by a woman writer, and according to the cover, the author had been much acclaimed for her previous book. With no one to talk to—and nothing to drink—Tessa decided that she might as well take an interest in it; clearly, she was the only person there who was.

But even with a book to hold she didn't feel much better. Someone, a man with hair even longer than Marcus's, bumped into her from behind and spilled red wine down one of her sleeves. "Sorry, darling," he grinned as he lurched off. "Ciao . . ."

Tessa slammed the book back on the table, got out a handkerchief and dabbed

321

at the stain. She was wearing an expensive cream silk blouse and the rose coloured mark above the cuff was infuriating. As she turned, someone—one of the white faced, kohl-eyed girls, shrieking with laughter—blew smoke in her face. At this point, Tessa considered leaving, pressing through the mob somehow, getting out into the air and finding a bus or taxi to take her home. She had had a quick chat with Gran on the phone earlier. She had sounded low—old, a bit out of touch. Tessa wished fervently that she had avoided all this and gone to see her.

There was still no sign of Marcus. She picked up the book again and started to flip through it. Pretentious, she thought, and ridiculous . . . she could tell instantly that it wasn't a book she would ever read. Behind her, she heard the smoker drawl.

"Why, there's Marcus Reardon. Isn't that Baby Wittering he's got in tow? I thought that was all over. You know he's getting his own column in the *Chronicle*." A giggle. Tessa half turned. The girl was leaning against her companion, an arm draped round his neck. "That's Baby all right. She's not looking *too* bad, considering . . . I suppose having all that money helps. They say he can't keep away from her although she's got lovers galore. Man-mad—what's the word for it? Darling, you shouldn't feed me all this dreadful wine."

"Nympho. But it's the dollar signs in the eyes that attract Marcus. He always has swarmed around rich women. Personally, I know you girls won't have it—but I've never liked him."

"Coo—just look. They seem cosy enough now those two."

Feeling sick, Tessa searched through the crowd. Marcus was standing with a fat, fair-haired woman who was lavishly dressed, and who had once clearly been extremely pretty. Marcus was bending down, saying something into her ear. She couldn't see his face. The woman looked up at him with a ravishing, and unmistakably intimate, smile.

Tessa let the book fall right where she was standing, and dived through a gap in the mêlée in the direction of the door. With spilt drinks, cigarette ash and plates of half-eaten cocktail snacks on every surface, the place had come to resemble a social battleground. Marcus caught up with her just outside the front door and took her arm.

"What an absolutely dreadful party," she said looking straight ahead.

"Oh did you think so? It seemed fairly standard to me as these things go. Here we are."

Tessa sat silently as Marcus backed the car and they moved off.

"I did warn you that it wouldn't be quite your scene, my sweet. Going to things like that does happen to be part of my job. I told you that too."

"Quite. And I noticed the work you were doing . . ." Although Tessa knew better, she couldn't help herself. "With that fat, dolled up *old* blonde," she added cruelly.

Marcus laughed. "Baby? Baby Wittering? She's an old chum. She once fancied herself as a writer and Daddy— he's Texas oil—bought her a magazine. It never came to anything. She's been hanging around literary parties for years."

"So *that's* what it was—a 'literary party'." Her voice poured hurt and scorn.

"Tessa, don't be a silly girl." His hand

324

found her thigh and stayed there. "We're off to sample a newly opened restaurant in the King's Road. Called Edward's because Edward Cairn owns and runs it. I'm told it's about to become London's most chic watering hole. We'll give it the once-over. Yes?" He glanced quickly round at her. He was smiling.

Seduced by the warmth of his hand, her anger at his abandonment of her at the parties receded. She pushed the cynical, gossipy conversation which she had overheard to the back of her mind. Melting, wanting his touch so much—*so much*—she put her hand over his.

"That's more like it."

Getting out of the car in Chelsea he said, "Now come here and give me a kiss."

They walked into the restaurant hand in hand.

After a glass of wine from a bottle of "decent" red, approved by Marcus, Tessa began to feel human again. She looked round. The restaurant had a blue and white tiled floor, ladderback chairs and lots of fresh green plants. All the paintwork was spanking white.

"I like it here," Tessa said, looking at

the trailing philodendron with professional approval. "It feels like being abroad."

"It's supposed to, my darling. An up-market Italian trattoria. It's got a good look, no doubt about that." Marcus picked up the menu. "Let's not come to any hasty conclusions. What do you fancy?"

During the meal, Marcus's eyes were constantly darting round the room—a characteristic which Tessa was coming to know. It was filling up with a young, casually dressed crowd, many of whom seemed to know and hail each other loudly. One or two faces looked familiar to Tessa.

"Very classy, this place," Marcus commented ironically as he refilled their glasses. "Many debs' delights. A duke. One young royal . . ."

"Who?"

"Take your time and look behind you."

Tessa did—and found herself looking directly at a young man with brown hair and a weak chin. He was dimly recognisable from photographs in the Press. Tessa turned back to Marcus, looking disappointed.

"Well?"

"He's supposed to be wet and he

certainly looks it. Tom met him somewhere, at a party not long ago. Who else
have you discovered?"

"Among others, Edward the proprietor.
Sitting in the corner eating his own food.
How's your veal, by the way?"

"Fabulous. But I have a bone to pick—
not that it was exactly your fault." The
wine and the pleasant atmosphere had
relaxed her. She lifted her arm and showed
him the stain on the cuff. "Some drunk at
that awful party poured plonk over
me . . ."

"Good God child, don't you yet know
what to do with red wine spills?" he
scolded, summoning a waiter. After a
couple of minutes' consultation he told
her, "He's gone to get a napkin soaked in
soda water. It should get it out. I told him
the damage had been done at a previous
party."

He was looking at her as though really
seeing her for the first time that evening.
She was getting used to that aspect of his
personality too; emotionally elusive; so
often preoccupied by his own thoughts.

"You look very pretty. Young. Fresh.
Delicious. That's a beautiful blouse." He

studied her appearance. "That creamy colour does something good to your skin —and the hair. Tessa, Tessa . . ."

Their hands met across the table, then the waiter returned and with a few expert wipes the stain had all but vanished.

"So much for your literary parties . . ."

When they were having coffee, Tessa looked up to see a tall gangling young man hanging over their table. Marcus stood up.

"Hello, Edward. I did spy you over there and I wanted to have a word. Let me introduce Tessa Selway, Edward Cairn."

They shook hands and Edward drew up a chair. Tessa thought he looked more like a schoolmaster than a restaurateur—shy, stammering and boyish.

"So—Edward." Marcus lifted his glass towards him. "All goes well, I'm glad to see. You're not going to need a plug in my column or anywhere else. You've got all the toffs in here already. It looks good. Edward; it has a nice uncluttered feel. Pleasantly casual. And I must say, we've had a splendid meal, haven't we Tessa?"

Tessa nodded and smiled.

"Really?" Edward Cairn blinked "Actually, we're turning people away thes days. We . . . we . . . must be doing some-thing right. But something in print in the . . . the r-r-right place never hurts, Marcus. Delighted you could come and see us, b-both of you."

On their way back to Parloe Square, Marcus said, "He's not particularly impressive, I know. But Edward's a trained chef and he's got very strong opinions about what's wrong with eating out in London. This is a good first effort. I think he'll go far." He looked at his watch. "I must get home. I've got two important calls coming in tonight, one from France. Checking something out that might be a plum. I'll tell you when it happens. Plus one or two bits and pieces to write up."

Tessa glanced at him. He looked edgy, tapping his nails against the steering wheel while he waited for the lights to change. She could see that he was genuinely nervous about how the column would be received; he knew that this was his big professional chance. Perhaps it was this that was making him so moody—warm one moment, cold and unreachable the next.

"You're going to work tonight? But Marcus it's late . . ."

"My best time. It's when I concentrate most clearly. The next few days are going to be frantic—and the weekend too. We go to press after lunch on Sunday. That's final. I should know by the end of the week which way the wind is blowing; whether I've got something to build on." It was as though he was talking to himself. "Sorry to be obsessive," he added as they turned into the square.

"But when will I see you?"

Her voice was hardly above a whisper; she felt the touch of despair, near panic. Desperately, she wanted to scream: *But last night, Marcus, last night . . .*

They were parked outside the house now. The streetlights shone softly; behind their glow rose the dark outlines of the houses. One or two people walked by, sauntering in the warm night. Marcus turned. "I'll give you a ring when I can see what's happening. After Sunday. I'm sorry, Tessa my sweet, but I'm going to be hard at it—non-stop—until then. That's just the way it is."

She didn't say anything so he took her chin in his hand and made her look at him. "Tessa." He spoke gently. "You've got to take me as I am. I told you that before. I warned you. We're taking risks, both of us."

She shut her eyes.

"Sweet Tessa—it's a difficult thing for a man to say but I was very moved last night. Please know that."

"Oh God . . ." Tessa fumbled for the handle, got out and fled up the steps to the front door; hands shaking as she pushed her key into the lock, not looking round, not hearing the car, knowing he was still there. She slammed the door shut and stood in the hall.

A couple of minutes later, she heard the car start and move off.

"Oh God," she said aloud. *"Oh God . . . What am I going to do?"*

"Blimey, that's a long face." Joan was doing the vases when Tessa got to the shop the next morning—taking long-stemmed white roses, one by one, from a shallow

331

cardboard box. "And yesterday you were full of the joys of spring. What's up with you then?" She pushed the box to one side and felt in her pocket for her cigarettes. "You wouldn't be in love by any chance, would you? Something soppy like that?"

Tessa managed a wan smile.

"Well—would you?" Her expression was warm and caring, belying the flippant words.

"Oh Joan . . ."

She hadn't slept much for the second night running, thoughts and emotions—all quite new to her—churning through her mind. Her nerves were raw. More than anything else she was bewildered—by Marcus, by the passion and turmoil of her own feelings. Tears came quickly.

"Poor Tess." Joan put a strong hand on her shoulder. "That journalist chap, is it?"

Tessa nodded.

"I thought it must be because of the *Chronicle* lying around the place every day."

Tessa tried again to smile—but couldn't.

"I've only seen him once when he came in here looking for you." She struck a match. "Your Dad won't like it, you know."

"No fear." Tears were streaming down her face now and she dashed them away with her hand, sniffing.

"Come out to the back." She shepherded Tessa into the work-room and handed her a wad of paper tissues. "Poor old love, go on then, sit down and have a good weep . . ." The shop doorbell rang. "Bloody hell, they would. I'll go. Back in a sec."

Whoever it was took at least fifteen minutes and by the time Joan came back, Tessa was reasonably composed but still sniffing and red-eyed.

"Sorry. I didn't mean to do that to you. You're a brick, Joan."

"Look—I don't know the first thing about affairs of the heart. I was born an old maid." They smiled at each other with affection. "I'm probably putting my foot in it, but you know if you ever want to use the mews . . ."—Joan kept a tiny mews house round the corner where she stayed the occasional night—"it's yours. Any time. I can never wait to get back to the country even if it does mean getting up before dawn to go to the market. Here you go." She took some keys off a peg and handed them to Tessa.

Tessa laughed a bit shakily. "I'm sure I shan't need it, Joanie. But thanks all the same." She sighed. "It's good to be able to talk to somebody—it does help."

"I don't want to pry. Whatever you do is your own business. I'm a great believer in that. But you know I'm always around if you need me, any hour of the day or night. I never sleep much these days. By the way, I see Reardon's doing something new in the paper. A column of his own, is it?"

"That's right. It starts next week—he's very involved in it . . ."

"Well—as long as you're happy." Joan stared doubtfully at Tessa's reddened eyes and the dark circles beneath them. "Not married, is he?"

Tessa shook her head. "No, he never has been."

"He's a lot older than you, Tess." Joan smoked away thoughtfully. "Of course, I only saw him that once . . ." She wanted to say something but didn't quite know how. "He didn't look—well—what I would have expected for you. That's all."

"He isn't, Joan. That's the trouble."

Joan dragged away at the cigarette. Then she asked suddenly, "Is he kind?"

"No—I don't think he is." Tessa blew her nose.

"All I can say is, I hope he's worth it."

Late that afternoon, Oliver came charging into the shop, all elbows and shoulders, narrowly missing a vase of peonies with his briefcase. Tessa, who had been moping about all day not really settling to anything, cheered up at the sight of him. When she phoned to thank him for returning her shawl, he had said he expected to be around here today. But she had forgotten.

"Oliver, you've found us. What a lovely surprise!"

"I had to call in at a shop near here—about some curtains for the house, actually—and I couldn't resist dropping in on you. I hope I'm not in the way."

"Of course not—don't be silly. I'm *so* pleased you did. And we're not busy now either. The rush usually starts again when people begin to drift home from work."

Oliver looked round with interest.

"What a delightful shop. It feels very personal and cosy. I'm hopeless at flowers —I hardly remember any names, but these all look so fresh and pretty."

Tessa introduced him to Joan who grinned at him, sticking out a wet hand. She looked at them both with interest.

"Why don't you two hop out the back and have a cup of coffee? Go on. I'll hold the fort out here, Tess."

Tessa plugged in the kettle and made them mugs of coffee while Oliver hoisted himself on to one of the work-stools.

"Where are the curtains for?" Tessa asked, stirring in sugar for Oliver.

"The drawing-room. I don't expect you noticed the other night, but the ones I've got now are in shreds." She hadn't. "And I thought I'd treat myself to some new ones and hope they buck up the room until I can get it painted. Here . . ." He put down the mug and began foraging in his briefcase. "These are the sample bits I've just picked up round the corner. This is

336

the one I've decided on. What do you think?"

Tessa looked doubtfully at the small piece of coarse, putty-coloured fabric.

"Isn't it a bit dull? I mean—you can get material in such wonderful colours and chintzes, it seems a shame not to use them." And in a beautifully proportioned room like that, she thought, it would be hard to go wrong.

"Oh no, something plain is definitely best," Oliver disagreed confidently. "The curtains there always have been. I wouldn't want anything splashy. Those wide tassel ties will dress them up, so the woman in the shop says. And they're going to make them."

It was all sounding worse and worse to Tessa, but she knew from Tom that once Oliver's mind was made up he rarely changed it. Not that his curtains were any of her business.

"I expect they'll be splendid," she said tactfully. "Are you snowed under with work?"

"God, yes. You can't see my desk under all the paperwork I haven't yet got down to . . ." He finished off his coffee and looked at his watch. "I must go back and get down to it. But before I go, could we make a date for lunch? That's really why I came in—to pin you down. There's a decent little French restaurant I know a couple of streets away from here." He slid off the stool and looked at her intently; his face was unusually serious, his huge frame seemed to fill the small room. "As a matter of fact, since I'm not in court this week, what about tomorrow?"

On their way out, squeezing past arrangements waiting to be collected, he complimented Joan on the shop as he said goodbye. He had parked his car at a crazy angle, half on and half off the pavement. After waving him off, Tessa came back smiling, some colour in her face. For the first time that day, she felt like a human being.

"What a super young chap," Joan commented, looking at Tessa and blinking.

"Yes, he's nice, isn't he? I've known him for ages—through Tom. Oliver *always* seems to cheer everyone up."

13

WHEN Tessa came in from work on Friday, quite late, she felt tired and grubby. She had heard nothing further from Marcus since he had dropped her back after dinner earlier in the week. That morning in the *Chronicle*, as part of the final stages of his publicity build-up, there had been a grainy photograph of him taken during the war, in flying suit and goggles, clambering into an RAF plane; underneath, a brief resumé of his celebrated record which was made to sound glamorous as well as extremely courageous.

Reading it in snatched moments many times over, Tessa felt alternately buoyant and despairing. Once, in a fit of heart-stopping blackness, it occurred to her that she might never see him again.

"Saw old what's-his-name in the paper this morning," Joan said cheerfully as she helped Tessa clear up the mess in the workroom. "So he was one of the boys in blue was he? I bet he broke a few hearts in his time." She added tactlessly, "They were the very devil with the girls, that lot."

On and off throughout the day Tessa asked herself: was he working at the paper, in his flat, or scouring the continent for whatever story he was after? Although she would not, *would not,* get in touch with him (she had some pride, she told herself unconvincingly), the photograph made her think of Gran. She went straight to the desk and telephoned her. Vi took such a long time to answer that Tessa was about to give up when the phone was picked up—clumsily. Tessa realised that she had woken her up because she seemed not to recognise her granddaughter immediately.

"Oh Tessa, it's you," she said, her voice shaky. "I was having a bit of a lie-down . . . Sam's funeral knocked me out rather and I've been a bit under par . . . Tonight? Well, if you feel like coming over, darling . . ." She sounded doubtful. "All right, then, we'll have something on a tray, with Charlie."

Tessa remembered when she got home

that they hadn't said anything about time. So she would change and get there early. Gran had sounded tired, quite worryingly so. She wouldn't stay late.

About to descend to Ella's flat for a quick chat as she always did when she got in from work, Tessa heard voices—and stopped. There was a peal of feminine laughter, a man's deeper response and then Ella's soft, faintly Welsh sing-song. Without any doubt, it was Tom and Angie and Ella. And they seemed to be having a very jolly time.

Tessa sighed and hesitated. Facing Angie again so soon after their lunch was the last thing she wanted. She was feeling glum enough as it was. But realising that there was nothing for it but to join them, she called out and went down.

They were in Ella's comfortable sitting-room, the long windows open on to the terrace. Angie, mint fresh in a white linen dress, was sitting in the rocking chair, Tessa's special place. Morgan was lying curled in her lap, encircled by her long and lovely arms.

"There you are, Tess. I said you'd be n soon if they waited a few more minutes." Ella, her eyes bright with excitement, was positively glowing. Tom had always been her favourite, although, fair-minded as she was, she had tried to conceal it. She had been worried about him recently. He hadn't seemed to be enjoying his work; he had kept away from Parloe Square. He and his father were as quarrelsome as ever, the pair of them. And now, suddenly, here he was with this beautiful girl, both of them looking happy as the day was long. They made such a handsome couple; she couldn't wait to tell Maggie even though you couldn't go jumping to conclusions . . .

"H'llo Tess." Tom was sprawled on the sofa, still in his formal black coat and striped trousers, looking through some papers.

"You do look exhausted, poor Tessa. Was it a dreadful day at the shop?" Angie said, looking at her with rather too much sympathy for Tessa's liking.

"Not too bad," she said shortly, plonking herself down next to Tom.

Neither made any mention of their lunch together.

"I did so want to meet Ella." Angie

smiled straight at her. "I'd heard so much about her that I pestered Tom to bring me when he finished in Chambers early today. We had a good, strong cuppa, Tessa, and a piece of Ella's wicked chocolate cake."

Dazzled by Angie's flattery and her beauty, Ella murmured, "A little bit of what you fancy, as they say, does you good —and you can't be worrying about your figure all the time."

"Oh, I don't. And I had a tour of the house, didn't I, Ella?" Looking back at Tessa, Angie said, "I think it's absolutely lovely. All the antiques and the paintings . . . and the curtains in the drawing-room, that heavenly purple, are so smart."

"Do you think so? We've always loathed them, haven't we Tom?" Tessa knew she sounded sullen and ungracious—and didn't care. Seeing the charming picture Angie made—her hair pulled loosely back, rocking gently as she stroked the cat—she was depressingly conscious of her own untidiness and creased cotton skirt.

Tom looked up. "Have we?" he asked mildly. "They don't look too bad to me."

"Tom you *hated* them, you know you did, you said they looked like royal mourning . . ." Tessa spoke vehemently, her cheeks flushed.

"Now, you two," Ella said indulgently. "We don't have 'words', not at your ages. Morgan really seems to have taken to you, Angie; he won't go to everyone." Morgan, hearing his name, raised his head, yawned, and went back to sleep. You traitor, Morgan, Tessa thought bitterly. And we *have* always loathed those beastly curtains, Ella too.

"Tom used to sit in that rocking chair when he was waiting for the taxi to come and take him to the station to go back to Marlborough. He used to rock the chair until I thought it would come apart, all neat in his grey suit, waiting for the front door bell to ring. Remember that, Tom?"

"I suppose I do." He put the papers he had been holding on one side. "I expect it was nerves." He gazed at Angie.

"Did you go away to school, dear?" Ella asked kindly.

"Er—no." Angie's glance swerved away from Tom. "No, I didn't. I hated school as a matter of fact. Towards the end, I hardly turned up at all."

"Gracious," said Ella, puzzled. "We

never wanted to send you away, though, did we Tessa?"

Tessa jumped up without answering. "I must go and get changed. I'm going over to see Gran tonight, Ella. I'll have something to eat with her. She sounds a bit lonely."

"Just as well you're going, dear. I meant to pop over myself this week but somehow the time flies by what with this and that —even though there's not the rush with Mr. Selway being away . . . Oh, you know Tom went to the office, Tess?"

"To Selways? Whatever for?"

Tom pushed his hand through his fair hair and looked faintly embarrassed. "I thought I'd look in, see what reports Pa's lieutenants had been getting back from the States, how things were going. Actually, they gave me these—copies of some of the correspondence to do with the company he's trying to buy. It's one of the largest electrical companies over there." He handed her a piece of newsprint. "This is quite interesting. It's an article from the *New York Times* headed The Brits Are Buying. Lots of English companies over there on fishing expeditions at the moment, apparently . . . and Papa and Selway Electric are mentioned."

"Goodness, Tom." Tess glanced at the cutting. "This is the first time I've *ever* known you take the remotest interest in Papa's affairs. Why on earth now?"

"Oh, I don't know . . . it's a very big deal, this one. I suppose one ought to take some pride in the old man's achievements. They've housed and educated us, after all. Apparently, if all goes well they hope to close the deal in a week or two. It's in all the financial pages." He sounded sheepish.

"I should think you *would* both be terribly proud of your father," Angie put in sharply. "I'm sure he'll be pleased to hear you took the trouble to go to the office, Tom. And did you tell Tessa that we're going to see your mother in Dorset this weekend?"

"How did you get hold of her, Tom?" Their mother steadfastly refused to have a phone and could only be reached, with difficulty, via the village post office.

"I spoke to Marie and she sent the taxi over and phoned me back. We're going on Saturday. I don't suppose you want to come do you?" It was not an enthusiastic invitation and Tessa declined.

"I will go down soon, though," she said.

"That's all right then." Tom sounded relieved, stretched—and began jingling the change in his pocket. "I'll tell her. It's best to write, really—otherwise she tends to forget and there's nothing but bread and cheese in the house and Felix spends the whole time apologising. Heaven knows," he said to Angie, "how our half-brother Max grew up into such a normal kid with her eccentric mothering."

"I really must be going now," said Tess.

"Give my love to Gran," Tom called after her.

"I fancy a drop of brandy, Tessa darling," Vi Delmore said, waving in the direction of the drinks tray. "Help yourself to what you want. It's all there. Not sure about the ice . . ." She sounded vague. And she didn't look well. Tessa saw this the moment she opened the door. In the few weeks since Grandpa Delmore's funeral and Flora Flood's party, her appearance had altered noticeably. Her cheeks looked sunken and she seemed to have lost weight. She stooped. Although she had on a good silk dress and her pearls, she was wearing slippers which flapped as she walked.

"Lovely to see you, darling," she said as Tessa handed her the brandy. With a sigh, she settled back into her habitual corner of the sofa. The cushions there were deeply creased and there was a woolly rug beside her on which Charlie was asleep. The ashtray was full of half-smoked stubs. Tessa had a hunch that she had spent most of the day there. She had a bad colour; she looked haggard. Tessa frowned: should she say anything? Suggest a doctor?

"I hope you've been looking after yourself, Gran," she said finally, sitting in an armchair with her shoes off and her feet tucked under her.

"Oh—well enough. I'm not much interested in 'looking after' any more. What about yourself, darling? I hear you've seen Marcus Reardon once or twice. He can be fun when he tries, can't he?"

Something inside Tessa fluttered and quickened. "He saved the day rather after

Papa and Tom had that row at the gallery. Yes," she said airily, "I do like him. He's good company. Very interesting. And he's got his own column now—did you hear?"

"He popped in and told me. Long may it last say I. He's not famous for sticking to jobs." She took her brandy glass in both hands.

So she knew. And he *had* been in to see her.

"I think he's away again, isn't he?" Vi sounded confused. "I got a card from him just the other day." She put down the glass and pushed at a heap of papers on the table beside her. "It's around here somewhere . . . I can't think where exactly."

Tessa sipped her drink, frowning. Gran wasn't herself tonight. The blue eye-shadow was messy and her mouth, always so carefully painted, was an orange blur.

"Tom sent his love, Gran. He's got a new girl. She's called Angie and she's a model. She's very beautiful. Actually, Tom met her through Marcus."

Vi didn't appear to be listening properly.

"No, I can't find that card he sent

349

anywhere." She stopped riffling through the papers and collapsed back against the cushions. "France, I think. Yes, that's it. Tom met her, this girl, through Marcus you say?"

"That's right."

"In that case," she said decisively, "she can't be anything to write home about . . ." She took a swig of brandy. "That much I can tell you. Nice if he takes you about a bit, darling, Marcus. He has his points; I regard him as a friend." Her eyes half closed.

Tessa said desperately, genuinely worried now, "Tell me—what have you been doing with yourself, Gran?"

"Me?" Eyes opened again. "Living in the past, to tell you the truth. And I find I like it better these days—than the present, that is." She smiled groggily.

Tessa swallowed. What on earth was she talking about? Surely, she thought, horrified, she can't be going soft in the head? Not Gran?

"What part of the past?" Tessa asked cagily.

Vi seemed not to have heard her. "I was sorry about Sam, after all," she said clearly, as though to some invisible listener, some unknown contemporary, not Tessa. "You could say we grew up together, all those years and years ago. Guilty? Well —I must have felt a bit, mustn't I? Leaving him like that, poor Sam, in that ghastly house. After he died, a thread snapped. I could feel it going." She was looking beyond Tessa, not seeing her, somewhere into the distance. "Before that, I think I thought David was going to walk in one day. I didn't really believe, not until Sam went, that he was dead." She looked back at Tessa, focused again. "Funny, the tricks the mind plays, isn't it? You mustn't listen to me, darling, I'm fast becoming a silly old woman." She reverted briefly to her normal, brisk manner.

"But now I feel as though I've only got Ben. And Charlie." She shivered, lifted the dozy dog on to her lap, and pulled the rug round both of them. "I'll have a drop more, Tess, please." She held out her glass.

"Ben?" Tessa got up and poured a very small amount of brandy.

351

"Ben Levson. You remember him, don't you?"

Tessa thought back. "Didn't he wear hats all the time?" she asked.

"In the end he did, when he was with me here—in Eaton Square. He always said his ears were cold in this country. He said the hats kept them warm and to hell with the conventions." She laughed happily. "They all came from that place in St. James's—you know the one. Lock's. They're still there, in the dressing-room."

"And something else I associate with him, Gran. Cigars. I remember being with him—here? At Chalcot? And thinking he smelled of cigars."

"Quite right. And always the same ones. A most peculiar sweetish scent they had The first time I met him, in the South of France—at luncheon on his yacht, that very first time—I asked him if he was ever, ever, without a cigar in his hand. And he grinned, he had very white teeth and of course he always went marvellously brown, and he said, Jesus lady not when I'm f——. My dear, I was *so shocked*. You've no idea how sheltered we were in those days."

"Gran . . ." Tessa was appalled, scarlet in the face. *"Gran . . ."*

"And that was when it all began, of course," she went on imperturbably. "Such fun we had over the years, in all the best places . . . He was so *clever*, Ben. And terribly, terribly rich on account of those face creams his great aunt used to make in Hungary." Tessa blinked, still reeling. Gran had never spoken like this with such breathtaking candour; she was only just managing to follow her. "He always came back to me after those dreadful wives. Four of them—or was it five? He only liked the first one, but she was put out to grass long before I came on the scene. Once, he telephoned on his honeymoon and told me to fly straight out to wherever he was. In one of those noisy old planes, so slow . . . He sent the wife packing—and that was the end of her. He always said he kept acquiring them because I wouldn't marry him. And he adored the idea of being married—it made him feel so *respectable*. All the same—I think I was right there. I'm sure of it. Sad in the end when he was so ill and nothing, not even all that money, could help him."

She was staring out into space again.

"Shall I get us something to eat?" Tessa asked. "You probably haven't had anything all day. Ella meant to come and see you this week . . ." And how I wish she had, Tessa thought. "Don't move. I'll go and have a look in the kitchen."

"Phyllis left some bread and butter—and I think there was something else . . ."

"But not much," Tessa said aloud, surveying the almost empty refrigerator. In it was a bottle of milk, an aged lemon, some smoked salmon and, curiously, four packets of digestive biscuits. The bread and butter was on the table. Beside it was a scrawled note. "Dear Lady D. Ever so sorry but I shan't be in next week what with my sister's boy getting married. Ta for now. Phyllis."

That settled it. She would tell Ella without mentioning it to Gran and they would decide what to do. She couldn't stay here alone. She really needed someone living in, looking after her. She peered around the kitchen. There was a damp floor cloth under the sink which was beginning to smell; the old linoleum floor didn't look very clean. In fact, the whole flat, despite the beautiful objects, was looking dusty and run down. It couldn't have had a lick of paint for years.

Tessa threw out the lemon and put the bread and butter on a tray with the smoked salmon—fresh and good, obviously ordered that day from the fishmonger round the corner. In a cupboard, she found the remains of a jar of instant coffee so she filled the kettle and put it on.

When she took the tray into the drawing-room she saw that Vi had generously refilled her glass.

"Heavenly salmon, Gran," she said, "but you're living very sparsely these days as far as food is concerned." She looked pointedly at the glass. "Here you are. Now eat up."

Tessa was starving and ate quickly. Vi picked at hers for a few moments and pushed it away. "Not hungry, Tess. Here —finish mine up. I'm sorry, darling." She sounded genuinely contrite. "I should have taken you out somewhere or got more food in. You were always such a tomboy as a child," she added obscurely.

"I expect it was having an old brother —Tom."

They were quiet for a bit, then Vi asked, "How's George? He's gone off somewhere too, hasn't he? I don't know what's happening to my memory these days."

"He's in the States, Gran. With Poppy. Doing some tremendous deal, according to Tom."

"Good old George. He must be making a packet. Of course he inherited plenty— and the business—from his father. But that was before you were born . . . Getting on with him all right, are you?"

"So-so. Life is more peaceful when he's not around, Gran."

"That's right. I never did like him much though I suppose I shouldn't say so— although I don't know why not. He was middle-aged even as quite a young man. Rigid. We all thought he'd look after Jennie, who was so dim. It all seemed quite suitable."

"Well, it *wasn't*, Gran."

"No indeed. Quite the opposite. I never really blamed Jennie for getting out. I don't think people should be expected to

356

live unhappily—*I* didn't. We all make mistakes. Although it was mightily inconvenient at the time. And of course the shocking way she did it. Tasteless and very nasty, I didn't approve of *that*. I don't expect you remember."

Tessa did—but she said nothing.

"We came down to Chalcot for lunch on a Sunday and had a bit of a council of war. Jennie was in that dreary cottage with Felix by then, Max well on the way. Ben always thought Jennie was so beautiful when she was a child—and after . . . he took quite an interest in her, in fact. Galleries and things like that," she said vaguely. "Anyhow, about Jennie going off . . . the Floods were marvellous, bless them, and I found Ella. Everything works out in the end," she finished bleakly.

"You've hardly touched your coffee, Gran. It must be cold. Shall I make you another cup?"

Vi shook her head. "I'll stick to the brandy, darling." She tipped back her glass and took a generous mouthful. "And Tess—I do love the hair; keep it short like that, it looks very soft and pretty . . . nice colour and you won't lose it, either. That gingery hair stays."

"I'm glad you like it, Gran," Tessa said smiling and reached out to touch her hand.

"And there's something else. It's been bothering me all evening. You look— better. Different. *Glowing*, yes that's the word. Happy, are you?"

Tessa blushed. "More or less. Well— *yes*, in a way. You feel cold, Gran. Are you sure I can't get you another blanket or anything? I've got to get going soon because I'm doing the market at Covent Garden in the morning . . ."

Apparently out of the blue, Vi said clearly, "You know, I think Marcus is going to be very successful at last. I feel it in my bones. Nice that you two get along." Tessa started and blinked. "I thought—I don't know—that he would get you out of a rut. Different to what you're used to. Know what I mean?" She yawned.

After a pause, blushing, heart hammering wildly, Tessa murmured, "I do know, Gran."

She thought: Incredible. She's a wily old girl for all her apparent mumblings and confusion. She had deliberately thrown

Marcus and her together . . . she had suspected as much all along. Where—and how?—was it going to end?

Pulling herself together, she remembered it was time she was off. She got up and stood looking down at Vi and Charlie huddled together on the sofa. She hated leaving her alone like this. She looked so old and small and vulnerable. For all her canniness, she sounded frighteningly out-of-touch.

"If there's nothing you want, Gran, I really should go home."

"That shop of yours, I suppose . . . well, off you go darling. Lovely to have you with me."

Tessa kissed her cheek. "Ella wants to come and see you soon, Gran. Maybe tomorrow."

"All right, darling. I'll remember. You won't mind if I don't see you out? Charlie and I must get ourselves organised for his constitutional—a breath of air will do us both good. 'Night, 'night, darling Tessa . . ."

14

IN bed with Marcus the following Sunday evening, Tessa propped herself on her side, leaning on her elbow. The bed was so narrow, almost a cot, that it was the only way she could talk to him without falling out.

"You must go and see Gran again," she said. "She looks terrible and she sounds dotty. I'm quite worried about her."

Marcus shifted on the pillow. They had been in bed, intermittently sleeping and making love, since lunchtime. Tracing the outline of her neck with his fingers, he began kissing her breasts for the hundredth time.

"Marcus, be serious." But her senses were already beginning to respond. . warming, melting, not to be resisted. She knew there was a world away from all this Somewhere . . . "Marcus . . ."

"I am . . ." he eased his body beneath

hers, "very serious about you—us. We'll talk later, there's a good girl."

When they were dressing, Tessa said, "Gran seems to be letting go, living on brandy and digestive biscuits, of all things. She either makes no sense at all—or too much. Her conversation is *most* peculiar. Her daily has packed up. Ella goes round most days but Gran obviously doesn't want her there, she says. Can you go and see her?"

"I did pop in the other day and she seemed all right. About as usual, but all right, I will. This week."

"Try."

"I promise." He looked at his watch and Tessa saw him.

"Do you want to go to the paper?"

Although they had obliterated the past few hours, Tessa had some idea of the nervous tension which had been building in him. The presses would be rolling now. That first important column—all done; too late to change. For better or worse.

He yanked at the bedclothes, "No. What I really feel like is some exercise. Of a different kind." He kissed the top of her

361

head. "Walking around, a pint in a pub, then I'd like to pick up a first edition of the paper somewhere, somewhere anonymous like anyone else will. See how it looks . . ." He sounded edgy, restless.

"I'll come with you."

"I'd like that."

"Haven't you got something warmer to wear?" It had been a cloudy, showery day and she had come out in a cotton skirt and blouse and a mac. She shook her head. Marcus opened a drawer and tossed her a sweater.

"Here. Put that on."

They left the flat around ten. It had stopped raining but the sky was still leaden, streaked with grey and yellowish clouds. They started walking, fast but aimlessly—through Soho, across Piccadilly, down the Haymarket. They didn't talk much. A soft rain began to fall and they went into the nearest pub—poorly lit, smelling of spilled beer, the sort of place Tessa would never see in her usual life. Marcus ordered a pint of bitter and Tessa a lemonade. He downed the beer quickly while Tessa took a gulp of the lemonade, grimaced—and left it. By the time they came out, the traffic had fallen off noticeably and there weren't many people about. A drying breeze had sprung up.

Once, he stopped. "My poor Tessa. Are you exhausted?"

"No."

"Where does Ella think you are?"

"At Joan's mews house."

"You're very good to me," he said humbly.

He took her arm as they plunged across Trafalgar Square. Soon after, they stopped at an all night café and ate sausages and chips washed down with pots of tea. Then they walked on . . . across Waterloo Bridge, leaning over the parapet to watch the dark, flowing river.

It was well after two when at last they stood outside Charing Cross Station and saw the vans begin to arrive. Bundles of newspapers, first editions, just off the presses; chucked out and wheeled off to the trains. Cleaners pushed at piles of rubbish with stiff brooms. An odd taxi trundled past. London was slowed, mysterious with night.

"Come on, let's go and get one." Tessa

pulled his arm, genuinely excited, looking back at him. "I'm dying to see it . . ." She was. He didn't move. His expression was impassive.

Tessa realised quite suddenly that he couldn't face it. Not even after all the work, the doggedness, the hectic pace. The lightning-quick ideas—nosed out and followed up. Everything that he was had gone into this. It was, he believed, his last chance.

She put her arms round him, standing so close that the open raincoat he had slung on—hours and hours ago it seemed —encompassed them both. He held her very tightly, his face dropped, buried in her neck.

What was he afraid of? Failure? Tomorrow's column which was now today's? His reputation—himself—on the line? Some anguish from the past intruding?

She stared over his shoulder into the blackness. A sort of wisdom came to her. Self-preservation perhaps. Quite calmly. She knew that she loved him—and that there was no hope for it. Just like that.

Soon, she said quietly.

"Let's go and find Marcus Reardon in the *Chronicle,* shall we?" And he grasped her wrist and they started walking to the deserted news-stand.

By the end of the week, it was clear that The Marcus Reardon Column in the *Chronicle* was already creating a stir. And after two weeks, his success was certain. Marcus's photograph appeared above it. The muddy newsprint accentuated his gauntness; he looked, if not handsome, at least photogenic. He had the sort of face which the public seemed to expect of a journalist.

Each day in the week before the column first ran, short, biographical "puffs" about Marcus Reardon (hammering away to make the name familiar) appeared in the paper: they cited his journalistic stints, his interviews, his solid pieces of investigative reporting.

No one needed to know that he had never stayed on any paper for long; that his best work had been freelance; that he had a tendency to heated arguments when crossed professionally. That when fired—or after storming angrily out of a newsroom—he would take off, usually alone, and head for the continent, where he would stay for as long as the money held out—return, and start the same cycle again.

His new editor, who had known Marcus since the war, had long had his eye on him. He had always considered that Marcus had *style*. And it happened that he heard of Marcus's latest upset just at the time when he had determined to create a new Name on the *Chronicle*—sales needed a boost, circulation had been slipping over the past few months. The paper, he felt, was too anonymous, too bland; he wanted a seasoned writer whom readers could come to identify with, turn to automatically so many mornings a week—be *entertained* by.

The brief was broad: London's social, political and arts scene—part gossip, part news background, part comment. Pithily and intelligently presented. With the Marcus Reardon touch and point of view. He had a hunch, which proved correct, that Marcus had the ability and the charisma to do the job and start to build a following.

He did—but he was also lucky, even in that first column which he and Tessa pored over in the early hours of Monday, drinking tepid cups of coffee in the glaring light of an empty all-night café. Because he happened to have hit on a story which, however ephemeral, had, put crudely, gut appeal.

It had come to him by chance and he was in two minds whether to include it among the rest of the material he had for that day. Fortunately, he did—because it was immediately picked up by the rest of the Press. It made a brief news item in the quality dailies; headlines in the tabloids. Importantly, it resulted in the *Chronicle* being hit by a libel action brought by a member of the Cabinet. This ensured, from the word go, that Marcus Reardon was a journalist in the know—one to be read and reckoned with.

All this stemmed from Marcus having *suggested*, among several other topics that first Monday, that a Member of Parliament's recent trip to Paris, supposedly to investigate French farming methods, was in fact no more than a short holiday at the taxpayers' expense—with his mistress in tow. Coming at a time when the public had been asked to tighten their belts—taxes in the previous budget increased on both beer and cigarettes—alert editors seized on this as a hot item. The whiff of sexual scandal, the blonde mistress-cum-secretary, added spice.

While Marcus sat back, hugely enjoying the commotion and getting on with his work, conscientious reporters started digging. Questions were asked in the House of Commons. And a day or so later, to Marcus's delight, a photograph appeared in a down-market daily—of the politician, his girlfriend and a delegate from the Soviet Embassy in Paris, at Maxim's, all smiling stupidly and looking slightly drunk.

A predictable scenario followed: a terse statement was put out by the Foreign Office citing the importance of trade links, shared agricultural knowledge, bridges to be built with communist countries etc, etc. The politician was seen (photographers from the Wire Services tipped off in advance) leaving his London house with furrowed brow and briefcase, accompanied by his wife, smiling bravely, and a clutch of children. The afternoon papers carried the report that he had instructed his lawyers to sue the *Chronicle*.

When the fuss had begun to die down, Marcus's editor and the politician, who had known each other for years, shared a good bottle of claret at one of London's exclusive clubs. The "unfortunate business" was mentioned once only, as they were waiting to get their coats. Brief, tough remarks were exchanged on both sides. The two men then shook hands, sent best wishes to their respective wives by name, and went their separate ways.

That afternoon, a tame apology was drafted which would run in the *Chronicle* the following day. After a brief consultation during which the draft was read over the phone, the politician's lawyers agreed to withdraw the action. The story was dead. (It had been a nine-day wonder, anyhow.) But The Marcus Reardon Column had taken off . . .

Well pleased, the editor phoned Marcus at the flat where he was bashing out copy. Sleeves rolled up, tieless, a pot of coffee by his elbow. Few people knew his home number. He had always been cautious about this. When he got his stories, checked and re-checked his sources, this was where he concentrated hardest, not in the noisy, frenetic newsroom.

"Glad you approved," Marcus told him, cradling the receiver, eyes still on the copy in front of him. "You settled with old so-and-so, then." He mentioned the politician.

"Yes, that's fixed. And he's lucky to get out of it so lightly. You saw what we're printing?"

"Nicely ambivalent."

"That's right. And I like the piece of yours we're running tomorrow, Friday. I've got the proofs here now. Just keep it up, that's all. Keep it up."

Tessa came in later, arms full of packages from the delicatessen. She was breathless and excited.

"A hectic day, we never stopped. I'm exhausted. And it's my turn to go to the market tomorrow. Still hard at it?" she asked sympathetically, glancing over at his desk. He took the packages from her. "But your next deadline isn't until Sunday . . ."

"True—but deadlines have a nasty way of sneaking up on one. This smells good. What is it?"

"Roast chicken—and other bits and pieces. The remains of one of Ella's apple pies. I went home from the shop on my way . . ." Marcus took the bags into the kitchen and Tessa removed her cardigan and inspected the plant she had given him.

"I see you're looking after the lily," she called out. She flopped into a chair as Marcus came in with two glasses. "And there's something I really want to tell you, something exciting . . . Papa phoned from Chicago. They signed the deal today, this morning their time. Selway Electric now owns Butanes, which is also an electrics company but about ten times larger. I knew it was likely, that's why Papa rushed over there, but it seemed terribly remote. Now that it's actually happened, I suppose I do feel rather thrilled."

"So you should. Actually, I did know . . ." He was fiddling with the ice bucket.

"But how? It's not being announced until tomorrow, Papa told me. How could you have?" She looked crestfallen.

371

"I spent much of the day in the newsroom at the *Chronicle*—and these are the sort of things that get talked about there. You're looking very sweet, dearest Tessa. Come and give me a kiss. A decent one. Over here. I need resuscitating."

"Are you stuck with the work?" she asked after a while. "And could you move your arm a bit? That's better." He pushed a cushion off the sofa with his foot.

"No worse than usual." He closed his eyes. "Writing—it's like breaking stones."

The sudden despair in his voice shocked her. She turned to him. He looked exhausted, white, like a figure carved on a tomb. "But you can do it, Marcus," she said helplessly. "You make it seem so easy; it reads so well, just as if you were there, in the room, talking . . ."

"Sometimes." Eyes still closed. "It's a discouraging business."

They lay there quietly for a couple of minutes. "All the same," Tessa said sensibly, "you've had the most marvellous run with the column. The MP story picked up, the bit about the statue with its toes missing . . . and people are talking about you. *They are*, Marcus. When I was getting dressed someone I heard on the radio said "Marcus Reardon in the *Chronicle* mentions . . ."

He folded his arms tightly across her back. "I know. You brought me luck," he said.

After a large whisky, over supper, he cheered up. The cold chicken she had brought was moist and delicious and he had foraged in the refrigerator and made a presentable salad.

"I'm busy on Thursday," Tessa said casually. "I'm having dinner with Oliver."

Since the column burst, Marcus was frantic almost every waking moment. Tessa never knew when he was going to phone, as he had that afternoon, telling her he was free, he was missing her, please come . . . *which she did.* She worked in the shop and at the market efficiently; but inwardly she was in turmoil—rushing to answer the phone, half-hoping it was Marcus, half glad when it wasn't. She was evasive with Ella. She had caught Joan looking at her anxiously. It had occurred to her several times that she felt more than anything else as though she had caught some minor illness—heady; heartstopping; miserable.

And Oliver was making a dead set at her since his party. There was no mistaking that. He phoned constantly; they had thoroughly enjoyed lunching together and he had insisted on a firm date for dinner on Thursday.

If only, if only it had been last winter —before Marcus.

"Good old Oliver. There's a nice bit of cheese somewhere . . ." Marcus peered into various tins. "Ah, here we go. I must say, he knows how to throw a party, does Oliver. In fact, I'm dining in the Commons on Thursday. And I had thought of popping in on Vi on my way there."

With Oliver, dinner, Marcus thought, slightly more ruffled than he would have wanted. *Piqued*—and he would be the first to say so. Ridiculous—and he had seen that night how much they had in common. Backgrounds. Tom's friend. Almost shared childhoods apparently. And seeing him turn up with Tessa at his party had given him a jolt all right. That had been obvious—at least to Marcus.

"I wish you would—you'd cheer her up", Tessa was saying. "Ella says she's a bit better. She went out and got her hair done today. But she still gets muddled and lies a lot—says she's eaten when she hasn't, maintains the daily still comes which she doesn't. I don't think she can be bothered with people any more. But she'd love to see you, I know."

"I won't tell her I'm coming. I'll just appear. No cheese?" Tessa shook her head.

"No thanks. I wonder how Tom and Angie got on with Mother and Felix. Angie phoned Ella and told her they were driving down last Sunday. By the way, Ella thinks Angie is wonderful. I suppose Tom knows about the Selway Electric deal. He seems to have kept in touch with the London office ever since Papa went over, casing this deal. It's extraordinary, quite unlike him. He usually never bothers about the business at all, says how much it bores him, how it has completely taken over Papa's life."

"I suppose it has. Your Dad must be in line for a knighthood now as long as he doesn't blot his copybook—and makes a few hefty donations in the right direction."

"Wow—were they saying that in the newsroom too?"

"You learn everything quickly."

"Rotter . . . try some of Ella's pie. It looks a bit battered but it tastes divine."

"When is he coming back, by the way?" He took the pie, regarding it cautiously.

"Papa? In about two weeks. He and Poppy are going somewhere—Palm Beach, I think. I spoke to Poppy too today. She's become terribly American all of a sudden. Papa has been overworking, she says, and they simply have to have a 'vacation'. Not a holiday—a *vacation*."

"You are unkind about the woman. If she keeps your father occupied, you should be pleased."

"If he becomes Sir George, she'll marry him, that's the trouble," Tessa said gloomily. "And then she'll be my step-mother." She scraped the last of the pie on to Marcus's plate. "You know, the way you get your information is a mystery to me. You never told me how you got on to the story of the Paris junket. Did someone tip you off?"

Marcus shook his head. "Do you

remember that restaurant I took you to? In Chelsea?"

"Of course."

"Well, I saw our friend the MP lunching there with another man. I know the mistress lives round the corner; I've known her for years as a matter of fact. She's an obliging girl." He forked some pie. "I simply thought that I'd give her a ring as she was likely to be alone, see if she had anything interesting to say. And it all poured out, giggle, giggle. She also told me that the chap from the Russian Embassy had his hand virtually up her knickers all the time they were at Maxim's. But I thought I'd leave that bit out in the interests of world peace."

"Good heavens, I should think so. But isn't she livid that you printed it and there was all the fuss?"

"On the contrary, she became queen for the day . . ."

"You are so cynical."

He shrugged. "Perhaps. But I assure you she's remained friendly. I've spoken to her since several times. I told you, she's an obliging girl. And she even gave me the number of their room at The Bristol. So checking it out was no problem."

"Do you think she wanted to—well, embarrass him—the politician lover?"

"Clever Tessa. Indeed I do—and so she did. He's a mean bugger and he's been promising her he'll leave his long-suffering wife for years. At least now she knows he never will."

The phone rang and Marcus went into the sitting-room to answer it. He came back, tossing his hair—which now very badly needed a cut. He had been asked, he said, to appear on the prestigious late-night news and comment programme on television. That night. He knew one of the producers and someone had let them down at the last minute and could he fill in.

"So I said I would. It's the best possible publicity for the paper. And me, of course." He glanced at his watch. "Look, I'll have to have a quick shave and change. One of the reasons they got hold of me is that I live so close and apparently they're desperate. Sorry to leave you and dash off like this, Tessa love."

"Heavens, Marcus. *Tonight*—that really is exciting. What on earth are you going to say? Don't you get nervous?" She looked impressed—happy, delighted for him. Wide-eyed, soft, pretty. "You see, things really are going well for you." She turned and began stacking the plates. "You'll have to hurry. What time will you be on? I must watch."

"Where?"

"At home, of course." Then she said —although she knew better—"Or here. I suppose I could square it with Ella, and stay." She put the glasses carefully in the sink.

Marcus came over to her and held her. "Could you?" he said. "Stay?"

Everything, except for his nearness, told her *no*. Marcus went on holding her, his mouth moving across her cheek, finding hers . . .

He had thought, moments before—none of his women ever, ever stayed. Hence the narrow bed in the monastic room. No matter what the time, the circumstances, the passion, even. He would drive them to kingdom come to be finally rid of their presence—however beguiling. He must wake up with the place to himself. Always. No clothes or combs or pins or general

379

female clutter. Even lingering scent displeased him. These were his rules, the rules he had made years and years ago; the basis of his unashamedly self-centred life-style.

"Please do," he said, still holding her. "Please, Tessa."

It was late by the time he got back to the flat. The show had gone well and he had been asked to stay on for a drink with two other guests—an economist and an actor—and the producer. Looking at his watch, he had reluctantly agreed. He couldn't afford to pass up that kind of conversational opportunity. In fact, he had picked up one or two interesting leads.

His key in the lock, he opened the door cautiously. There was one light left on in the sitting-room. He looked into the bedroom. He remembered later that he hadn't felt such an overpowering sense of relief since the days when, after a heavy night of bombing, he saw the lights of the familiar home airstrip beneath him . . .

"I was so proud—you were marvellous," Tessa said sleepily, out of the darkness. And he had been. At ease, informed a couple of short jokes so expertly told tha he had them all laughing without a trace of self-consciousness. He had looked good too, with his bony face, just the right amount of grey around the temples, hair brushed back so the length didn't really show. And he had remembered to wear a blue shirt.

He went over and sat on the bed. "You've no idea how glad I am that you didn't run out on me," he said lightly. "Not tonight, at least."

Tessa moved her head on the pillow. "But I did. I'm at Joan's house. You know that."

"Of course."

"I've set the alarm for five. I won't wake you."

He stroked her arm—gravely, tenderly. "What on earth have you got on?"

"The sweater that you lent me before. Remember?"

He threw off his jacket, loosened his tie. It was only moments before his hands—*those hands*—slid up her soft skin, beneath the rough wool, up and up. . . the sweater pulled over her head landing on the heap of Marcus's clothes. Their bodies together—so quickly. One, really. Both said things, deeply meant, which were not possible, although they did not know it, did not know anything except each other, not in those quick white-hot seconds. Several times Tessa cried out, although she did not know that either. Almost immediately, they slept, arms round each other, Tessa wedged up against the wall. And when the alarm went off, she thought at first that she would never be able to get up or leave that warm, narrow bed, with Marcus's leg flung across hers and her head against his shoulder.

She didn't bother to make coffee. Washed and dressed, she crept back into the bedroom. He had hardly stirred when she somehow disentangled herself and climbed out of bed. There was a grey half-light. She felt chilly, so she pulled Marcus's sweater off the tangled pile and put it on over her shirt.

That was when he woke.

"Tessa?" His arm shot out and pulled her back on the bed. "You were leaving . . .without saying goodbye . . ." His head buried in her lap, his voice muffled. She looked down at him.

"Yes," she whispered.

*She wanted to go and never see him
again. (Goodbye, goodbye.) Now, while
she still could; for both of their sakes.*

She wanted never to leave.

Painfully, she tore herself away—
throwing off his arm—picked up her bag
and ran out of the flat. She raced down
the stairs which were still quite dark and
out into the quiet street. Breathless,
shaking, she got to where her car was
parked. For a moment, she leant against it
. . . then she found her keys, got in, and
started to drive off towards Covent
Garden.

15

"**H**AVE a lovely time, you two," Ella called out as Tessa and Oliver left the house and walked to his car. They both turned and waved at her; she was standing at the open door watching them, looking so pleased—the last pink fingers of sun striking the fanlight above her. Neat and white-haired, she hadn't changed much since she had arrived on that same doorstep years before. Seeing her there as Oliver searched for his keys, Tessa felt a rush of affection.

"You're so sweet with her—with Ella," Tessa told Oliver as they roared up the square. "She adores you, you were always held up as an example to Tom." They both thought that was funny. And then it occurred to Tessa that Oliver was nice to everyone. He simply had a sunny, outgoing disposition which meant that he naturally made the best of people and situations. It was just Oliver. "She was thrilled you asked her to have a drink with us upstairs—and that you really talked to her and asked about Maggie and where they were going for their holiday."

So he had. But Oliver had the knack of making *whoever* he was talking to seem as though they were the only people in the world who mattered to him at that moment. As he liked most people anyway, and was always interested in what they were doing—very often, they were.

"North Wales again, she said. I hope they get a glimpse of the sun." He changed gears noisily, accelerated—and the car stalled. Oliver had a reputation for eccentric driving. Tessa had noticed that the bumpers of the car, which resembled a large black beetle, were badly dented. "Hell. Sorry about that." He got it going after a few tries and grinned at her. "I always have been a clumsy so-and-so and I've never got on terribly well with cars . . . Here we go . . . Oh Ella, I do like Ella. She's a really good sort. Mother was ill on and off all the time I was growing up and when we were at Marlborough I used to envy you and Tom having her fussing over you both. I shouldn't say that, I suppose. Mother did her best—it can't have been easy for her being ill and also the war . . ."

"Ella is the most marvellous looker-after. Thank heavens Gran found her. Papa must have been desperate, having us on his hands. Plus everything else—the divorce, the house, Selways. And she's very keen on Angie, by the way. Tom brought her back for tea the other day. What do *you* think about Tom and Angie, Oliver?" Tessa asked. He was, after all, Tom's oldest friend and they had both avoided discussing her until then.

After the slightest pause, "She's a stunning girl, all right. Tremendous poise and all that. They came round for a drink the other night so I got to know her a bit better." He frowned. "I'm not *absolutely* sure . . . How about you?"

"The same."

"When Tom turned up at the party with her I knew I'd seen her before somewhere. Fiona recognised her at once—and now, of course, I seem to see photographs of her wherever I look. Frankly, Tom seems deliriously happy with her, very contented —and that's the point, isn't it?"

He turned and smiled and looked at her

for such a long time that Tessa simply had to tell him to keep his eyes on the road.

"Quite right. By the way, I'm taking you somewhere new . . ." Squeezed between a bus and a taxi, Oliver narrowly missed both as Tessa flinched. "I thought this was a good opportunity to try it. Lots of friends have said it's excellent." He whipped past the taxi as the driver blew furiously on his horn. Oliver, unperturbed, waved merrily back. "It's in Chelsea which is why we're heading up this nightmare of the King's Road. It's called *Edwards.*"

Oh no, Tessa prayed, *Oh please God no* . . .

"You haven't been there, have you?"

"No," she lied, thinking: *It's sure to be crowded and Edward Thing wouldn't recognise me even if he saw me. But of all the restaurants in London . . . I suppose because it's new—and fashionable.*

"Good, I'm glad about that. I expect we'll see masses of people we know."

"I have heard about it," Tessa said faintly.

They were sailing on up the King's Road rather too fast when Oliver suddenly applied the brakes. The car screeched to a halt, and again horns blew about them. Tessa grabbed the door-handle.

"People *are* so impatient. I only slowed down." Oliver leant forward to read the street signs. "I think it's this one . . . No, must be the next." They lurched forward. "I'm not terribly sure of my whereabouts down here—London, as they say, is a series of villages. And this isn't mine."

They found the street and parked—some way from the kerb. Tessa almost fell out of the car as Oliver rushed to open the door. To Tessa's relief, the restaurant was full. All the smart magazines and Sunday papers had given it good reviews. It was becoming extremely popular among the educated, affluent young, and a stylish boutique, under the same ownership, had already opened next door with similar success. Both were now considered the last word in chic informality.

There was a crush of people waiting for tables in the tiny bar by the door. Oliver had booked so they plunged straight on downstairs with his broad shoulder clearing the way. He took Tessa's hand protectively, leading her down after him

At least four people—obviously old friends—shouted to him noisily as they went.

He waved back.

"I told you we'd know people here," he said happily, looking round once they were seated. He waved again. "So far," he leant across the table, smiling directly at her—his particularly bright, warm smile which lit up his otherwise plain face. "So far, I've seen two chaps I was at Oxford with, one girl I've seen about a bit and someone in the Guards I did my National Service with. Awfully jolly place this. I like the atmosphere. Now what are you going to eat?"

Despite being afraid to look round too eagerly in case she was spotted by Edward, Tessa suddenly started to enjoy herself. Several couples stopped at their table to chat on their way in or out. Oliver's enthusiasm for almost anything was infectious. He put on his glasses and worked his way down the menu, pleasurably anticipating the meal. His comments were informed; he seemed to know something about food and wine.

"To tell you the truth, Tess, I've been

waiting to come here until I could get hold of you. I thought, somehow, that it would be a nice thing for us to do together." He put down the menu and watched her steadily. The glasses made him look more than ever like a friendly bulldog with large ears.

"That's so sweet of you, Oliver." She was feeling very guilty. Except for a brief mention of Angie and her thanks for his returning the shawl, they had so far not talked much about the party. Or Marcus. Even during a long, talkative and merry lunch.

"Not thoughtful—*meant.*" Again, the level gaze. Tessa blushed. All her life, Oliver had been in and out of the house with Tom. As a schoolgirl she had visited his rooms at Oxford. Once or twice since he had taken her to a cinema; they had been to dances and parties together—but always as part of a group. It was only at the Hunt Ball last winter that he had suddenly and briefly shown his interest in her; quickly, it seemed, forgotten. At least, until his party . . .

To Tessa's considerable relief, the waiter intervened—offering suggestions.

Oliver started talking about his house. "Yes, it's splendid, isn't it? I'm so lucky to have it. My grandmother always promised I should, but somehow I didn't think . . . Anyhow, there's a bit of money, not much, but enough, and I hope that in time I'll be able to restore it to a beautiful family home. That's what it was always meant to be. And overlooking the Canal and the barges—it does make it special, doesn't it? It's not called Little Venice up there for nothing. And it's so central. I'm determined to cheer the house up this Christmas to hide the shabby bits until I can afford to get it properly painted—the curtains should help. You shall decide on the trimmings—a tree, holly and so on. I'll become your customer—or is it client?"

He spoke gaily, obviously proud of the big, mid-Victorian house and its unkempt garden which he had inherited. It must have been beautiful once, years ago. Tessa knew that it was where his mother was born and had grown up; this, and his memories of her, must make it particularly important to him.

"Customer—definitely. But your first

Christmas tree will be my housewarming present, properly trimmed . . ."

"That's something to look forward to. And I'll have to get into the garden sooner or later. It's the most terrible mess, as you saw." He looked glum. "There really is so much to be done to the place. The garden is rather low on my list of priorities, I'm afraid. Speaking of gardens, tell me more about the shop—it certainly looks thriving."

So Tessa told him how she had met Joan in the first place, taken on what she thought was the most temporary of jobs—liked it, and stayed on. She described some of her mates, the "characters" she met in the market, the jobs they had been commissioned to do during the summer, and the new "Garden" they were beginning to plan. In fact, she said, Joan had already got some figures out of their accountant and they hoped to go over them together after work tomorrow. And Joan had been in touch with some estate agents. They both thought that getting the right kind of premises in the right position for a price they could more or less afford was the key. And it *had* to have something about it—character—like the small bow-fronted shop in Chelsea.

"It sounds fascinating, good for you, Tess. And Joan. I do admire you for going out and doing something, not just hanging about . . . putting your back into a project and making it work. I'm sure your father must be terribly proud of you." Tessa made a face and Oliver, knowing George Selway, laughed. "No really, I'm sure he is, even if he doesn't show it. You must get your acumen from him." He signalled a waiter. "A glass of wine would be nice, wouldn't it? Service doesn't seem to be one of their strong points here . . . I've had one or two interesting cases myself lately, lucky breaks, really."

They ordered, and Oliver chose a bottle of wine.

Tom had told her how well he was getting on at the Bar—and she could believe it. He was beginning to carve out a name for himself, Tom said. Like Tom, he had always been academically clever; they had been friendly rivals at school, then university. His concerned manner inspired confidence. He was good with clients, Tom thought; they felt they could trust him. And he was impressive in court, on his feet. He had an excellent voice. He didn't get rattled—and he wasn't easily bullied.

He was specialising in criminal work and he told her a little about a sensational and particularly appalling murder case, which had been in all the papers quite recently. As Tessa knew, he had been mentioned a good deal when the trial was reported; he found himself Junior Counsel for the prosecution.

"And do you know, the first day, the evidence was so dreadful and involved those two young children—that I blanked out. The thought of those kids, the cold-bloodedness . . . The case was being heard in Essex and when we'd finished for the day, I found myself driving and driving and I ended up at a pub miles from anywhere. God knows how I got there—I simply don't remember. I didn't get home until midnight. I suppose it must have been the strain. We'd been working on the case until all hours. And then actually facing the horrific facts, the cruelty. I was perfectly all right after that, even when the cross-examination got really tough. It's funny how the mind and body react to extreme stress."

He dismissed the incident, shrugging it off with a smile. "I say, you are looking beautiful, Tess. What colour exactly would you call that dress? Raspberry? I thought so too at my party—that you were looking beautiful—radiant. It went off awfully well, the party, didn't it?"

Now that the subject of the party had at last been more than casually raised, it could no longer be avoided. Tessa braced herself and fiddled with her necklace—a Victorian gold chain studded with garnets —which her father had given her for her last birthday. Out of the corner of her eye she had seen Edward, hopping chattily from table to table.

"It was fabulous, Oliver. Everyone was having a marvellous time. And it was lovely seeing the house. I hadn't seen Fiona for ages . . . we had masses to chat about, I must give her a ring and we'll have lunch."

She babbled away nervously, hoping to avoid the serious talk which she sensed was coming—and keeping an anxious watch on Edward's progress.

"That chap you brought, Marcus Reardon . . ." Tessa's heart dropped. "Is he a good friend of yours?"

"Marcus?" She tried to sound surprised. "Yes—yes, he is. Actually, he's a friend of Gran's. I haven't known him very long." With no effort at all, she sounded perfectly composed. She had absolutely no intention of telling Oliver how they had met—and she was certain Tom wouldn't have done either.

"His column in the *Chronicle* seems to have taken off with a bang. He must be very talented at what he does. I saw him on television the other night. He was most amusing, I thought."

"Did you?"

Tessa stared down at the white cloth, at the pool of light cast by the lampshade. To her horror, even then she felt the faintest ripple of sexual excitement.

"I'm told, and I hope I'm not saying the wrong thing, that he's a bit of a slippery customer."

Tessa looked up at him; grey eyes very clear. Her hair, which had been trimmed that day, curled sleekly. "Really," she

396

said, her eyebrows raised. "In what way, exactly?"

"I couldn't be specific. I haven't the facts—that wouldn't be fair." His elbows were on the table, arms crossed. His neck and shoulders looked massive—and he sounded clipped and professional. "I've heard his services as a journalist are available—for a price."

"You mean he sells gossip to the newspapers, that he can be bribed?" She was very matter-of-fact. She surprised herself.

"That sort of thing. As I say, I can't be exact. It's hearsay, I grant you, mostly from one or two of my contacts in the police. And I do know he had a tremendous war record."

"He did. He was David, our uncle's, best friend. You know that?"

He nodded.

"And from what little I've seen . . ." Tessa paused, "he takes his work very seriously indeed." She was beginning to feel uncomfortable, and determined not to show it. Also, she could see Edward working his way slowly but surely towards them across the crowded restaurant. And Oliver, gregarious as he was, would be certain to know him. Surely he wouldn't recognise her, not from that one brief meeting when she was with Marcus?

"Hmm, well, the fact is . . ." Oliver's elbows slid across the table towards her. "The fact is, Tess, that I don't like to see any man with you. Reardon particularly. I hadn't realised it before that night, but suddenly—at the party—it came to me. Just like that. Absolutely clearly." He squared his shoulders and his chin. "I mean it Tess, seriously. You and me . . . we *belong* somehow. I'm absolutely convinced. So there you have it."

"*Oliver* . . . but I mean . . . we haven't, you never . . ."

Tessa was thrown into confusion— surprised, flattered, appalled, all at the same time. For years, she had dreamed of Oliver paying her some attention, not just as Tom's younger sister; last winter, dancing with him again and again at the Hunt Ball, she could swear that he was treating her as a woman—and an attractive one at that. Differently.

But nothing had come of that wonderfully happy evening. And now there was Marcus. Why, in real life was the timing often so awkward, so badly—so *painfully* —out of synch?

"I have now." He looked so determined. "I have now, Tess. All my cards on the table. I believe in quick, intuitive decisions in personal things—and I think they work in the law too."

Tessa couldn't help smiling at him. He looked so sure, so pleased, so happy. Confident, without a trace of arrogance. "But Oliver," she said, playing for time, taken completely by surprise, "I thought Tom said you had a girlfriend, a serious one . . ."

"You mean Julia? That was never anything much. Physical attraction, mostly. And in any case, it's over and done with." *Julia*—the deliciously pretty fair girl she had seen at the party, coming in with a group just behind her and Marcus. "It was a fling—rather a painful one at times. A sort of temporary madness. As though it had nothing to do with my real self at all."

"I can understand that."

"I thought you might." Tessa didn't answer and her eyes dropped away from his. The restaurant suddenly seemed very noisy. He put his hand, wide and strong, over hers. "We've known each other for a long time, Tess. Think about it, will you?"

But before Tessa had a chance to reply, a voice above them said, "W-would I b-be interrupting if—if I said 'Hello' and thank you for coming. . . ?"

It was Edward Cairn. He stood over them like an awkward, lanky schoolboy. Oliver sprang to his feet, shaking him warmly by the hand. "The great man himself! This is a treat, Edward; we're loving it, aren't we Tessa? Have you met Tessa Selway? Tessa, Edward Cairn, we were at Oxford together."

Tessa and Edward Cairn spoke simultaneously.

He said: "Of co-course, weren't you here the other n-night with. . . ?"

She said, clearly: "No, we haven't, how do you do?" and put out her hand.

Their eyes met and Edward blinked nervously. "Oh quite. S-so nice you're here," he stuttered. "I th-think I know your brother . . ."

"Tom?" said Oliver. "That's right. You would, of course. From Oxford. We must bring him along, Tessa. Tell him what he's missing. Clever old Edward, the ideas man, packing 'em in, while the rest of us slave away at the ill-paid professions . . ."

"Go on Oliver, you love it, being a barrister," Tessa teased, nicely pink in the face, hugely relieved that the awkward moment had passed. Edward had definitely twigged. If he wasn't used to situations like that, then he should be. "He fancies himself in that wig and gown," she said to him gaily. "I can just see Oliver as a judge, presiding, can't you?"

"Some of us have to keep the system going," Oliver grumbled good-naturedly. "But congratulations, Edward. A really good show. It's a rather special night for us, isn't it, Tessa? And we mean to come back. With Tom. If we can ever get in through the door that is. *Ha Ha.*" A waiter was hovering with plates. "We're just about to get going on the grub—and the vino," he added, as a bottle of wine appeared. "We'll let you know what we think on our way out."

During the meal, Oliver did not refer again to his personal declaration. Instead, he kept Tessa amused by chatter about his work and his plans for the house. And he

told her about his five female cousins—
"they're like sisters, really"—and their-
on-and-off romances. "They drive my
poor aunt and uncle mad. Even Fiona,
who seems to be the most rational."

When they had almost finished, a couple
they both knew stopped at their table. The
girl had been at school with Tessa. "And
you're looking great, so svelte I hardly
recognised you," she told her, while Oliver
watched proudly. It was her birthday and
they were celebrating, going on to a night-
club—The Hibiscus—and wouldn't they
join them there?

"Is that all right with you, Tess?"
Oliver asked. "Not got to be up with the
lark for Covent Garden tomorrow, have
you?"

"Not tomorrow—Joan's turn."

"Then we'd love to. You two go on and
get a table there and we'll join you . . ."

Oliver parked in his usual cavalier fashion
and they crossed the street into the mews
where music from The Hibiscus was just
audible. It was at the far end and they
walked towards the flower-covered trellis,
spot-lit against white-washed walls. In the

muggy summer night, it looked almost Mediterranean. Tessa remarked on this and Oliver agreed, tucking her arm through his. They could hear the music loudly, liltingly now—and laughter, as the door opened and a group came out.

"What luck that we met Mark and Susie at Edward's . . . I haven't been here for months," Tessa said happily. "I *am* enjoying this, Oliver."

He stopped and looked at her— seriously, not like his usual genial self at all. "I'm so glad, Tess. So awfully glad."

Later, when they were dancing on the tiny, crowded floor, Oliver said into her ear, "You don't have to tell me Tess, but did Tom meet Angie through Reardon?"

Tessa moved her head slightly and looked at him—surprised. "Yes, he did. How did you know?"

"I saw them talking at the party. And I put two and two together. That's all . . ."

They went on dancing until Tessa saw Susie waving from the table, trying to attract their attention. They had been drinking champagne and now a small birthday cake had arrived.

"Let's go and help her blow the candles

out." Holding Oliver's hand, she led the way over.

It was late by the time Oliver got her back to Parloe Square. They stood just beyond the glow of the streetlamp outside the house. Oliver took both Tessa's hands in his and held them tightly against his chest. He bent and leant his forehead against hers.

"Remember? Will you? What I said about you being for *me?*"

Tessa giggled. She felt safe and, yes, happy. Astonishingly happy. Almost euphoric with relief in fact. More than content to be standing with Oliver, so close; delighted by his sound, familiar presence . . . She sniffed. He smelled clean and soapy and, just faintly, of lemon cologne. The bulk of his very broad shoulders was infinitely reassuring.

"Oh Oliver . . . you silly old thing." It was said affectionately. "I was just terribly surprised, that's all. And yes, I'll remember."

"You're sure?"

"I'm sure." Lamplight caught the sparkle from the gold and silver threads in the shawl round her shoulders. "And thank you for such a wonderful evening, Oliver. I loved it." And she had. Oliver's calming, buoyant presence had steadied her; she had felt herself again. It was almost as though she had awakened from some tantalising, troubled dream. At Edward's—yes, even there—and after, in the noisy nightclub . . . For the first time since Aunt Flor's party—*since Marcus*—she had felt tranquil. She had been close, she sensed dimly, to losing her head altogether. To doing heaven only knew what. Oliver, that evening, had pulled her back from the brink.

"I was extremely proud to be with you. You looked so pretty—everyone said so."

"*Oliver . . .*"

But she had—and she knew it. Her deep pink dress, made of silk taffeta, flattered her shoulders and her small waist. Her skin had a lovely sheen. Oliver's open declaration had been exhilarating—and very gratifying, almost taken her breath away . . . This friend of Tom's whom she had hero-worshipped as a child . . . More than anything, she had found him such fun to be with. But how could she reconcile

405

her affection for Oliver with her passionate response to Marcus's every word and move?

"We're going to the theatre next week. I'll get tickets. Don't forget."

"I won't, I won't. Honestly." Laughing, Tessa tried to extricate her hands from his vice-like grasp. She failed.

"Not until you've sworn to give me a chance. To get to know me better. Like we are now."

"I swear."

At the door Tessa turned, still laughing, and blew him a kiss. Oliver was standing in the full light of the street lamp, his broad face creased in a huge grin like an india rubber.

"And I swear never to give up. *Never.*" The grin disappeared. "And I'll fight for you if I have to. I mean that. Goodnight, Tess."

He dived into the oversize black beetle which seemed much too small for his huge frame.

In the hall, Tessa met Ella who was mooching about in her old blue dressing-gown. She seemed to go to bed later and later these days. Tessa thought that her arthritic hip was giving her a lot more trouble than she was willing to let on.

"We had the most marvellous evening Ella, such fun—but what on earth are you doing still up? I thought you would have been in bed hours ago."

"Just pottering, dear, you know how I do. I *am* glad you had a good time . . . I can tell that just by looking at you. Oh, a gentleman rang for you. Twice."

Marcus . . . he rang *twice*. Thrilled; apprehensive . . . her emotional life was becoming frighteningly intense.

Ella sounded guarded.

"Was it Marcus Reardon? What did he want?" Tessa asked casually, one hand already on the bannister.

"That's the name. Nothing the first time." Then more disapprovingly, "The second—and it was very late indeed—to tell you that he had to go out of London for the day and he would phone when he got back tomorrow night."

"Thanks, Ella." Tessa yawned, and started up the stairs. So he was off somewhere tomorrow. I wonder if he dropped in on Gran?

He rang—*twice*.
She said goodnight to Ella and went straight up to bed.

16

EARLIER that evening, walking through Eaton Square, towards Vi Delmore's flat, Marcus thought, *Oliver will be calling for Tessa at Parloe Square about now.* Ridiculous how it rankled—had done all day. He rang the bell.

Vi opened the door and greeted him without surprise—although she had not known that he was coming—and led the way into the drawing-room. She was wearing a long pink housecoat, trimmed with satin and wispy ostrich feathers. It looked slightly tatty, a remnant of nineteen-thirties' elegance—as it undoubtedly was. Charlie was tucked under her arm and she had a cigarette in her mouth, the ash drooping.

"Drink? Help yourself," she told him. "And top this up, would you?"

She handed him her brandy glass and dumped Charlie among the dishevelled cushions on the sofa beside her.

"*You* look pleased with yourself," she called after him, reaching for an ashtray. "So you're going to be a success are you? You have that look—creamy, catlike. About time too, is all I can say."

Marcus laughed and splashed soda into his whisky. "I'm becoming respectable—almost establishment, you might say. It does make a change." He came back with their glasses. "Cheers, Vi."

"In that case, your hair needs cutting."

"You always say that."

"Only because it always does. You'll have to give up the unpleasant stuff too. The hush money." She eyed him beadily. "Blackmail, they called it in my day."

Marcus settled in his usual chair opposite, legs flung carelessly, arm hooked over the back.

"Oh come now, Vi." He smiled at her indulgently. "I think that's going a bit far, even when I was on my uppers."

"No it isn't. It's a fact," she snapped. "And you know it. You never could resist the money. It was all too easy. And all for some depressing bit of human frailty."

"We won't split hairs."

"I've got one of your new pieces round

410

here somewhere. Charlie and I tottered out and bought it, didn't we Charlie?" She looked round vaguely. "It's here some-where. A bit of rubbish about an MP taking his floozy to Paris. As if there was anything new in that, I ask you . . . I thought the rest of it was rather good. Not that I can ever find my glasses these days to read much of anything."

"The column's being read and talked about, Vi. That's the thing. I was bloody nervous about it when it came to the point. I can tell you that."

"You must keep at it," she told him severely. "No rows or fallings out with the people in the office. You've got talent; you must use it responsibly."

"You sound just like my editor."

Marcus studied her affectionately, nursing his scotch. He had always enjoyed her company—and was doing so now. They were birds of a feather in a way, he supposed. Loners; not without style; generally cold in human relationships.

"Do I?" she said vaguely, dabbing at her mouth with a crumpled handkerchief. "Now there was something I—wanted—

411

to—talk—to—you about . . ." she was practically mumbling.

"What was that, Vi?"

Tessa, out on the town with Oliver—doing whatever Bright Young Things did these days—drifted in and out of his mind too often for comfort. This was absurd. He would concentrate on Vi. He considered, and rejected, asking her whether she knew Tom's great friend, Oliver Bingham . . .

Vi. Why on earth was Tessa so concerned about her? True, he had never seen her in this kind of déshabillé and the place looked a bit of a shambles, dust everywhere.

But she was getting on, after all; she had clearly been affected by old Delmore's death, for whatever reason. The funeral had been a strain and she had apparently put on a good show as the widow. Tessa had been exaggerating her condition and her sudden access of senility. He said, "Tessa thinks you're living on brandy and digestive biscuits. She's very fond of you and she worries."

"Rubbish. Not that there aren't worse things—to live on I mean. And I wish she wouldn't send that Ella round here

412

snooping. She's a good woman but she irritates me greatly. I'm perfectly capable of managing on my own."

"Yes—well . . ." Marcus never missed much of what was going on around him and he noticed that she had the silver-framed photograph of Ben Levson, obviously taken years ago on his yacht, on the table beside her. She had moved it from its usual place on the mantelpiece. He remarked on this.

"I *adored* Ben. I like having him here with me." She patted the table and lay back on the cushions with her eyes closed. "You only met him when he was old and ill and sad, didn't you? After the war. You can't imagine how brilliant he was, that first summer. I'd escaped from poor Sam, with the children, to the Floods in the South of France. Oh but it was divine then, not trippery, not spoilt . . . nobody there, just the locals and a few artists and writers. That American couple, the Murphys, they started it all—the summer thing down there, that's when it began . . .

"A bit of heaven . . . the colours, the blues, the sun, the dazzle. Funny twisted

413

trees so green on the headlands. Swimming off the rocks . . . long, lazy lunches. Lizards slithering across the terrace of the villa at midday. And the red striped canopy all along. It looked so *gay*. David went brown as a nut, diving and swimming until we dragged him out. And mademoiselle always insisted Jennie wore a hat, she was so fair . . . and I think— yes, I *think*—that was when she started to go quiet, secretive . . ." She tried to concentrate. "After that summer she changed."

Marcus watched her attentively. Best to humour her, he thought. "Go on. And Ben?"

"Oh *Ben* . . ." She smiled lovingly. "He looked like an ugly pirate. A swarthy swashbuckler with a grating New York accent. One of those awful cigars was always clenched between his teeth. But such charm, such vitality, you cannot imagine. The cleverest, the most interesting people in the world were captivated —Passas, the singer, Marbessa the artist. Politicians. And it *wasn't* just the money, the yacht. Simply—he knew how to live well, how to entertain.

414

"He was a Jew, of course, and proud of it. People, the people *we* knew, thought that was rather odd in those days. I never gave a damn. It meant nothing to me one way or the other. In fact I liked it—his being different. Anyway, he simply over-powered me and I fell for him, just like that."

"Lucky Ben."

"Perhaps . . ." Her eyes flew open. "But *all* the women were mad for him. He was," eyes slowly closing again, "quite *wickedly* sexy . . ."

"You naughty old thing, Vi. Tut tut . . . the Viscountess Delmore."

"Don't patronise me just because I'm old," she said crossly. "It makes no differ-ence as you'll find out yourself soon enough. He liked that, of course, the handle. Ben did. And I was amusing. I knew how to dress. Terribly girlishly boyish we were in those days with shingled hair and striped jerseys and waists round our bottoms. Your drink all right, is it?"

"Fine," Marcus said. "It's fine, Vi." He glanced at his watch. He was on his way to the House, he told her, breaking in on her thoughts. When he got back to the flat, he might risk ringing Tessa. He *might*. (With luck, unless they were making a late night of it, she would answer. Not Ella.) Just to hear her voice —that was why—no point in beating about the bush ... He was missing her terribly; he hadn't been able to concentrate, not the way he liked, blotting out everyone and everything, all day.

Opposite him, Vi seemed to have nodded off.

"Vi?"

Marcus leant forward.

"You're not going to sleep on me, are you Vi?"

She looked very crumpled, half lying there on the worn brocaded cushions, her chin sunk deep into the feathery pink.

"Vi?"

He touched her. For the first time, he felt some alarm. She straightened up. Then she said, looking right at him, in a perfectly normal voice, "David is dead, isn't he?"

A pause ... Marcus considered. So Tessa was right after all. He sighed. Oh dear, oh dear.

"Yes."

"It was the girl, Pamela, who did for him, wasn't it?"

"What do you mean?" he asked sharply.

"That girl, the one he was engaged to. Pretty but flighty, I always said so. She couldn't stick it—the way he looked. After the burns and the skin grafts on his face."

Briefly, vividly, and after so many years, Marcus heard Pamela's high heels drumming against the polished floor as she fled from David's room up the long hospital corridor, disappearing through the swing doors, never to be seen again. He, Marcus, left helpless, staring after her; having to go back, slowly, and tell David—who knew in any case, whose face, what was left of it, was already turned to the wall.

"It wasn't easy for any of us, Vi, least of all David," he said quietly. "I don't think one should be too hard on Pamela."

"No, no I suppose not. Pretty girl, good family. A bit more of this with water, would you, Marcus, please?"

To his considerable relief, she seemed content to leave it at that. He refilled her drink, making it mostly water. Her mind passed on to other things. "I'm glad you're getting along with Tess." She took the

417

glass, sniffing at its contents. "That was a marvellous idea I had, bringing you along to Flora's opening. I knew you were just what Tessa needed." She sounded genuinely, and rather childishly, pleased. "She looked lovely the other night. What's the word. . . ?" She stopped, muddled. "*Blooming*, that's it—blooming. She really did. So important for a woman, a good lover. Essential really. It will stand her in good stead later on."

Marcus, rarely at a loss gaped. He stared down at his nearly empty glass, one side of his mouth twitching. Jesus, what a witch of a grandmother this Vi was . . . He could think of absolutely nothing at all to say—which seemed wisest.

"As long as you don't go getting any silly ideas, either of you. About respectability for one thing. Just because you're getting some recognition all of a sudden."

Marcus still didn't answer.

"You heard what I said, Marcus?"

"Yes."

"Well?"

"I said, I heard you."

"Good. You make sure you did. I'm a canny old woman—and I know the form.

418

Now can you find me a cigarette?" She poked about helplessly. Marcus eventually retrieved the cigarette box which was stuffed between two cushions under the sleeping Charlie. He took one out and lit it for her.

"I didn't care for Tom's girl, by the way," she said after one or two puffs. "They came the other night—yesterday was it? An adventuress, I thought. Quite a minx. And common underneath that put-on accent. Not that I mind that but I thought she was hard, hard as nails."

"She is. Tom met her through me. Did you know that?"

"Tessa told me; so I was prepared, you might say, for anything."

Marcus raised his eyebrows and let that one pass.

"They went down to see Jennie and Felix at the weekend, they told me. Jennie won't care tuppence although she always did seem quite fond of Tom. George Selway won't be pleased. Except the girl is spectacular. He'll like that. Tom's a bit wet, between ourselves." She flicked some ash towards the ashtray—and missed. "He always was. Wishy-washy. There's a lot of his mother in Tom, except he's clever. I've always thought he needed taking in hand. Perhaps this young woman will give him a bit of backbone."

She yawned, putting her glass on the table none too steadily. Really, she seemed to be saying, I can't be bothered with all this any more . . .

She looked exhausted, her rouged cheeks sagging, her eyes almost hidden in deep wrinkles. Marcus again looked at his watch. Vi's head lolled sideways. She started to mumble. "Are we invited for luncheon, Flora? I've got that jaunty peaked cap, so right with the white trousers. I got it at Marshall's and hid it in the wardrobe . . . What *would* they say if they saw me like this in Hertfordshire? I can see the launch coming to pick us up . . . Yes, a marvellous show, we've seen it twice. My dears, everyone has. Even Sam didn't snooze . . ."

Marcus went and sat next to her and held her limp hand. Poor old Vi, bless her. He felt infinitely sad. There was no point in trying Tessa yet; but of course he would later. She was absolutely right; Vi was coming and going. Disorientated. She

420

needed someone with her; she shouldn't be left on her own, not like this.

To his amazement, still without opening her eyes, she started to sing—quietly and musically, word perfect.

> "In lives of leisure
> The craze for pleasure
> Steadily grows,
> Cocktails and laughter,
> But what comes after?
> Nobody knows."

She stopped abruptly.

"Noel Coward, isn't it? Well done Vi." Marcus said gently. She sat bolt upright, blinking, looking down at his hand which was still holding hers.

"Oh—it's you Marcus. I must have dropped off. I've been feeling a bit done in, to tell you the truth. It was Sam and the funeral—all that. I seem to be living in the past a lot these days. What time is it, anyway?"

Marcus stood up. "Time I was off, Vi. Can I get you anything at all? What about some supper?" He removed her glass and took it into the dining-room. "Shall I get you something on a tray before I go?" He didn't like leaving her the way she was, didn't like it at all. "Ella comes in most days, doesn't she?" There was no doubt at all that her mind was wandering . . . it could still be delayed shock from Delmore; David's death brought back. He'd had a nasty moment just now when she started on about that—David's accident.

Ben Levson's memory. Loneliness. She could well get back to her old form given time and the right care. And someone constantly with her.

"She's not coming tomorrow, not if I can help it," Vi said stoutly. "She's bringing that sister of hers, the nurse, one of these days. Checking up on me, the pair of them," she added darkly.

"Quite right too. You need it. And you must get someone in to help you, Vi. It's not sensible."

"Now don't you start fussing over me. What did you do with that glass, anyway? And speaking of sensible . . . Yes, that's exactly what I wanted to talk to you about, the very word. I've remembered." Her face cleared; she looked completely well and alert. "Go on Charlie . . ." She pushed him quite roughly off the cushion and brushed the hairs away with her hand. "Go and get ready for your nightly outing, go on. Where was I? That's it, sensible." She looked up at Marcus who didn't reply. He was an attractive man, no doubt about that. She hadn't always thought so—but she did now. "Oh dear," she said, "I see." She caught something—a certain expression—on his face. She knew him, after all, very well.

"See *what?*" Marcus said, irritated, pushing his long hair back. He was prepared to be sympathetic, sorry to see her like this, but what was she on about now?

"As you are perfectly well aware, Marcus, I'm talking about Tessa. You're getting too fond of her."

Marcus sighed. The old witch. In addition to losing her marbles, she appeared to have acquired second sight. Dammit.

"Look," he said, smiling a bit, "she's a sweet kid—and yes, I am fond of her. We see each other sometimes. That's it, that's all. OK?"

"*Rubbish,*" replied Vi. "You can't fool

me, neither of you. I'm all for it—it's exactly what I thought might happen. But no nonsense about respectability. That's not the point at all. For either of you."

Marcus bent and kissed her cheek. "Don't move, Vi. If you're sure there's nothing I can do for you . . ." He put his hand on her shoulder. The bone felt frail beneath the flimsy material.

"Promise, Marcus," she insisted. "About Tessa."

"All right. I promise."

"Good. Now you see you stick to it."

17

IT had been a long and exhausting day and by the time Tessa and Joan walked over to the little mews house, round the corner from the shop, they were both whacked. They had been decorating a church for a wedding tomorrow. They had started early and only just finished. Both were delighted with their work. "It looks a dream, Tess. Just the way I'd pictured . . . lovely wafting greenery with streams of colour, *floating* in it," Joan had said. She handed Tessa a gin and tonic and slumped on the sofa. "We've never done anything better. Cheers."

"I agree. But we're going to need more staff than Jilly if we go ahead with our plan." Tessa nodded towards a table where she had dumped a pile of papers. Bullied by Joan, their accountant had rushed out a basic financial plan of operation for the anticipated "second garden". They wanted to go through it together, add a few ideas and suggestions—and then go straight to the bank manager while he seemed so encouraging. "It's now or never," Joan declared.

"That won't be hard, Joan, finding good help, as long as we can offer a decent wage. And we've agreed that's a must, whatever other corners we cut. We can always advertise and ask around. I've got to know quite a few people through seeing them at the market—and I'm sure you have too. It's finding a place that's going to be right for us that will be the difficulty. We want something that's going to fit in with our way of doing things, our look. *And* in the right neighbourhood . . . What did the estate agent say?"

"He's got a couple of possibilities that are worth looking at. He's sending the particulars. We'll know straight away if they're any good. The best way to handle it is for one of us to see a property—and if we think there's hope, the other can come round. That saves time and means there's someone other than Jilly in the shop. I'll show you in there," indicating the accountant's blueprint, "what the price guidelines are. He's got it all worked out: mortgage, salaries, approximate fixed overheads, working capital . . . all based on this shop, of course. But it's exciting stuff, isn't it?"

"It certainly is. And to think that it all really did come out of 'Joan's garden', the real one in Sussex."

Joan gave her heartiest, jolliest laugh. "Now it's going to be a 'Tessa's Garden ' —I like that best. 'Joan's and Tessa's' is a bit of a mouthful."

"Really?" Tessa looked pleased. She said brightly, "We'll save that for the third."

"That's all right by me, but let's get the second off the ground first. Calling it 'Tessa's' does make sense. The accountant and I both agree that one of us will have to stick to each of the shops to start with, to keep this one going, up to scratch, while the other one—we hope—begins to take off." She grinned at Tessa. "And the next one's your baby . . ."

"Fair enough. And let's go through the ideas and the finances, or what he's estimated, tonight. Don't you think?" She had forgotten her tiredness; her enthusiasm was fired. "We never get time at the shop and it's so easy to put it all off

427

week after week. Gosh, Joan, think of how you'll have to trawl the antique stalls for yet more bits and pieces and general clobber . . ." She was feeling more relaxed now, her imagination blazing with the reality of a new shop. And she was so glad that today's job was over; pleased that it had turned out so well. The bride, as well as her mother, had been genuinely delighted. And both she and Joan had a feeling that it would lead to more good work. "We must have another pretty window like the present one. A sort of trademark . . . I mean, you take one look at the shop and you know instantly it's not a conventional florist, so it either appeals or it doesn't. 'Tessa's' must be like that too."

Joan got up. "Exactly. And we've too much stuffed in this shop as it is, plenty there for 'Tessa's' for a start. We'll put all the papers out on the table and get 'Tessa's Garden' mapped out in our heads so that we know exactly where we are, what's possible and what isn't. But later. We must eat first. Scrambled eggs. OK?"

"Perfect."

"You stay put—there's only room for one of us in there anyhow."

Tessa looked about while Joan went into the small kitchen in the back. The house consisted of one big living-room on the ground floor with a spiral staircase leading up to the bedroom and bathroom.

"It's such a cosy little place, Joan," Tessa called through. "You should use it more often. Now that you've got a decent gardener in Sussex whom you can trust to get on with things, you shouldn't do all that driving back and forth." The sitting-room was simply and sparsely furnished— but comfortable, and with some attractive touches. A huge pottery vase filled with dried grasses; a pretty, gold-framed mirror. The times, recently, that she had allegedly been staying here, she thought ruefully. Good old Joan; what a friend.

"I might, although I'm always glad to get out of London. I say, Tess, I purposely haven't said anything . . ." Joan called back. "Didn't feel it was my place . . ." Tessa heard her beating up the eggs. She could tell from her voice that the cigarette was still in her mouth even when she was cooking. "But I've been wondering how

429

your love-life was going? To tell you the truth, I've been a bit worried about you."

"Hectic," Tessa shouted back at her through the gallery door. (The eggs were cooking now, the fork scraping round and round the saucepan.)

"Sounds good. Still seeing the journalist chap? Saw him on the box the other night looking very glamorous."

"He is, at least in some ways . . ." Ways on which she would not, she thought, elaborate. Even to Joan. "And he's extremely interesting, worldly, I suppose."

Marcus walking in from the studio, coming into the bedroom, tearing off her sweater—no, *his* sweater . . . his hands, so sure. He had phoned her twice last night. Where was he? Out of London, on the trail of someone to interview, probably. She could smell toast—and realised she was very hungry.

"Who else is on the scene then? That big chap with the nice face who keeps popping into the shop? That was a slap-up lunch you had with him the other day."

"Oliver? Yes, he is too, now." All this carried on from one room to the next, loudly, while the eggs cooked away. Tessa thought it was comforting—and rather funny—to be discussing her private life like this. It made her see the amusing side. "So you see I'm very much in demand at the moment, Joan. One chap seems to have snared the other. Oliver saw us together—Marcus and me—and it seems to have done something to him, although I suppose it must have been there all along. I've always had a bit of a thing about him . . . Perhaps that's how it works —feast or famine. Anyhow, it may just be your gin, but I've decided to take it as it comes and hope it all works out for the best." But she felt a lot less confident than she sounded. Her mixed emotions both confused and alarmed her.

"And I'll fight for you if I have to. I mean that," Oliver had said—fierce, determined. And Tessa believed he meant it.

The scraping stopped and Joan appeared in the kitchen door, red-faced and smiling merrily back at her. "Bloody good," she said. "That's the stuff. Leave the blokes cooling their heels and concentrate on the work. Grub's up, so come and get it. And

431

then 'Tessa's Garden' is going to get itself born tonight."

The moment she got back to Parloe Square she heard Tom's voice calling out.

"That you, Tess?

"Tom?"

What on earth was he doing here at this time? Ella's door opened and Tom appeared. He was ashen.

"Tess, come down here a minute would you?" He ran his hand distractedly through his hair. "I know it's late but something has blown up. I've been rattling on to poor Ella. I hoped, actually, that you might be in."

Ella was sitting in her rocking chair with the evening paper spread out in front of her. She looked worried. Tom must have been there for some time because there were coffee cups about and an overflowing ashtray.

"What on earth is the matter with you?" Tessa asked, looking from one to the other. "What's happened? Nothing bad from New York—from Papa?" Just as she felt the first twinge of alarm, she caught sight of the headlines in the paper. *Man-*

*about-town arrested on gambling charge
. . . socialites believed to be involved . . .
Guy Loden, well-known figure in the
racing world, was today arrested in his
Kensington home and charged . . .*

"Is that why you're here, Tom?" She leant forward and pulled the paper towards her.

"Of course."

"What does it mean exactly?" She looked uneasily over to Ella who was twisting her hands together and rocking away in the chair.

Tom's head jerked up. "Just what it says. Loden has been charged with running that house in Aberdeen Road as a gambling casino. Which of course he does. Everyone in London has known that for years. The police have been staking the place out, ready to pounce. Now they have —and you may be sure they've got their tackle in order. And however one may think that the law needs changing, it's still the law. Angie is bound to be a key witness, and lucky not to be arrested herself. She got out just in time, as it happens. Late this afternoon—just before

433

I got in—she had a phone call. Threatening, ugly . . ."

"But why? I mean, it wasn't her house, she wasn't responsible for what went on there. She doesn't live there any more. He —Loden—did her bodily harm." Tessa wondered what on earth Tom had been telling Ella. "What can anyone do to Angie?"

"Don't be an idiot. Angie knew exactly what was going on at Loden's." Tom spoke impatiently. "Even if she has repudiated the whole ghastly mess in the meantime. And gambling wasn't the only illegal activity taking place on the premises. She broke down and told me the whole story tonight—after that call."

The whole story? I wonder, Tessa thought, I wonder. She hated seeing how Angie was twisting Tom round her little finger; look at him—pacing desperately around at this time of night. Bringing his troubles down here to Ella as he had done since he was a schoolboy. And what on earth did *she* make of the sordid web Tom's beautiful girlfriend was dragging him into? No wonder she looked so upset.

"What story?" Tessa asked.

"The house was used as the nerve centre of a drugs network which fanned out over the whole of Europe and even the States. The gambling was a sort of flamboyant, if illegal, cover. The police undoubtedly know this and if they don't, they soon will. Angie is vehement that she had absolutely no part in it and of course she didn't; but she heard things, she can name names. To Loden and his gang she's a danger—as they made quite clear today."

"I see."

She didn't particularly. If you played around with people like that, this was what you got. She had used her looks and her figure and God knows what else to make a career for herelf. She hadn't needed to stay on with Loden. Now, since he was clearly besotted, Tom was making it *his* business—and getting himself into a fine old state about the consequences.

"You wouldn't like a cup of tea, would you dear?" Ella asked hopefully. Tessa shook her head. "Oh dear, I do think this Mr. Loden sounds a wicked, wicked man. That poor Angie. Wherever is it all going to end?"

"In a long prison term for Loden and

as many of his henchmen as the pros- ecution can make stick," Tom replied crisply.

"How did the man on the phone actually threaten Angie?" Tessa asked. Tom spun round and faced her. His eyes were pale, wild and frightened.

"Her face . . . acid. She'd never go in front of a lens again, he said, they'd make very sure of that *if she talked . . .*"

"Tom!" Tessa was aghast. "That's— that's terrible. Do you suppose they really mean it?"

"Yes I do."

He resumed his frantic pacing while Ella jumped up and began collecting cups, scurrying out to the kitchen.

"What are you—is she—going to do?"

"Cooperate with the police up to a point. We'll have to consider her position very carefully. She's gone to see her aunt and Paulo tonight. They're bringing her back . . ." he looked at his watch, "about now. I had wondered . . ." He stopped pacing. "I had wondered whether there was the slightest chance of Reardon bringing some kind of influence to bear on Guy Loden—whether some deal could be worked out. At the price of a certain amount of silence on Angie's part. He knows Loden. He might be willing to act as a sort of go-between. That's why I came here tonight—and waited for you to come back. What do you think?" He watched her closely.

"But that's ridiculous, Tom."

"Is it? Why? I'm pretty desperate, Tess."

"There's nothing Marcus could do. I'm sure of it."

"He's the *only possible* link we have, Tess, with Guy Loden. Only Loden could call off the heavies. Acid thrown in the face. Think of it . . ."

Tessa winced. "I'm sure Marcus wouldn't even try. I don't think he'd want to get involved. Not that it would help if he did."

"He would if you asked him."

Tessa sat there silently. She could feel all the excitement and confidence of the day draining out of her. The flower arrangements which looked so fresh and charming; supper with Joan; the concept for another shop which they had just finished hammering out.

If only Tom would stop going on and on about it. It was late, they were both tired and he, plainly, was badly overwrought. It was none of *her* business this terrible Loden affair. Who really knew the truth about Angie and her involvement with the goings-on in the Aberdeen Road house? And Tom hadn't even been at the flat when the threatening phone call had been made. Surely now, in London, nobody—not even hardened criminals—could make such a threat and expect to get away with it. It all sounded terribly farfetched to Tessa. She yawned.

"Marcus would listen to you, Tess, or at least give it some thought. And he might, he just might, be able to suggest something. If you asked him."

"All right," she agreed, exhausted. "I'll ask him. And if there's anything to report, I'll get in touch with you tomorrow. Now I'm going to bed."

Tom had scarcely left the house when the phone rang. It was Marcus.

"I hoped it was you," he said when she answered. "I think I wore out my welcome with Ella last night. I've just this minute got back from Oxford, interviewing some

438

appalling American who wants to be the next President. What about you, my love?"

"Tired and worn out." She sounded it. "And I've had Tom here . . . ."

"I'm not surprised. I saw the papers. I expect Angie will make a tremendous impression in the witness box; haughty pose on the steps of the court. All the camera boys will have a field day."

"Don't, Marcus," she said wearily. "It's serious—she's been threatened. Tom's in a dreadful state. He wants to know if you'll see Loden."

"What on earth for?"

"He thinks you can act as a go-between, let him know that there are certain things Angie won't say. Anyhow, he wants to see you."

A pause.

"I don't mind that . . ." His voice dropped. "Tessa, come over. Please." All pretence, all joking dropped. Oppression crept over her; the now-familiar loved and hated desire. Infatuation. Whatever it was. What he did to her—even his voice. And she was tired—so dreadfully tired. "Tessa, are you still there?"

"Yes."

She tried to concentrate on the shaft of golden light which cut across her father's desk. Her mind told her, coldly, to finish it there and then. Her throat was tight and her hands felt clammy.

"I'll give some thought to the Angie situation. I'd have to be convinced she was telling the truth. And I saw Vi last night . . ."

"What did you think?" Suddenly alert.

"Frankly, that she needs looking after rather badly. I'll tell you. Tessa, let me come and get you."

"*No . . .*"

"Then come yourself. Just tonight. Please, Tessa."

She whirled round her bedroom and slung some belongings into an overnight bag. She thought about nothing; her mind was completely blank. She flew down the stairs. Ella was in the hall, too distressed by Tom's revelations to do the final locking up and go to bed.

"Tessa, where on earth do you think you're going at this time of night?"

But Tessa already had her hand on the front door.

"I'm going to Joan's. We're in the middle of planning a new shop and we want to get our proposal together by tomorrow. I'll explain all about it soon." It sounded lame and ridiculous and no doubt Ella knew it. But she didn't care.

Ella waited until she heard her car shoot off up towards Knightsbridge before she turned off the last lights. She felt more deeply distressed and unhappy than she could remember. For years, ever since she had taken on the pair of them—no mother, the nasty divorce, Mr. Selway ill with malaria and at his wits' end—she had run number thirty-four Parloe Square with tact and common sense. Mr. Selway may not care to admit it but it was she, Ella Jones, who had got them through—even those first difficult years after the war. And they'd all turned out a credit: Mr. Selway with his name hardly off the business pages of the newspapers; Tom so brilliant and such a good cricketer; and Tessa—not quite what they'd hoped for yet, married and settled, but a sweet girl nevertheless, making a success of her shop. And with some of her Papa's good business sense, Ella thought.

Tonight, for the first time, the ordered world over which she presided had begun to slip away from her control. Shattered first by Tom, tales of this dreadful Loden man and Angie—and then by Tessa, tearing out of the house with some cock-and-bull story, about going to Joan's. As if she hadn't tumbled to that one. She'd seen that man, that friend of Lady D's, dropping her back here. He looked much too old for her liking, for Tessa. Not the right type at all.

Well, she sighed, they were adults now and they must do as they pleased. She found herself longing for Mr. Selway's return; perhaps then everything would go back to the way it had been just weeks before. The clock in the hall chimed midnight. Ella put her hand on her bad hip which was sending shooting pains down her side. Then, feeling old and weary, she took herself off to bed.

Tom, back in the Kensington flat, lifted the curtain and looked down on the dark, nearly empty street. He glanced repeatedly at his watch, fretting. Angie should have been back long before this. He had been surprised not to find her here when he got back. Paulo had promised to drop her right in front of the flat; he wasn't working at the restaurant that night. They would have a good supper, the three of them, cooked by Paulo. Angie could talk to them more freely without him; and they would bring her back, that was arranged. She didn't want to be left alone; she didn't even want to take a taxi. Not after the telephone call that afternoon.

She had told Auntie and Paulo this— omitting the phone call—when she decided on the visit after Tom came home. She was adamant that she wanted to tell them herself about Loden, and that she had severed all ties with him. It was only fair on them and the two youngsters, Angie told Tom, white-faced.

Tom agreed, dropping Angie at Auntie's and then racing to Ella in Parloe Square, to tell her everything—as he had always done—and hoping that Tessa would be around. When they were driving out to West Borwood, it was Angie who had said something about Tessa and Marcus.

"Marcus knows his way round all right," she had said in that hard voice, a bit Cockney, that made Tom uneasy. "He's got a name now, through the column. He's got weight, if he chooses to use it. *He* could reach Loden for us. And he might —for Tessa. She's got under his skin. I knew when I saw them together at that party. She's so different, I suppose. And young. *Posh.*" She almost spat the word. "Nothing like her has ever hit him before or probably will again."

Tom made up his mind, then and there, that even getting Marcus's advice was worth a try.

So where was Angie? He let the curtain drop and began pottering round the flat, touching books, edgily switching a lamp on and off. She needed protection, there was no doubt about that . . . and as far as he could see, there was only one way he could give it.

In a side-street some hundred yards away, a small car slowed and stopped, the engine still running. Although alert for the sound, Tom didn't hear it in the steady drone of traffic, even at this hour. The driver was a swarthy, overweight middle-aged man wearing an open-necked shirt. Sitting next to him was a pretty woman with faded grey-blonde hair and a worried expression. Angie uncoiled herself from the back seat, got out and waved them off. Once the car was out of sight, she started walking towards the flat, her hands deep in the pockets of her white coat.

Although the street was so close to a main London thoroughfare, it was quiet and ill-lit. Her footsteps echoed. She was almost at the corner, when a powerful car swerved into the street at high speed— a dense black outline, tyres shrieking. Instinctively, Angie veered on to the pavement, shoulders pressing against the wall. But to her horror, the car, its headlights fused into one blazing arc, accelerated and appeared to come straight at her.

For an instant, no more, she was mesmerised by the speed and the brilliant light. Then she flung herself ahead into the darkness—into the rapidly decreasing space between the car and the wall. The car missed her by inches, hardly braking as it turned out of sight.

Weak with terror, Angie raced for the house, pushing the key into the lock, clattering up the three floors, banging on the flat door with her fists. When Tom opened it, she was standing, her face as chalky as her coat, trembling.

"Oh my God, Tom," she gasped. "He's tried to kill me! And next time . . ."

He pulled her inside, sat her down on the sofa and gave her a brandy and made her tell him, slowly and precisely, what had happened, moments before, in the empty side-street where Paulo had dropped her. He stayed very calm, very controlled. He asked her questions of the same kind, and in the same tone, as he might have used in court. He said gravely, "I've asked Tessa to speak to Marcus. He might—just *might*—be able to get certain points across to Loden which we want him to know. And believe. She has more or less said she will. But this changes everything. I'm going to speak to Reardon myself." He glanced at his watch. "Now." Angie stared at him, the glass shaking in her hand, mute. "But first . . ."

Tom's face, which had been so strained, broke into a huge smile. He dropped on to one knee in front of her and put his hands on her arms. And he looked very handsome with his fair hair flopping forward, his tie pulled loose from his collar.

"Angie, my darling," he said, "Please marry me."

Driving up Park Lane, Tessa heard Big Ben—right across central London which was already dimmed and slowed—booming out midnight. There was still a fair amount of traffic about, and she drove impatiently.

The second she rang the flat bell downstairs, lights came on in the dilapidated hallway. She raced up. Marcus was waiting for her in the door of the flat. He didn't smile, just held out his arms. Once she was inside, he grabbed her—she almost collapsed against him—holding her tightly. Then he walked her into the bedroom, took her bag and started to undress her. Bone-weary, like a rag doll, she let him.

Neither of them spoke one word.

While Tessa kicked off her shoes, Marcus took a nightdress from her bag and slipped it over her head. She got into the cot-like bed.

"I'm for the sofa tonight." He bent over her. "Sleep tight, my love." He drew the covers up round her chin.

"What about Tom?" she whispered.

"I've spoken to him already. He phoned just before you got here. It is serious. I'll do what I can. I've arranged to meet him on Monday. Now—forget about it. Go to sleep." His hand was on the pillow by her head. Tessa moved and kissed it.

"Thanks Marcus."

He went to the door. "See you in the morning." He switched off the light. Her tears were a mixture of many things—love and regret and hope and confusion and tiredness. Mostly tiredness. She didn't make a sound and very soon she was asleep.

18

TESSA woke very early, and for a few seconds she could not think where on earth she was. She opened her eyes on to a wall of books and white curtains. Her heart pounded with anxiety . . . Marcus's flat. Last night. She must have been mad to come here. So late, so tired, so irrationally. Thoughts and worries came tumbling into her mind: "Tessa's Garden", Tom and the Loden case, Gran, Ella's face as she rushed head-long out of the front door.

Her heart thumped away under the covers. She could hear Marcus in the kitchen and smell coffee brewing. She called out to him.

"Marcus?"

"Coming . . ."

The door opened and he stood there—smiling that lopsided smile, looking very alert and rested. (He must have been able to sleep properly on the sofa.) Fully dressed, shirt-sleeves rolled up, sweater

449

slung casually round his shoulders. Those good cheek bones; seeming younger than he usually did; handsome. *Looking happy*.

Tessa sat up and smiled back at him, knowing then exactly why she had fled across London at midnight.

"Hello," she said. "Hello there . . ." She must look a sight, her hair a mess and the straps of her nightdress falling over her shoulders.

"You look delicious, charmingly crumpled. I wanted to see you here this morning just like this. My Tessa." He had brought her a mug of coffee. "I know you slept because I looked in on you later. You were a poor darling exhausted heap last night." He drew the curtains, letting in great shafts of sun. Then he sat on the bed and handed her the coffee. "Dearest, darling Tessa . . ." He leant over and kissed her shoulder where the straps had slipped.

"Don't. You'll make me spill," she warned. (Breath coming faster, excited by his mere touch.)

"It's fresh, I've just made it. Look, I told you that I'd seen Vi. And I do agree that she's fading—she really needs someone with her all the time."

"We've tried that on her already. She doesn't want it—and she's very stubborn."

"Oh, I know. Can't Ella persuade her to have a housekeeper? I'm sure she's not eating, just sipping brandy and soda all day long. And as you say, her mind goes in and out of the past—one minute she's rational, the next, off somewhere." He frowned. "Her health is all right, is it? I thought she seemed very frail . . ."

"As far as we know it is. She refuses to have a doctor near her, and she seems to be quite well. She still goes out a bit—at least the terrible Charlie sees that she gets dressed and has some fresh Belgravia air."

Marcus laughed. "There is that, although he's a horrible spoilt creature, isn't he? And another thing I told you last night, remember?" He dropped a kiss on her nose. "I'm seeing Tom on Monday. And Angie. I can't promise to be of any use, but I'll hear them both out and if I think I can do any good, I'll speak to Loden. They're hell-bent on shutting Angie up. There doesn't seem any doubt

451

about that. After all, they met through me —and I feel somewhat responsible. It *is* frightening . . ."

"About the acid, you mean? Tom told me . . ."

"And other things," he said evasively. "Threatening. I'm convinced she's being truthful; it's very worrying. He means business, Loden does. And Tom, as you know, is nearly out of his mind . . . Angie seems to have taken him over, completely, doesn't she?"

"He loves her," Tessa said.

"Yes."

Marcus looked at her, almost said something, but seemed to change his mind. Then, "It's a marvellous day, look . . ." Sunshine was pouring into the room, even here, in the dingy block in Soho. "It's not expected to last, so let's make the most of it. Let's go to the country."

"Where?" Tessa enquired, sipping coffee.

"To Dorset." Marcus was smiling at her, still holding one hand, stroking her arm.

"*Dorset*. But why?" She sounded dismayed.

"Sweet Tessa, you know you wanted to go down and see your mother. You said so. And I'd be fascinated to meet her. Let's make a day out of it. Why don't we?"

Tessa hesitated. For all the powerful sensations which his presence evoked in her, she would really rather not. Not there. Not to Dorset. Mother, the Floods, her wartime childhood . . . Something, some inner caution, warned her off.

"Marcus, I can't."

"But you can reach your mother through the Floods, can't you? Or the post office? Tell her we're coming down this morning. We'll start early—we won't stay there long. To be truthful, I've wanted to meet her—Jennie—for years. And Felix. You know what an inquisitive so-and-so I am. And I badly need to get out of London." He tipped up her face and kissed her lightly. "Some country air with you is just what I want. Say yes, Tessa mine."

"I'm going down to see Mother . . . I've just spoken to Aunt Flor, and she's getting Bea at the post office down the road to tell her," Tessa told Ella an hour or so later, avoiding her direct look. She had driven herself back to Parloe Square from Marcus's flat. Snatching a letter from Oliver off the hall table, she had started to fly up to her room. Ella called out and she had stopped on the first landing looking down at her in the hall. "Marcus Reardon, that friend of Gran's, is driving me down. He's picking me up here in about twenty minutes." She saw no point in lying more than she had to.

"I see, dear," Ella said evenly. Neither made any reference to her flight from the house so late the previous evening. Or to Joan and the shop. "Well, that's nice for you, isn't it? You won't have to drive yourself—or go fussing about with those difficult trains and all the changing. Maggie will be over in a little while. We're going to an early film and popping in on Lady D on our way there. I want Maggie to have a look at her—professionally, you might say. She won't hear of us getting in the doctor, although I'm pretty sure she's not eating properly."

"Oh Ella, I'm so glad about that— Maggie going to see her." Tessa said,

454

genuinely relieved. Gran had become a real worry. Something would have to be done, especially now that Marcus, too, was concerned. "She *is* being naughty. Do you suppose you could suggest a housekeeper —someone living in? Perhaps she would take it better from Maggie."

"You know how she is, Tess. A law unto herself. She's often quite breathless —it's this, really, that I want Maggie to look out for. She's very experienced, you know, and used to nursing older people. But when I spoke to Lady D this morning to tell her when to expect us, she sounded very chirpy. You never know with her from one day to the next."

"I'll have to tell Mother that she's not been too good . . . although I don't suppose we can expect any help from *her.*"

"Oh no, Lady D won't want her poking her nose in," Ella said decidedly. "Not that she's likely to take the trouble." She sniffed. "Give them all my regards won't you, Tess, the Floods as well?"

"Of course—and Ella, I might stay the night with Mother as I'm down there. I might. So don't worry about me . . ."

"Very well, dear." Ella didn't so much as blink. "I'll expect you when I see you, Sunday some time. Anyhow, have a nice visit. It's a lovely day for you."

Tessa quickly changed and packed a holdall. Marcus seemed insistent on their staying down somewhere, making a weekend of it. She could hear the warning signals ticking away again; but it was too late now. Turning, she saw the envelope on her dressing-table and ripped it open. She smiled. Oliver had written it in the train on his way down to Winchester where he had a case, in his most ebullient style. The car had "packed up" on his way back from "leaving you in Parloe Square last night". Out of petrol, he'd forgotten to fill up, and what a lucky escape she had had not getting stranded . . . Wasn't it a splendid evening, and she hadn't forgotten everything he had said, had she? And he had the theatre tickets—good seats too— and he might have to stay the night in Winchester (feeble case, not worth the trouble, but there it was) and the car was being mended and he really did adore her. And that was that. "All my love, Oliver

XXX" And a ps—"I'll give you a ring on Sunday."

It was all so typically Oliver. She pictured the car, and started to laugh. The bell rang and she ran down the stairs—thankfully, no sign of Ella—and she was still laughing when she got into the car with Marcus and they shot up to Knightsbridge and headed west. It was the thought of hefty Oliver and his dented and troublesome black beetle.

"What's so funny?" Marcus asked, noticing her giggles.

But she only said, "Nothing much. Nothing at all. I spoke to the Floods and we'll have a drink with them on our way. And don't expect much hospitality from Mother. Lunch is strictly bread and cheese —it simply never varies."

As the summery countryside floated by, and they had left the heavy traffic, Marcus relaxed and settled back into his seat. "Sorry . . . ," as he felt for her hand, "I'm being poor company. I'm childish about being thwarted by traffic." They had to yell at each other to make themselves heard above the engine.

"We're well on our way now. I told Aunt Flor we'd be there about twelve. We'll only stay for a bit—Hubie's not really up to seeing people these days."

"How far on from them is your mother's cottage, did you say?"

"Only about three miles, but the roads are very narrow and winding. It's deepest Dorset there, all right," Tessa yelled back.

The sun had broken through the greyness, lighting up the green fields and the hedgerows. Large patches of blue spread above them. Leaving the grime and congestion of London always induced a mild euphoria in Tessa. It did so then, despite all her misgivings at coming down with Marcus. He began fiddling with the radio. He found a brief news bulletin which was followed by a weather forecast of violent electric storms coming in from the west.

"That settles it." Marcus moved the stick easily through the gears. "We'll stay down for the night, don't you think? We've come all this way and there's no need to rush back for either of us. Particularly if that weather arrives . . . We can find a decent pub. Yes?"

"Well, perhaps." But she didn't want to. Despite the sun and the good feeling of being out of London with Marcus her uneasiness persisted. She thought of Ella and Maggie, off to a film, ringing Gran's doorbell; she thought about Oliver's letter lying on her dressing-table. "Let's see how the day goes, shall we?"

Marcus glanced at her quickly, sideways, and said nothing.

As they reached the first ugly straggle of houses which led into the pretty main street of Chalcot and the Floods' house, powerful childhood memories came flooding back to Tessa as they always did when she came here. Up the next street was the station, its two platforms still in use, where she had met Papa back from Burma. Almost a stranger in his redbraided uniform. She, petrified; and sweet peas in bowls all over Chalcot House.

"I don't know what you'll make of Mother," Tessa said as they reached the shops. "She's not in the least like Gran."

"So I gather. I'm looking forward to it, after knowing Vi all these years. And to meeting Felix as well. I looked him up, actually. He's very well-known in his

459

field." They were stuck, the engine idling noisily, behind a lumbering bus.

"He doesn't do much translation any more because his eyes are so bad. He's a darling, Felix is. He and Hubie were both linguists at Heidelberg at the same time. They've been friends ever since. It was Hubie, or so I've always been told, who got Felix out of France in the war. It's a dreadful story. His wife and daughter were taken from their apartment in Vienna by the Gestapo and disappeared into the camps. He never saw them again. Felix was away on an international conference somewhere . . . he was so eminent that he was allowed to leave the country even then. Anyhow, he escaped and was hidden in a cellar for years."

"Lucky chap. Extraordinary how he survived and turned up in the depths of the English countryside."

"And then met my mother."

"Even more extraordinary. But he must live with terrible memories. How did Hubie manage to winch him out of France, I wonder? The Germans had an amazingly strong grip on the whole country."

"Hubie was in the SOE. He had contacts."

"Was he really?" This immediately caught Marcus's attention. "He must have had some incredible experiences."

"Look, there's Chalcot House, at the end, set back from the street a bit. Can you see?"

"It's a pretty little place, Chalcot, lots of nice mellow red Georgian bricks."

"It is. And it never changes."

"When were you here last?"

"A few months ago. Tom and I always come for Christmas—without Papa. And it's all exactly as it was when we lived here in the war, Tom and Mother and I. You can't imagine how we missed it when Papa, whom we scarcely knew, dragged Tom and me off to Parloe Square."

Glossy magnolia leaves covered much of the façade of Chalcot House. Heavy curtains were partially drawn at the front windows. Tessa put her finger on the round brass bell as Marcus jerked back his hair and attempted to straighten his cravat. Behind the white door, they heard the sound of dot-and-carry-one coming down the stone-flagged hall.

"It's Marie," Tessa hissed at Marcus. "She's their French cook-housekeeper. I warn you—she's terrifying. They've had her since before the war."

The door creaked open. Marie stood to the side, dark and watchful, little changed from the way Tessa remembered her as a child. Only the hair, pulled severely back, was more obviously streaked with white.

"Bonjour Marie. Comment allez-vous? I've brought a friend of Gran's down. This is Mr. Reardon."

"Bonjour Téssa." As always, she pronounced her name with an accent on the e. She glowered at Marcus and turned, leading the way through the hall, talking at them in French over her shoulder.

"You have had a good journey? Monsieur and Madame are waiting for you in the garden. You should know that Monsieur is not in good health—we have already had the doctor today. You will see."

The Floods were outside on the lawn. The white wrought-iron table and chairs were set beneath the green beech tree, with a view right across the paddock and the fields to the low blue line of hills in the distance. As Tessa and Marcus walked out of the garden room, they saw Aunt Flor, enthroned in one of the chairs. She seemed to be wearing grey chiffon and her hair was piled strangely on top of her head.

Hubert Flood saw them first. He started towards them, his head grotesquely bent, dipping and swaying in their direction. Tessa was appalled. She had not known whether she would find him in better or worse condition than when she saw him last, but she had never expected this degree of disfigurement. In the weeks since she had seen him, the disease had taken hold. Tessa nerved herself as she went towards him.

"Hello, Hubie. Here we are . . . sorry we're late, the traffic out of London was bad. You remember Marcus Reardon?" She attempted to kiss his bobbing cheek.

"But of course, Tessa, my darling, what a lovely thing to happen." Tremors shook his entire body uncontrollably. "On your way to see your mother, are you? If Mr. Reardon could kindly open a bottle of champagne for us . . . My hands, you know, these days. Come and have a drop, do."

Even in illness, Tessa thought, his courtesy and his manners had not deserted him. And there didn't seem to be anything wrong with his mind, either.

"Thanks, Hubie, we'd love some." She took his arm with difficulty.

He moved sideways, crab-like, concentrating so as not to lose his balance. "Lovely of you both to have taken the time to drop in on us. We adore company." His head drooped lower. "Don't get enough of it these days, I'm afraid."

"Hubert." Flora Flood, shading her eyes with her hand, called out sharply. "Come and sit down. You're wearing yourself out. You know what Dr. Holford said. Come and sit down. Bring him here, Tess."

Marcus rearranged the chairs around the table. It was warm and hazy with a coppery sun lurking above the green beech.

"Hello, darling," Flora said to Tessa as she kissed the side of her aunt's face, barely missing the piled-up white hair.

464

"Sweet of you to come; I'm afraid we can't cope with lunch, even with Marie. You do understand, Mr. Reardon."

"Oh *Marcus*, please."

"Well then, Marcus, deal with the champagne, would you?"

Although she chatted away, not for one second did her eyes leave Hubie; she watched his every move with anxious, almost maternal, love. Eventually, when they were all settled, sitting with glasses, she turned to Tessa. "So you're off to see Jennie and Felix?"

"That's right, I promised I'd come down, and Marcus has never met her although he's heard about her from Gran for ages. Since David, actually . . ."

"Yes, I remember. They flew together, didn't they, David and Marcus? Ghastly tragedy, David's death. I don't know how we all went on, Vi especially." She sounded bleak, defeated, unlike her usual robust self. Hubert's illness had taken a toll on her too. "But of course we did. So many fearful things were happening at the time. Look at Felix and his family. One practically despaired. You were too young to know what was happening, mercifully."

She fumbled among the yards of chiffon and produced a crumpled packet of Gauloises. "All right, Vi, is she? She sounded quite potty on the phone the other night—going on and on about Ben Levson, I ask you. As if anyone remembered all those ages ago . . ." Impatient, drawing heavily on the cigarette, her eyes returned achingly to Hubie.

"Gran's not too bad," Tessa said carefully, the smooth and golden champagne —the best of Hubie's considerable cellar, Marcus told her later in some awe—was immediately going to her head, gently blunting her sadness at seeing Hubie. "She's a bit, well, vague, since Grandpa died. Ella's going round to see her this afternoon with her sister Maggie, the nurse."

"That's all right, then," Flora was hardly listening. "I expect she needs a good change."

On her right, Tessa heard Marcus engage Hubie in conversation about the war, occupied France . . . they were trading experiences, Marcus talking openly about some of his more nerve-racking flights over Germany. They had found common ground which genuinely interested both men. With two hands, Hubie somehow got his glass to his lips.

"How's the shop going, Tess?" Flora asked.

"Very well. We're tremendously busy. Even Papa is going to be surprised at our turnover this year. And we would like to open another."

"I *am* glad." But she was abstracted, turning again towards Hubie. Tessa followed her glance.

"He's gone down a lot, Aunt Flor," she said quietly.

"Yes, yes he has. It happened very suddenly, just like that. Young Dr. Holford keeps us all going. He seems less agitated now. He's enjoying talking to Mr. Reardon." She sighed, and stubbed out her half-smoked cigarette. "George and Poppy still in America, are they?"

"Yes. They'll be back in a couple of weeks. Papa has just done a tremendous deal for Selway Electric."

"Has he? Hubie always said he was a shrewd businessman. We don't bother much with the papers these days. Er, Marcus is a journalist Vi says . . ."

"And a successful one. He has his own column in the *Chronicle*."

"Has he now?" Her aunt eyed her with interest for the first time. "You're looking very paintable, child," she said kindly. "Strong colours suit you. I like that blue, cerulean, and cobalt yellow. That's a pretty skirt, rather like a Turkish peasant's. After all these years, I can only think of colours in terms of the canvas."

"I'm sure. Are you painting much now Aunt Flor?"

Flora Flood shook her head and the meringue-like nest of hair trembled. "I can't, you see. Well, how can I?" She shrugged. "We've had the most wonderful life together—but it's very cruel, this." She watched Hubie, whose tremor had subsided, and who was talking animatedly to Marcus. "Poor you, having to eat at Jennie's. Have you warned Marcus about the odd ménage up there?"

Tessa laughed. "I have, but it's hard to explain, isn't it? I'm sure he'll enjoy meeting Felix, anyhow."

It was very pleasant sitting there in the shade, looking back at the house. Roses climbed all round the long drawing-room

468

windows and pots of brilliant geraniums splashed the grey stone of the terrace. Tessa felt peaceful after the irksome journey; pleased that Marcus and Hubie were getting on so well. She chatted to her aunt about this and that—local people they both knew, Tom, Max's music scholarship —until after about a quarter of an hour Flora Flood leant across the table, interrupting Hubie.

"Top us up, would you be so kind Marcus? And then why don't you get Tessa to show you round the garden? It's looking very good." She eyed Hubie anxiously.

Marcus broke off what he was saying and stood up, taking the champagne from the bucket and glancing at the label before he carefully refilled the glasses. "Thank you, I'd like that. And I don't suppose there's any chance of seeing your studio, is there Mrs. Flood?"

"Of course, if you wish. The door's open . . . show him Tessa. It's the usual mess and not much work in progress."

"I think she must have kept every article she ever used in her still-life pictures,"

Tessa told Marcus as they looked round the light, lofty room which was crammed with objects of every description—pots of every colour and size and glasses and dried flowers, all faded with dust and age. Canvases were stacked deep against the wall. A half-finished oil painting of the summer garden rested on an easel. An ancient, sagging sofa and armchair, both covered with rugs and shawls, surrounded a black oil stove. The whole place smelled of turpentine.

Marcus strolled round, peering, touching. "How absolutely fascinating."

"It's the old stable-block, you see. Hubie had it converted into a studio when they came back from living in France at the beginning of the war, shortly before we came to live here."

They wandered out. There was no sign of Flora or Hubert Flood. Tessa stopped underneath the spreading beech tree. "Do you see this uneven patch of grass? This is where we used to dig in our sandals under the swing which was tied on to that high branch, there," she squinted up through the dappled leaves. "You can still see the grooves in the bark."

"I see." Marcus put his hand on her shoulder and peered up.

"Tom and I used to bet each other who could go higher. He always won. I can remember, just as though it was yesterday, waiting for Fred and his taxi to drive me to the station to meet Papa. I was terrified, you see—I couldn't remember him at all. And I swung up, up, up—head back, feeling quite dizzy, you know how you do when you're a kid."

"And you looked angelic, Tessa, in that blue dress with the sash." Tessa and Marcus turned in surprise. Flora Flood, the chiffon wafting about her, had come across the lawn to meet them. Her long silver earrings jangled.

"We were sure you were going to get it dirty. She was such a tomboy in those days. And I painted her, wearing the dress, sitting with Orlando, the cat we had then. He was a marmalade puss and his coat almost matched her hair."

"The painting in London? Above the mantelpiece in the drawing-room?" His hand stayed on Tessa's shoulder.

"Oh you've been there?" She sounded slightly surprised. "That's right. I always loved that one." She looked from Marcus to Tessa—and back to Marcus. She had apparently noticed his hand. With a jolt, Tessa thought: she doesn't like Marcus. He was marvellous with Hubie, but she doesn't like him. I wonder why.

"I think we ought to go off to mother's, Aunt Flor," she said.

19

"KEEP going on this road and it's about a mile down on the right. It's the only dwelling for miles around, so you can't possibly miss it. It's a hideous red brick semi-bungalow. Tom and I can never think why on earth it's called a cottage."

And neither, when he saw it, could Marcus. It was built close to the road with an intensively cultivated garden spreading out behind. A fair-haired woman in a faded cotton dress stood by the ugly iron gate, waving to them.

"There you are, Tessa . . . cooee!" She had a high, light voice. "Lovely to see you, darling, and such a surprise. Felix is thrilled, of course."

"Mother," Tessa said quietly to Marcus as they walked towards her. "You'd recognise her anywhere, she's so like Tom."

"*Darling,*" Jennie cried. Tessa barely brushed her mother's cheek. "And this must be Mr. . . ." Her eyes glowed, radiantly blue in the lovely face, as she extended her hand.

"Marcus Reardon, Mother. David's and Gran's friend, you remember." The mere sight of her mother irritated Tessa—and it showed.

"Yes, *of course*. I've heard so much . . ." Still smiling, vague. "Now do come in. You saw the Floods, did you? Felix is longing to see you—both of you and have someone intelligent to talk to for a change." Her hair was drawn back into a bun with wisps escaping about her slender neck. Her features, Marcus saw at once, were perfect. There was simply nothing wrong with them. Nose, chin, cheekbones —even the arc of her eyebrows. Her face was hardly lined at all. Like David, he thought bleakly, as he followed her, exactly like David would look now; his normal face, not the one they built.

Inside, an elderly man rose from an armchair where he was bent over, reading, and hurried towards them. He was slight and so round-shouldered that he appeared at first to have a hunchback.

"Tessa, my darling, you have been

neglecting us, for shame. Far, far too long since I saw you." He spoke with a pronounced, guttural accent. Tessa greeted him with noticeably more warmth than she had her mother, and Felix Morgenstern was clearly delighted to see her. His eyes behind thick glasses lit up at the sight of her; his smile and his manner transformed his unprepossessing appearance. He charmed instantly.

"Hello, Felix, I've missed you too." Tessa hugged him. "And I've brought you someone interesting to talk to, who knows all about your translations. This is Marcus Reardon, the journalist."

"Welcome, how good that you have bothered to come all this way to call on us. We are very, very out of everything down here, as you will imagine. Now, Marcus Reardon, let me see . . ." He clapped his hands together. "I have it, but of course . . . the *Chronicle*. My dear Sir, we are honoured. You see, books and newspapers are my lifelines these days. Sit down, sit down. We will be lunching in a moment. Now tell me . . ."

The two men started talking. Felix Morgenstern had the wonderful gift of being interested in everyone and everything. He inclined courteously towards Marcus, his eyes gleaming with intelligence, and immediately began enquiring knowledgeably about his work, even remembering an anecdote from one of his last week's columns. Tessa left them at it and went into the kitchen to find her mother.

"Is there anything I can do?"

"Nothing, darling. I expect you're both starving. We'll eat at once because I have to do some picking after. Perhaps you would give me a hand with the peas? I'm selling masses of our fruit and veg at the markets these days. How do you think Felix is looking? He's had a touch of rheumatism lately and I have worried rather."

Tessa thought, with an edge of bitterness: she is totally, totally absorbed in Felix and her own life. She hasn't even the normal polite curiosity about mine—her daughter's. Except for Felix, it's as though she has drawn a veil between her and the rest of the world. Nothing else, nobody else, exists for her.

They ate at a table in the corner of the sitting-room. On it were four plates and knives, four glasses—and cheese and homemade bread and pickles. Jennie Morgenstern carried in jugs of beer and cider. Tessa thought, briefly and regretfully, of Marie's cooking and the dining-room table at Chalcot House. She caught Marcus's eye and glanced away quickly.

"Hubie looked dreadful," Tessa said to her mother. "It was awful seeing him like that."

"Did he, darling?" Jennie looked round the table, her light and exceptionally luminous eyes, quite expressionless. "Do help yourself to everything, Mr. Reardon: cheese, pickles . . ." She cut large chunks of bread.

"Yes, he did," Tessa said sharply. "His tremor is so bad that he can hardly get around. Marie said they had had the doctor in this morning. When did you see him last?"

"A few weeks ago, I believe," Jennie said vaguely, offering bread. Tessa turned away impatiently.

"I know, I know." Felix looked across at Tessa gravely, nodding. "I was also there this week. There is nothing more that can be done for him. I spoke to Dr.

Holford and he believes that his condition may stabilise with the new drugs they are using, but it is a terrible illness, terrible."

Under cover of the conversation, Marcus assessed the room. It was barely furnished, only the row of books, a pile of newspapers and some records, all grouped round the chair in which Felix had been sitting, added some warmth and individuality. There were no signs of affluence whatsoever: a worn sofa, a couple of chairs, a rug. Also beside Felix's chair was an old-fashioned radio.

Circumspectly, Marcus studied Jennie Morgenstern. He had been conscious of something odd and remote about her the moment he met her by the gate. And he realised now that it was because she did not really *look* at anyone except Felix; only fussing ridiculously over his food, did she seem to focus. Her looks, too, were baffling. Her face, apart from some fine lines around the eyes, really could be described as timeless. There was no trace of make-up. She could be any age between thirty and sixty.

"These pickles are excellent," Marcus said helping himself to more.

"Mine," said Jennie, smiling radiantly at Felix, for all the world like a young girl in love. "I'm so glad you like them. Max, our son, is going to try and pop in for a minute. He's got a violin lesson later and he's having general tuition in Chalcot now. A teacher at the grammar school in Porchester is giving it to him. After the local school I'm afraid he has to get the rest of his subjects up to his music standard."

"Max is going to Hellston School in September," Tessa told Marcus. "He's got a music scholarship. He's a genius, isn't he Felix? We must have one in the family."

"Ah, Tessa, you are such a tease," Felix replied, going pink with pleasure and clearly believing it. "He is a good boy and tries hard at his work. I help him all I can but he needs someone who, how shall I say, knows the ropes. His music, that is different. Young as he is, he plays with *soul.*"

Tessa and her mother cleared the table. No coffee was offered. Jennie immediately suggested that she and Tessa go out in the garden to pick—and let Marcus and Felix go for a walk. She knew, she said, that

Felix was dying to cross examine Marcus about his work. "But not too far, Felix, nothing tiring. You won't let him, will you Marcus?"

Tessa and her mother, each with a large straw basket, tackled the peas. They worked on either side of the high, staked plants now dense with greenery.

"Tom was here the other day," Jennie called through. "With a girl."

"Angie. She's beautiful, isn't she?"

"Oh very. And I thought Tom seemed happy. Felix thought she wasn't quite the thing, not quite right."

"In what way?" Tessa, interested, briefly stopped picking.

"He didn't think she seemed quite, well, educated enough for Tom. But I can't see what on earth that matters. Your basket's not full up, is it?"

"Heavens no."

Tessa considered, and rejected, telling her mother about Gran's recent bout of odd behaviour. It wouldn't register, for one thing. Nothing ever did except for Felix—or Max. Or Tom, occasionally. And in any case, the last thing Gran would want would be Mother rushing up to Eaton Square. Through the bottom of the curly green plants, Tessa could see her mother's feet moving slowly ahead of her —bare legs and old brown sandals. Tessa sighed. She admired her mother for making a small success of this market gardening; it was hard physical work, and she supposed she made a bit of money, which they needed. But it was desperately boring. Hoping fervently that Marcus and Felix would come back soon, she went back to the picking.

Marcus was enjoying their brisk walk along a path at the edge of the downland. Peering ahead and using a stick, talking volubly, Felix kept up a brisk pace. Marcus strolled along beside him. They had turned back after some twenty minutes and were now approaching the gate. The sky had clouded over and it was very still. Marcus slapped at midges on his arm. There was thunder about.

They had been speaking at length about the early days of the war which both men recalled vividly from very different points of view. Felix had spoken very openly about his life and work in Vienna, the ominous grip of the Nazis which only he, of his entire family, had escaped. He was now telling Marcus how desperately he wished he could take his son back to Vienna one day, show him the apartment house where he was brought up, the graves of his parents and those landmarks of his earlier life that still remained. "It is my dearest wish," he said, his voice full of emotion. "And to go with Max, with the future generation—that would, if you understand, do much to exorcise the past." He turned to Marcus, clearly moved.

"I think I do understand," Marcus replied quietly. "As much as anyone outside that particular experience can."

"And you, as a writer, a professional, will understand when I tell you, very truthfully, that it was the written word, my own, which preserved my mind and my sanity through it all."

Marcus stopped, surprised. "I know your translations," he said, "and I know your very distinguished academic background. But I hadn't realised that you have published work of your own?"

Felix's face puckered into a smile.

"Ach—published, no. But written—yes."

"May I ask what?"

He leant on his stick with both hands. As he spoke, his accent became increasingly pronounced.

"It is a long story, very personal. Years have passed, the world has moved on . . . but for two years during the war I was hidden in the cellar of the house of a French family sympathetic to the Allies. During that time, I never went out, not even at night. Apart from whispered exchanges with the family, I was quite cut off from all social contact; from daylight, from wind and rain, from the everyday world, you might say. *Totally*. In private, helpless agony over the fate of my family."

Tessa had mentioned this wartime episode on their way down that morning.

"And you started writing?" Marcus asked, alert. "During the time you were hidden?"

Felix shrugged eloquently.

"Of course. Then it was the only way I knew to survive. And I had, I discovered, great tenacity, a great will to live—my

483

curiosity overcame the tragic circumstances. I had to hold on. I had to *know* what had happened to my wife, my daughter, colleagues . . ."

"You—started to keep a journal perhaps?" Marcus asked tentatively. But the hesitation was false. All his instincts for sniffing out a good story had been aroused. He had some idea of the quality of this man's intellect; he could imagine the depth of the writing.

"A diary, yes. They managed to get me pencils and paper. And I wrote, a little, every day. It was the discipline by which I lived. The family—their comings and goings, their private, domestic upheavals, became my own eyes and my own ears. And the Maquis, the British and French agents who used the house as a headquarters; and the Germans; two young officers were billeted in the spare bedroom for days, only feet from where I lay in the attic beneath shelves of apples gathered from the orchard. I lost all idea of time, of the seasons . . ."

"I'm sure," Marcus agreed, intent. "And you wrote also of your own feelings, the reactions of a hunted man, in isolation, a virtual prisoner?"

"That too."

"Were the British agents able to get word to Hubert Flood? That was how you escaped, wasn't it?"

Felix nodded.

"Eventually . . . and they were very good to me—*wonderful*—both Hubert and Flora. And yet, so soon after, I, who wished never to hurt anyone, was myself inflicting pain of a kind on others."

"This was when you met Jennie."

"Yes." Felix had been looking away across the chalky fields. Now, he turned his face to Marcus. Lined and sallow, yet it was transfigured with joy. "It is not easy to speak of such things," he said gently, "so let me just say that we both had suffered. And we recognised that each had the capacity to understand and heal the other. *Immediately*. And so it has been. Come."

He walked on, leaving Marcus no alternative but to follow.

Suffer? Jennie Delmore, now Morgenstern? And on a par with the tragic events of Felix's past? What on earth could he mean? Marcus was uncharacteristically stumped for any possible answer. He quickened his pace to reach Felix who was pushing on ahead.

"The diary," Marcus persisted, pulling up beside him. "Were you able to bring it with you when you escaped?"

"Ja. I have it still."

All Marcus's senses as a newspaperman were alight now. He was like a cat stalking prey. Its possibilities, he decided, might be enormous. He said casually, "It sounds like a most valuable record. Have you ever thought of—showing it to a publisher perhaps?"

Felix shook his head emphatically.

"*Never.* It is a personal experience, to be shown one day to my son only."

They had reached the cottage. In a woosh of air and a screech of tyres, a lad of about thirteen appeared from behind on a bicycle, stopped, and dismounted.

"Hello Dad, I'm not too late am I? To see Tess? I raced all the way back from Chalcot."

"Ah, Max, there you are . . . ." The boy was breathless and red-cheeked, the image of his father but with his mother's light blue eyes. "No, you're not too late. This is Mr. Reardon, a friend of Tessa's. My son, Max."

"How do you do, then?" Max said cheerfully, and quite unselfconsciously. He had his father's openness of manner. "Is that your car, the green one?" And when Marcus nodded, "Cor, i'n it smashing—I bet you don't half get up some speed in that."

"I'll take you for a spin if you like."

Max's face fell. "I've got a violin lesson, over in Porchester. Mum's taking me— and we'll be late if we don't get on over." He spoke with a slightly burred country inflection.

"Another time then . . ."

"Tessa is picking with your mother, Max. You know where to find them." Max went off wheeling his bike, Marcus and Felix looking after him.

"What a nice lad," Marcus said.

"A good boy, a very good boy. He is most patient with his decrepit old father. And he is talented, really. Hubert Flood has been wonderful to him, absolutely wonderful. He has arranged his music lessons since he was very young. And now that he won the scholarship, he has given him a very beautiful violin."

"He may go far," Marcus smiled.

"We shall see, we shall see."

Jennie, Felix and Max all saw them off. Felix had his arm round Max's shoulders; they were much the same height. Jennie stood close to Felix, her hand on his elbow.

"I hope you are going straight back to London?" Jennie called. "It's going to storm. Do go straight back, darling." She sounded almost motherly; concerned.

"I expect so—we'll meander. Good luck with the new violin, Max. I'll be down later in the summer, Mother."

Everybody waved and smiled to everyone else and they moved off down the dusty road.

Marcus, negotiating a difficult bend, said, "That was very pleasant. I liked Felix, he's fascinating to talk to. What memories . . . A 'story of our times' if ever I heard one. Max seems a pleasant lad. Felix obviously dotes on him."

"And what about Mother?"

Suffering, he thought, her *suffering*

. . . He said, "Her looks are pure Delmore —strikingly like Tom and David. But you're right, she's a bit unearthly. I wouldn't mind betting that there's a story there too, if anyone could get to it."

"Whatever do you mean?"

"I really don't know. A hunch. Just something I sensed." He felt like keeping Felix's revelations to himself for the time being.

"She only truly minds about Felix," Tessa said, peeved by her as she always was. "And Max, I suppose."

They drove on and had almost reached Chalcot when Marcus slowed the car to a standstill; there was another car coming towards them, a rattling old Ford. Tessa stared. "Oh heavens," she said, "it's Fred and his taxi. Speak of the devil . . . he uses this as a short-cut to Porchester. I'm going to duck." Which she did, her head bent close to the floor. The two cars passed with smiles and salutes all round. Marcus seemed amused.

"What on earth did you do that for?" he asked, once the Ford was well clear and Tessa upright.

"You'd be surprised how fast news travels in these parts," she said primly.

Marcus laughed. They had driven back to Chalcot—the Floods' house was just visible ahead in the high street.

"What a funny girl you are. Now, shall we turn up here and follow our noses to the other side of the county, and see where we land up?"

20

IT was after that, later, that everything started to go wrong. The weather darkened and grew sullen—and with it, Marcus's always unpredictable mood. He hardly spoke; he was withdrawn, totally preoccupied with his own thoughts. He had turned his mind away from Felix's diary and was pondering his assertion that he and his wife were fellow sufferers, that it was this which had brought them together so surprisingly in that back-of-beyond corner of wartime Dorset. And they did indeed seem an incongruous pair. They stopped once to walk through a village which was a well-known beauty spot. A few miles on, just outside a small town, Marcus spied a pub. It was attractively sited some way from the main street, overlooking an escarpment which dropped steeply to a valley. He parked and went to investigate and came back to the car, where Tessa was still sitting, to report that The Fox was just what they were looking for. He sounded more cheerful.

"A bedroom with a pretty view and a double bed. Spotless bathroom nearby. So I booked us in. All right?" He pulled a small case out of the boot.

Tessa thought that it wasn't—and said so. "Why can't we have a drink and a meal and then go back to London?" she pleaded. She sounded and felt panicky; close to hysteria. The greyness, the rain, Marcus's soured mood. She hated the very thought of staying in this godforsaken spot, miles from anywhere, out of touch, so far from Parloe Square, from Ella . . . For the first time in her life that she could remember, Tessa wished she had listened to her mother and insisted they went straight back to London from Chalcot.

"Tessa, *for God's sake.*" Marcus turned on her, irritated. "I told you I needed to get away. And I'm damned if I'm driving for three more hours today. Particularly with the weather getting worse by the minute. That's final. Now grow up and stop acting like a spoiled child."

Equally cross, Tessa saw that there was

nothing for it but to give in. It had started to drizzle steadily.

"I haven't got anything that could pass as luggage," she muttered, dragging her holdall off the back seat.

"No more have I," Marcus told her casually. "But nobody's going to mind." He gripped her arm as they walked into the hall, ducking under a low beam.

"Now what's wrong with this?" Marcus asked when they got to the room. It was charming. White-washed walls and dark beams; the bed, in an old fashioned wood frame, was covered in a faded patchwork quilt. The window faced down over the valley.

"It's not too bad," Tessa said gracelessly; knowing that she sounded just as he'd said—spoiled and childish.

They went down to the bar and drank tepid gin and tonics.

Marcus joined a group of locals playing darts. Watching, Tessa saw the curious glances he drew from the stocky, red-faced men who came in, calling out familiarly to the couple behind the bar. Marcus had a good eye and a steady aim. He played with utter concentration; he was determined to win. His casual, well-cut clothes, the long hair, the suede shoes, contrasted almost laughably with the stout boots and serviceable working clothes of his opponents. Marcus beat them all, nodded, thrust a fiver on the bar to indicate drinks all round, and took Tessa off to the small dining-room.

They quarrelled miserably over a dinner of excellent home-made steak and kidney pie. She hadn't liked the arrogant, competitive way he had played darts, and told him so. Marcus didn't seem to know what she was talking about. Or care. She nagged on about going back to London; there would be no traffic now, they could easily make it in a couple of hours. Marcus looked tense and tired and scarcely replied. He said suddenly, "I was interested in Felix. I didn't tell you on the way over, but I prised something very interesting out of him on our walk."

This—whatever it was—must have been preoccupying him ever since, Tessa thought wearily.

"Did you—what?" she asked indifferently.

"We were talking about the war, as a matter of fact. He kept a diary. All the time he was hidden away in the cellar. He told me a bit about it." Marcus pushed his plate away, half finished. "It must be an astonishing record. A 'personal experience', he called it. Knowing his ability and the background I should say it is a remarkable piece of work." His fingers beat on the table. "I'd give anything to get hold of it."

"Why?" Tessa asked coldly. "I can't see it's any of your business."

Marcus looked at her and laughed. "Why? To auction it off to the highest bidder—or publisher, of course. Film rights . . . I'd have to see it first, but he's already got a distinguished reputation as a translator. That alone would mean it was noticed. There's a good deal of interest in that kind of war memoir just now. It might turn out to be a most rewarding project. Who knows?"

Marcus laughed, pleased—and Tessa flushed.

"Felix would never agree to that," she said heatedly. "*Never*. All he wants is to live quietly, in peace, in the cottage. He

495

would hate any kind of publicity, surely you can see that. Particularly over something so sensitive. You know that his wife and daughter both died in the gas chambers. For years, long after he came to this country, he didn't even know what had happened to them. How could you contemplate anything so—so *crass?*"

"My poor little innocent." Marcus was smiling. "Haven't you learnt yet that everyone has their price—even you?"

It flashed through Tessa's mind: Oliver would never say or believe such a thing. The difference in values between the two men hit her forcibly. Facing Marcus, her chin jutting, the thought of Oliver brought a rush of warmth and familiarity.

"That's not true!" she blazed. "It's *not . . .*"

"I think it is." Still smiling; very cool. "And I'll tell you why in this case. The boy, Max. He adores him. The cottage is nothing," he said dismissively. "But he will want his son to have everything, all the opportunities. And if the diary is good, and a publisher makes a reasonable offer . . ." He shrugged. "Why not?"

"He wouldn't do it. Don't you see?"

496

Tessa hissed angrily. "Dredging up the tragic past; Hubie helping him get to England, then running off with Mother . . . exposing his innermost feelings under pressure, in captivity, really. To the world. He wouldn't do it—not for *anything*. Don't you have *any* concept of reticence?"

"Professionally not much, frankly. Coffee?"

Tessa shook her head. It was heavy and thundery and she had the beginnings of a fierce headache. Marcus looked at his watch and ordered coffee for himself.

"He won't want to see the boy lacking for anything, particularly if he's talented."

"His name is Max and he happens to be my half-brother," Tessa said coldly. She remembered what Oliver had told her about the recent trial concerning young children brutally murdered, and that at the end of the day's hearing he had driven for miles and miles, aimlessly, his mind quite blank.

"So if I decide to approach Morgenstern about the manuscript," Marcus said crisply, ignoring the reproach, "that's the line I would take. The boy."

Tessa looked at this stranger whose cold grey eyes stared across the room, away from her. Then she pushed back her chair and left the table.

Her head was throbbing badly now. Very decisive, very controlled, she collected her things from the bedroom, swallowed two aspirin, and went in search of the bath-room. She found it at the end of the corridor, spartan but clean. The huge taps gushed soft, warm water. She lay and soaked, letting her mind flit from one thought to the next.

The warnings she had ignored; plunging headlong, mindless . . . Joan's concern, Ella's, Angie's harsh innuendoes . . . her own sense of danger, the exquisite physi-cal excitement. She closed her eyes, remembering.

Until Marcus had stumbled upon the existence of Felix's diaries, the day had gone well enough, although she had been reluctant to come at all. She understood, with a spurt of anger, that Marcus had manipulated her into this sudden dash down to Dorset to see Mother, the Floods. It was that cold-blooded curiosity of his, and now his absurd preoccupation with Felix's sad story. Poor Felix.

She turned on a dribble of hot water with her toe.

Next week, Marcus would meet Guy Loden. She believed, or hoped, that he would do whatever he could to smooth that situation. At least Tom and Angie would have a point of contact with the dreadful man. And next week, her heart quickening with pleasure, next week she would see Oliver. He would phone tomorrow, he said. She would insist that they drove back to London early.

By the time she got back to the room, she was feeling calmer.

Marcus had commandeered the single chair and reading lamp and was writing, surrounded by scattered sheets of yellow paper. He had a bottle of scotch on the table and two glasses. He looked up. "Oh there you are . . . Are you all right, my love? You're sure?" There was no reference to her abrupt departure from the dining-room.

"Yes." She sat on the bed and watched him steadily. He looked so lost in whatever it was he was doing; just talking to her—

caringly, as he was trying to—was an effort. It interfered with his total concentration. She saw that clearly now. "How's it going?" she asked evenly.

"Interesting. As a matter of fact, I'm noting down some of the things Felix and Hubert Flood told me today. About the war. Riveting stuff. You never know when it might come in useful . . . I nipped down to the bar and got a bottle. Feel like a drink?"

She shook her head. The bath and the aspirin had made her sleepy, but her head was better. "I think I'll curl up."

"You do that." He went back to his work. "I shan't be long."

The storm finally broke in the early hours of the following morning. Thunder, lightning and torrential rain burst simultaneously. Tessa woke up. She saw Marcus, fully dressed, standing by the window looking out down the valley. Lightning briefly illuminated the room.

"Marcus."

"What a sight." He was talking to himself; perhaps it was that which had woken her, not the storm. Another bolt of lightning flared and forked as the thunder cracked. "Fires all over Berlin. . . exciting . . ." Marcus was smiling, holding a glass. Tessa was wide awake now. She had no idea what time it was or how long she had been asleep.

"Come to bed, Marcus. It's late." She sat up. As she spoke, rain lashed the window, rattling the panes, and thunder rumbled, echoing off the steep hillsides.

"I loved those fires." He hadn't heard her. "They were the best moments, shooting up and blazing in the blackness, meeting in one huge inferno far down below. Knowing we'd hit—those seconds before the flack and the searchlights got too bad and started reaching us. Two seconds, one second . . . and then we turned. I was always high—we all were, grinning like monkeys, making fists, mission accomplished. But I always thought of David then. Always. And if he was flying, I thought: Don't let it be David, not tonight. Me if I must. But not David . . ." He stared, not moving, out at the wild night.

Pulling the coverlet round her, Tessa went and crouched down beside him. It was as though she was hearing Marcus Reardon—the true Marcus—for the first time. She remembered the intensity with which he had spoken to Hubie and Felix; some of the memories which all three of them had unleashed that afternoon on the peaceful Dorset countryside.

She was suddenly filled with a terrible apprehension. "David *was* shot down . . ." she said quietly.

"Yes. He made it back across the coast. His crew must have been dead by then. He baled out over Kent. It was September and they were harvesting." He was talking mechanically. "The farmer who saw him said—and I'm quoting him precisely: he came down out of the sky like a long, flaming torch. They reached him quite soon and beat out the flames." Tentatively, Tessa touched his arm.

"And they saved him," she said.

"That time, yes."

"And when he was stronger, they worked miracles on his face, his hands, in that special unit in Sussex, didn't they?" Tessa watched him warily.

"They did indeed. It was no picnic for anyone . . . not for David, not for the

502

staff. Some of the skin grafts took, some didn't." Without looking at her, he poured another drink. It could only have been his second; the bottle was almost full. "Eventually, they rebuilt his lips and his eyelids; the nurses were marvellous, of course. And there were no mirrors so he didn't see much except for the bandages. Vi and I and one or two of the other chaps who saw him regularly got pretty hardened. And on the whole David's morale was good. He was hopeful then— he talked a lot about writing, maybe journalism."

"And what about the girl, the one he was engaged to?" Despite the hour and the strangeness of Marcus's demeanour, Tessa was mesmerised. In her mind's eye, she kept seeing the photograph in Gran's drawing-room, David in his early twenties, in uniform, fair-haired and confident and smiling. And so like Tom. But to her, from childhood, a glamorous and mysterious figure. Now Marcus standing; speaking so oddly.

"Pamela, pretty Pamela." Marcus looked down into his drink and swirled it round. "David met her at a party the summer before he was shot down. He was mad about her, and she about him. Why not? He was immensely attractive, even if he did know it. Anyhow, Vi brought her to the hospital—she thought David was looking well enough mended by then—but she couldn't take it. I've never blamed her, never. She was all togged up in a pale blue suit and one of those silly hats pulled down over one eye. Silk stockings and very high heels. (Funny, the things one remembers.) Anyhow, she walked into the room and put her hand over her mouth. She saw his new lips; his eyes were mostly bandaged still. I suppose we were lucky she wasn't sick on the spot. She gave a sort of scream and fled. I've never seen her since, but I believe she married quite soon after. David was very good about it. Vi and I felt completely, utterly helpless."

Tessa hugged the cover to her. It was quieter now. The violent summer storm was passing over out there in the blackness.

"He got better after that, didn't he?"

"Yes, he really did. He put his back into getting well; his one thought was to rejoin the squadron. He went somewhere to

504

recuperate and then had a jolly, long leave in London, staying in Eaton Square, going out and about. We had dinner together once or twice. There was a lull in the raids and London was surprisingly full of gaiety and booze and attractive women. No, it wasn't until the following year, early in the summer of '44, that he did it . . ."

Tessa went cold and hot and cold again. "Did it?" she asked.

"That's right. Killed himself." Marcus rocked back on his heels.

"But . . ."

"An accident? A stupid, elementary mistake on a training flight by an experienced pilot like David?" He turned and faced her for the first time. It was too dark to see, but Tessa knew that his eyes were icy. "Even at that time, nobody really believed that. But only I *knew.*"

Tessa willed herself to stay calm.

"How did you know Marcus?" To her amazement, her voice was quite normal. All of a sudden his body, which had been rigidly upright, crumpled; he slumped into a chair and set the glass on the floor beside him, among the sheets and sheets of paper.

"A letter, of course. He couldn't stand

people staring at his new face. He used to be so handsome—like Tom, only with a stronger personality. But after all the plastic surgery . . . He didn't actually say much in the letter, just that he had thought it through and this was his decision. But he got his timing wrong."

"How?"

"I'd been away on a forty-eight hour pass. I came back early—I don't know why. He hadn't expected me until the next day. I found the letter on my bunk. I was still holding it—and this is the worst . . ." He put his hand over his eyes. "I was still holding it when I saw him through the window, walking out to the hangar . . . and I did nothing. I just sat there until they came and told me."

Tessa swallowed. Her heart was beating suffocatingly. But she said steadily, "It probably wouldn't have made any difference in the long run—anything you could have said. Don't blame yourself, Marcus. You mustn't."

"Bless you for that. I've always thought so, or wanted to, myself. But it's a hard memory to live with. Alone."

"Gran never knew or suspected?"

"I don't *think* so . . . if she did, she never said anything."

He dropped his hand and looked at Tessa. The first faint glimmerings of a calm and rain-washed dawn filtered through the window. He looked utterly exhausted. "I'm so sorry," he said, "so sorry to have burdened you with this."

"It's all right." When he put out his hand towards her, she took it.

"I knew from the beginning that I'd have to tell you—everything or nothing—when you asked. Nobody else. I've never told anyone else. Only you."

"About David?"

"Yes." His voice was quite hoarse. "Good, generous, loving *lovely* Tessa." He spoke each word very distinctly. She stared at the floor. Little by little the room —the beams, the bed, the sloping white walls—was materialising out of the darkness. "It was all wrong, you and me, despite the attraction . . . too many risks of one sort or another . . . age, experience." He rambled, tiredly. "I tried to— prevent it."

He had.

507

"Tessa—say something. Why don't you? Was it all so bad with me?"

She turned her wet face away. "You know that it wasn't."

"Yes. I know . . . The trouble was, I started to love you."

As you loved David who was, after all, my uncle. In his way—as much as he could, perhaps he had.

She was drained; bone-weary. Flat. Exhausted by Marcus's frank revelations which had been inspired, she supposed, by his discovery of the existence of Felix's secret diary. All her powerful, ambivalent emotions towards him seemed to have vanished. In their place, now, only a distant affection. And pity. She looked down at his hand which she was still holding. Even then, the faintest involuntary quiver . . .

Parloe Square; Joan and the shop; Oliver . . .

She knew with utter certainty that she must get away from here, from Marcus, and stay away, now and forever. That this was her chance for happiness.

He muttered, "Felix . . . the diary . . .

508

I understand. I won't press. His and the family's privacy . . . You're right."

His head fell forward and he was sound asleep.

Tessa's mind raced. Wait, she thought, wait. There was a station, they had passed it yesterday. It couldn't be more than a mile or so away. She had money. With luck, once he was deeply asleep, he wouldn't wake for hours. She watched him for ten minutes, perhaps a quarter of an hour. When she began to move, she found she was cold and stiff. She dressed in seconds, wiping her face with a handkerchief, pushing her new belongings into her canvas holdall and dragging a comb through her hair. She glanced at her watch. It was nearly five.

With one hand on the doorknob, she turned. Marcus hadn't moved. Impulsively, she picked up the blanket and tiptoed over to the chair. He stirred a little as she tucked it round him.

She crept down the stairs, clinging to the side. In the small reception room, the grandfather clock ticked loudly and reassuringly. She tried the front door.

Locked. Looking closer, she turned the giant iron key and shot back the bolt. Silence again. Nobody seemed to have heard. She pushed open the door and stepped out into the promising new morning. The air smelled wonderfully fresh and clean after the storm. Early sunlight splayed through the pinkish sky, dispelling the dewy mist rising from the grasses.

She took a deep breath and started down the lane towards the town. By the time she reached it, she was running as fast as she could through the empty street, bag hoisted on to her shoulder, long legs flying. She stopped a startled milkman to ask the way to the station. The birds chorused cheerfully.

The stationmaster rubbed his eyes and looked her up and down curiously. She made a fine old sight, this big and beautiful young woman with her high colour and coppery hair. "London, eh?" he said, consulting his pocket watch.

She was quite contented, chugging through the green countryside, stopping at every station on the line, listening to the jovial shouts and the clanking milk churns. She had a huge, happy sense of relief which somehow matched this morning which was turning warm and golden. She would not think of the sad revelation of the past night; it had, after all, become part of her life now. It was a secret which she and Marcus would share forever in their quite separate lives. Marcus would sleep late and when he woke he would look and perhaps reach for her.

No, she would not think about that either.

21

TESSA felt lightheaded, as though she was recovering her strength after a bout of long, debilitating illness. Deliberately excluding whatever might be painful—not yet, later, plenty of time for that—she thought of the ordinary things in her life carefully, and with pleasure. She was really looking forward to getting back to the shop tomorrow, slipping into the daily routine.

And what would happen to Tom and Angie, she wondered, her head lolling back against the plush seat. He was desperately in love with her all right; he wouldn't get over it easily. And she saw the other night, in his frantic worry about her being caught up in the Loden case, a resolution she hadn't known in Tom before. He had seemed more manly, less the promising boy who excelled at everything without having to try. Angie herself was an enigma; and Marcus had said that she and Tom were babes in the wood as far as Angie was concerned, whatever that meant. It was best not to judge, but how would Papa take it?

Gran. She looked through the dusty windows on to the reaches of the New Forest, stretching as far as the eye could see, rushing past (clack clack clackety clack) in a blur of green woodland and yellow broom . . . She needed a housekeeper to live in and look after her. Finding the right person wouldn't be easy, but she and Ella would tackle it somehow. Just the thought of Ella in her sitting-room with Morgan curled up asleep on the rug was comforting.

So it was the early afternoon before the taxi set her down in Parloe Square. She handed the driver a tip, turned and there were Ella and Oliver Bingham—Oliver?— talking at the open front door. It was the look on both of their faces—serious, stricken—that gave Tessa the first hint that something was amiss.

She and Ella rushed towards each other, exclaiming simultaneously, "Tessa, there you are, thank the Lord, where *have* you been . . ." And Tessa, looking from one to the other, "What happened, what's wrong, *tell me?*"

Oliver got them inside and sat Tessa down on the hall chair and half knelt and held her hand very tightly while Ella told her, her voice wobbling, that her grandmother had died peacefully, at home, early yesterday morning. "In her sleep, Tessa love, she can't have known anything at all. Maggie and I . . ."

"No, no, no . . . Oh Gran, no . . ."

Tessa dropped her face into her hands and broke into wild, uncontrollable sobbing while Oliver put his arms round her and held her and rocked her and comforted her like a child. Soon, the telephone rang in the study and Oliver nodded to Ella above Tessa's head. Ella, standing watching her, helpless, twisting her hands together. Oliver stayed with Tessa as she wept, stroking her hair, holding her against him, not once telling her to be quiet or to stop this extravagant mourning. He was completely unselfconscious. Ella reappeared holding out a clean handkerchief which Oliver took. She went away, not bearing to watch Tessa's pain.

Eventually, partly through the comfort

of Oliver's nearness, partly through sheer exhaustion, she calmed. She leant weakly against him.

"Shall we go down to Ella's?" Oliver asked quietly.

Tessa nodded, sniffed, hiccupped and rubbed her pale face with her hand.

"Here." He gave her the handkerchief. She stood up with difficulty; her legs had no strength in them and Oliver supported her like someone very, very old as they moved slowly down the stairs.

"Tom?" Tessa asked once she reached the sofa and collapsed on to it. "Where's Tom?"

"I was with him yesterday, actually," Oliver said. "He's got a lot to tell you in another direction. But I'll leave that to him. He had something he had to see to, but he should be here soon. He phoned me around lunchtime and told me about your grandmother—which is why I came over straight away. To be with you. Just to see if there was anything I could do or be of any help."

"You already have been, Oliver," Tessa said, smiling at him wanly, meaning it. The enormity of Vi Delmore's death had wiped everything else from her mind. It seemed somehow quite natural that Oliver should be here in the house, his huge frame uncomfortably filling one of Ella's hard wooden chairs which she had brought from Wales.

"I was very close to my own grand-mother too," he said, picking up Morgan and starting to tickle him under his chin. "She was very good to me after Mother died. You could say that she was someone very special in my life because of the circumstances. A bit like the way Lady Delmore kept an eye on you and Tom all these years . . . So in a way, I do understand."

Tessa blew her nose. "I know you do," she said indistinctly. She could hear Ella rattling teacups in the kitchen. "What are we going to do about Papa?"

"That's been seen to. Ella managed to get hold of him in New York yesterday morning. He's decided to fly back immediately."

"And he'll be here in about an hour, Tess." Ella came in with a tray; Oliver jumped up and took it from her. "That was him on the phone from the airport just now. The car is meeting him and he'll be coming straight back to the house. He'll take charge of the arrangements then."

"And Mother?" Tessa's eyes met Ella's. "We phoned the Floods immediately," she said quietly. "Poor Mrs. Flood was so upset as you can imagine; they were such devoted sisters. We found her, you see, in the flat. Maggie was with me which was fortunate. She didn't answer the door when we got there even though she was expecting us. And we could hear Charlie yapping in the hall. I had the key with me, luckily." She leant forward and covered Tessa's hand with both of hers. "She looked lovely, dear, ever so peaceful, just like she had gone off to sleep. It was her heart, the doctor said. It could have happened at any time. So you must be glad she went easily, Tess, and not grieve too much. I think she knew it would be soon."

Tessa shut her eyes and bit her lip and fumbled for the handkerchief in her pocket. Ella poured the tea.

"So Mother does know? She got the message?" Her eyes were swimming. What with the shock and the sadness, nothing was making much sense to Tessa any more. All her reactions seemed very slow.

"Yes. I have spoken to her, and Tom has; she said Mrs. Flood sent the taxi over to the cottage as soon as she heard and she telephoned later on."

Oh God—Fred's taxi . . .

Now everything was horrifyingly clear. They had passed it, by inches, soon after they had left Mother and Felix. So Fred *had* come with an urgent message; he hadn't been using the back way to Porchester after all. Aunt Flor must have expected that she was still there.

"I see," she said miserably. She felt Oliver's eyes on her.

Tessa and Oliver went out and sat on the weathered teak bench which was set among the flowering tubs on the terrace, not talking much, each lost in their separate thoughts, listening to the summer insects buzzing. Oliver found, and held, her hand.

"I miss Tom," Tessa said suddenly.

Oliver squeezed her limp fingers. "He'll be here any minute, honestly. Tess?"

"What?"

"When Ella couldn't find you yesterday —and you can tell me it's none of my business—were you with Reardon?"

"Yes." He didn't say anything. He looked down and traced circles on the back of her hand. Tessa thought, irrelevantly, that he had a surprisingly delicate touch for someone so big and bearish—and who was inclined to be clumsy.

"We went down together to see Mother and Felix and the Floods. But I came back alone. I won't see him again. I'd rather not say any more if you don't mind, Oliver. Except that I would like to think it *was* your business. Now. And I'm sorry." She could only just manage the words. She held the wet handkerchief up to her face. Oliver put his arm round her.

"My dearest Tessa. I want to believe all that. You will never know how much."

There was another easy silence between them; Tessa pulled close to him. And something odd seemed to have happened to her mind. She sat there, blankly, for minutes, and then something she had forgotten, something important which was hovering on the edge of her consciousness, surfaced.

Tom—where was he? Why was Oliver deliberately not telling her something about him? Papa would be here soon, Ella said. The plane from New York . . .

Charlie . . .

She sat bolt upright. "What on earth has happened to poor Charlie?"

"It's all right, Tess." Oliver sounded embarrassed. "I've got him at home. There was a panic yesterday and it seemed a bit much to leave him with Ella when she had so much to cope with. So I picked him up and took him back to the house. Fiona is staying with me for a few days so he's being nicely spoilt."

For the first time since she had got out of the taxi, Tessa smiled properly. "Oh Oliver," she said, sensibilities so fragile that she was ready to burst into tears all over again. "Oh Oliver . . . I loved your letter, it was so like you, and it made me laugh and laugh."

George Selway and Tom arrived at the house within minutes of each other. As always with George Selway, his arrival was dramatic. His barely controlled nervous energy generated a sort of electricity which

520

could almost be felt. The moment he stepped into the hall, the quiet and sunny house sprang into life. He was looking very distinguished, razor-thin and slightly tanned. His wiry hair, like Tessa's, had kept much of its colour. He looked well despite the long journey; every inch the gentleman industrialist in his immaculately tailored grey suit and papers under his arm.

"Tessa!" he shouted. "Tessa . . . yes, I'll have a cup of tea, Ella, thank you." Barking orders to the chauffeur about the luggage: "No, not there, upstairs," and asking for Tom.

Tessa, hearing the commotion, came running in from the garden and threw herself at her father. She didn't say anything in case she lost control again. The sight of Papa, the familiarity, made her throat catch. She felt the tears coming.

"I'm so sorry, Tessa my darling," he said as she disengaged herself. "It's sad news. But you're all right, are you?" He looked at her keenly, possessively, holding her arms. Obscurely worried about her as he always was. "Yes? Yes?"

She nodded. She didn't trust her voice.

"It's a nasty shock for you, I know. I was very fond of Vi myself. She didn't suffer, thank God, couldn't have known anything about it." And catching sight of Oliver's bulk hovering discreetly behind her, held out his hand, glad to see that he was with her. He approved of Oliver. He liked his manner and the sensible way he had of tackling things. He had often, ever since they were boys, wished that Tom could be a bit more like him in his ways. Now was a case in point. Here was Oliver, making himself useful—and Tom nowhere to be seen.

"How are you, Oliver? Awfully good of you to come along. Sad business, poor Vi."

"I thought I might be able to be of some help to you and Tom, sir. There'll be a lot to be seen to . . ."

"Quite right. We'll have to get down to the funeral arrangements. I believe they're quite simple. Fortunately, Vi consulted me about the will and what she wanted done last year sometime. I've got a copy of all the particulars in my study."

"We've been watching the Selway Electric success story in the papers, haven't we

Tessa?" He nudged Tessa with his elbow. "You must be delighted, sir."

"That's right. Well done Papa," Tessa said dutifully with a grateful glance at Oliver.

"Hmm . . . It's not over yet, but I think we're on to a winner there. I'll have to be going over again before long. Take you with me, Tess." He grasped her arm again. "Get you away from the flower market for a bit. What do you think?"

Tessa tried to smile—nodded. "I'd like that."

"Good journey, sir?" Oliver asked.

"Not bad at all, although it's a devilishly uncomfortable business. It was lucky Ella managed to get me and I could hop on the next plane. I've left Poppy in New York, by the way. She'll be following in a day or so. And where is Tom?" he demanded testily. "I really do think—"

"He's here, Mr. Selway. I saw his car pull up." Ella came rushing from the kitchen with a cup of tea, a bit flustered as she invariably was when he came charging into her comfortable household. "Here he is now."

"Right. Well, let's all go up to the

drawing-room, shall we?" He glanced at his watch and swallowed some tea. "All my letters and so forth are in the study, Ella, are they? Tom, there you are. At last."

Tessa immediately thought—and she realised later that she had been right—that something about Tom looked different. There was a determined tilt to his jaw; he seemed older. He greeted his father and came over to Tessa and hugged her, which he rarely did these days.

"It's awful, Tess, isn't it? I can't believe it, can you? We'll miss her a lot. Thanks for your support, Oliver, again." They seemed to catch each other's eye over her shoulder and smile.

"Come along now, come along, we're going upstairs, Tom," George Selway said. "We must decide what has to be done immediately and what can wait. The papers for one thing. *The Times . . .*"

"I'd like a word with you in private first, Father, if you don't mind. It won't take long. Could we go into the study for a minute?"

"For God's *sake*, Tom."

"In the study, Father." He sounded

very firm, very much in control. "Tess, you and Oliver go upstairs. We'll follow you up."

"Very well then, but make it quick." George Selway looked annoyed. As the study door closed, Tessa said to Oliver, "What on earth does Tom want to talk to Papa about, and in private? Now of all times?"

"He'll tell you himself. Let's wait for them upstairs as Tom said."

"Is it . . ." Tessa stopped on the curve of the landing. "It's not about Angie, is it? I mean, he doesn't want to *marry* her. . . ?"

"I've told you. I'm sworn to secrecy." Oliver grinned. "But between you and me, you're on the right track."

An hour or so later, when she finally got to her room, Tessa thought: this has been the most extraordinary day. She sat on her bed and looked round at the familiar pink striped walls and curtains. She was so tired that her mind darted about incoherently.

It was a day that had begun in another bedroom; more of a night, really, that had petered out and ended.

Was Marcus back in London?

David, in his flying gear, walking out towards a plane for the last time; Marcus watching, holding his letter . . .

Tom must tell him about Gran tonight, before it was announced in the papers. That was only right. They had been such good friends. (Tears pricking again.) And he had promised to help with Angie's problem.

Tom and Angie . . . *Tom*.

Because, after what seemed a long time, he had burst in on her and Oliver in the drawing-room, his face positively glowing with happiness, pulling Angie after him and declaring, "We've told Father, Tess; you're next . . . *we're married!* And you happen to be standing beside our best man. I hid Angie in the car until I'd bearded the old man. Isn't she gorgeous?" She was. "Now where's Ella?"

So for the second time that afternoon Tessa had reason to be grateful for Oliver's hand on her arm as she stammered out a combination of surprise and congratulations. And there was nothing for it but to kiss them both—Angie ravishing in pale pink silk, looking every bit as happy as Tom—and ask all the expected questions.

They stood there, holding hands, smiling foolishly at each other. Both pleased as Punch. Until Tom turned serious and said, "We would have done it sooner or later anyhow, Tess. I simply told Pa that because of Angie's family situation we didn't want any fuss—so we just picked up old Oliver here and popped round to the registry office. Which is true in a way. I thought it was best not even to get you, Tess, not without Pa. But the Loden thing has become ugly, and Angie will be more protected this way. I'll see to that." Still holding her hand, very confident.

"I'm the luckiest girl in London," Angie said, going on smiling like a Cheshire cat with her curving mouth and her slanting green eyes and giving Tom a kiss on the cheek.

And she looked it.

Then George Selway came in, bringing Ella—and this to Tessa was the strangest of all—looking genuinely pleased. She always knew at once with him. He did. And while Ella was ooing and aahing and wiping away a tear or two, she saw he was looking at them with a good deal of satisfaction. *Papa was*. And an exceptionally handsome pair they made, too.

In fact, George Selway was thinking, amused: Good old Tom, never thought he had it in him. A damn beautiful girl, by God. No background of any kind, it appeared . . . still, no tiresome relatives to be dealt with either which was a blessing. No dreadful wedding to be suffered. They could organise a drinks party here in due course, a suitable time after Vi—poor old Vi. His eyes narrowed as he raked Angie's waist; he assumed she wasn't in the family way. Unlikely. *She* knew her way around all right—hard as nails. Do the boy a world of good. Might even make a man out of him. They'd met through that deplorable journalist fellow, friend of Vi's. Funny, but he'd had the oddest feeling at that gallery that Tessa might get mixed up with him. He'd been wrong, thank heavens.

He wondered briefly, and with the slight ache of an old wound, what Jennie would make of it all. "Look here," he said, breaking in on the general laughter—

528

Oliver was relating how the ring was bought on the way to the registry office— "we'll have a bit of dinner here tonight. Drink your health, Tom and Angie. Vi would have wanted it if she had known . . . Rustle something up, can we, Ella?"

Ella could, of course.

Amazing, Tessa thought, simply amazing. He's delighted. And then she excused herself and went off for a rest.

22

ELLA was used to producing decent meals unexpectedly to fit in with the hectic pace of George Selway's business life. She was a good plain cook, and never failed to rise to the occasion. That night, she prepared to serve soup and roast chicken and a chocolate mousse. Once she had the preparations under way, she started to hum and to feel her normal cheerful self again. Goodness, what a lot she had to tell Maggie when she found a moment to speak to her. There was nothing like a spell in the kitchen when there was upset in the family she had always thought. And the past twenty-four hours had brought them all both excitement and sadness.

When she woke (in a panic of not knowing where she was or what time of day it was), Tessa bathed and dressed and went down to the kitchen to help.

"You'll never know how glad I was to see you this afternoon, dear," Ella told her. "Right after Oliver rang the bell . . . When Mrs. Flood said you weren't at the cottage with the Morgensterns, I was so worried what with everything else and Mr. Selway flying all that way home. I didn't know what on earth I was going to tell him. All's well that ends well." And she left it at that, giving Tessa instructions over the mousse while she basted the chickens. "And isn't it thrilling about Tom and Angie? Now I wonder where they'll live, they won't be able to stay in Tom's flat for long, will they? That's right, whip the cream a bit more, Tess. I've done the table, the best silver. Why not, I thought? Ever so rushed, the wedding, wasn't it? But as long as they know their own minds, and it isn't as if she has any family very much."

"I knew Tom was determined to marry her. I knew that." Tessa licked the bowl.

"I think I did too. It's the way he looks at her, isn't it? I'm glad Lady D met her, at least. Following her husband, both gone within weeks."

Angie sat between Tom and George Selway at dinner, looking demure in yet another stunning frock; dove-grey this time with her black hair pulled back into a sophisticated chignon. (Tessa knew that designer clothes were a perk of her job; but whatever she threw over that long-limbed frame would look divine. Maddening.) She was listening with apparently rapt attention to her new father-in-law's hectoring pontifications. Droning on about the American economy and cost efficiency and the work ethic . . . Tessa felt like yawning.

The big family dining-room overlooking the square, with its deep red walls and curtains, was both elegant and comfortable. Ella had made the table pleasantly festive with a bowl of sweet peas in the centre and creamy candles. The silver and glass gleamed against the old polished table. Outside, the fading light of the lovely summer evening glimmered through the trees.

Watching Angie across the table, Tessa thought what a consummate actress she was. Whoever would have believed that night, only weeks ago, when she had arrived at Marcus's flat with that lovely face—now leaning so deferentially towards

George Selway—bruised and swollen. Tom got up to pour more wine. He was slightly flushed and his straight fair hair fell forward on to his face. He touched Angie's shoulder possessively as he refilled her glass.

She's a complete mystery to us, thought Tessa. We'll probably never know the truth about the Loden affair and Angie's involvement. Marcus was right there. But as long as she goes on making Tom as happy as he looked tonight, who cared? Not Papa, obviously. The pair of them were laughing away, getting along famously; Angie had obviously got him off his economics lecture. She was, after all, only too used to handling wealthy middle-aged men; Papa was clearly not immune to her dazzling charms. And she was sure that Gran, who had never cared much for the conventions, would have felt the same. Sad, Tessa thought with a sudden stab, that she wasn't here with them tonight.

"Do you think I should say a few words?" Oliver was whispering beside her. "A bit awkward under the circumstances. But I was the best man—or witness, rather. What do you think? I don't want to do the wrong thing."

Who could imagine Oliver ever doing the wrong thing? "I think you should," Tessa whispered back. "Just briefly."

"All right, then. Here goes."

Oliver rose and tapped his glass lightly. The high pinging noise silenced them all immediately. George Selway, Angie, Tom, Tessa—and Ella, coming in from the kitchen with an enormous bowl of chocolate mousse.

"I'd like you all to join me in drinking Tom and Angie's health." Oliver began.

"Hear, hear . . ." George Selway got stiffly to his feet, joined by Tessa and Ella. Tom reached for Angie's hand. Oliver looked round the table, perfectly at ease, his powerful frame dominating, even though both Tom and George Selway were taller than he. He was used to speaking on his feet, and it showed. He had an excellent voice. It wasn't a pose, exactly, but the fingers of one hand were partially thrust into his pocket. He waited until they all held their glasses and then he continued smoothly, "There are others who care for Tom and Angie's future as we do but who are not with us tonight. I know they would want to join in this toast, and I ask that we remember them." He paused. George Selway cleared his throat. "Would you all raise your glasses with me . . ." They did so, Ella, close to tears, clutching at Tessa. "Good luck, good health and happiness. God bless Angie and Tom."

Tessa carried the coffee tray up to the drawing-room and Tom brought out the brandy and cigars. George Selway had become increasingly expansive towards Angie and was showing her some brochures from the briefcase he had brought back with him.

"It's going to be a huge concern," he told her, taking a cigar from the box that Tom offered. "Huge. We've got all the technology over here; really very advanced stuff. We always have had of course, but we have never been able to exploit it. Some of the best ideas have been pinched from under our noses. And we've allowed it. Over there, they've got the industrial know-how, the efficiency, the mass markets. Put them both together *without losing control of the product*—and it's bound to succeed."

Angie and Tom sat together on the sofa. (Tom and Tessa had listened, bored, to this kind of talk for as long as they could remember.) Tessa and Oliver drifted over to the window which Tessa had opened on to the warm night. The smoke from the cigars drifted up towards the high ceiling.

"You know, you ought to reconsider coming into the business, Tom. I really do believe you should, so hear me out for a change." George Selway spoke forcefully, fixing Tom with his most hypnotic stare. "There are lots of ways we could use a young fellow like you. A legal training is a good background in any business. And after me . . ." He shrugged. "Well, there's a tremendous opportunity and challenge there for the taking if I'm not mistaken."

"I might, Pa. I might." Tom swung one leg over his knee. Relaxed now, his eyes returned again and again to Angie.

"After all, you're a young chap with responsibilities now Tom. I don't fancy your wife is going to want to live in that dingy bachelor flat forever. Isn't that right,

Angie?" Perfectly confident of *that*, George Selway reached for his brandy. This hasty and unconventional marriage of Tom's might well work out, was his considered opinion. Might be the making of him, Tom. Angie said nothing but turned to Tom half smiling her beautiful, green-eyed cat's smile.

"I think your father is making a lot of sense, Tom," she said. Over by the window, Tessa and Oliver exchanged incredulous looks.

"You did the toast splendidly," Tessa told him quietly. "You were absolutely right to mention the others, whatever Papa may have thought."

"Your Dad needs standing up to rather firmly, don't you think?" Oliver murmured back.

"Indeed I do."

"*Tessa*," George Selway slewed round in his chair. "Where have you got to? There you are. What are you two whispering about?"

But before Tessa could reply, the telephone rang and she went out into the hall to answer it.

"It's probably the Delmores," George

Selway said, his cigar still in his mouth. "They said they'd phone back if they got hold of the vicar."

Tessa came back after some minutes and stood by the double doors. "It's Mother," she said, looking straight at her father. "She wants to talk to you about Gran's funeral and various other things. It's important, and I think you should speak to her. Perhaps you should take it in your study." He got up very slowly, very deliberately, and carefully stubbed out his cigar. Then, while his children watched, walking slightly stooped—like a much older man—he started down the stairs.

The study door was still closed when Tessa and Oliver crossed the hall and slipped out of the front door. When the minutes passed and George Selway didn't come back up to the drawing-room, Oliver said tactfully to Tessa that he felt like a breath of air—and what about a turn around the square? Tom and Angie were giggling over an old photograph album.

It was a balmy night; the tops of the trees rustled gently in the lightest of breezes. They had only walked a few steps when Tessa stopped. "Do you know, Oliver, this is the first time our parents have spoken to each other for years. They haven't said a word since that day Papa came back from Burma, and in the afternoon she went off to Felix. I know because Mother has told me. Literally, Papa has never mentioned her name that either Tom or I can remember. Any communication, and there wasn't very much, was through Ella and the Floods. And the lawyers, I suppose, during the divorce. It was Ella who told us when Max was born."

"Well, Lady D's death has mended that fence, perhaps."

"Perhaps," Tessa said doubtfully. "But you know what a tough old bird Papa is. Perhaps they're having the most almighty row." She looked worried. Oliver laughed.

"I doubt it. Emotional fires don't last forever."

"Don't they just. You don't know my Papa."

"Let's leave them all to it at number 34 Parloe Square for a bit," he suggested sensibly. He put his arm round her and they strolled on.

"Gran has left Mother the flat. I know

that because it was all discussed a year or so ago. Her pearls to me, which is lovely. Tom and Max and I get anything else between us. So Papa is going to have to acknowledge Max's existence at last, too." They walked on in silence.

"Did you hear what Tom said when your father suggested he came into the business?" Oliver asked. "I could hardly believe my ears. He has always said that working with your father is about the last thing he would ever do."

"In the past, yes. But I don't think he has been enjoying the Bar. Gran didn't think so either."

"I agree. He's found it irksome, all the waiting about, the paperwork. It's very tough going. You've got to be absolutely determined it's what you want. Really dedicated." He sounded unusually serious.

"Like you are." She looked up at him.

"I am, yes. And I've had some lucky breaks."

But it wasn't only luck; that was too simple. For his age, his career was already outstanding. Tessa didn't say so then, but she had seen, that night at dinner, during those few minutes when he had proposed

Tom and Angie's health, the natural way he would address a court. He had confidence and timing; and a hint of the dramatic. He was, she knew, a patient worker too. Tom, for all his brilliance, was quickly bored. The faster moving world of business might, after all, be better suited to his talents. And Selway Electric, now so large, could absorb both Tom and Papa.

"I'm pretty sure Angie has been pressing for Tom to go into Selway's. She thought he was mad to pass up an opportunity like that. She told me so. But what has really amazed me tonight is the way Papa has accepted her."

"Tom was pretty concerned about that, I can tell you. Even if he didn't show it. The Loden case is still worrying. Apparently Angie had the most horrible scare—Tom didn't tell me what. He just went white and said he never wanted to think about it again. But he decided to marry her at once, then and there. And she obliged. She's been to the police, I do know that. She'll be a witness for the prosecution as Mrs. Tom Selway and not, to be blunt, as Guy Loden's ex-mistress. The chances are that if nothing more sinister turns up—*if*—Loden will get off with a fine and a short sentence. There's a good deal of feeling that the gambling laws are antiquated and need changing. But it will be a sensational trial all right."

"Did Angie's aunt turn up for the wedding?"

"Yes she did. She seemed very nervous and didn't know what to expect. To tell you the truth, we put a good face on it, but Tom and I weren't too sure of the form either." They laughed. "We got there terribly early and Tom got all white and nervy—you know, the way he does. Anyhow, Angie's aunt seemed all right. She must have been pretty when she was young. She's got something of Angie about her. But she looks very—well, worn. I shouldn't think she has had an easy life."

"Neither has Angie."

"No. Her name, by the way, is Angélique."

"That sounds romantic. And her father?"

Oliver shook his head. "Père inconnu. The aunt said her sister was 'a bit of a one with the boys.' So perhaps no one ever did know. Anyhow, she pushed off when

542

Angie was a baby—she thinks she's living in Australia—and the sister simply brought her up. She's got this common-law husband, the Italian waiter, and two kids of her own. She seemed glad that Angie was getting herself settled, but it was all a bit sad."

"Oliver . . ."

"What?"

"Do you think Angie loves Tom?"

Oliver considered the question. He said carefully, "Certainly not the way he's head over heels about *her*, if that's what you mean. Although he's an attractive lad is our Tom and they're exactly the same age, by the way, twenty-nine. She's knocked about a good bit. But there's something direct about her. Hard but direct. I have a feeling your father may have sensed that. He took stock with that very quick, practical brain of his and decided he could have been faced with much worse. I think she wants to live well in a conventional middle-class way; she wants comfort and stability. And with Tom, she will have that. And yes, to answer your question finally, I do think she will make him a good wife."

"Oliver," Tessa said, putting her arm round his very broad back, "you are such a comfort."

When they got back to the house, Tessa hung back on the steps. Tom and Angie's laughter floated out through the drawing-room window above. They couldn't hear George Selway.

"Do you think he could still be talking to Mother?" Tessa asked "All this time?" Oliver put both hands on her shoulders.

"You've been worrying about this ever since she rang, haven't you?" His face was always so full of expression, as it was then, that people thought of Oliver as an attractive man. Thinking it herself, Tessa smiled back at him.

"I suppose so. She's so dotty, my mother. You know she hasn't got a phone? She must be at Hubie's. I don't suppose you remember her?"

"Only very vaguely, from when I used to come over when I was staying with the cousins in the war. And after that she wasn't there. Look, I think, seriously, that you should let them sort their lives out themselves. There's nothing you can do about it . . . and they might surprise you rather nicely. If you could turn your mind to *us* for a moment, there are one or two things I'd like to mention."

There was a fresh burst of laughter from the drawing-room where now they could also hear Ella's soft, slightly sing-song voice. When she didn't answer, Oliver said, moving closer and clamping his arms round her waist.

"Tess, I know you're going to the States with your father for a holiday when he goes back . . ."

"Yes—yes I want to do that," she interrupted. "And you know about the new shop, a second 'Garden'? Joan and I are both keen on that. We've already got a couple of places to look at . . ." She went on talking wildly to stop Oliver saying what she was afraid he might. She couldn't.

"Tessa. Be quiet and listen to me." She did. His voice was firm but his expression was vulnerable. If she hadn't known him better, she might have thought he was afraid. "I've had some nasty moments, but I told you, I never give up."

She put her hands on his shoulders. She

could hear Tom's loud laugh above them; Angie, Ella talking. The fog which had blanketed her mind and her feelings suddenly lifted.

"I'm so glad you don't Oliver. So *glad*," she said passionately. "Do you mean that?" He was deadly serious now.

"Yes."

"*Tessa.*"

Part Three

Endings

1

SHROUDED and padded in an ocean of tissue paper, the dress hung from Tessa's wardrobe in a fall of the palest pink slipper satin. She had wanted pink from the first; she always enjoyed wearing it because with her bold colouring, it made her feel a bit dashing.

Standing in front of it in scruffy jeans and her oldest sweater, Tessa stared. Less than a day to go now; she felt the first twinges of panic. Mother had promised to come in and have a chat and a last inspection. It seemed the right thing to do. Tessa looked at her watch. She noticed that her hands weren't quite steady; wedding nerves . . . It was almost six o'clock. Where on earth was Mother?

"You can't possibly even think of it, Tess," Ella had said when Tessa first broached the idea of the dress. "A bride in pink?" Her sense of propriety was outraged. "I never heard of such a thing. What would people say?"

"I thought brides always wore white—the first time, anyhow," her mother had remarked last winter, as she bent to cut a cabbage from the frost-bound soil. "Although as a matter of fact, I wore a silvery dress when I married George. I believe it was rather the thing at the time. Fishy, like a mermaid." Tessa looked surprised. It was the first time she had ever heard her mother so much as mention a garment. For as long as she could remember she had worn nondescript baggy skirts, shirts and sweaters; Felix's socks over thick stockings in the winter. The divine face, which hardly changed, disembodied above . . . "And pull up a few carrots, would you Tess? Felix really does prefer them although the cabbages are marvellous this year."

It was Angie, in the end, who supported her. "I don't think I would personally, but if it's what you want . . ." She shrugged. "Why not? I expect the weather will be dreadful. It usually is in April. The church will be freezing, so at least you'll look warmer. Oliver is in seventh heaven, and

I don't suppose he'd notice if you wore a sack."

So for her wedding to Oliver—tomorrow afternoon at three—Tessa would be going up the aisle on her father's arm wearing delicate pink, the long Delmore family veil, and carrying a cascade of pink and cream spring flowers superbly chosen by Joan.

Tessa was beginning to feel tired. Joan and all the girls from both shops had taken her out for a late dinner the night before. After a lot of searching, and just as both she and Joan had been beginning to despair, they had found a small vacant shop in a popular shopping street off Knightsbridge. The rent was more than they had anticipated; but there was a possibility that the leasehold could be bought in the near future. (George Selway, brought in as a consultant, was quick to seize on this.) The bank manager gave his approval and Joan brought her decorators up from Sussex to paint the place soft apple green and white. They worked until all hours to get it done—Tom and Oliver lent a hand over one weekend. And just before Christmas, "Tessa's Garden" opened. Tessa worked there fulltime now. Joan was scrupulous in letting Tessa get on with it herself. She had made mistakes, hired more than one assistant who hadn't proved suitable, but it had the Joan and Tessa stamp all right; it was getting known; by the end of the year, they hoped, it would be paying its way.

So far, so good as far as the shop was concerned. But soon after they became engaged on New Year's Eve, Tessa quickly realised that Oliver wasn't keen to have a wife who worked flat-out five days a week, and who frequently rose before dawn to do the buying at Covent Garden. He admired her hard work in principle; in practice, he was a lot less sure. At first, Tessa ignored his barbed hints—but both their feelings exploded in a full-blooded row one evening when Tessa's work coincided with a cocktail party given by Oliver's head of chambers.

"What do you mean, you'll be late and meet me there?" Oliver bellowed down the phone like a wounded elephant. "We belong together and we'll go to the party together. It's all arranged. *Don't you understand?*" His hand crashing down on the papers which covered his desk.

What Oliver didn't say, but what Tessa knew and resented was—in addition to being proud of his new fiancée, this was also a useful occasion for his career. And he was professionally very ambitious.

"But what about *my* work?" Tessa yelled back from the crowded shop. "I'm running a successful business, not just playing about in my spare time. It's very important to me. *Don't you understand that?*"

In the end, Tessa gave in. Joan was amenable and agreed to work late herself that evening and use one of their part-time helpers. So Tessa turned up at the party on time, with Oliver, her hair gleaming and wearing a black taffeta dress which rustled charmingly when she walked. But inwardly, she was still seething, and later, when they went out for dinner by themselves, she told him so.

"Darling Tessa," Oliver murmured contritely, "I'm sorry about the tantrum. Truly." He picked up her hand and dropped a kiss on her fingers next to the sparkling sapphire engagement ring. "You shouldn't have made me love you so much. I'm too possessive. It's all your fault."

"You can't charm *me,*" lied Tessa, melting. "This is serious, important to our future. We've got to talk it through."

Oliver's grin reached right up to his warm brown eyes.

"Tomorrow," he said.

So over Tessa's job, they compromised. She had a frank talk with Joan and they agreed that Tessa should never work later than five—even though it meant getting in extra help which would reduce her monthly drawing. She was already training one of the new assistants to do the buying; Tessa would only go to Covent Garden in an emergency, or if there was an exceptional job. She duly reported this to Oliver who seemed more or less satisfied.

In other ways, too, as their engagement progressed and the wedding plans got under way, Tessa was finding that what Oliver said was not always what he meant. The house overlooking the canal, which Tessa was coming to love almost as much as Oliver, nevertheless became something of a battleground between them—usually affectionate, occasionally sharp. One of

George Selway's wedding presents was a cheque to spend on the redecoration. And although Oliver insisted that this was what he wanted, Tessa found him quite stubbornly resistant to change. It turned out that he continued to see the house through his mother's and his grandmother's eyes; he wanted it cleaned up and painted, yes, but he also wanted it to end up looking much the way he always remembered it.

After a difficult afternoon when Oliver had lovingly but firmly vetoed the colour of paint she had chosen for the drawing-room, Tessa rushed back to Ella.

"Leave it, Tess," Ella counselled wisely over a strong cup of tea. "The more comfortable he feels, the happier you'll both be. Oliver doesn't take to change easily. Some people don't, and you must accept it. It's part of his nature; his conservatism, his soundness. And it could have something to do with the years his Mum was so dreadfully ill when he was a baby. A touch of insecurity."

"There might be something in that," Tessa agreed, sipping her tea thoughtfully. "There might be . . . it must be terribly important to him that the house looks more or less the same—because he hates me to feel unhappy for a second."

Ella leant forward and put her hand on Tessa's knee. "You've got a lifetime to get the place the way you want it, Tess, little by little. Don't rush it, not just now. But you stick to your guns over the bedroom and that lovely bright chintz."

She did.

What with getting the new shop off the ground, Oliver, the house and the commotion of the wedding, Tessa had very little time to herself at all. Occasionally she wished, always with sadness, that her grandmother could be there, could have known how happy and excited she was. Shooting through Soho one night, she thought she glimpsed a sleek green sports car. It was nearly dark and she couldn't be sure. And if her heart skipped a beat or two, it wasn't enough to stop her going on chatting to Oliver.

There was a knock at the bedroom door and Jennie Morgenstern's head appeared at last. She was laden with an assortment of bags. "There you are, Tess. I'm so sorry to be late . . . we did a bit of shopping and then we couldn't get a taxi. I

556

didn't want Felix to be worn out waiting about for a bus. Truly, I don't know how you manage London at all. We're simply exhausted." Which Tessa thought odd because her mother worked harder physically—hoeing and weeding and pruning and lugging produce around— than anyone she knew. "Oh there it is. Do let me look. Yes, it's a very pretty pink, isn't it? Like a sweet pea."

"It's wonderful, just what I wanted. I thought we'd have a nice drink, Mother. Frankly, I could do with one. I'm starting to feel a bit jittery. What have you done with Felix?"

Jennie Morgenstern, who was wearing a loose black coat and dress, without adornment of any kind, sat on the bed. Her hair was pulled up more tidily than usual, accentuating the pale oval face, the blue and tranquil gaze. "I've left him in the study with your father. George has opened one of his best malt whiskys. They're going to listen to the news—and they're having a nice chat about shoes. George says his shoemaker in London has begun to charge the most outrageous prices and we have this marvellous little man in Dorset, not terribly far from the cottage."

Tessa bit her lip. "That's all right, then. I'm going to get us some champagne; I won't be a minute."

Flying down the stairs towards the kitchen, she burst out laughing. So this was what it had all come to—the years of Papa's bile and bitterness, the war hero betrayed by the gentle and beautiful wife at home, the righteous father . . . it ended up with Papa and Felix, his ex-wife's lover, now husband, drinking malt whisky together and discussing—*their feet.* "I can't wait, Tessa said aloud, I can't wait to tell Oliver."

"What on earth's so funny, Tess?" Ella asked, looking at her hard and hoping she wasn't getting hysterical. Strange things could happen to brides at the last moment. "I've just heard on the wireless that it's going to be a lovely sunny day tomorrow. Now do you think your mother and Mr. Morgenstern will want to stay for a bit of cold supper? I don't want it to be late, dear. We've still got a lot of packing to do."

"I don't know Ella. I'll ask."

Tessa grabbed the icy bottle and two glasses and dashed back upstairs.

After Jennie's unexpected telephone call to Parloe Square when Vi Delmore died last summer, the thaw between the Selway and Morgenstern households set in. The terrible rift which had begun in a bedroom at Chalcot House in the summer of 1945 at last began to mend. That night, George Selway and Jennie had spoken for almost an hour—and told no one, not even Felix, what was discussed. When George finally emerged from his study, he simply announced that he was all in and was going to bed.

After that, to everyone's surprise, Mother had started behaving quite sensibly. A telephone was installed in the cottage and Tom and Angie were invited for the weekend. Max was sent off to boarding school. The ancient car was exchanged for a small new one. Largely thanks to Ella, the flat in Eaton Square was cleared and sold. And after Tessa and Oliver got engaged the following Christmas, Jennie Morgenstern showed a little interest. She at least seemed to understand that as mother of the bride, certain things were expected of her.

So one cold January day, she and Felix lunched at the Ritz at George Selway's invitation to cement the reconciliation and discuss the spring wedding. It was apparently a perfectly friendly meeting. Felix Morgenstern enjoyed one of the few really good meals he had had for years and perused the wine list knowledgeably. Towards the end of the meal, George Selway looked round expansively and remarked that as long as Tessa and Oliver agreed, this seemed as good a place as any for the reception, didn't they think?

It was then that Jennie looked up at the enchanting painted ceiling and seemed to remember something—something which amused her greatly. Because she put her hand to her mouth and her head fell back and she started to laugh until tears ran down her cheeks.

"Liebchen . . ." Felix put his hand gently on her arm.

"What on earth is it, Jennie?" George Selway asked, irritated, remembering how trying she could be with her otherworldly vagueness. A waiter hovered and George Selway signalled for the bill.

"Do forgive me," Jennie gasped. "I just remembered something and it seemed terribly, terribly funny. All over now. Shall we go? Your stick, Felix."

"Ella says it's going to be a sunny day tomorrow," Tessa said, handing her mother a glass. "And she wants to know if you and Felix will stay for supper. After that we've got to pack all this stuff." She gestured towards the chairs piled high with the clothes Tessa was taking to France. She and Oliver were spending their honeymoon in Cannes; they would see Oliver's father, who lived in a converted farmhouse in the hills behind the coast and who was not well enough to come to the wedding.

"Oh no we can't," Jennie said quickly. "Stay for dinner, that is. But do thank Ella. Felix mustn't get overtired. He's had enough for one day—and all the excitement tomorrow." She lifted her glass to Tessa. "Happiness, darling."

"Thanks Mother. You know Tom is taking Oliver out for a stag dinner—I suppose he had to as best man. He told

Oliver only to invite his closest friends, and it turned out that Oliver has fifteen of them. Oliver, of course, would. Expensive for poor old Tom. I can see that I'm going to spend the rest of my life feeding and talking to Oliver's best friends and their wives." She didn't sound as though she minded very much. "Angie won't be seeing much of Tom tonight."

"Isn't it *exciting* about the baby? In two weeks, is it? Then I'll be a gran. And I think it's so wise of Tom to have gone into the business. George does seem to have mellowed a bit and Tom never was very happy in the law. Not like Oliver. I adore Oliver. We all liked him when he was a boy, I remember. I was wondering, Tess."

Jennie got up and walked to the window, looking out onto the clear April evening, over the new green treetops to where rows of old chimneys were outlined against the light sky.

"Will you wear Gran's pearls—her good ones, the ones she left you?"

She turned and held out her glass. Seeing her fairness against the shapeless black clothes, the flat black lace-up shoes, Tessa was struck by her mother's extraordinary appearance. What a baffling woman she was. Because in her inimitable, eccentric way, she did have style. Her own style, which was what it was all about. She simply didn't look like anyone else at all.

"Gran's pearls?" Tessa refilled their glasses. "Oh yes, *of course*. Nice to think I've got something of Gran's on tomorrow. Why?" When Jennie didn't answer, she said again. "Why Mother?"

"I just wondered," Jennie said slowly. "I just wondered whether you knew who had given them to her. Do you?"

"It can't have been Grandpa Delmore. They didn't have enough money to get the roof mended, let alone buy pearls . . . I suppose it must have been the lover, the American."

"Ben Levson."

"That's right. I hardly remember him. No, wait a minute. I've got something to show you. I'd almost forgotten." She rummaged in a drawer and brought out an old snapshot. "I found this in the attic the other day when I was going through some boxes. It was taken at Chalcot." Hubert had taken it, one Sunday afternoon, soon after Jennie had departed. "Oliver's in it so I kept it. That's me, holding Orlando. Remember Orlando? And there's Gran. Aunt Flor and Papa. And Tom." She stood close to her mother. "And that's Ben Levson, sitting by Gran. Look."

Jennie took it from her and stared. The photograph had kept well. It was still sharp and clear.

"Yes," she said quietly, "that's Ben. Goodness how he changed."

"Did he?" Tessa asked indifferently. "He must have been quite old then—it couldn't have been long before he died." She glanced at her watch. She wanted to have a word with Oliver before he was hijacked for the night by Tom. And why had Mother, when she had been sounding like a normal person for a change, suddenly gone off on this tangent about Gran's boyfriend and the pearls? It was all such a long time ago, Tessa thought impatiently, and not very interesting.

"I remember Ben. And the pearls. The Floods had a party at their villa, Les Garoupes. It was August, August 1925. We were staying there for the summer— Mother and David and I. It was a big party, very grand, with a dance-floor laid outside over the terrace. There was a band. And fireworks. Mother had only just met him—Ben Levson—but he was with her constantly."

Jennie Morgenstern was still standing in front of the window. Behind her, the sky was beginning to darken.

"She was a daring old thing, Gran, wasn't she? Walking out on Grandpa Delmore like that—becoming, quite openly, a sort of kept woman. I suppose Papa and Felix are all right down there . . ." Tessa looked at her mother uneasily. Jennie's face was slightly flushed; there was an odd, intense look about her eyes.

The hot, still night and the sound of cicadas. The smell of pines, the sea. Jasmine hanging along the wall outside her window. All day, waiters had been rushing round with trays, laying glasses, plates and cutlery on spotless white linen. A sense of excitement mounting through the hot midday hours. Mademoiselle fussing—her wide floppy hat that she hated; David fractious when they were made to rest, rest . . .

By the evening, it was a little cooler. The band arrived and the caterers. There were massed tubs of flowering plants, silver coolers for the wine. Candles on small round tables by the swimming-pool, waiting to be lit. (The grown-ups—Mother, Hubie, Aunt Flor—had disappeared.)

Jennie watched all this—flitting about like a wraith—silvery hair rippling down her back, keeping just out of Mademoiselle's gaze. Smooth, skinny legs and sandals racing beneath the white shorts—down paths, between tables, in and out of the brilliant shrubbery.

She was behind a tree in the wild part of the garden beyond the swimming pool when she saw them. Her mother and Ben Levson. Her mother had her back to her. He was doing something to her neck, fastening something, something that caught the soft evening light. Pearls.

He looked up, over her mother's shoulders, and saw her. Part girl-child, part nascent woman; mouth soft and open, eyes staring. A curtain of hair. His dark, mobile face broke into a dazzling white smile. At her. She turned and disappeared, *running and running back up to the house, to her cool room—and Mademoiselle. Sitting on her bed, knees together, panting . . . Mademoiselle scolding.*

"Mother, Mother . . . are you all right?" Tessa asked. "Here, why don't you sit down for a bit." She wasn't used to London and she probably didn't have much lunch. The wedding; the excitement. Two glasses of champagne. She hoped she wasn't going to pass out on her. "Close your eyes for ten minutes. It's quite early. I'll go and see what Papa and Felix are doing."

"I think perhaps I will. I'm perfectly well, darling," she said, sounding it. "I shouldn't bother in the least about those two. Get on with your packing." She put her head back and shut her eyes. "I'd like you to stay here with me."

They were determined to stay up for the fireworks, she and David. But David, who was so much younger and who had been swimming for most of the day, slept as soon as his head touched the pillow. In the next room, Jennie lay awake—listening to the voices and the music and the laughter, the whole gay crescendo of the party. The hat, the pine smell . . .

She knew who it was the moment the door opened. Her heart beating like a hammer. She could tell from the shadowy outline of his white dinner jacket. When he came close and stood looking down at her, the aromatic cigar smoke clung.

He was laughing very softly as he pushed away the sheet, lifted the white cotton nightdress; whispering to her not to be frightened, that he was not going to hurt her; that he was going to love her and make her happy and feel good.

She lay on her back, her arms straight at her sides, looking up at the grotesque shadows on the ceiling.

After the first moments, she had no fear.

His hands—very soft, very sensitive—played over her beginning breasts. They moved unhurriedly over her stomach, parting the narrow thighs. He bent and kissed her there, over and over, those supple lips moving higher, back over and around her stomach to finish where one day soon her breasts would be.

That was all he did; that was all he ever did.

As he left—it was only minutes—he put one finger over her mouth.

"A secret between us."

And he was gone.

"Go on, Mother, you're having a bit of a nod off. It will do you good." Tessa was standing by her, arms full of brightly coloured bathing suits and towels. "I've been down to the study. Felix and Papa are watching the news and Papa has ordered you a taxi. I'll wake you in a quarter of an hour."

"Thank you darling." Her eyes closed again.

So whom should she have told? Mother? Aunt Flor? Mademoiselle?

Appalled; ecstatic; terrified; uncomprehending. Half longing in a dim, unrealised way . . .

She could tell no one. She turned the only way she could—inward, on herself. From that night, a wall came down between her, Jennie Delmore, and the rest of the world.

*Nothing happened again that summer;
not even when he had driven her into
Cannes, by herself or with her mother, as
a special treat.*

*Once, while Vi was having her hair
coiffed at Antoine's, he had taken Jennie
to a shop and bought her some bauble. A
gold charm bracelet. After, they had sat
under the striped awning of a café and
eaten pistachio ice-cream while Jennie
swung her legs and turned her wrist this
way and that admiring the jangling
charms.*

*"You'll spoil her, Ben," Vi had said
indulgently. Later, taking his arm. (They
were on the Croisette in brilliant
sunshine.) "Where is she going to find
someone to treat her like you do when
she's grown up?" And they laughed.*

Jennie walked silently behind.

*The summer ended—and they returned
to England.*

*It was a year or so later, after Vi had
left Sam Delmore and when she and the
children were living in the big flat in Eaton
Square—decorated to within an inch of its
life—that it happened again. Ben Levson
was in London on business; seeing Vi,*

preparing to sweep her off to some exotic place although Jennie had heard the maids say he had married someone or other which she found extraordinary.

One afternoon, he tore into the flat, in a belted camelhair coat, homburg hat rammed down to his ears, a haze of cigar smoke, and announced he was taking Jennie round the galleries. She didn't seem to have anything to do with herself—"So why the heck not, Vi?"

Vi agreed. She was getting her face done later; and in any case, "so improving" for Jennie. How kind . . . why not indeed? They were driven to the Ritz where Ben Levson always kept a suite when he was in London. Up in the lift, along a dim corridor. Deep carpet . . . She stood looking at him in the huge, hushed bedroom.

"Undress," he said, rolling the cigar round in his mouth. The dark eyes staring hypnotically. Obediently, Jennie took off the black velvet dress with the lace collar, the high white socks, her underwear. He pointed to the bed. She climbed on to it and lay on her back looking up at the ceiling as she had that night in France.

He repeated precisely what he had done to her there.

He never spoke. When he had finished, she simply got off the bed and dressed. Immediately after, he rang for the chauffeur and told him to drive her first to the National Gallery where he was to spend half an hour with her—and then back to Eaton Square.

From then on, this took place whenever Ben Levson was in London, perhaps three or four times a year. What he did to her never changed by so much as a single caress.

But Jennie changed.

When she was fifteen, what had been excruciating became, instead, exquisite. The only outward sign she gave of this was closed eyes and a wash of colour across her pale face. But her agonising dilemma became worse.

She grew up, came out. Vi Delmore presented her at Court in white satin and feathers and she became known as "that beautiful Delmore girl with nothing to say for herself. So lovely—but like a statue—and about as interesting."

She married, at eighteen, the first man

*who asked her—George Selway. She saw
no other way out.*

She never saw Ben Levson again.

*Having money and servants and George
Selway's controlling ways, she got through
somehow. Her beauty, which was like
something that didn't belong to her,
defined her. The house in Parloe Square,
two children . . . and then the War.*

*On a bitter winter night in the Floods'
kitchen in Dorset she met Felix Morgenstern. That first look, a kiss dropped
on her hand—warmth, gentleness,
some innate understanding—touched the
broken spring inside her. And she started
to mend.*

"Come on, up you get. The taxi will be
here any minute." Tessa shook her
mother's shoulder. Jennie started.

"What's that? So sorry, Tess, I think I
must have slept after all. Now let me get
everything together." She began collecting
the bags, and the worn leather sack of a
handbag she carried everywhere.

"Mother, before you faded, you were
talking about Gran's pearls. You sounded
so upset, as though you didn't want me to

573

wear them for the wedding. Is it because *he* gave them to her—Ben Levson—not Grandpa?"

"Oh no, darling, I just wanted to tell you about when Ben Levson gave them to Gran at Les Garoupes, the night Flora and Hubie had a party, and it rather set me off. I've been dreaming about it, I think. So vividly . . . I haven't thought about it all for years and years. One day perhaps I'll tell you, and perhaps I won't." She smiled at her warmly. "But do wear the pearls, darling. For Gran. She would have wanted it."

That's all right then, Tessa thought, relieved. There's nothing wrong with her. She'd started to get rather worried, but it was just some trivial childhood memory concerning Gran and the pearls and that man Ben Levson. She must have needed the rest; she looked sparkling now, like a young girl. She hung the rest of the carrier bags over her mother's arm.

"I'm longing for tomorrow," Jennie said as they walked down the stairs. "I know you're going to be the loveliest bride ever. And I know you're going to be happy."

"Oh Mother . . ."

But she sounded so sure and so happy *for her* that Tessa couldn't help but be a little moved. She took Jennie's hand.

"I'll phone Oliver straight away and tell him what you said, and how you said it."

"Do." Jennie squeezed her hand back.

When they got the first landing, they saw George Selway and Felix waiting in the hall, looking up at them. And even George Selway was smiling.

2

IT was a wonderful wedding. Everyone agreed on that, hat meeting hat over glasses of champagne at the reception in the Ritz; the conversational buzz high with excitement. The bride so pretty and natural—and the divine dress, such an unusual colour, and the flowers, my dear, a positive bower of springtime . . .

And whoever saw a more rumbustiously happy bridegroom than Oliver Bingham? He beamed with happiness, greeting everyone with great hugs, holding on to Tessa's hand, stepping on the hem of that lovely dress until admonished (he always had been a bit ham fisted, dear boy though he was), not letting her away from his side for a second. Quite as though they didn't have the rest of their lives to spend together. Not that his bride didn't seem equally delighted, eyes alight and that pretty gingery hair so charming with the dress and the écru lace of the old Delmore veil.

And as for Jennie Morgenstern, Selway that was, words failed. For years, it had been put about that she was living like a gypsy in the depths of the countryside with that German professor—so much older, and not a penny piece to his name —after up and leaving the lot of them. Yet here she was, with her indestructibly perfect face, moving round the room, chatting to everyone, reminding people of darling Vi. And she had always been so tiresomely shy and withdrawn, never a word to say for herself in the old days.

And as for her husband, the professor (over there, quick, talking to that pretty cousin of Oliver's), he was charming everyone, particularly the ladies, and the young ones at that. Whenever Jennie looked over to him, which was often, he was surrounded by admiring girls, friends of Tessa's and Oliver's, who flirted with him outrageously. His quick brown eyes taking everything in, asking all the right questions; such quaint, courtly, old-fashioned manners. *Quite* a way with him he had.

Everything went supremely well, like clockwork. The music in church, supervised by Oliver, was exceptionally fine. During the service, the sun, striking the windows at exactly the right moment, haloed the bride and groom just as they were taking their vows. Oliver, speaking very firmly, turned towards her; the bride, naturally, a bit trembly. Many of the women present dug about for handkerchiefs. The men cleared their throats or looked up at the vaulted nave.

The star of the day, after the bride, was undoubtedly the bride's mother. Anyone who saw her there would agree with that. The photographs, in any case, would prove it. Jennie Morgenstern had taken herself off to Harrods at nine o'clock that morning—leaving Felix to fend for himself for a change—and emerged at lunchtime a very different woman. She had bought a brilliant blue silk dress and jacket and a matching cartwheel hat; black shoes, gloves and bag. Her hair had been washed and put up and her nails—well, at least made the best of. Even her children scarcely recognised her. Shorn of her baggy tweeds, she turned out to have almost as good a figure as Angie Selway in her modelling days.

"I just can't believe it," Angie whispered to Tom as they walked out of church to the triumphant organ music. "She looks ravishingly sophisticated. I'm quite envious and very impressed."

"She looks normal, that's what I can't believe," Tom said out of the side of his mouth.

Angie gave him a surreptitious dig in the ribs.

"The son and heir was very active during the service," she murmured through beautifully made-up pink lips.

"He must have liked the music old Oliver put on. And it was good, wasn't it? Particularly the Elgar." He bent towards her affectionately. "Feeling all right are you darling? We're not going to have to make a dash for it before we can get to the old man's fizz are we?"

Angie smiled her satisfied cat's smile and took his arm possessively. He was looking very debonair in his morning coat, so tall, so fair. And she was in the last days of a trouble-free pregnancy. Her face had filled out becomingly, and she was enormous. But with her height and clever, tent-like dressing with matching shoes and stockings, she still looked elegant.

Some months before, she had been a key witness at the sensational Loden trial; photographed entering and leaving the court each day, perfectly turned out; beautiful, dignified; her husband always at her side.

Once the whole farrago was over, the outcome was much as Oliver, in his hard-headed, professional way, had expected. A short sentence and a stiff fine. Guy Loden was even made to seem a perversely attractive figure in his Edwardian suits, and immaculately cuffed shirts. Raffish but not unappealing. There were no further sinister revelations. The whole truth of the matter of Loden and his circle and their lifestyle, as was hinted in the Press, never really came out. London was full of rumours at the time—it was said that Royalty was involved; that at least two members of the cabinet were seen regularly at the Loden gaming tables. However, nothing was substantiated and within days the matter was forgotten.

Tom and Angie (with George Selway's help) had bought a charming house in

Chelsea. Vi Delmore's small legacy took care of the decoration. The top floor was now a nursery, painted pale blue because Angie was absolutely certain that the child was a boy. (Nicholas Thomas George—to be called Nick.) Since marrying Tom, she had become very social, very domesticated —edging her way on to several important charity ball committees; starting to give small, interesting dinner parties; acting as George Selway's hostess on more than one occasion.

The moment Tom joined Selway Electric, Angie packed in her modelling career. George Selway thoroughly approved. He was finding this daughter-in-law—who stood up to his temperament without batting an eyelid—more and more to his liking. Tessa and Oliver occasionally had mild arguments over which of the two was tougher, her father or Angie. On the whole, both favoured Angie. But Tom was wildly happy, proud and home-loving. And he made a good start in the business. As George Selway shrewdly realised, Angie's push plus Tom's natural abilities would see to that.

George Selway and Jennie Morgenstern

received with the bride and bridegroom. After admiring the colour of her wedding dress, almost everybody remarked to Tessa on her mother. "I had no idea she was such a stunner, Tess." And Tessa would say, meaning it, "Yes, she's looking wonderful, isn't she?" and pass on to the next in line who would tell her a variation of the same thing. One guest—was it Fiona?—was wicked enough to make a comparison with Poppy Renfrew who was *not* looking her best in a purple dress and a feathery mauve hat.

Flora and Hubert had been driven up from Chalcot that morning. Hubert's health was remarkably improved. The doctor had found tablets which agreed with him and which lessened the effects of his illness. He sat during the reception with Flora, ever watchful, at his side, and greeted a procession of friends with his usual vivacity. He hugely enjoyed Tom's short and witty speech, murmuring to Flora that "you couldn't beat a legal training for dealing graciously with words."

However, when it came to the bride-groom's reply, Oliver's euphoria got the better of him. He went on and on and on . . . often amusingly, but for much too long. Guests started swaying on their feet, looking about longingly for more champagne or a cup of tea. Not a moment too soon, Tessa's satin shoe found and rapped his ankle—and he finished abruptly.

Marie came with the Floods, the only female in the room wearing black. But it was a new suit of fine wool, beautifully sewn. Earlier, she had helped Tessa dress, which miffed Ella slightly, but Tessa insisted. She knew there was no one like Marie for giving a dress the right tug or pulling down a hem. At the reception she loped about, seeing the Floods were comfortable (Flora was looking terribly gaunt with the strain of Hubert's illness, everyone said)—and keeping an eye on young Max. He had come up with the Floods that morning, neat in his grey school suit, and was having the time of his life merrily scoffing everything in sight, with several glasses of champagne slipped to him on the side by Tom.

At one point, after they had cut the cake, Tom told Tessa, with much hilarity, "Mother has just been overheard telling someone that the cottage is much too small, they need somewhere for Max to practise and for Felix to put all his books, and it is high time they looked for something larger."

"She's joining the human race," Tessa laughed, as Oliver pulled her with him to talk to someone.

"About bloody time," said Tom.

It was early evening before Tessa went upstairs to change. Marie and Ella came with her to help with the dress and veil which they would later pack away. Her going-away outfit, and everything else she needed, was already hanging in the wardrobe, everything thought out to the last shoe and earring; the luggage packed and waiting in Oliver's car. Oliver wouldn't tell Tess where they were spending the night. They were flying off to the south of France the next morning.

When she was zipped and buttoned into her new navy suit and pleated silk blouse, Marie and Ella took one last look round, brushed off some imaginary specks, and Ella, verging on the tearful, was then firmly marched back downstairs by Marie to let everyone know that the bride was about to re-emerge.

Tessa was sitting at the dressing-table when there was a light knock. It was Angie.

"Almost ready? Is it all right if I come in? I adore that suit . . ." She sailed in and shut the door. "It's all been wonderful, Tessa; everyone says it's the best wedding they've ever been to. And you were so right about the dress, the pink. You stuck to your guns over that."

Tessa turned from the mirror, holding a comb. "Only because you backed me up."

"Listen, Tessa . . ." Angie sank on to the bed, sitting very straight. "I've got something to tell you. I've been debating . . ."

"Go on." She knew what it was before she started. And she knew it would be truthful. She had come to have a healthy respect for Angie's bluntness.

"Yesterday, Tom took me out for lunch. The last outing before The Event. We went to Soho."

Then she knew for sure. She braced herself.

"I honestly didn't know what to do. I

didn't want to spoil anything today. I didn't tell Tom—you can't tell men things always can you? They don't get it right. Anyhow," brisk, leaning across to turn down Tessa's little velvet collar, "here goes . . . Tom had to rush off to some meeting so I stayed on to finish my coffee. God knows when I'll get out to a decent restaurant again. I looked up and there he was. Marcus. He sort of materialised."

"I see."

"He's doing marvellously. He's writing a book, something about the War, and he's been shortlisted for editor of one of the top quality dailies. I read it somewhere the other day."

"Has he?"

Tessa had read it too, the same paragraph, several times over.

"Yes—and likely to get it, Tom says. He heard so in his club."

You brought me luck, he said.

"Well," Angie went on rapidly. "We chatted for a few minutes. There's a lot I like about Marcus. I always said that. He helped us over Loden. And I owe him Tom, remember . . . He made a few rude remarks about my tum."

How did he look? Who was he with? Did he ask. . . ?

"We neither of us mentioned your name but he must have known about the wedding. Tell her good luck, be happy, give her my love, he said. And then he was gone. That was all. I didn't know . . ." A brief, searching look. "It was just my instinct. A message from a friend, I thought . . ."

Tell her good luck, be happy . . .

"I'm glad you told me, Angie. Honestly. It was absolutely the right thing to do." And she was smiling.

"I thought it might be." Angie stood up. She was not normally demonstrative, but she bent and kissed Tessa's cheek. "That's that then."

When Angie had shut the door, Tessa went to the window and looked out on to the early spring evening. But she did not see the freshly green park or the streaming traffic. Certain memories which she would keep forever came to her. Last summer, now a world away . . . The narrow bed in the Soho flat; hands splayed on a steering wheel; from somewhere, a musky

587

hawthorn scent. Regret—so quickly stifled.

Give her my love, he said . . .

She turned and stared right across the heart of London's teeming West End. And she called out, her voice steadying, "And the same to you, Marcus, the same to you. Good luck, be happy too."

Down the stairs she came, the long red carpet, familiar faces glimpsed among the bobbing crowd of Papa's and Poppy's business and city friends. Hats a bit awry now; faces a bit flushed. The talk and the laughter submerged in a roar of, "There she is, here she comes . . ." And shouted, louder than all the others, *"There's Tessa, come on darling . . ."*

Oliver, standing at the bottom, now wearing a suit, looked incredibly happy; reaching out, one arm firmly round her as they all closed in.

"Tessa, Tessa . . . Good luck, darling, God Bless . . . Doesn't she look sweet? Lucky chap . . . Long life . . . Such an adorable pair . . . Look after her, Oliver."

They pushed through their wedding

guests together . . . Oliver's arm still round her, loving, protective.

"Goodbye Papa." A quick kiss. "Thank you for everything, it's been wonderful, all I could ever have dreamed . . ." Was it possible his eyes were moist? Then it was Oliver's turn. "I'll look after her, George. Never fear. Thank you for *her*—oh, and the fabulous wedding."

Mother, hat and hair still perfectly in place, holding on to Felix's arm. The Floods, Hubie managing to stand to see them off, Flora looking proud. Ella in tears now—"Cheer up, Ella darling, it's my wedding, you know—and we'll be back in two weeks." Marie—yes, smiling.

"Goodbye goodbye!" Blowing kisses, waves, lots of hugs. Fiona, a bridesmaid, still carrying the bouquet Tessa had thrown her when she went to change. Joan and Jilly and the new girls, "You were amazing, the flowers were everywhere. You did us proud; we'll never forget it."

They were nearly at the entrance now. Tessa, exasperated, tugging at Oliver's arm; he wanted to go on talking to everyone. Angie, stately and beautiful, whispered; "I'll try and wait until you two get back before I pop, but I can't promise." Poppy Renfrew, quite overcome with emotion, champagne, or Mother's dazzling appearance flinging her arms round her; something she had never done before. "Dear, dear little Tessa." Almost sobbing.

With everyone at their heels, pushing and shoving in a not very mannerly way, they emerged into the pale April evening light. And *wham*—Tom and Max caught them full in the face, masses and masses of confetti showering handful after handful while everyone yelled in delight behind them, picking it up, joining in.

Hand in hand, Tessa and Oliver ducked into the black beetle of a car, decorated by Tom, God knows what tied on behind.

"Goodbye, goodbye . . . Have a wonderful time in France." More kisses blown, more waves. It was all a blur to Tessa now.

They moved off, Tom's devilry clanking at the rear. The guests had now spilled on to the pavement, determined on a last look, laughing, loving every minute . . .

Until moments later, the inevitable happened—at least, it had all the hallmarks of Oliver's driving experience. Tessa heard strange sounds coming from the engine, and said so.

"Nonsense, darling," Oliver pooh-poohed gaily, giving one last wave in the mirror, buzzing round into Piccadilly. "Imagination, or a bit of Tom's rubbish."

Clunk, clunk, clunk . . .

"There it goes again. *Listen*." Tessa clutched at Oliver's arm as the car shuddered and began to lose speed.

"*Bloody hell* . . ." He manoeuvred it towards the pavement where it gave up the ghost and died. "*Oh my God. Of all* times for something like this to happen." He groaned and grimaced and ran a finger around inside his collar. For Oliver, he looked almost embarrassed. "Darling, I'm most desperately sorry. My fault. It has been behaving badly, not starting properly, and I meant to get the blasted thing checked. Oh my God . . . Forgive me?"

"I'll think about it." Tessa was on the verge of wild, hysterical laughter. They couldn't have been more than a few hundred yards from their guests. She would have given anything to see the expression on their faces if they had known.

"It's just one of those maddening things . . ." He slid an arm round her shoulders. "No bones broken. It's only a heap of metal, after all." Oliver was rarely put out for long. Unbelievably, he changed the subject, dismissing the car as an irrelevance. "I know I messed up the speech. I meant it to be short and funny like Tom's. And it wasn't. I fluffed it. Darling Tess, did you think you'd just married a pompous so-and-so?"

"I did a bit." Really laughing now; and at the same time mildly vexed. "I thought you were never going to stop, but I still love you—even if we have broken down and I don't know where we're going."

"That's simple. Home, darling, to more champagne, the house decorated by Joan and a meal cooked by Marie and brought up from Chalcot this morning. You didn't guess, did you? We all threw out masses of false clues."

"Oh Oliver, it's the best idea you could have had." Relenting, kissing his cheek.

He hugged her. "Glad I got something

right at least. I say, did you see your mother when . . ."

They sat there for a while, fairly near the kerb of Regent Street, traffic swerving around them, talking over the wedding, admitting how nervous they had been when they took their vows. Passers by turned and stared at the small black car with its rusty cans and drifts of confetti and "Just Married" scrawled across the back inexplicably stopped, and the young couple in front, heads close together, talking away—oblivious. Without exception, they smiled.

After about ten minutes, Oliver got out and hailed a taxi. He transferred their brand new luggage and handed Tessa in as the cabbie gawped. (He too had sighted the shambolic car.) Then Oliver solemnly untied Tom's tin contraption and got into the taxi with it.

"Where to then, guv?" the driver asked, swivelling round, grinning from ear to ear.

"Ask my wife," said Oliver.

GUIDE
TO THE COLOUR CODING
OF
ULVERSCROFT BOOKS

Many of our readers have written to us expressing their appreciation for the way in which our colour coding has assisted them in selecting the Ulverscroft books of their choice.

To remind everyone of our colour coding—this is as follows:

BLACK COVERS
Mysteries

*

BLUE COVERS
Romances

*

RED COVERS
Adventure Suspense and General Fiction

*

ORANGE COVERS
Westerns

*

GREEN COVERS
Non-Fiction

THE SHADOWS
OF THE CROWN TITLES
in the
Ulverscroft Large Print Series

The Trial of Charles I — *C. V. Wedgwood*
Royal Flush — *Margaret Irwin*
The Sceptre and the Rose — *Doris Leslie*
Mary II: Queen of England — *Hester Chapman*
That Enchantress — *Doris Leslie*
The Princess of Celle — *Jean Plaidy*
Caroline the Queen — *Jean Plaidy*
The Third George — *Jean Plaidy*
The Great Corinthian — *Doris Leslie*
Victoria in the Wings — *Jean Plaidy*
The Captive of Kensington Palace — *Jean Plaidy*
The Queen and Lord 'M' — *Jean Plaidy*
The Queen's Husband — *Jean Plaidy*
The Widow of Windsor — *Jean Plaidy*
Bertie and Alix — *Graham and Heather Fisher*
The Duke of Windsor — *Ursula Bloom*